KISSED BY HER CAPTIVE

"Ye need something," Ruari said. "I can see it in your eyes. They are huge, dark pools of longing."

"I need ye to release me before I reopen a few of your wounds," she said, but knew her threat lacked strength. Her voice was low and husky, robbed of the steel needed to relay a warning.

"Ye need the heat of passion in your blood to burn away all the dclusions besetting ye."

Before Sorcha could reply to his arrogant statement, he brushed his lips across hers. All thought fled from her mind. Sorcha uttered a soft, low moan as he began to kiss her thoroughly. She greedily opened her mouth when he prodded her lips with his tongue. The slow, heated stroke of his tongue caused her to tremble from the strength of desire racing through her . . .

Books by Hannah Howell

The Murrays

HIGHLAND DESTINY
HIGHLAND HONOR
HIGHLAND PROMISE
HIGHLAND VOW
HIGHLAND KNIGHT
HIGHLAND BRIDE
HIGHLAND ANGEL
HIGHLAND GROOM
HIGHLAND WARRIOR
HIGHLAND CONQUEROR
HIGHLAND CHAMPION
HIGHLAND LOVER
HIGHLAND BARBARIAN
HIGHLAND SAVAGE
HIGHLAND WOLF
HIGHLAND SINNER
HIGHLAND PROTECTOR
HIGHLAND AVENGER
HIGHLAND MASTER
HIGHLAND GUARD
HIGHLAND CHIEFTAIN

The Wherlockes

IF HE'S WICKED
IF HE'S SINFUL
IF HE'S WILD
IF HE'S DANGEROUS
IF HE'S TEMPTED
IF HE'S DARING
IF HE'S NOBLE

Vampire Romance

HIGHLAND VAMPIRE
THE ETERNAL HIGHLANDER
MY IMMORTAL HIGHLANDER
HIGHLAND THIRST
NATURE OF THE BEAST
YOURS FOR ETERNITY
HIGHLAND HUNGER
BORN TO BITE

Stand-Alone Novels

ONLY FOR YOU
MY VALIANT KNIGHT
UNCONQUERED
WILD ROSES
A TASTE OF FIRE
A STOCKINGFUL OF JOY
HIGHLAND HEARTS
RECKLESS
CONQUEROR'S KISS
BEAUTY AND THE BEAST
HIGHLAND WEDDING
SILVER FLAME
HIGHLAND FIRE
HIGHLAND CAPTIVE
MY LADY CAPTOR
WILD CONQUEST
KENTUCKY BRIDE
COMPROMISED HEARTS
STOLEN ECSTASY
HIGHLAND HERO
HIS BONNIE BRIDE

Seven Brides for Seven Scotsmen

THE SCOTSMAN WHO SAVED ME
WHEN YOU LOVE A SCOTSMAN

Published by Kensington Publishing Corporation

My Lady Captor

HANNAH HOWELL

ZEBRA BOOKS
KENSINGTON PUBLISHING CORP.
http://www.kensingtonbooks.com

Chapter One

Scottish border—summer 1388

"Sweet Mary, Sorcha, I cannae go down *there*."

Sorcha Hay understood her pretty cousin Margaret's hesitation, one bred of a horror she shared. At the base of the small, windswept hill they stood upon sprawled the men who had fallen in the latest skirmish between Sir James Douglas and the English Lord "Hotspur" Percy of Northumberland. It was a bloody squabble. This one had been over a banner which the Scots had stolen while raiding in England, causing Hotspur to vow to get it back. Word was that the Scots had won, even capturing Hotspur himself, but it had cost them Sir James Douglas, a brave knight. Sorcha doubted that many of the men scattered on the rocky ground below her felt particularly victorious as they breathed their last.

A gust of wind slapped a hank of her thick chestnut hair across her face. She welcomed the way it obscured her view for a moment. The sight of so many dead men was a painful one. She was also terrified that one of the broken figures on the ground was her brother Dougal. A heavy sigh escaped her as she more securely tied her hair back with a length of blackened leather. She could not give in to her own fears and weaknesses. She had to be strong.

Firmly taking the plump and timid Margaret by one dimpled hand, Sorcha tugged her pale, wide-eyed cousin down the rocky hillside. In her other hand she clutched the worn reins of her sturdy Highland pony Bansith. She prayed she would not need her little horse to carry Dougal's body back to Dunweare.

The human scavengers were already approaching the dead. If Dougal was down there and still alive, Sorcha knew she had to find him before they did. Any man still clinging to life would swiftly have his throat cut even as his pockets were stripped clean. The cold-eyed men and women who scurried over such battlefields wanted no witnesses to their ghoulish thievery. Sorcha hoped she and Margaret had the skill to act as debased as the scavengers.

In an attempt to ease some of her fears, she briefly touched the small bow and quiver of arrows she carried on her back. She and Margaret also wore swords and daggers made specifically for them by their clever armorer Robert. They were not totally helpless.

"Those corpse-robbing corbies will kill us," whispered Margaret, tugging her thick, dull-brown cloak more tightly around her voluptuous figure.

"Not if we join in their thievery," answered Sorcha.

"Nay? If they have no qualms about cutting the throats of helpless, dying men, why should they be troubled about killing us?"

"I am not saying they arenae dangerous, but if we go about the business of picking o'er the corpses as if we do so all the time, they will probably ignore us." Sorcha

stopped by the body of a young man, thinking sadly of
how short his life had been.

"I cannae touch him."

"Then hold Bansith's reins, Margaret, and keep a
very close eye on those scavengers."

As Margaret took the reins, Sorcha crouched by the
young man's body. Murmuring a prayer for his soul, she
gently closed his empty, staring eyes, careful not to let
the others roaming the field see her acting so kindly.
She collected up his sword, dagger, and all else of any
value, silently promising the youth that she would do
her best to see that his belongings were returned to his
kinsmen. Sorcha took careful note of his appearance,
her only real clue to his identity, before putting her
booty in the panniers slung over the strong back of her
pony. Reluctantly, her stomach knotting as she fought
down queasiness, she moved to the next man.

Sorcha did not stop by every man, performing the distasteful task of stealing from the dead only enough to as-
suage the keen suspicions of the scavengers. All the
while she and Margaret looked for Dougal, but without
success. By the time she crouched by the fifth man she
felt forced to rob, she was feeling distinctly ill. Although
she found some cause for relief in not finding Dougal's
body, she was still worried about his fate. It would be a
particularly cruel twist of fate to stain her soul with the
crime of robbing the slain men only to have to leave the
field with no certain knowledge of what had happened
to her brother.

"This mon is verra finely dressed," Sorcha murmured
then froze, her hands still upon the ornate buckle of his
scabbard, as his broad chest rose and fell with a deep
breath.

"Touch that sword, ye foul, thieving corbie, and I will

send ye straight to hell," the man said in a deep, soft voice made hoarse with pain.

She could not fully stifle a soft cry of alarm as he clasped her wrist in one large hand, the mail of his gauntlet cutting into her skin. A quick glance at Margaret told her that her cousin was too intent on watching the scavengers to notice her current difficulty. Trying to hide her fear, Sorcha looked at the man, shivering inwardly over the fury glittering in his pain-clouded dark green eyes.

"Ye dinnae have the strength to kill every corbie slinking o'er this bloodied field, my fine knight," she whispered.

"Ere I die, I can make sure that a few of you will ne'er pick at a mon's bones again."

"Aye, and ye *will* die if those other corbies ken that ye are still alive. Howbeit, if ye will heed me ye might yet leave this cursed field alive."

"Who are ye talking to, Sorcha?" asked Margaret.

"Weel, cousin, if ye will babble at me at all the appropriate times, mayhaps the others will believe I am talking to you," replied Sorcha.

"Is that mon alive?"

"Aye, for the moment." After another swift peek at Margaret assured Sorcha that the girl had the sense not to stare at her, Sorcha looked back at the knight. "The first thing ye can do, sir, is to let me go about the ill deed of robbing you."

"Oh, aye? So ye can steal all I own more easily ere ye cut my throat?" he snarled.

"Nay, fool, so the other thieves slinking o'er the battlefield dinnae ken that ye are alive. We could all be slain then, for they will realize that Margaret and I are *not* what we pretend to be." She did not waver beneath his hard stare. "Ye had best decide quickly. They will soon wonder why I linger here." Despite the tension of the moment, Sorcha almost smiled as she heard Margaret deride Dougal in colorful terms for his insistence upon joining the neverending battle against the English.

"Why is that girl talking to you?" grumbled the man.

"So that the others dinnae guess that ye still have the breath to speak," replied Sorcha. "After all, we both ken that they are watching us, and I must be talking to someone. Ye are supposed to be dead."

"If ye are not here to rob the dead then what are ye about?"

"My cousin and I are looking for Sir Dougal Hay, laird of Dunweare."

"Ye willnae find that brash laddie here. The English took him."

"I thought the English lost this battle."

"Aye, but they managed to drag off a few of our lads as they fled the field."

Sorcha cursed, ignoring the man's startled look. "Do ye think anyone else on this bloodied field survives?"

"There may be a mon or two, but they willnae be breathing much longer. What the English didnae finish, the thieving swine tiptoeing amongst the bodies will, be they English or Scot."

"Shall I wander about and see if I can find another survivor?" asked Margaret.

"Only if ye truly wish to, Cousin," replied Sorcha, resisting the urge to rub her wrist when the man eased his hold on it.

"Now that we have seen that this mon still lives, I think I must."

"Dinnae be too obvious about what ye are doing and 'twould be best if ye leave the horse behind."

"How will I help anyone if I cannae move them?"

"If ye find a live one, we will consider the problem then." Sorcha shook her head as she cut loose the man's purse and added it to her booty. "Try to get the fool to hide. I will need time to think of how we can walk away with this mon or anyone else." She smiled faintly when Margaret whispered a mild curse. "Be careful." As soon as Margaret left, Sorcha turned back to the wounded knight. "Who are you?"

"Sir Ruari Kerr, laird of Gartmhor. I fought with the Douglases."

"And they show their gratitude by leaving ye here to rot. Why didnae the English take ye for ransom?"

"I fell as the English fled with our men snarling at their heels." He closed his eyes. "Once those Sassenach dogs cease to run they will be gathering their ransoms for the men they captured."

Sorcha tensed, a chill seeping through her body. That would not be long for the battle had taken place on the English side of the Cheviot hills. The English did not have far to run to be safe enough to tally their losses. She had been a fool to think her troubles were over simply because her brother's chosen side had won the battle. Of course the English would demand a ransom. It was the only reason to take the highborn soldiers captive. What the English could not know was that they could demand a ransom for Dougal till their tongues fell out, but it would gain them nothing. Sir Dougal Hay might be a laird and may have been dressed as fine as the Douglas himself, but he did not have two coins to rub together.

Dougal was doomed, she thought, her heart heavy with worry and a building grief. Then she looked at Sir Ruari Kerr. She recognized the name and the lands he held. Unlike with Dougal, one could trust in the richness of Sir Ruari's attire. Although she hated to even consider the possibility of holding the handsome knight for ransom, she could not immediately discard the idea. It could be the only way to get the coin needed to buy back Dougal's life.

"I heard that the Scots captured Hotspur himself," she said.

"Aye, they did," he replied, partly opening his eyes to look at her.

"So, willnae the captured Scots be returned to us in trade for him?"

"Only those who are asked for. If your brother is weel kenned by the Douglas clan . . ."

"He isnae."

"Then ye shall probably have to buy him back."

"And since the English suffered such a resounding defeat, they will no doubt ask for large ransoms in an attempt to salve some of their bruised pride."

"Aye, they will."

"Cousin," Margaret whispered as she hurried up to Sorcha. "I found another mon still alive, a lad actually."

"Where is he?" asked Sorcha.

"On the right-hand side of the field, nearly half the distance down 'twixt here and the trees at the far end of the field, in a thicket."

"Aye, I see the thicket. He is in there?"

"He is now. Using my skirts and cloak to hide his movements, I stood guard while he squirmed into the bushes. Have ye thought of a way to help these men flee this field?"

"How weel was the laddie dressed?"

"Not as fine as this knight. Aye, and his attire is fair ruined by rips, blood, and mire."

"Then we shall claim him as kin and say we are taking his body home."

"We cannae claim this rogue as kin. No one with a kinsmon dressed so finely would be robbing the dead."

"I wouldnae wager too heavily on that, but aye, 'tis what these dogs will think." She frowned at Ruari for a moment then smiled crookedly as she realized what she planned to say would not be a complete lie. "We shall say that we want to take his body back to his kinsmen, for anyone dressed so finely must be important, and his kinsmen will surely reward us for finding his body. Both men must play dead." One sharp look from Ruari's green eyes told her that he understood.

"We cannae carry both men on Bansith. She is just a wee pony."

"True. We must make a litter. Ye will have to fetch what is needed, Margaret, as I daren't leave our pony or this mon unguarded."

"Ye havenae tended to his wounds, Sorcha."

"We are pretending he is dead, Cousin. Ye dinnae bind the wounds of a dead mon," Sorcha explained in a gentle voice. "We will see to his injuries as soon as we are out of sight and reach of these human carrion." Sorcha began to fully detail what she would need to make a litter.

Ruari covertly studied the two young women he was now dependent on. The one called Margaret was a well-rounded fair-haired beauty with wide blue eyes and all the dimples any man could ask for. The woman called Sorcha was the one who drew his keenest interest, however, and he found that curious. Margaret was far more suited to his usual taste. Sorcha's heavily lashed, huge brown eyes were her best feature. They were dark pools reflecting a keen wit, strength, and determination, qualities he had never considered flattering in a woman. She had a small face, her fine bone structure clear to see. Ruari suspected that if she ever curved her full, tempting mouth in a smile, there would be no sign of a dimple. Her hair was thick and hung to her tiny waist, the rays of the setting sun touching upon reddish highlights in its rich chestnut depths.

Inwardly frowning as he recognized his attraction to the woman, an attraction strong enough to be stirred despite his pain and weakness, he carefully inspected her tiny figure. The drab gray gown she wore was snug, hugging every slim curve. Small high breasts, a tiny waist, and slim, shapely hips stirred his interest even though such a figure had never caught his eye before. She moved with a lithe, easy grace he had to admire.

What troubled him more than the fact that he was attracted to a woman who met none of his usual requirements was that this tiny woman was saving his life. That was surely going to produce a lot of jests from his kinsmen. The highly praised and honored Sir Ruari Kerr saved by an insignificant lass from an insignificant branch of the Hay clan? Ruari winced as he all too easily imagined the laughter of his kinsmen.

The sound of a footfall drew him from his bout of self-pity. One of the scavengers was approaching his rescuers. Ruari hastily assumed the posture of a dead man, praying he could keep his breathing shallow enough to be indiscernible. He heartily cursed his wound and the loss of blood which left him so weak. It insured that he could not fight. If death approached, he would like to be able to at least try to strike out at his killers before they cut his throat. All he could do was lie silent and pray that Sorcha Hay was as clever as she seemed to be.

Sorcha warily eyed the tall thin man as he stopped in front of her. She did not like this sign of strong interest on the part of the battlefield thieves. She definitely did not like the delay this intrusion caused. Now that she knew Dougal's fate and what she needed to do to help him, she was anxious to leave this place of unshriven dead and the treacherous humans who preyed on such misery.

"I see that ye build a litter," the man said, his voice soft and cold as he fixed his dark, unblinking stare on Sorcha. "Have one of you injured yourself?"

"Nay, sir, but I thank ye for your concern," Sorcha replied, cautiously setting her hand on her sword beneath her cloak. "We but need something to carry two bodies."

"Two bodies? Why do ye wish to remove the dead from the field?"

"Not all the dead, sir. Just two."

"Dinnae be clever, lass," he muttered, pointing one long, bony, and filthy finger at her. "Ye had best tell me what I wish to ken or ye and your bonnie companion may join these corpses."

"My cousin found one of our kinsmen upon the field, and we wish to take him home. We intend to take this mon as weel."

"Oh, aye? And I am to believe that he is a kinsmon, too?"

"Nay. I didnae claim him one, did I? He is richly dressed, of a breed not often left to rot on the battlefield. I thought that returning his body to his kinsmen may weel bring me a coin or two."

"Ye ken who this mon is?" the scavenger asked, eyeing Ruari speculatively.

"Aye, weel enough. The markings on his scabbard and his clan badge tell me to take him to the Kerrs of Gartmhor. I ken where that is."

"They are a wealthy clan," the man murmured, idly caressing his sword.

"They are, but I dinnae think they will pay so much for a corpse that 'tis worth ye dying to gain it." She nudged back her cloak so that he could see that she, too, had a sword.

When Margaret stepped up beside Sorcha, her hand on her sword as well, the man held his hands out in a conciliatory gesture. "Be easy. Ye have claimed the booty, and I honor your rights to it."

The moment the man slinked away Sorcha ordered Margaret, "Take Bansith and get that laddie ye found, then come right back here so we can toss this hulk of a mon on the litter."

"Are we to leave this place now?" asked Margaret as she grabbed the pony's reins.

"As swiftly as we can. The glint in that adder's eyes made me verra uneasy."

"But he said he would honor your right to the booty."

"That mon wouldnae ken what honor was if it grew legs and walked up to spit in his skinny face. Go on, Margaret, and be verra careful."

"Shouldnae ye go help her?" asked Ruari after Margaret left.

Sorcha looked at Ruari, wondering how he could speak, yet still maintain his pose of death. It was so good a pose it made her uneasy. "That mon recognized your worth, sir. 'Tis best if I dinnae leave ye unguarded," she replied, keeping a close watch on the scavengers and trying to talk clearly without moving her lips too much.

"And ye think a wee lass like yourself can stop him from taking whate'er he pleases?"

"Aye. The mon is a stinking coward. As long as he must fight to gain what he wants, I hold the advantage. I could not, howbeit, regain something once it is taken.

So, the wisest, safest plan is to keep a verra tight hold on what I have."

"And ye think your cousin can do the same?"

"Aye, and verra weel, too. One thing it is *not* difficult to make Margaret understand is when she is in danger, and she has been weel trained to defend herself."

Ruari had no opportunity to respond as Margaret returned. He was astonished at the speed with which she had accomplished her chore, but even more so when he saw the youth draped over the pony. His young cousin Beatham had disobeyed orders and joined the battle against the English. Ruari prayed the boy's wounds were not severe if only so the rash youth would soon be well enough to be disciplined. Just as Ruari thought to say something to his errant cousin, Margaret and Sorcha moved him onto the litter. Although the women were gentle and surprisingly strong, pain tore through his battered body, stealing his ability to think. It took all his will just to keep from crying out. Despite his efforts, a shaky sigh escaped him as they settled him onto the litter.

"Hush," Sorcha ordered, removing her cloak to spread it over him.

"He is sweating badly, Cousin," Margaret whispered.

"Dead men arenae supposed to sweat."

"Ye had best cease talking to this dead mon, then," Ruari said, his voice a hoarse shadow of itself.

"Aye," agreed Sorcha. "And I had best cover that poor ghastly face of yours."

He closed his eyes even as she tossed the hood of the cloak over his face. When the pony began to move, dragging the litter over the rough ground, his pain increased. It would be easy and undoubtedly advantageous to let the blackness fluttering at the edges of his mind sweep over him, but he fought it back. They were not out of danger yet, and, despite his helplessness, he wished to be aware if it struck.

"That mon is walking our way, Sorcha," Margaret said, looking back. "He appears to be encouraging a few of his companions to join him."

"Curse the fool." Sorcha stopped, turned, and readied her bow, expertly notching it. "I fear I must remind the dog of his own cowardice."

"Ye arenae going to kill him, are ye?"

"I cannae think of any mon who deserves to die more than that one, but nay, I willnae kill him. I will only show him that I can if I wish to."

She smiled faintly and shot her arrow. It pierced the ground at the man's feet, bringing him to an abrupt halt. He stared at the arrow then at her. When he took another wary step toward her, she calmly fired a second arrow. Again it landed directly in front of his feet. He took a few hasty steps back. His companions immediately deserted him, scurrying back to the far safer task of stealing from dead men. A moment later, he joined them.

"Do ye think he will leave us be now?" asked Margaret.

"I think so, but we had best keep a close watch on our backs. Hurry along, Margaret." As Margaret tugged the pony into its plodding pace, Sorcha followed, but kept a cautionary eye on the scavengers. "We need to place a goodly distance between this dark place and ourselves. Not only do I wish to be away from those dogs, but we are too close to the English here for my liking. In truth, I think we may be in England itself."

"Ye dinnae ken where we are?"

"Oh, aye, I do. I just dinnae ken who lays claim to it this year." Sorcha laughed softly as she watched Margaret's expression waver between fear and confusion. "Dinnae trouble yourself, Cousin. I may not ken exactly whose lands we stand on, but I ken weel how to get back to Dunweare. We will be home on the morrow. Now, we must try to reach a safe camping place and tend to the wounds these two fools have gained in this unending squabble with the English."

Chapter Two

Ruari cried out, opened his eyes, and saw only blackness. It was a moment before he could subdue his panic enough to realize he was still beneath Sorcha's cloak. At some time during the slow, torturous journey he had lost his grip on consciousness. He felt smothered, and struggled to move his wounded right arm enough to tug the covering from his face. His awkwardness made him curse even as the cloak was pulled from his face. Taking a few deep breaths, Ruari stared into Sorcha's rich brown eyes.

"We are about to camp for the night, sir," Sorcha said. "As soon as the campsite is readied, I will see to your wounds."

"And the lad?" he asked.

"Margaret has helped him o'er to a tree. His wounds arenae severe. Once we were out of sight of the battlefield, he sat up on the pony. We believe he was banged on the head, fell, and was left behind."

Slowly turning his head, wincing as even that small, cautious movement brought him pain, Ruari looked around the camp until he espied his young cousin Beatham. Despite his anger over Beatham's disobedience,

Ruari was relieved to see that Sorcha was right; the youth did not appear badly hurt. In truth, the boy was clearly well enough to indulge in a little flirtation if Margaret's smiles and blushes were any indication.

Still moving cautiously in an attempt to minimize his pain, he watched Sorcha prepare a fire and then looked over her choice of camp. He had to admire her selection. It held enough trees and undergrowth to allow them shelter yet not so much that an enemy could approach them completely unseen. It was also on a rise that allowed her a good view on all sides. Someone had taught the girl well, he mused, and wondered why. The expert way she set up camp only added to his curiosity.

All interest in her strange skills fled his mind, thrust aside by his pain, as she and Margaret shifted him from the litter to the bedding Sorcha had spread out by the fire. His wounds were serious, made all the more so by the long hours they had been left untended. As the women removed his armor and clothes, the urge to slip into the blackness was strong, its promise of sweet oblivion from his pain a great temptation. He clung to what few shreds of awareness he could, however. Ruari did not fully trust his rescuers yet.

"Ye would ease our distress greatly if ye would swoon," Sorcha muttered as she washed the blood and dirt from his body.

"Our distress?" Ruari spoke through gritted teeth, even her gentle touch almost more than he could bear. "I am the one in pain, woman. What trouble can it cause you?"

"I have always found such stubborn bravado troubling. I ken that ye cling to your senses as if ye held the Holy Grail and I am some heathen trying to snatch it from your hands. Ye allow yourself to suffer needlessly. That, my fine knight, is the act of a fool."

"The mon is in great pain, Sorcha," Margaret said. "'Tis unkind of you to insult him."

"He deserves such insults."

"Heed me, woman," Ruari began.

"Hush, fool. Ye can bemoan my impudence later. Bite on this," she commanded even as she stuck a thick piece of leather between his teeth. "Ye have three deep gashes that need stitching—the one on your right arm, the one on your belly that nearly cost ye your innards, and the one on your left leg. Either ye were attacked by a veritable horde of Englishmen or ye were too stupid to fall after receiving your first serious wound."

"'Tis a miracle he has not already bled his life away," murmured Margaret.

Sorcha thought so, too, but said nothing, concentrating on closing the worst of his injuries. She closed her ears to the sounds of pain he could not fully stifle. Although she detested adding to the man's agony, she comforted herself with the knowledge that she had no choice. The moment she tied off the last stitch, she looked at his face. His eyes were so glazed with pain they had lost all color, as had his face, and she knew he was barely conscious. She urged Margaret to go and finish tending the youth's minor hurts, and bandaged Ruari herself.

Now that she had finished the more onerous task of treating his injuries, she found herself taking an unsettling interest in his battered form. He was a big man, tall and strong, yet not bulky. His was the lean, hard strength of a wild animal. His skin was smooth, taut, and several shades darker than her own, almost as if he had allowed the summer sun to touch every inch of his body. As she wrapped clean strips of linen around his wounds, she found it difficult to resist the urge to smooth her hand over his skin to see if it felt as good as it looked. There was no hair on his broad chest. Tiny dark curls started just below his navel, ran in a straight line to his groin to provide a soft protection for his manhood, and diminished to a light coating on his long, well-shaped legs. He was, she decided, an exceptionally fine figure of a man.

Inwardly cursing her own weakness, she quickly finished bandaging him and covered him with her cloak. It was fortunate that his wits were dulled by pain or he would have noticed her ogling him like some greedy whore. She brushed the sweat-dampened black hair off his face, realized she was lingering over the chore and flushed guiltily. Sorcha wondered what ailed her as she tugged the piece of leather from between his still-clenched teeth.

"Are ye done mauling me, woman?" Ruari asked, astonished at how weak his voice was.

"Aye," Sorcha replied. "Ye may yet live."

"He is going to be all right?" asked the youth as Margaret helped him over to the fire.

"'Tis in God's hands," Sorcha murmured as she began to prepare a meal of oatmeal and barley bread. "Howbeit, he survived for many an hour with no aid. A mon that stubborn should do weel once he is clean and mended."

"And still awake?" The youth cast a nervous glance toward Ruari then paled.

"Aye," Ruari said, his voice strengthening as his pain eased.

"'Tis glad I am that ye have survived."

"Ye willnae be so glad when I regain my strength, laddie."

"Now, Cousin . . ."

"Cousin?" Sorcha asked, looking from the youth to Ruari and back again.

"I am Beatham Kerr," the lad replied. "Sir Ruari's cousin."

"Who was supposed to stay at Gartmhor," Ruari grumbled.

"But, Cousin," Beatham protested, "how am I to become a knight if I am always left behind with the women and children?"

"There is many a mon guarding the walls of Gartmhor who wouldnae appreciate ye calling them women or bairns."

"I am twenty now, Ruari. I shouldnae be coddled so."

"Asking ye to see to the protection of my keep isnae coddling ye."

"Enough," Sorcha snapped as she moved to Ruari's side. "Neither of ye are weel enough for this childish squabbling." She ignored both men's glares as she helped Ruari raise himself up enough to sip from the wineskin she held to his lips.

"'Tisnae wine," Ruari complained.

"Nay, 'tis a fine cider. I have little stomach or head for wine and I hadnae anticipated entertaining guests."

"Ye are verra sharp of tongue, wench."

"So I have been told. Ye must rest. That is a fact whether I tell ye sweetly or tartly. We have a long way to go on the morrow over rough ground and mayhaps farther still on the next day. That will depend on how much ye slow us down."

"We have traveled a fair distance already."

"Aye, though not as far as I would have liked."

"Ye must live verra near to the border with the English."

"Sometimes too near, but Dunweare is a hard keep to take, as ye will soon see. 'Twas built for defense." She shook her head as she returned to the fire and the food she was preparing. "And now ye have me talking with you as if we are but guests at some banquet. Ye need to lie quietly, fool."

"And while we speak of fools, which one of your kinsmen allowed two wee lasses to travel o'er this dangerous land to a battle?" Ruari winced as he tried to move into a more comfortable position only to restir the worst of his pain.

"We are hardly sweet, helpless lasses. Margaret and I can fend for ourselves. We left Dunweare not long after my headstrong brother did. We wished to be close at hand if he should need some help. Since he slipped away alone, we felt that was verra possible. At times my brother forgets his responsibilities."

"There is naught wrong with fighting the English. Your brother could bring great honor to your clan."

"At times, sir, a clan may need the mon far more than it needs honor. Now, be silent. I dinnae ken where ye get the strength to talk or why ye should be so eager to do so."

"I think 'twas all those hours of lying on the field alone, unable to help myself and with little hope of anyone coming to my aid." Ruari spoke in little more than a whisper, then closed his eyes, startled that he had spoken so honestly. He decided Sorcha was right. He badly needed to rest.

"Here now, isnae that just like a mon. He pesters a lass until she fair wants to scream, but just when she needs him awake, he sleeps."

The soft, husky voice, so close to his ear, as well as her words brought a swift halt to Ruari's descent into sleep. Her remarks carried a distinctly sexual meaning to his mind, but he sternly scolded himself for such thoughts.

Then he opened his eyes and met her gaze. The glint of mischief was clear in her dark eyes, and he frowned.

"Ye should choose your words with more care, lassie," he warned. "Someone could mishear them."

"Nay, I think not. I fear I have the habit of speaking most plainly. Margaret, prop this fool up so that I may try to put some food in his belly."

Although Margaret's softly rounded form was a pleasure to lean against and the plain fare Sorcha fed him was remarkably tasty, Ruari found that he lacked the strength and wit to appreciate either very much. A fierce will to live had kept him clutching at life and consciousness. Until his wounds had been tended, he realized he had feared slipping into unconsciousness, had feared that blackness would lead to the neverending oblivion of death. Now that someone had taken care of his needs, his battered body called out for sleep. He began to find even the simple chore of eating too much for him.

"Enough," he finally said, turning his head to avoid the spoon Sorcha held to his lips.

"Aye," agreed Sorcha. "Ye ate weel for a mon so close to death. It appears that eating has made ye cease to be so stubborn and recognize that ye need to rest."

"Truth. I must regain my strength." He closed his eyes. "There are at least two people I must discipline."

Sorcha smiled faintly when she saw how alarmed young Beatham was. She did not know Sir Ruari well, yet her instincts told her that the young man did not really have much to fear. If Ruari did anything more than loudly scold his cousin and perhaps insist that he do some less than knightly chores for a while, Sorcha would be very surprised. Her instincts told her that, concerning his family and friends, Ruari Kerr was more bark than bite, and at Dunweare her instincts had long

been notorious for their accuracy. It was that confidence
that, despite knowing that she was the second person
Ruari felt he needed to discipline, kept her from being
concerned about his threat. The only thing she did
worry about was how he would react when he discovered he was to be held for ransom. That could easily put
her on the side of his enemies in his mind. Sorcha was
sure that having Ruari Kerr as an enemy was something
any wise person would avidly avoid.

Inwardly sighing, she sat legs crossed before the fire
and began to eat her meal. Ruari would undoubtedly
be furious when she told him that he was her captive.
The fact that he had relinquished most of his original
distrust of her would only enhance his anger when she
informed him that his clan would have to pay to get him
back. Sorcha was startled at how sad she felt as she considered Ruari's anger. She did not even know the man,
yet the thought of him being angry with her, seeing her
as his enemy, was highly distressing.

Unsettled by her thoughts, she attempted to distract
herself by watching Margaret and Beatham who sat
across the campfire from her. It was amusing to watch
the youth flirt with Margaret. She clearly enjoyed Beatham's attentions, which was not surprising. Beatham
was a very handsome young man with his thick blond
hair and fine blue eyes. He was a perfect match for Margaret. Even in his wit, Sorcha thought with an inner
shake of her head.

After another few minutes of watching the pair,
Sorcha grew uneasy. Margaret and Beatham were doing
more than idly flirting. There was a natural rapport between them. Even though she knew it was not true,
Sorcha got the sense that Margaret and Beatham had
known each other for a long time. She was going to

have to have a long talk with Margaret and prayed the girl would be in the mood to understand. Beatham and his cousin were prisoners. Even if Beatham was willing to forgive that, Sorcha did not believe that Ruari would. Anything more than a mild flirtation between Margaret and Beatham was certainly doomed.

"Margaret," she said, gently interrupting a murmured confidence between the young couple. "I think Beatham should rest now." She turned to the youth. "Ye should bed down next to your cousin. Margaret and I must take turns standing guard so we cannae watch over him as weel."

"I can help ye guard the camp," Beatham offered.

"Nay. Your wounds—"

"Arenae that serious."

"True, but they have weakened you. They were left untended for far too long. Ye havenae got the strength to be a guard tonight. Howbeit, ye will have enough to tend your cousin if he needs aid."

"And that will be a great help, Beatham," Margaret said. "After all, if we had to stand watch *and* care for Sir Kerr, we would get no sleep at all."

Sorcha inwardly grimaced as she listened to Beatham talk grandly about the honor of helping such bonnie lasses. She cleared away the meal and, ordering Margaret to help Beatham spread out his bedding next to Ruari, went to get the bed pack she and Margaret would share. Her pony playfully nudged her as she reached his side, and she took a moment to see to his needs. Margaret joined her just as she finished watering the animal.

"Do ye wish me to take first watch?" Margaret asked, idly scratching Bansith's ear.

"Nay, I will." She handed Margaret the bedding. "Spread this near the fire and keep your weapons close at hand."

"Aye, I will." Margaret studied Sorcha for a moment before asking, "Does something trouble you?"

Sorcha briefly pondered a way to gently explain her concerns to Margaret then decided that directness was best. "I think ye would be wise not to get too friendly with Beatham Kerr."

"Why? He seems a nice young mon."

"Oh, aye, a sweet boy."

"Boy? He must be your age, twenty or so."

"True, but there is still a boyish air about him," Sorcha said, smiling faintly. "How I feel about him doesnae matter. I but try to stop you from losing your heart to a mon ye can ne'er have. He will soon count himself your enemy."

"Why? What could we e'er do that would turn the Kerrs against us?"

"Hold Sir Ruari and Beatham for ransom."

"I dinnae understand."

Checking to be certain Beatham was still too far away to overhear her, Sorcha replied, "Dougal is being held by the English. They will demand a ransom for him. Ye ken as weel as I that we have naught to buy his freedom with. The Kerrs of Gartmhor have some riches. As soon as I ken what the English demand for Dougal's life, I will ask that much from the Kerrs. I really have no choice," she added when she saw how crestfallen Margaret looked.

"But Beatham has played the courtier even though he kens he is a prisoner for ransom. Mayhap that means the Kerrs willnae hold it against us."

"He doesnae ken he is a prisoner yet." Sorcha idly rubbed at her temple, vainly attempting to massage away a beginning headache. She cursed Dougal for his impetuousness, for his mad search for glory which would now cost his family dearly. "I havenae told him or Sir Ruari."

"Why not? It seems they have a right to ken we are *not* the rescuers they think we are."

"They do, and I detest this deception, but it must be played out. They must not ken our plans until we are at the gates of Dunweare. We are but two lasses. Aye, they are wounded men, and we have fighting skills, but 'tis far safer if we play this game. If they ken my plan they may try to escape. Weel, I need not tell you of all the trouble that could come down on our heads."

"Nay." Margaret sighed and cast a longing glance Beatham's way. "He is such a sweet, bonnie mon. I felt a true softening toward him."

"I ken it. 'Tis why I felt I must warn you."

"Mayhap Beatham would understand and forgive us."

"He may, but Ruari is his laird, and that mon willnae forget and forgive."

"Aye, I think ye are right. How sad."

"I am sorry, Cousin."

"'Tisnae your fault. 'Tis Dougal's. He put himself in jeopardy. Although he can be an utter fool at times, our clan needs him. Ye must do all ye can to get him back. 'Tisnae your fault that I feel drawn to Beatham either."

"If it will help any, what I ask of ye now may just make the end of that courtship come sooner than later."

"What do ye mean? Dinnae ye think I could win the heart of a mon like Beatham?" Margaret demanded.

"Of course ye could. Aye, I suspect ye could draw a promise of marriage from him ere we reach Dunweare. And then he could meet our kinsmen and kinswomen." Sorcha smiled crookedly as she watched a look of understanding slowly transform Margaret's pretty round face.

"Oh, them."

"Aye, them. Mayhaps ye can find some solace in the fact that my actions now will save ye from suffering through that confrontation. They would all gather at Dunweare if there was a wedding. Beatham does appear to be kind and sweet of nature, but e'en he may balk at taking the Seven Sisters into his family."

"Aye and they are but a small part of the problem. I love my family dearly, but there are times when I wish I had been born into another clan."

Sorcha laughed and nodded, in complete sympathy. "Go and rest. I will take the first watch."

"Are ye sure we must be so vigilant? Ye must be as weary as I, and I could use far more than the few hours of sleep I can allow myself."

"Margaret, we are in the land both Scotland and England claim, yet neither can rule. 'Tis an area that teems with rogues, thieves, and men banished from both countries. Our family has suffered from living just on the edge of this wild land. Aye, we must guard the camp. Shelter the fire so that 'tis enough to keep wild animals at bay yet not so large it will act as a beacon for the villains who call this land home."

Nodding, Margaret left to spread their bedding out by the fire. Sorcha sighed, checked her weapons, and strode into the wood encircling the camp. She would establish a circular guard out of sight of the camp. As she studied her shadow caused by the moonlight shining through the trees, she realized she would present a small obstacle to any ruffian who wished to attack the camp. Her skill with bow, sword, and dagger was good, but it could never fully compensate for her lack of size and strength. Shaking off a brief attack of fear, she began her steady, watchful pace around the camp.

With each step she cursed her brother. He knew he was

needed, desperately so, to carry on the line. While it was true that she could take his place as laird of Dunweare, that whatever husband she might gain could stand for her in court or in battle, it was not the same. The line could weaken, losing the strength it would gain in going from son to son. Eventually the Hay name itself could fade. Dougal had bred no heir yet, had not even tried to find a wife. It was his responsibility to ensure the continuance of the line before he threw his life away on some battlefield. He had been told that since boyhood, so he had to know, yet he continuously shirked his responsibility. This time his inconsideration, while not fatal, had seriously affected her and Margaret. If Sir Ruari Kerr was the vengeful sort, it could even affect the whole clan. It was past time someone forced Dougal to listen to reason.

"Better yet, mayhap I should slap some sense into his empty head," she muttered then nervously looked around, her voice sounding far too loud in the quiet forest.

She sighed, kicked at a stone, then silently cursed as her toes painfully reminded her that her soft rawhide boots were not much protection against such nonsense. It alarmed her a little, but she had to admit that some of her anger at Dougal was because of Ruari Kerr. She did not understand why she was so attracted to the man or why the feelings had become so strong so fast, but she could not deny it. Because of Dougal's foolish act, she was forced to make Ruari an enemy. That both infuriated her and saddened her. All she could do was let matters take their course and pray that Ruari would not turn the whole incident into a long, bloody feud.

Chapter Three

"A prisoner?"

Sorcha stared at Ruari in surprise, amazed at how loudly he could shout. He looked so furious, so prepared to leap off his pallet and do her physical harm, she began to worry that she had told him the truth too soon. They were only yards from the heavy gates of Dunweare, a welcome sight after three long days of travel, but it might not be close enough.

"Aye, a prisoner for ransom," she replied, signaling Margaret to urge the pony to a slightly faster pace. "I intend to ask your clan to buy you and Beatham back."

"Ye would stoop to this when your own brother is being held for ransom?" Ruari demanded.

"I stoop to this *because* my brother is being held for ransom. I need the coin to buy the fool back."

He cursed her and started to sit up. Sorcha put one small, booted foot on his chest and pushed him back down. That she could accomplish such a feat told her how weak the man was. The way he glared at her through his tangled black hair revealed how furious that made him. Sorcha quickly removed her foot, pleased to see that they only had a few feet left to go and that the people within Dunweare's imposing walls had already moved to greet their arrival.

She glanced toward Beatham who, weakened from travel, rode on Bansith. He also looked furious although, on his softer features, the expression was more sullen than threatening. Beatham made no attempt to escape, however. Sorcha suspected his compliance was due mostly to the fact that Margaret held Bansith's reins. To break free, Beatham would have to strike her down. It was clear that no matter how angry he was, he could not bring himself to do that.

Cries of welcome from within the walls of Dunweare caught Sorcha's attention. It was not going to be easy to make her family understand why she was doing what most of them would consider a crime. Taking a person for ransom had not been the way of her clan for many a year. After a quick glance at a fierce-eyed Ruari, she hoped her family would have the strength to hold firm to their prisoners until the ransom was paid.

Ruari cautiously shifted his position on the litter in order to get a good look at Dunweare before he was dragged inside its walls. What he saw made him curse. It could well prove impossible to escape from such a stronghold.

Dunweare sat atop a rocky hill, the path to its gates little more than a twisting, narrow rut. Its high thick walls seemed to grow out of the rock itself. Little more than moss, thistle, and wind-contorted thornbushes grew all around, providing little cover for an attacker, or for anyone trying to flee the dark towers of Dunweare. Near the base of the hill where its incline softened and was greener, was a circle of cottages, an excellent first line of defense. The people living there would certainly make it difficult for anyone trying to cross the moat ringing the two sides of the hill that did not border the river. If a family had to live in one of the most dangerous places in Scotland, the Hays had chosen the best place to do so.

And, he thought, turning enough to glare at the huge, wooden, iron-studded gates he was being dragged through, such a stronghold had cost a lot to build. Sorcha had to be lying when she tried to justify her actions by claiming poverty. It struck Ruari as decidedly odd that he found her dishonesty more infuriating than her actions themselves.

A moment later his full attention was caught by the people crowding around them as they entered the bailey. He shifted a little, made uncomfortable by the dozen or more pairs of eyes fixed upon him. He frowned as he realized the curious crowd consisted mainly of the very young, the old, and women. There were a few armed men, but he would not deem them soldiers. A quick look up at the walls revealed only a few more men. He was certain Dougal Hay had come to the battle alone. This scarcity of soldiers puzzled him. He looked around, hoping that someone would say something that would answer at least a few of his questions.

Sorcha grimaced then laughed as four of her five aunts living at Dunweare rushed up to hug her. They all talked at once, their greetings and questions blending into an indecipherable babble. She breathed a sigh of relief when she saw Robert, the armorer, elbow his way through the crowd. He stood before her, his big hands on his hips, and stared first at Beatham, then at Sir Ruari, and finally at her. "Where is Dougal?" he asked, his voice so deep and authoritative everyone else grew quiet.

" Alive." She waited for the mumbles of thanksgiving to ease before adding, "But taken captive by the English."

"Curse that foolish boy. The Lord clearly made him pay for his bonnie face with his wits. Aye, I am glad he is alive, but I must ask for how long? We havenae anything to buy him back with."

Grizel Hay, the next to youngest of Sorcha's seven aunts, stepped up next to Robert. "If we try verra hard we may be able to gather together a small ransom. We cannae just shrug our shoulders and leave poor Dougal to his fate."

Sorcha smiled at her plump little aunt, noticing fondly that Grizel's big brown eyes held her usual expression of sweet optimism, and her brown hair was untidy as always. "I fear, Aunt, that a small ransom willnae do. The English lost the battle, and Sir Henry 'Hotspur' Percy himself was captured. The English will ask a heavy ransom to soothe their pride and try to recoup some of what they will lose when they must ransom their own men."

"Then Dougal is doomed," wailed Bethia Hay, Sorcha's spinster aunt, a too-thin, frettish woman who appeared to be one tiny bundle of dull brown from head to toe.

"I hate to agree with the old woman," Robert said, ignoring Bethia's soft gasp of outrage, "but I fear she may be right. When the English discover that we cannae buy Dougal back, they willnae just send him home out of the kindness of their hearts."

"I ken it, Robert, but I think I have the answer to our trouble right here." She idly waved a hand at Beatham and Ruari, directing everyone else's attention back to her prisoners.

"Weel, I did see that ye had brought a few companions

back with ye. Your kindness in helping the poor lads does ye honor, but I dinnae see how they can help us."

"I fear 'twas not just kindness that prompted me to drag these two carcasses off the battlefield."

"Ye wouldnae ken what kindness was if it reared up and spit in your eye," grumbled Ruari.

Robert kicked the litter, causing Ruari to hiss a curse of pain. "Dinnae speak so to our lady Sorcha."

Sorcha lightly touched Robert's muscle-thickened arm. "Nay, good friend, allow him his anger. I deserve it."

"Ye? Never!"

"Aye, me." Pointing to each man in turn, she introduced her captives. "This is Sir Ruari Kerr of Gartmhor, and this is his cousin Beatham. I have taken them for ransom." She waited as their shocked expressions slowly changed to consideration tinged with reluctance.

"'Tis a sad business to take a mon for ransom," said Robert, and several people murmured in agreement.

"I am glad ye think so," said Ruari. "Now mayhap, ye can talk some sense into the lass."

"Weel, sir, being only the armorer, I dinnae carry the rank to scold her," answered Robert, smiling faintly at Ruari's surprise. "Howbeit, I do take the liberty now and again."

"More now than again," grumbled Sorcha, but Robert ignored her, his attention fixed on Ruari.

"This time, Sir Ruari, I fear I must bow to her wishes. None of us likes the taking of men for ransom. 'Twas often done in the past, but in her father's father's time, the Hays of Dunweare cast aside the practice."

"Yet now ye are willing to cast aside their wishes and shame their memory."

"Aye, and I believe they would approve. Dougal must be returned safely to Dunweare." He moved to unhitch the litter from the pony. "We will care weel for ye and your cousin. Have no fear of that."

"Has all been weel, Robert?" Sorcha asked as he and two other men moved to help Ruari and Beatham into the keep. "'Tis most odd, but every time I leave Dunweare for longer than a few hours, I often get the feeling something back here requires my attention."

"And this time ye were right to think so. I believe wee Euphemia will soon be a woman."

Sorcha cursed, and a quick glance at Margaret revealed that her cousin was distressed by the news. She prayed the Kerrs would not be at Dunweare too long. The various oddities amongst the members of her family were often difficult for people to accept, but they were the least of her troubles. Young Euphemia making the transition from child to woman would bring to the fore all the reasons the Hays of Dunweare chose to live in such a remote place. Sorcha prayed that Ruari and Beatham would be ransomed early, too soon to discover all of Dunweare's dark secrets.

"Has it become a large problem yet?" she asked Robert, trying to keep her questions obscure so that Ruari and Beatham did not know what was being discussed.

"'Tis just beginning, but 'twas more sudden and stronger than I can recall any others being." Robert shook his head as he and the stablemaster hefted Ruari's litter up the narrow stone steps inside the huge tower house. "My innards tell me this will be a difficult one."

"Has Euphemia noticed?"

"Aye. And, ere ye ask, she hasnae cast aside her peculiar notions yet."

As she moved to help Margaret with an unsteady Beatham, Sorcha wondered what she could do. Her first thought was to confine Ruari and Beatham in a securely

locked room, but then realized that was a foolish idea.
The trouble hanging over Dunweare like some storm
cloud could not be locked out. Instinct told her that
Ruari Kerr was about to experience the full glory of
Dunweare's curse. She told herself it did not matter and
knew she lied.

Ruari bit back a cry of pain as he was lowered to the
bed. He wondered how he could endure so much—the
battle, the long rough journey to Dunweare, and the pain
of being moved from litter to bed. It seemed that such
pain ought to be fatal. It also seemed unfair that, now that
he was no longer so strongly in fear of his life, he found
it difficult to swoon and escape his pain.

"Where have ye taken Beatham?" he demanded when
he looked around and did not see his young cousin.

"Into the chamber next to this one," replied Sorcha as
she set a basin of water on a table near the bed and
began to wash the sweat from his body. "Ye have gone
and made yourself all asweat."

"'Tis hard work being carried about."

She ignored his sarcasm, turning to Robert, who
stood by her side, everyone else having gone to help
Margaret settle Beatham in his room. "Where is Neil?"

"Should be here soon," Robert answered.

"Ah, aye, I would prefer a mon tend to my needs," said
Ruari, frowning when Sorcha and Robert just grinned.

Before he could ask what amused them, the door to
his chamber was thrust open so powerfully it slammed
into the wall. He turned to see who had made such an
abrupt entrance and gaped. Striding toward the bed was
the biggest woman he had ever seen. She had to be six
foot or higher. Although she did not appear to have an
ounce of fat on her, she was buxom, sturdily built, and
obviously strong. When she stepped up to the bed, her

hands on her well-rounded hips, he slowly looked up the impressive length of her voluptuous body. He was a little surprised that she had light green eyes and not the brown so common at Dunweare, but his true interest was fixed on her hair. Tumbling over her square shoulders in a thick wavy mass to her waist was the reddest hair he had ever seen.

"Ah, Aunt, I am verra pleased ye are here to help," said Sorcha. "This is Sir Ruari Kerr." Sorcha was unable to control her grin as she looked at a still-gaping Ruari. "And, Sir Ruari, this is my aunt, Neil Hay."

"Neil?" Ruari shook free of his fascination with the woman and stared at Sorcha. "Did ye say Neil?"

"Aye, she said Neil," replied Neil, scowling down at Ruari. "I was the seventh of seven daughters. Papa couldnae think of another lass's name." She shrugged. "Aye, and he may have hoped that, if I was given a laddie's name, I would become the son he so badly wanted."

"Neil," Ruari muttered, shaking his head, but no one paid him any attention.

"Do ye really think this battered piece of flesh will gain ye enough coin to buy back my foolish nephew?" Neil asked Sorcha.

"Aye," replied Sorcha. "The Kerrs of Gartmhor are wealthy enough to spare a sack or two of coins to get their laird and his cousin back. We will wait until the English ask their price for Dougal and then ask the same of the Kerrs for him and the lad."

"No profit made in that."

"Weel, I dinnae do this for profit, Aunt, but out of need."

"Ye keep speaking of need, but I see none," snapped Ruari. "This is a fine sturdy keep, larger than most and stronger than any I have seen, save mayhap for my own. It had to have cost ye dearly."

"Verra dearly indeed—in coin and in lives," replied Sorcha. "What wealth our clan had was eaten away by this keep ere my father was born. Living on the edge of such a lawless stretch of land and so near the English requires a strong, dependable keep. Building such a place requires a great pile of coin. Aye, a great pile, and my forefathers were skilled at gaining that coin. 'Twas rare that a day passed without some poor soul wandering the halls of Dunweare awaiting his kinsmen and the ransom they would bring. And many a raid was made into England, raids that cost us the lives of our men."

"And ye now reveal that the blood of those reivers runs fast in your veins." Ruari started in surprise when Neil suddenly swung a tight fist at him, the blow quickly halted by Robert who grabbed the woman by the wrist. "I see her temperament matches her hair," he murmured as, after a brief staring match between Robert and Neil, she yanked back her hand.

"Mayhap we just havenae learned to accept insults as graciously as ye, sir," Sorcha drawled, pleased to see a hint of color tint his high-boned cheeks. "While my father was still a beardless youth, the true cost of this keep became painfully clear. We had bled Dunweare of its manhood."

"Here, lass, I dinnae think ye ought to tell the mon such things," Neil said.

"He and his cousin will be here for a while, Aunt. They would have to be blinded to stop them from seeing the truth for themselves. And, I believe Sir Ruari is warrior enough to have already seen that Dunweare could be successfully protected by a handful of suckling bairns."

"Aye, I saw that clear enough," agreed Ruari, his

reluctance to admit it evident in his deep voice. "Aye, and so too have I seen the lack of men-at-arms. I had thought the men had gone to battle, then recalled that Dougal came alone."

"Dougal kenned that no mon would go with him nor allow him to go if he revealed his plans." Sorcha moved to collect a blanket from an ornate wooden chest beneath a narrow window slot. "We depend upon Dougal to replenish the male half of Dunweare, sir, to replace the blood our forefathers so carelessly spilled onto the dirt of so many battlefields." With Neil's help, Sorcha spread the blanket over Ruari. "Ye *will* be held for ransom, sir, for we have no other choice. For nigh on fifty years our wee clan hasnae played the ransom game, a game most all others consider a fair one, even an honorable one."

"But ye *will* play it now."

"Aye, Sir Ruari, we will and dinnae think that because our army consists of the old, the verra young, the crippled, and women that we will play it poorly." As she spoke she tucked the blanket up over his chest and leaned closer to him. "Ye will be treated weel, kindly, and with the respect that is your right, but dinnae mistake any of that as weakness. If ye try to escape, we will stop you. If ye somehow manage to slip beyond our walls, we will hunt ye down. Ye are our captive, sir, and though ye may scorn your captors, dinnae let that arrogance prompt ye to act foolishly. I promise ye, we will make ye regret it."

Sorcha suddenly realized that she was staring at his mouth. It was a fine mouth, just full enough to be interesting. That mouth tempted her, drawing her closer, and that startled her. She quickly turned her gaze up to meet Ruari's more directly. There was a look of growing curiosity in his rich green eyes that warned her that her distraction had not gone completely unnoticed. Sorcha swiftly straightened up.

"I pray I have made myself understood," she said, inwardly thanking God for the steadiness of her voice.

"Aye, completely," Ruari replied.

"Good, then if my aunt doesnae object, I shall leave you in her care for now."

"Ye go, lass," Neil said. "I will see to the lad's care. Ye go and have a wee talk with Robert. He has a few things he has been wanting to tell you."

"About Euphemia."

"Aye, wee Effie. I fear we have a few troubling months ahead of us."

Although dreading all she was about to hear, Sorcha nodded and left with Robert. She felt a pinch of reluctance over leaving Ruari. He had been in her sole care for almost three days, but she knew that was not the source of her hesitation. Despite his anger, she had enjoyed being near him. It would be the first time since she had found him that she would be away from his side. The extent of the unease that caused her was a real concern. It was obviously not enough to remind herself that there was no hope of a steadfast attachment between herself and Ruari. She decided she needed to put some distance between herself and Sir Ruari Kerr, to dim her fascination with the man by concentrating on the troubles at Dunweare.

"Now ye may speak more freely about Effie," Sorcha told Robert as they walked down to the great hall.

"The trouble began but hours after ye and Margaret went chasing after Dougal."

"There was no hint of its onslaught?"

"Nay. 'Tis why I feel we are going to suffer a long, unsettling time. The spirits just descended. Aye, with a

cursed vengeance. Everyone kenned that Effie was
coming of age and expected the trouble to begin, but
even those of us who have been through this time and
time again, found the first onslaught so strong as to
cause us some qualms."

"Do ye think someone could actually be hurt this
time?"

"I will admit I am a bit afeared of that, yet there must
have been some bad times before, and I have ne'er heard
it told that any harm came of it."

"True. How is Effie reacting to all of this?"

"She refuses to believe 'tis happening because she is
to be a woman soon."

"Weel, I didnae want to believe it either when it happened to me. 'Tis a frightful thing to leave one's childhood behind, but when ye must face that change with
mischievous spirits hurling things about and being a terrible nuisance, 'tis a sore trial indeed. And there are
Effie's fancies to consider. The child seems truly convinced that she is a changeling, a bairn left behind by
the fairy folk. She probably thinks fairies dinnae suffer
the afflictions of mortal women."

Sorcha silently began to consider all she could say
to Euphemia in an attempt to make the girl accept her
coming of age with calm resignation. Calm was the
best. It was the one truth her family had uncovered
about the curse that haunted them. The calmer the girl,
the less violent the activity of the spirits. The noises
were muted, fewer objects were thrown about or stolen
and hidden away, and all the other nuisances grew easier
to bear. There was an herbal drink her grandmother had
brewed that would keep the girl calm, even sweetly
blissful, for hours at a time, but Sorcha did not like the
idea of using it.

Robert pushed open the heavy door to the great hall, and Sorcha stepped inside. She came to a halt so abruptly, Robert walked into her. Sorcha ignored his soft curse in favor of uttering a few of her own. The great hall was a mess. Two nervous women were picking up scattered candelabras, plates, and tankards and righting the tipped-over benches. It looked as if a wild revel had just ended, but Sorcha knew that was not the cause of the disarray. Even as she stepped into the room, a large shield hanging over the huge stone fireplace crashed to the floor. The two maids screeched, took a few deep breaths, and continued to pick up. Robert sidled around her and walked over to the shield. Sorcha followed, pulling a high stool over so that he could put the shield back.

"'Tis bad," she murmured, holding the tall, three-legged stool steady as he climbed on it.

"'Tis also far too constant, too unrelenting, for my peace of mind. The spirits are mightily stirred up this time."

"Mayhap Euphemia's change from child to woman will be a swift one." Sorcha grimaced when Robert gave her a telling glance as he jumped off the stool. "One can always hope."

"Hope all ye like, lass, but as ye do so, plan what we must do to ease this turmoil. Mayhap ye can speak to your own spirits. One of them may ken how to stop this."

"They dinnae seem to. I have asked them before. In truth, my ghosties dinnae seem to ken much at all. And I would prefer that they stay away for a wee while. I may be able to explain away things hurling themselves about or noises in the night, but I doubt I can explain a ghost or, since Ruari willnae be able to see my spirit, my talking to someone who isnae there."

"Ah, I hadnae thought of that."

"All the whispered tales and fears that forced our clan to move to this desolate place have faded. If Sir Ruari and his cousin become aware of our secrets, those dark stories could begin again. We have no other place to run, Robert."

"So what can we do?"

"Pray that Sir Ruari leaves here thinking no more than that we are all quite mad."

Chapter Four

Wincing slightly as he awoke, Ruari instinctively tried to move and as his battered body protested, he warily opened his eyes. It did not really surprise him to find someone by his bed. He had sensed that he was being watched. And he had not been left alone once in the three days he had been at Dunweare. What did puzzle him was why the Hays would make such a young, delicate girl his nurse and guard. The slim elfin-faced girl staring at him so intensely could not have reached womanhood yet. He began to squirm inwardly beneath the steady gaze of her huge blue eyes and he scowled at her.

"I dinnae think ye should be in here, lassie," he said, frowning even more when she idly brushed a thick lock of blond hair from her angelic face and nodded.

"Ye are uneasy," she said, her voice soft and melodic. "'Tis to be expected. Most of the mortal folk I meet are uneasy around fairies."

"Fairies?" Feeling thirsty, Ruari carefully inched himself into a sitting position only to find the tankard and ewer of water no longer on his bedside table.

"Aye, I am Euphemia, a fairy and a changeling. The

fairies took the true Euphemia the day she was born and set me in her cradle. Of course, these poor deluded folk have raised me as one of their own. They simply willnae heed me when I try to tell them the truth."

"Trying to make folk listen to ye can be a tiresome chore," he agreed, wondering if there was insanity in the Hay blood.

As he thought over the events of the past three days, he began to think that a deep strain of madness did indeed taint the Hays. He had heard strange noises in the night—crying, moaning, even a chilling laughter— yet no one could explain the sounds when he inquired about them. Now this young girl talked of fairies. With her fair hair loose and tangled, her gown light and flowing, and a coronet of wilted ivy in her hair, she did resemble one. It had the taste of madness as far as he could see. Ruari eyed her with an increasing wariness, wondering if she was the one making all the noises in the night and if she was dangerous. The idea of being murdered in his sickbed by a tiny, pale girl-child who was not in her right mind was acutely distressing.

"Have ye seen my water?" he asked, hoping he could turn her mind to more mundane and sane matters.

"I suspect the spirits took it. They have been most troublesome of late. Sorcha claims 'tis because I am soon to be a woman, but that is foolish. I am of the fairy folk. Ye would think the spirits would ken that and cease to haunt me." As she spoke she climbed onto his bed.

Ruari edged back as she leaned closer, one tiny hand on either side of him, her long hair tickling his chest. "What is this talk of spirits?"

"Mayhap they havenae troubled you, but surely ye have heard the noises in the night?"

"Aye, I have heard them." When she straddled his

body with hers, Ruari felt a distinct thrill of alarm. "I thought perhaps one of your kinsmen was troubled in his mind."

"Nay, 'tis but the curse of the Hay women. 'Tis said an old Pictish witch put this curse upon us." She leaned toward him, placing her hands on the headboard of the bed on either side of his head. "Whenever a girl of this clan approaches womanhood, the spirits come to torment us. 'Tis a bother, but to tell the truth, I am not sure I believe in curses. If 'twas only that, someone would have discovered a way to put an end to it all." She edged her face closer to his. "There are so few men about Dunweare."

"I did notice that." Sweet heaven, the child is trying to seduce me, Ruari thought, and struggled to move away only to discover that he had no room left to move. He was already backed up hard against the headboard. "I am verra thirsty, child. Could ye go and see what happened to my drink?"

Euphemia ignored his request, her wide gaze fixed upon his mouth. "Mayhap Sorcha is right when she says I am now a Hay and will soon be a woman, that when the fairies left me I ceased to be one of them. If she is right and I am soon to become a woman, that makes the lack of men at Dunweare verra troublesome indeed."

"Weel, ye cannae use me to ease *that* problem," Ruari snapped and tried to reach out, grab her, and push her away only to discover that such a movement caused him more pain than he wished to endure.

"Why not? Ye are a mon, and I am now more woman than child."

"Mayhap, but I am eight-and-twenty, lass. Old enough to have fathered you. 'Twould be best if ye cast your eyes elsewhere." Ruari gently raised his right arm, fought to ignore the way the movement pulled achingly at his wounds, and tried to push her away. He was unable to give her a push hard enough to dislodge her, however, for it caused him too much pain.

"Ye are certainly older than I would like, but as I have said, there isnae much choice at Dunweare."

Before Ruari could respond, she clasped his head between her hands and pressed her mouth against his. He did not have time to fully experience his shock over the young girl's brazen attack, however. The sound of something crashing to the floor quickly grabbed his full attention. Certain that someone had entered the room and misinterpreted the scene, Ruari shoved the girl aside, cursing at the pain that ripped through his body. He frowned when he saw no outraged kinswoman.

"I thought someone was here," he muttered then cursed as the water bowl and ewer were hurled across the room. Even as he tried to turn and shelter Euphemia, the girl leapt to her feet on the bed.

"Enough! I grow weary of these tantrums!" she yelled, shaking her small fists toward a chest as it was shoved away from the wall.

Unable to pull her down and out of the way, Ruari wriggled down to avoid the objects tossed around the room. Euphemia neatly ducked each object as she continued to curse the air. He turned his attention to the door when he heard someone banging against it. The door was not locked, yet whoever was on the other side was having great difficulty opening it.

"Curse it, let me in," cried a voice Ruari recognized as Sorcha's.

"No one is keeping ye out," he called back.

"Is Euphemia in there? I think I hear her."

"Aye, she is here."

Sorcha cursed and fought to open the door. She could

tell by the way an unseen hand held the door closed and the noises coming from within the room that the spirits were making themselves known to Ruari. What she wanted to know was what Euphemia was doing in Ruari's room. The girl had been specifically ordered to stay away from the prisoners. Sorcha swore that, when she got into the room, she was going to make Euphemia sorely regret her disobedience. Even as that angry thought crossed her mind, the door flew open, and Sorcha stumbled into the room. As she caught her balance and her breath, she looked around the room, noticed that the disturbance had ended, and turned her full attention on Euphemia.

"What are you doing in here?" she demanded, walking to the bed and yanking the girl off it.

"I came to visit our prisoner," the girl replied, fruitlessly trying to wriggle free of Sorcha's grip as she was dragged to the door.

"Ye were told to stay out of this room. Aye, told firmly to stay as far away as possible."

"Ye have no right to tell me what to do."

"I will show ye how much right I have later and I am sure your mother will be glad to repeat the lesson." Sorcha pushed her young cousin out of the room. "And dinnae try to hide. I *will* find you."

"Ye are just trying to keep him all to yourself," Euphemia complained as she stumbled into the hall.

"Dinnae be such an idiot."

Sorcha slammed the door behind her still-complaining cousin. She had a deep well of sympathy for little Euphemia, but the girl sorely needed some discipline. As she moved to tidy the room, she thought over Euphemia's parting words and she began to get very suspicious. Neil had recently complained that Effie thought of nothing but men, often bemoaning the lack of them at Dunweare.

Sorcha suddenly knew exactly why her cousin had disobeyed everyone and crept into Ruari's chamber. She turned to look at Ruari, only to find him staring at her in fury and confusion.

"And just what were ye doing with that child?" she demanded, hoping that an abrupt attack would divert him from the questions she knew he wanted to ask.

"I was doing nothing at all. That mad girl came in here, babbled something about fairies and spirits, and then decided I was here for her amusement." Ruari winced as he tried to shift his battered body into a more comfortable position.

"And of course it ne'er occurred to ye to try to use her silliness to devise an escape." Despite her sharp words, she quickly moved to give him some gentle assistance.

"Nay, I had no time to be so clever. That foolish child decided I was brought here to help her change from a child into a woman. Then somehow she made things fly around the room. 'Twas then that ye arrived." He watched her as she checked his wounds. "I demand ye tell me what game ye are playing."

"Game? What do ye mean?" She frowned when she noticed he had nothing to drink. "What happened to your tankard and the ewer?"

"Gone. And the game I speak of is those noises no one will explain and all that just occurred here. That lass spoke of spirits, but I am not such a fool."

"Mayhap not, but I suspect ye are thirsty." Sorcha went to the door, opened it, and, seeing her aunt Bethia, asked the woman to fetch some food and drink for Ruari.

"I grow verra weary of this," grumbled Ruari as Sorcha returned to his bedside and he grabbed her by one slender wrist to hold her by his side. "Ye will tell me what I wish to learn. I demand some answers."

"Ye are a verra demanding sort of gentlemon, arenae ye."

"And I begin to think ye and all of Dunweare are mad. There is that woman Neil who isnae only as big as any mon I have seen, but ofttimes acts like one. Then there is that wee birdlike woman who fusses o'er everything, talks without drawing breath, yet says naught."

"My aunt Bethia."

"Aye, her. And then there is the woman who says not a word and flinches each time I but blink."

"My aunt Eirie. She is a timid woman."

"Timid as a much-whipped cur. And let us not forget that wee deluded lass who was just here. She spoke of being a changeling and of spirits. From what little I have seen of Robert, he appears to be a sensible mon save that he heeds what all of ye say. Oh, aye, and let us not forget the curse the child spoke of."

"Ah, she told ye of our curse, did she?"

Before Ruari could reply, Bethia scurried into the room. She cast Ruari a nervous glance as she set a jug of mead, a small tray of bread and cheese, and a tankard on the table next to his bed. She paused, shifting from foot to foot when she saw how he was restraining Sorcha, but a quick shake of the head from her niece sent her hurrying out of the room.

"I have only been here a few days, but I begin to understand her skittishness," muttered Ruari.

Sorcha twisted free of his grasp. Ignoring his scowl, she moved to pour him a drink. She handed him the tankard, pleased to see that he had recovered enough to drink without help. As she cut him some bread and cheese she briefly debated with herself on how she should answer his persistent questions. He already suspected that the Hays

were all mad, so she decided to tell him the truth and let
him deal with it however he chose to.

"What *is* all this talk of spirits and curses?" Ruari asked
as he picked at the bread and cheese she set before him.

"'Tis said that far back in the thick mists of the past,
one of the Hay women roused a fierce jealousy in a Pictish witch. The witch cursed her and every Hay woman
to follow her. Whenever a Hay woman of Dunweare is to
become a woman, she must suffer through the torments
inflicted by ill-tempered spirits. 'Tis those spirits ye hear
at night, Sir Ruari. 'Tis those spirits who took your
drink. They are verra fond of hiding things. 'Tis those
spirits who put your bedchamber in such disarray."

"And ye believe this nonsense?"

She shrugged. "Why should I not? Each time a woman
of Dunweare begins the change from child to woman the
troubles begin. We have all suffered through it. 'Tis Euphemia's turn now."

Ruari took a deep drink of the sweet mead to wash
the food down then shook his head. "I was of the opinion that ye had some wits, but 'tis clear that yours are as
scattered as those of the rest of your clan."

"I see that ye have your doubts about what I am
telling you."

"Doubts?" Ruari laughed, wincing at the pain it caused.

"While ye are feeling so amused, I may as weel tell
ye the rest."

"There is more?"

Sorcha found his ridicule more annoying than she
knew she ought to. "The women in my clan are often
born with special gifts."

"Vast imagination?"

She ignored him. "I can see the spirits who walk the
land, see them and speak to them."

"Then why havenae ye had a stern word with the ones hurling your possessions around?"

"I can neither see nor hear those spirits and I fear the ones I do speak with ken little or naught about those troublesome ones. None of the Hay women with the gift has been able to reach them and reason with them."

"How inconvenient. Tell me, can ye call upon any spirit ye wish to?"

Sorcha could hear the heavy note of mockery in his voice. To her dismay, it hurt. She was not sure why, but she wanted Ruari to believe her, to accept her completely. That could prove dangerous. She knew she was doing a pathetic job of protecting her feelings, her heart. It was why she had done her best to avoid him since their arrival at Dunweare, but her family had begun to grow too curious about how she was acting. Telling him the full truth about herself could so disquiet him he could kill her growing infatuation with his own words. Sorcha just wished it did not have to hurt.

"Nay, I cannae call on anyone I wish," she replied. "I must settle for those spirits who decide to appear to me. My grandmother could reach out to others, but I have ne'er tried. I see and hear quite enough." She crossed her arms over her chest. "I realize ye find this amusing—"

"Why shouldnae I? 'Tis naught but a jest."

"'Tis no jest. Did ye not just see what happened in here?"

"Aye, and I mean to learn how ye played that trick. If ye think to afrighten me, it willnae work."

"To what purpose should I wish to afrighten you?"

"Who can understand the workings of a woman's mind?"

"Opinions such as that could cause ye a great deal of trouble at Dunweare, sir."

"And ideas such as yours can cause ye a great deal of trouble."

Suddenly Ruari was angry and, to his astonishment, afraid for her. He reached out, grabbed her by the arm, and pulled her close. Her closeness proved a distraction. He became intensely aware of her clean scent, the touch of lavender that wafted from her hair and clothes. Her thick, dark braid rested on his chest, and he could all too easily envision it undone, its silken waves caressing his skin. When he realized he was staring at her full mouth, hungering for a taste of her lips, he forced his thoughts back to the matter at hand. He could not believe she was mad or simpleminded, so she had to be suffering delusions bred of her kinsmen's wild tales. It was time someone made her aware of how lethal such delusions could be in a land rife with superstition.

"I am fully aware that my gifts are not widely accepted," Sorcha murmured.

"Not widely accepted? Such a gentle way of speaking, especially from a lass who has proven to have a sharp, stinging tongue. Such ideas can get ye killed, ye fool lass. Ye speak of things people dinnae understand, things people fear. Such tales can raise talk of the devil, and ye must ken what dire fate that can bring."

"Aye—death."

"Then why babble on so?"

"I dinnae babble and I rarely speak of these things. I but felt ye deserved the truth since ye are caught up in our trouble through no choice of your own. And I think seeing ghosties isnae truly something that would rouse people's fears to a deadly height. It does make them uneasy. That can stir up some verra dark gossip and much unpleasantness."

"Then cease talking such muck."

"'Tisnae muck, sir. 'Tis the simple truth. I cannae change that. I am what I am."

Ruari stared into her huge brown eyes. He saw no glint of madness or amusement that would prove she was playing some jest. The girl truly believed what she said. After what had just happened, he discovered there was a part of him that believed her and he swiftly subdued it. He had often heard of those who could peer into the shadows so many people feared and see what lurked there, but he had always scoffed at such tales. Ruari sternly refused to relinquish his skepticism.

He grew strongly aware of how alluring her small, heart-shaped face was and allowed that fascination to take hold. Being tempted by Sorcha was preferable to hearing her speak of ghosts and ill spirits. He decided the wisest thing to do was to ignore her talk, neither to ridicule nor accept it. He wished she was as easily ignored.

"Mayhap ye think ye speak to the spirits because ye are lonely," he said, his voice quiet and soft as he moved his hand just enough to stroke her thick braid.

"Lonely? Dunweare swarms with my kinsmen."

Sorcha found herself all too aware of their closeness, but she was unable to pull away. Her gaze was fixed upon his mouth, each movement of his lips causing her pulse to race. Men were scarce at Dunweare, and thus far she had escaped all knowledge of how tempting some of them could be, both physically and emotionally. She heartily wished she had remained so blissfully ignorant. Ruari Kerr's allure reached so deeply inside of her it was frightening.

"Ye are lonely for a mon, sweet Sorcha. How old are ye?"

"Twenty," she whispered, knowing she was being

seduced by the soft caress of his deep, rich voice, but unable to fight him.

"Long past marrying age. Mayhap, my bonny brown lass, ye are pining so for a mon ye have conjured one up in your mind."

"And ye claim that *I* speak nonsense," she muttered, but her brief flash of irritation was swiftly smoothed away by his sudden smile. The man looked so good when he smiled Sorcha was sure it was a sin.

"Lasses can grow as lonely as any mon. Your wee cousin Euphemia is proof of that."

"My wee cousin needs a sound cuff offside her empty little head."

"And what do ye need, Sorcha Hay?" Moving carefully to avoid any pain, he reached up to follow the fine lines of her face with his fingers. "Ye need something. I can see it in your eyes. They are huge, dark pools of longing."

It was hard for Sorcha to subdue a blush. The man saw too much. She prayed he did not see that her longing was not for just any man, but for him alone. The intense feelings swirling inside of her were exciting, frightening, and confusing. His touch, the way his lightly callused fingers moved over her face, made her want to lean closer and pull away at the same time. She was indeed filled with longing, but it pulled her two ways. She ached to find out just how good Ruari Kerr could make her feel, but she also longed to flee from him, to forget him and all the new confusing emotions he stirred up.

"I need ye to release me ere I reopen a few of your wounds," she said, but knew her threat lacked strength. Her voice was low and husky, robbed of the steel needed to relay a warning.

"Nay, I think ye but try to flee from what ye truly need. Ye hide in tales and imagination, locked away from the touch of a mon." He threaded his fingers into her thick, soft hair and tugged her mouth down to his. "Ye need the heat of passion in your blood to burn away all the delusions besetting ye."

Before Sorcha could reply to his arrogant statement, he brushed his lips across hers. All thought fled from her mind. She doubted she could put two sensible words together upon pain of death. A shudder tore through her when he gently nibbled at her mouth. She put her palms upon the bed to push herself away from him but lacked the strength to complete the move.

"Ye are a strange lass," he whispered as he teased her lips with small kisses. "Boyish in some ways, quite mad in others, yet thoroughly tempting. Enough play, I think," he growled and kissed her.

Sorcha uttered a soft, low moan as he ceased his teasing and began to kiss her thoroughly. She greedily opened her mouth when he prodded her lips with his tongue. The slow, heated strokes of his tongue inside her mouth caused her to tremble from the strength of the desire racing through her.

Suddenly Sorcha panicked. She tore her mouth from his, stared at him in open-mouthed shock for a moment, then scrambled off the bed. Without another word, she fled the room. Ruari Kerr had certainly shown her how good he could make her feel. If one small kiss could so enflame her, she was not sure she wanted to discover any more. Even as she ran away, however, she fought the urge to return to him, to his kisses and his touch.

Ruari eyed the door closing behind Sorcha with speculation. He idly touched his lips, still warm and damp from their kiss. He savored how her sweet taste lingered on his tongue. Sorcha Hay was all that he considered unsuitable in a bride, despite her good birth, and he had a few hard questions concerning her sanity. It had been a long time, however, since any woman had fired his blood with one short kiss the way Sorcha did. He decided his stay at Dunweare could prove to have some benefits.

Chapter Five

"Ye told him *what*?"

Sorcha grimaced at Robert's bellow. She had run straight from Ruari's room to the armory shed and Robert. For a few minutes she had fidgeted about, babbled aimlessly, and paced the room pretending to watch Robert put the finishing touches on a scabbard for Dougal's sword. Robert had finally cursed and demanded to know why she was plaguing him. She could not tell the man she was upset because one kiss from Ruari Kerr had her aching to crawl between the sheets with the man. Instead she explained how she had told Ruari the secrets of Dunweare and allowed Robert to believe she was upset about such disclosures.

"I told him all our secrets. Weel, the ones concerning the spirits leastwise. Euphemia went to his room, and he got a verra good look at the worst of our curse. I couldnae even get the door open. The spirits held it closed."

"Ye could have told him the door was stuck."

"Robert, we have spent the past three days mouthing such lies. He has heard the complaints, the crashes, the thuds, and all the noises that plague us all through the night. We have all twisted our tongues into knots trying to explain away those things. When Effie decided to creep into his room and play the budding whore, her ill-tempered spirits became quite enraged." Sorcha sighed and sat down on a stool made from a thick old log. "I fear there was no lie big enough or clever enough to explain away all he saw."

"Mayhap, but I am not sure 'twas wise to tell him the truth." Robert moved to stoke up the fire in his forge.

"He didnae believe me."

"That cannae be a surprise to you."

"Nay, yet I wish he had. I fear he now thinks we are all quite mad. Effie telling him all about being a changeling, a fairy caught in a mortal life, certainly didnae help." She smiled faintly when Robert leaned against the wattle-and-daub wall of the armory and started to laugh, although she was not sure what he found so amusing. "I am not sure I see the humor in all of this."

"Ah, weel, ye would, lass, if ye werenae so heartsore for the lad."

"I am *not* heartsore for Ruari Kerr," she snapped, jumping to her feet, but Robert just smiled.

"Oh, ye are. 'Tis why ye have been hiding from the mon since ye first brought him here. 'Tis also why ye came running in here to hide now and looking like a weel-kissed lass. If he is behaving too boldly, ye just tell me. The two of you can play all the games ye want, but I will-nae abide a mon taking advantage of you, or forcing ye to do what ye dinnae wish to do."

Sorcha cursed and kicked at a stone, sending it rolling out the door. "The mon will begin to think we have brought him here to play the stud for a paddock full of mares in heat." She ignored Robert's guffaw. "He holds a strong allure for me, Robert, and 'tis a dangerous thing."

"Dangerous? How so? Ye are both gentle born." Robert moved to stand near her, slouching against the doorframe.

"I believe he is higher born than I."

"Not by much."

"He is also a great deal richer than I. I dinnae e'en have a dowry."

"There is truth in all its ugliness."

"And he thinks we are all quite mad."

"He may change his thinking about that."

"He may or he may even prove to be a mon who finds a touch of lunacy in a lass an attractive thing." She exchanged a brief grin with Robert. "Howbeit, I have taken him prisoner for ransom."

"Aye, and unless he is a verra forgiving mon, that could pour water on the fire in his heart."

"Verra strangely said, but true. Nay, I dinnae think Sir Kerr will forgive this ransom matter verra easily. I am certain that his being taken by two lasses makes the bruise to his pride all the more tender."

"Do ye think he will return to Dunweare armed and eager for battle?"

"Nay," Sorcha replied and, after a moment of thought, knew she was as confident of her reply as she sounded. "He willnae raise his sword against us o'er this. I believe some of his anger is aimed at himself. Even though his first sight of me was upon the battlefield as I picked o'er the dead, he began to trust me."

"And instead of rescuing him, ye took him prisoner. Aye, that would make him wonder if he had been a wee bit of a fool. 'Tisnae a feeling any mon enjoys. Is that why ye are fighting your interest in him?"

"I am *not* interested in the mon. Not in the manner ye infer."

Robert snorted. The sound was so full of scorn it made

Sorcha curse. She opened her mouth to reprimand him only to frown when he tensed and stared out into the inner bailey. Looking in the same direction, she saw the too-thin figure of Robert's only son, Iain, hurrying toward them.

"Do ye think something is wrong?" she asked Robert.

"I think we are about to have guests," Robert replied even as he moved to greet his son.

"Father," Iain cried then paused to catch his breath. "Three men wait outside our gates. They are English and they ask to speak to someone concerning Sir Dougal."

"The ransom demand," Sorcha murmured. "Give me a few moments, Robert, then bring them into the great hall. Try to keep them from seeing our weaknesses too clearly."

"I will, lass," Robert said. "Howbeit, if they have the wit to see our weaknesses, they will also see our strengths. Dinnae worry o'er that. Just think on getting that fool Dougal back."

Sorcha nodded and hurried back to the keep, cursing her brother with each step. She dreaded dealing with these men. They would be scornful when they realized they had to talk over a ransoming with a woman. She would have to be strong, to make them believe she could take on the task as well as any man.

As she entered the great hall, she saw her aunts seated in a circle near the huge stone fireplace arguing with the newly arrived Annot over what color yarn would best depict their father's hair in the family tapestry they were working on. Sorcha hurried over to them, determined to enlist their aid. Although the Englishmen might be scornful toward one small female, she knew they would find confronting seven women a daunting experience. It was true that her nervous aunt Bethia and her shy aunt Eirie were not strong women, but when placed shoulder to shoulder with their more determined sisters, they were very skilled at pretending.

"The English have come to ask the ransom for Dougal," she told them as she reached Neil's side.

"Ah, ye want us to leave," murmured the tall, silver-haired Annot, the eldest of her seven aunts.

"Nay, I want ye to sit at the head table with me. Hurry now," she said as she shooed them all toward the long, heavy oak table set on a low dais at the head of the great hall. "I think even an arrogant Englishmon will be set aback when confronted with seven weelborn women."

"Ye want us to look stern and forbidding," said Grizel as she settled her short round body into the seat to the left of the high-backed oak chair Dougal usually occupied.

"Exactly." Sorcha took Dougal's chair, smiling faintly as her aunts lined up on either side of her.

"Do ye wish our help in the negotiations?" asked Neil as she sprawled in the chair on Sorcha's right.

"Weel, ye may put in a word or two, Aunt Neil," replied Sorcha. "I mean no discourtesy," she told her other aunts.

"None taken, m'dearling," Bethia assured her. "Long ago I learned how imposing we seven sisters can be when we array ourselves as one against someone or something. Howbeit, Neil is the one who can hold onto that strength even when she speaks, putting hard steel behind her words. I fear the rest of us begin to waver when we talk."

"Here they come," whispered Annot, who then clasped her hands in front of her and assumed a stony expression.

Three Englishmen strode into the hall, followed by Robert and his son. Their steps faltered slightly as they caught sight of the seven women staring at them. Sorcha saw Robert quickly hide a grin and knew he understood what game she played. She saw two more well-armed men take up the post of guards on either side of the wide door.

Robert left his son standing behind the three Englishmen and moved to stand on Sorcha's right. She was glad of his presence as she met the cold, steel gray eyes of the tallest of the three men.

"I am Sir Simon Treacher, and these are my men, Thomas and William," announced the man, his voice as cold as his eyes. "I am here to discuss the ransoming of Sir Dougal Hay. He is your liege lord?"

"He is," replied Sorcha, fighting the urge to shift nervously beneath his steady look. "What are your terms?"

"You expect me to discuss such a matter with women?"

"If ye want your blood money—aye. I am Sir Dougal's closest kin, his only sister."

"Ah, you are the Lady Sorcha Hay."

"I am."

"He said I would need to deal with you, but I assumed he was jesting. In England we do not allow women to play the lord of the keep, nor to take a part in such manly business."

"'Tis probably why your twice-cursed country is in such disarray," muttered Neil, glaring at the man. Simon ignored her, but the sharp lines of his long, narrow face grew noticeably tighter.

"Sir Dougal also mentioned a Neil Hay," he drawled, hinting that Dougal had not said anything he considered complimentary. "I believe I would prefer to discuss the ransom arrangements with a man."

"Ye may prefer it, sir, but I fear ye will be disappointed," said Sorcha. She waved her hand toward Aunt Neil. "This is indeed Neil Hay, Dougal's aunt. Now, do ye wish to discuss Dougal's ransoming with his sister or his aunt?"

"His sister," the man spat. "M'lady"—his tiny bow was riddled with mockery—"shall we begin?"

Sorcha nodded, mildly amused by his irritation. She ordered a page to fetch a bench for the men to sit on as well as wine for them to drink. Her amusement faded quickly when Sir Simon named his terms. He wanted a great deal for Dougal's life. For one solid hour they bartered, always polite, yet each determined to win the bargaining. At one point Neil rose to her feet in anger, slamming her fist on the table, sending several tankards bouncing hazardly close to a fall, and causing all three Englishmen to forget their manners, staring at her in gaping wonder. Sorcha took quick advantage of their astonishment, but only gained a small decrease in the ransom.

Throughout the negotiations Sorcha's unease grew. Sir Simon Treacher only took his eyes off her once—when Neil stood up in all her infuriated glory. The man was certainly trying to use the power of his unblinking gaze to make her bow to his demands, but there was more. As he bargained, a gleam of interest entered his eyes, a hungry look that made her skin crawl. She fought the urge to concede to his demands just to make him leave. Robert's increasingly dark look told Sorcha she was not imagining Sir Simon's lecherous stare.

When the negotiations were complete, the price and the place of exchange agreed to, Sorcha rose from her seat. She eyed Sir Simon's approach and extended hand warily, but could not ignore him. Such an insult could easily cost Dougal his life. He took her hand, slowly drew it to his lips, and kissed her fingers. There was nothing specifically offensive in the way he kissed her hand, but she could not shake the feeling she had just suffered an unwelcome advance. The moment he left, she sat down, poured herself some mead, and took a long restoring drink of the sweet honey wine.

"I feel as if I have just been privy to a seduction," muttered Robert as he helped himself to some mead.

"Aye," agreed Neil, scowling at the door. "That Sassenach wriggled in here like the adder he is and was eager to coil himself around our Sorcha."

"How verra colorfully put, Aunt Neil." Sorcha sighed, slumping in the chair and idly drumming her fingers on the ornately carved arm. "Between his looks and his touch, I do feel almost ravished."

"Mayhap someone else should go to the meeting to pay for Dougal's release."

"Nay, Aunt. I must go. The English may scorn the idea of a woman dabbling in a mon's business, but they understand that I act as laird in Dougal's place. They could deem it an insult if I send someone they consider an underling. And, if they dinnae see the emissary they expect, they could also fear a trick, and that would endanger Dougal."

"Aye," said Robert, "and we cannae afford to insult the English. They need no new reason to raid our lands." He looked at Sorcha. "Howbeit, that mon looked too eager to get his hands on you. Ye will go to that meeting with at least four men and Neil. 'Tisnae a big enough force to cause any alarm or insult to those cursed English, but enough to make Sir Simon Treacher think again about attempting to sate his lust for you."

"Mayhap ye are right, although I dinnae like the idea of taking men away from Dunweare."

"We can spare them. Now, ye had best prepare the message ye wish to send to the Kerrs of Gartmhor."

"I shall take great pleasure in throttling my brother when next I see him."

"Sorcha, I cannae find Beatham," Margaret cried as she raced into the hall, not slowing in her reckless pace until she stumbled to a graceless halt in front of the table.

"I dinnae think he has escaped," Sorcha said as Neil handed the disheveled Margaret a tankard of mead.

"Then where is he? He certainly isnae in his chamber."

"The lad was up and about this morning," said Neil. "He was also asking a great many questions about his cousin Sir Ruari."

"Have ye looked in Sir Ruari's chamber, Margaret?" Sorcha asked.

"Oh. Nay." Margaret gulped down her mead and headed out of the great hall.

"If ye dinnae find him there, we shall begin a search," Sorcha called after her cousin.

"Mayhap ye ought to go with her," suggested Robert.

"As soon as I decide what message to send to the Kerrs, I will go and see what our prisoners are doing." She sighed wearily and shook her head. "They are no doubt plotting an escape. The good Lord clearly feels I dinnae have enough trouble upon my table."

"I dinnae think ye look weel enough to attempt an escape, Cousin," Beatham told Ruari as he helped the man get a drink of hearty cider.

"I will be in another day or two." Ruari winced and softly cursed as he eased his aching body into a seated position. "Most of my pain has eased, and my wounds already begin to close."

"True, but ye are still weak." Beatham made himself comfortable at the foot of the big bed.

"It willnae be long before I have the strength to crawl out of this vulture's nest."

"Vulture's nest? Come, Cousin, 'tis not so verra bad here. I ken that being held for ransom isnae something to be enjoyed or wished for, but the women here seem verra nice."

"They are all quite thoroughly mad, their wits scattered to the four winds like thistledown."

"Margaret's wits arenae scattered."

"Margaret simply lacks enough wit for it to be scattered."

"Here now, ye shouldnae speak of her in such a scornful manner."

"Cease acting the outraged suitor, ye great dolt, and cut me some bread and cheese."

"Weel, ye still shouldnae speak that way about Margaret," grumbled Beatham as he moved to obey Ruari's command.

Ruari studied his young cousin for a moment, taking careful note of the youth's sulky expression. Beatham was a good-hearted lad, but his fair looks far outweighed his intelligence. He had thought Beatham sneaking off to battle, despite all orders to the contrary, was a problem, but realized that it was a petty nuisance compared to the trouble he could see his cousin courting now. As he chewed on the plain but hearty fare of bread and cheese, he watched Beatham retake his seat.

"Ye can cease wooing that lass," he said bluntly, his suspicions confirmed when Beatham blushed.

"She is equal in birth to me," Beatham protested. "And she doesnae push aside my attentions."

"I dinnae care. Ye arenae to get yourself entangled with a Hay."

"And why not?"

"It appears ye have forgotten that she is one of those who hold us for ransom."

"'Twas her cousin Sorcha's idea, not Margaret's, and she must obey Sorcha just as I must obey you."

"Aye, and ye do that so weel, too." He held up his hand when Beatham began to protest. "Dinnae trouble yourself to explain your disobedience. Your rushing to the battle despite my orders that ye stay at Gartmhor is the least of my concerns. Ye are to cease playing love games with Margaret Hay for many reasons. She is poor, and your family cannae afford ye making a match for love or passion alone. By taking us prisoner and demanding money for our lives, the Hays have destroyed what meager chance they may have had of making any marriage with the Kerrs. And your lass's heart will surely go cold when I exact my revenge for this insult."

"Ye dinnae mean to go to battle with the Hays, do ye?" Beatham demanded, going a little pale.

"Nay, but there is little else I will try. I willnae let this affront pass without some revenge. I cannae."

"But, Cousin—" Beatham began, only to jump to his feet when the door opened. "Margaret."

Margaret frowned as she strode over to Beatham and grasped his arm. "Ye shouldnae be in here. I was verra worried when I looked into your room and ye werenae there."

"Did ye think your full purse had fled?" Ruari drawled, earning a cross look from Beatham.

"He isnae weel enough to be out of his bed. He suffered quite a blow to his head and could easily grow faint." She started to tug Beatham toward the door. "Ye shouldnae have him in here, Sir Ruari. 'Tis most inconsiderate of you. Ye should have more sympathy for Beatham's injuries."

"Er—actually, Margaret, I came in here of my own accord," Beatham said.

"Then he should have had the sense and kindness to order ye back to your bed."

Beatham fought Margaret's pull long enough to say good-bye to Ruari. For a long moment after the door shut behind his cousin and Margaret, Ruari stared at it in amazement, then shook his head. It was a shame Margaret was poor and a member of Sorcha Hay's family. She and Beatham made a perfect match, he decided, and laughed softly. They would undoubtedly have the most beautiful and the most witless children in all of Scotland.

Ruari finished the last of his cider and was just wondering how or when he would get more when Sorcha arrived. She shouldered the door open, her hands full with the heavily ladened tray she carried, then kicked it shut behind her. He watched her closely as she took away the empty ewer and tray and replaced it with a full one. Despite his efforts not to, he thought about the kiss they had shared earlier and felt his whole body tighten with an eagerness to enjoy another one.

"So, your young cousin came by to visit, did he?" she asked as she gathered a bowl of water, a cloth, and bandages to clean and redress his wounds.

"Aye. Your cousin dragged him away not an hour ago." He bit back a curse as she eased off his bandages. "Any sign of poisoning in the wounds?"

"Nay. Everything appears to be healing swiftly and nicely." Trying to be gentle, yet knowing there was no way to avoid causing him some pain, Sorcha bathed his wounds. "Within a few days the stitching can be removed." She sighed and shook her head. "There will be scars, although I believe my stitching will prove good enough to make them neat and, mayhap, less noticeable than they might have been otherwise."

"Your healing skills are to be admired."

"Thank ye," Sorcha muttered, his tone making it clear that she had very little else he considered admirable.

"I will soon be returned to my full strength." As soon as she rebandaged the last of his wounds, he started to sit up, reluctantly accepting her assistance.

"And then ye mean to try to escape." She poured him a tankard of cider. "'Tis what ye and young Beatham discussed whilst he was here, was it not?"

"Nay." He smiled faintly. "We didnae have the time. Your cousin arrived to drag Beatham away ere we could make any plans. I did, of course, advise him against succumbing to your cousin's lures and wiles."

"Did ye? *I* advised *her* to stand strong against his attempts to seduce her." She was pleased to see that her slur on Beatham annoyed him as much as his insult to Margaret did her. "Ye shouldnae waste your strength trying to plot an escape. Ye willnae be here much longer."

"Have ye finally come to your senses and decided to stop this dangerous game?"

"I wouldnae call sending ye home without collecting a ransom, thus allowing the English to cut my brother's throat, coming to my senses."

Knowing that she would not fight him, at least for a while out of fear of damaging his wound, Ruari grabbed Sorcha by the arm and pulled her close. Once she felt he was healed enough to endure a little rough treatment, he knew he would not get ahold of her so easily. He intended to use his advantage to its fullest while he still held it. The annoyance darkening her deep brown eyes made him smile, for lurking behind it was the passion he had so briefly tasted earlier.

"I see that 'tis dangerous to stand too near you," Sorcha murmured, gently trying to wriggle free.

"It could be e'en more dangerous if ye get on this bed." He curled his arm around her tiny waist and tried to pull her slim body on top of him, but she tensed just enough to prevent his doing so without pain.

"Aye, verra dangerous indeed, especially for a mon with as many stitches in him as the tapestry on yonder wall."

Ruari laughed softly, grabbed her thick braid, and pulled her face close to his. He brushed his mouth over hers, and his body echoed the faint tremors rippling through her. Sorcha Hay was a passionate woman, the heat in her veins equal to his; Ruari was certain of it. He ached to enjoy that fire in its full glory. For now he would have to satisfy his hunger with a few stolen kisses.

Sorcha did not fight him as he took her mouth in a fierce kiss. She savored the heat it ignited within her. It was a dangerous path she was allowing him to pull her along, but she knew he did not have to pull too hard. When the kiss ended, she remained still in his arms, fighting to catch her breath as he traced the lines of her face with tiny soft kisses.

"I am a wee bit surprised ye wish to kiss a madwoman," she whispered. "Are ye not afraid of catching my madness?"

"Nay, I dinnae fear succumbing to your delusions. I do wonder, howbeit, if 'tis your touch of madness that gives your kisses that hot sweetness." He touched his mouth to hers, lightly sucking on her lower lip. "Ah, lass, I wish I wasnae injured. I am eager to spend the night all asweat with you."

Sorcha abruptly shook loose of the haze his kisses had plunged her into. She scrambled free of his hold and stood by the bed, torn between hitting him for his insulting words and accepting his crude invitation. He was looking at her as if he knew her thoughts, and she cursed. Fighting the temptation to pour the jug of cider over his head, she strode out of the room, swearing to herself that she would fight his seduction. She viciously silenced the voice in her head that laughed mockingly.

Chapter Six

"This isnae good," muttered Neil as she moved to stand next to Sorcha in the inner bailey. "Nay, this isnae good at all."

Sorcha grimaced, rubbing her hands up and down her arms as the evening chill began to add a bite to the breeze swirling through the inner bailey. She had been watching Margaret and Beatham play with four active puppies in front of the stables for twenty minutes. The pair were so engrossed in the puppies and each other that they had not noticed her scrutiny. They were, in truth, oblivious to everything and everyone around them.

She had warned Margaret several times, the last one only two days ago, moments after leaving Ruari's arms and realizing the depths of her own weakness. Margaret was not heeding the warnings any better than her own heart heeded the ones she gave it. Sorcha could heartily sympathize with her cousin. Beatham Kerr was a handsome, sweet-natured young man. It was also clear that, unlike his older cousin, Beatham's passion for Margaret was not simply a carnal one. It was difficult to know what to do or even if there was anything she *could* do.

"I have warned the girl many times," Sorcha said, sparing a quick glance up at her scowling aunt.

"So have I. E'en muddle-headed Bethia took the lass aside for a wee talk." Neil shook her head. "Margaret smiles, assures us all that she kens what we mean, thanks us kindly for our concern, and blissfully carries on just as ye see her now. Either she is more witless than I kenned she was or she is being polite when she does that. She is simply too kindhearted and sweet to tell us to mind our own houses."

"I think 'tis a wee bit of both. Beatham is no help either. He is as sweet and as witless as she is. I begin to think that they both believe that, despite all that has happened and all that will happen, they will get what they want—each other."

"Mayhap ye can speak to Sir Ruari. He may be able to knock some sense into the lad."

"I am sure Sir Ruari has already done so."

"I dinnae ken how ye can be so certain when ye havenae been near the mon in two days."

"I have been verra busy. There has been no time to coddle the fool." She scowled up at Neil when her aunt made a sharp mocking noise. "And what was that for?"

"Ye are a poor liar, child." Neil crossed her arms beneath her ample bosom and met Sorcha's look squarely. "Ye have been hiding from that mon for most of the time he has been here."

"That isnae true."

"Hah. If ye were animals, he would be the wolf and ye the poor trembling hare. Ye have ne'er had to be so cautious about your feelings, dearling, so ye cannae expect to suddenly become skilled at concealing them."

For a minute Sorcha considered continuing to strenuously deny what Neil—and too many others—thought.

With a sigh of resignation she decided it was useless. Neil was right. She was not used to concealing what she felt and was undoubtedly doing a very poor job of it. It might also help to have someone she could talk honestly with.

"And what do ye suggest I do? Pin my heart to my sleeve and wave it about as a banner heralding my stupidity?"

Neil laughed, then quickly sobered when Sorcha glared at her. "Nay, lass. And just because your heart goes in a direction ye dinnae wish it to, doesnae mean ye are witless. When I was a young lass, I suffered from a fever of the heart."

"Truly?" Sorcha immediately regretted her blatant surprise, afraid it would hurt Neil's feelings.

"Aye, truly. I ken I seem a hard woman, but as I said, I was young."

"Ye are but three-and-twenty now. 'Tisnae old."

"I was but sixteen when I lost my heart. The mon was no good, but I refused to see that. Weel, my heart did. My head kept telling me to be careful, but I was too fevered to heed that good advice. Didnae heed anyone else's good advice either. He was tall, strong, and handsome. I thought I had ne'er seen a bonnier face."

"I suppose Ruari Kerr does have a bonnie face," Sorcha murmured.

"Oh, aye, 'tis pleasant enough"—Neil exchanged a quick grin with Sorcha—"To make a long, dreary tale short, I loved that rogue with all the blind heat a young lass can muster. My own good sense and the warnings everyone gave me proved to be true. He didnae abide with me long. We were handfasted, but that was just so he could share my bed without one of our kinsmen threatening his life. The mon didnae e'en stay the year and the day. A few months and he disappeared into the mists, ne'er to be seen again."

"How is it that I ne'er learned of all this?"

"I was living with my sister Fenella in Stirling. Once I realized the fool wasnae returning, I came back here. 'Tisnae spoken of because no one wished to open old wounds. Now that I have spoken of it, I realize those wounds are healed now."

"I am sorry, Neil."

"Nay, no need to be sorry for me. I was sorely hurt, but once the pain eased, I realized I had no deep regrets. I had myself a fine time while that rogue was with me. Aye, I would cleave the maggot's head in twain if I e'er saw him again, but I am now able to recall all that was good, and those are some verra sweet memories."

"I am not sure I understand what ye are telling me," Sorcha shivered and wrapped her arms around herself in a vain attempt to protect herself from the chill air.

"What I am trying to tell ye is that ye should do as ye please." She draped her arm around Sorcha's shoulders and nudged her niece toward the keep. "'Tis growing chill and damp. We had best go inside. Staring at those two willnae change what is to be. 'Tis all in their hands. And your own fate is all in yours."

"Ruari will be gone soon," Sorcha said as she fell into step with her aunt.

"Weel, our lads willnae reach Gartmhor until the morrow or the next day," Neil said. "Then they must discuss the ransom, and then it must be gathered. The Kerrs will need about three days to come here. So 'twill be a week, mayhap more, ere Sir Kerr leaves. Ye dinnae have to ransom Dougal until twelve days from now. I suppose ye can continue to hide and your problem will ride away in a short while."

"Or?"

" 'Tis up to you, lass. True, ye think the mon can ne'er be yours and ye are probably right. What ye must ask yourself is which ye will regret the most—following your heart, taking a wee chance no matter how small it may be, or continuing to hide and never even trying to grab what ye want."

"Hard choices."

"Verra hard. But, ye will ne'er be faulted for whichever one ye decide to take."

"Thank ye for that comfort, Aunt. Mayhap I shall wander up to the great laird's chamber and see how he fares. Another visit with the arrogant fool may be all I need. But first, have ye seen Effie?"

"The child huddles in the great hall. She was banished from the kitchens this morning and refuses to understand why," Neil replied as they entered the keep.

Sorcha sighed, broke from her aunt's light hold, and strode into the great hall. She had spoken to Effie at least once a day since her return to Dunweare, but the child was not interested in listening. The girl's own mother, Eirie, had been reduced to tears just yesterday out of pure frustration and some fear for her child's sanity. Just as so many others had, Eirie had thought her daughter would cease to speak of being a changeling once she was on the threshold of womanhood.

She found Euphemia curled up on a bench near one of the narrow windows encircling the great hall. The girl looked so forlorn, Sorcha felt a strong tug of sympathy, but hastily shrugged it away. It was time to be firm, even scolding. There may have been too much kindness and not enough authority. Mayhap Effie had been too coddled.

"So, here is where ye have come to sulk," Sorcha said, sitting on the stone sill of the window.

"I am here because I have no wish to speak to anyone," Effie grumbled, staring down at her hand, her lower lip protruding in a childish pout.

"What ye wish matters verra little to me just now." Sorcha almost laughed at the shocked look the girl gave her. "'Tis far past time ye ceased feeling sorry for yourself and gave a wee bit of thought to others."

"And why should I think of them when they drive me away?"

"They didnae drive ye away. 'Tis just the mean spirits ye are tugging about that they dinnae want."

"There are *no* spirits!" the girl cried, leaping to her feet, her delicate hands clenched into tight fists.

"Sit down," Sorcha ordered, a little surprised when the girl obeyed her. She stared into Euphemia's big blue eyes and saw a deep fear lurking behind the childish expression of defiance. "It seems verra strange that ye can believe in fairy folk and changelings, yet not believe in spirits."

"I believe in *your* spirits."

"How kind. Euphemia, if there are well-behaved spirits who do little more than visit and talk, why cannae there be ill-tempered spirits who make noise, steal things, and toss things about?"

"Weel, they can just go and trouble someone else."

"That would be fine indeed, but they willnae. Ye are changing from a child into a woman—"

"I am not!"

"Effie, ye can shout and stomp your tiny feet all ye wish to, but 'twill change nothing. Ye are soon to be a woman."

"This isnae supposed to happen to fairies."

Sorcha stared at her young cousin for a moment as she began to understand Euphemia's delusions. "I suspect fairies have some similar affliction. After all, there must be new fairies from time to time, or they would disappear." She moved to sit next to Euphemia and took the girl's hand in hers. "Euphemia, becoming a woman may not be nice, may even be a wee bit frightening, but denying it willnae stop it. All ye are accomplishing at the moment is to make those troublesome spirits louder and stronger than they might be."

"Why do they have to be here at all?" She cursed when the shield over the fireplace crashed to the rush-strewn floor again. "Go away," she yelled.

"If ye would cease to fight the truth, ye would hear less of that. The more upset and angry ye are, the more upset and angry they are. 'Tis as if they are bred of your emotions, and the stronger your feeling, the stronger they are."

"Ye mean that if I am quiet and peaceful they will go away?"

"They willnae leave completely, but they will grow less bothersome. When ye are finally a woman, they will fade away. Ye must accept that as all the Hay women before ye have. God decided lasses must become women in this way, and ye cannae change His plan. I dinnae ken who or what decided we must do so with these spirits about to add to our misery, but that cannae be changed either. Mayhap someday a woman of the Hay clan will stumble upon the secret of banishing them, but until then they must be accepted."

"It seems to me the Hay women must shoulder a great many burdens." She scowled at her feet for a moment then glanced sideways at Sorcha. "Do ye think that, when I do become a woman, I shall gain a special gift as ye did?"

"Aye, ye may. Many a Hay woman has. Ye have drawn

these troublesome spirits so swiftly and so strongly it
would seem likely. Now, child, my mother's mother did
brew a potion that will help ye stay calm—"

"I dinnae want to take a potion."

"I didnae say ye had to. I but mention that there is
one. Ye may weel find yourself so weary of these spirits
ye crave a moment's peace. The potion will give ye one.
I just wished ye to ken that 'tis there." She stood up,
kissed Euphemia on the cheek, and then smoothed
down her skirts. "Now I must go and see how our prisoner Sir Ruari is."

"Sorcha, will ye tell the mon how sorry I am I acted
so foolishly when I went to his room?"

"Aye, I will, but I shouldnae worry much on how he
thinks of you. I am certain the mon believes it was just
some odd whim of a woman-child and has ceased to
consider it." She winked at Euphemia and was pleased
to see the girl smile briefly.

As Sorcha climbed the stairs to Ruari's chamber, she
felt her steps grow weighted with her nervous reluctance to see him. Not seeing him solved nothing, however. She continued to think about him. She blushed to
think of the times she had caught herself staring at nothing as she recalled the kisses they had shared. No
amount of work banished those heated memories. Neil
was right. Hiding from the man served no purpose at
all. Sorcha opened the door to his room and heartily
wished she could find the solution to her inner turmoil
before she did something she would regret.

Ruari sat up the moment Sorcha entered the room
and smiled at her. He had begun to think he had scared
her away. It did not please him to discover that he

missed her, but he reluctantly accepted the truth of it.
She was too thin, knew far too much about a man's ways
and had some very strange ideas, but he could not conquer a growing fascination with her.

"Have ye decided to grace me with your company for
a few moments?" he asked.

"Aye, if ye behave yourself." She collected a bowl of
water, a washing cloth, and clean bandages.

"Do ye truly think this is necessary?" he muttered as
she prepared to tend his wounds.

"We shall see." She removed his bandages and studied his wounds, astonished by their condition. The man
was healing with an almost miraculous swiftness. "I believe ye dinnae need the bandages any longer. Your injuries will fare better if allowed to breathe. Ye are a
wondrous healer," she murmured as she gently bathed
his wounds and dabbed them dry. "I dinnae believe I
have e'er seen wounds heal so swiftly."

"I was always quick to heal."

"I wouldnae be surprised to discover that these sword
cuts began to heal ere your enemy finished inflicting
them. Ye tell me that my talk of spirits could cause me
trouble. Weel, I suspect this rapid healing has roused a
question or two."

Ruari scowled, not pleased to be reminded of how odd
his ability to heal quickly was. It had caused him a few
uneasy moments. He attributed it to his own strength,
but others often wondered if it was a gift from God or the
devil. When so many suffered poisoning in their wounds,
death, or a crippling fever, his continued good health, no
matter how severe his injuries, was not often seen as the
blessing from God he considered it to be.

"It has been a week since I was cut down. I didnae

grow feverish nor did my wounds fester, so 'tis no great miracle that I continue to regain my strength."

"A weel-practiced answer, I think," she drawled as she put away her nursing tools.

"'Tis but the simple truth." Ruari frowned when he realized she was not listening to him.

Sorcha cursed as she caught sight of a familiar shadow in the corner of the room. It was an inconvenient time for one of her spiritual companions to seek her out. As the shape grew clearer, she cursed again. It was Crayton, the spirit who visited regularly, and could be somewhat of a nuisance. The fact that his image was so distinct, only slightly faded below the knees, told her he was not feeling playful. The scowl on his young, handsome face made her uneasy. Crayton was in a sour mood.

"Ye dinnae need to coddle the oaf as much as ye do," said Crayton.

A quick glance at Ruari assured Sorcha that he heard and saw nothing. She was never quite sure if Crayton spoke aloud as mortals did or if she heard him only in her head. At times she was certain of the latter, but the former was never as easy to discern. The one thing she was sure of at the moment was that she wanted Crayton to leave. She tensed as he moved to the bed and glared down at Ruari.

"Go away," she whispered and grimaced when Ruari eyed her warily.

"I should like to leave, mistress, but I was made to believe I was a prisoner," Ruari said.

"I wasnae speaking to you." With a distinct flounce of irritation Sorcha sat down on the edge of the bed and stared at Crayton. "I ken that ye dinnae believe a word I say about spirits and ghosts, but I fear one has come to annoy me."

Ruari frowned and looked around then wondered why he bothered. Did he really think he would see proof that she was not a victim of strange delusions? He realized that her claims of being able to talk to ghosts were not as unsettling as her actually doing so.

"I cannae see anyone," he said, watching her warily as he wondered if her madness was truly the harmless kind.

"Of course ye cannae. If ye could see him, ye wouldnae be eyeing me as if ye fear I will suddenly begin to drool, babble, and tear at my hair. Believe me if ye will or think me a sad, addled lass, I really dinnae care at the moment. All I can say is that I speak the truth when I tell you there is a ghost in this room. Nay," she cried when, cursing softly, Ruari got to his feet.

Sorcha could not move quickly enough to stop Ruari from walking through Crayton. All she could do was catch Ruari as he swayed and began to fall. The grin on Crayton's face annoyed her. She waved him out of the way as she helped Ruari back to his bed.

"I must have gotten to my feet too swiftly," Ruari muttered as he laid down.

"Weel, that may be some of your trouble," agreed Sorcha as she helped him get comfortable. "Howbeit, what ye were just afflicted with happens when ye walk through a ghostie."

"I walked *through* him, did I? He wasnae gentlemon enough to step out of my way?"

"Nay, he wasnae, and ye need not speak so bitingly." She poured him a drink of cider and handed him the tankard. "Dinnae ye believe in ghosts at all?"

"Nay, I dinnae believe in anything I cannae see and hear."

"Ah, then ye have spoken with and seen God, have ye?"

"Dinnae be impertinent. That is quite different. And, since ye mention God, why would He allow spirits to wander the land when He has so many places for the souls of the dead to go?"

"I wouldnae be so blasphemous as to try to explain God's ways."

"Verra clever," he snapped. "Have ye *any* explanation for why spirits would wander the earth, *if* they do, and why they should choose to speak to a wee lass?"

"Does the fool think ye are some bottomless font of wisdom?" asked Crayton dryly.

"Hush, Crayton. Why dinnae ye go and visit with my Aunt Neil?" suggested Sorcha.

"She cannae hear me. She just kens that I am near and talks to me."

"Then wait for me in my bedchamber. Ye should have more concern for this mon. He was wounded fighting the English."

"Do ye think he saw the mon I search for?" Crayton asked, drawing near to the bed again.

"Nay, of course he didnae. Ye were murdered when my mother's mother was but a bairn. Your killer is long dead now and having his toes roasted in hell. I dinnae ken why ye willnae heed me when I tell you that." Sorcha sighed when Crayton glared at her then left, fading into the wall. She turned to find Ruari staring at her a little too intently for her comfort. "He is gone."

"Ye didnae answer my questions. Why are there ghosts, and why should they come to ye?"

"I dinnae ken why these spirits linger," she replied. "My mother believed it was because they had left something undone, and until they felt that all was cleared away, they wandered the earth. As far as I ken, none of my kinswomen have met a spirit who died peacefully, his priest at his bedside, and his death not only expected but accepted. The spirit who spent the most years with my mother was a young woman named Mary who had been cruelly murdered by her husband. It took years for the truth to be discovered but when it was and the mon was punished for his crime, she left and my mother never saw her again."

"And ye said this Crayton was murdered." Despite himself, Ruari was interested, although he tried to convince himself that it was simply because he liked a good tale.

"Aye. An English raiding party stumbled across him and his lover, Elspeth. The poor lass was raped and murdered before his eyes, and then he too was murdered. The men responsible must all be dead by now, for it happened so long ago, but Crayton lingers, needing someone to be punished."

"He cannae find many Englishmen here."

"Nay, but he died not far from here, and I think he may be stuck here. Why do ye ask so many questions if ye think I am mad?"

"Mayhap I but try to see the reasoning behind your delusions."

"And mayhap ye are just bored." She stood up and moved to the door. "Ye will have to seek your entertainment elsewhere, sir. I dinnae really like being the source of your amusement."

Ruari sat up as she opened the door. "Ye cannae expect everyone to believe ye without question."

"Nay, I dinnae ask that of anyone. I do not, howsoever, expect to be thought mad or made an object of ridicule."

He winced when she left, shutting the heavy door behind her with a distinct thud. Sending her away angry and offended had not been his plan, he thought as he slumped against his pillows. When she had arrived after hiding from him for two days, his first thought had been to cheer the opportunity to steal another kiss and to hope for more, much more. Instead she had begun to speak of ghosts and talked to someone who was not there. He, in turn, had acted as if she were foaming at the mouth and waving a bloodstained battle-axe around. That was no way to accomplish a seduction.

"But she speaks to the air," he muttered angrily then took several deep breaths to calm himself.

Many people believed in ghosts. Even though he had never met anyone who thought he could talk to them, he had no right to scorn her beliefs. She was right to get so angry. He stared at the door and wondered how long she would hide from him this time.

Chapter Seven

"Ye cannae sleep because this isnae the bed ye wish to be in."

Sorcha cursed as that familiar soft voice echoed in her head. She pounded on her pillow then sighed, sitting up and lighting the candle on the table by her bed. Although she knew light or the lack of it made no difference to Crayton or to her ability to see or hear him, she preferred it. She poured herself a small drink of mead and stared at the vague shape beside her bed. Tonight she could only see Crayton's head and shoulders clearly. It was not her favorite of all his various manifestations.

"Ye should have a little more respect for the lateness of the hour," she scolded him,

"If ye want that mon, why not go to him?" Crayton asked. "'Tis what my Elspeth did,"

"Aye, and it got her killed." She grimaced. "I am sorry. That was cruel."

"'Tis the truth. That mon has been here for almost a fortnight. His kinsmen will come for him soon."

"And then my troubles will be over."

"Nay, they willnae be. Ye will just grow weepy."

"I have *never* grown maudlin," she snapped, then banged her tankard down on her bedside table and blew out the candle. "If ye dinnae mind, I was trying to sleep," she grumbled as she laid back down.

"Ye cannae sleep and ye ken it as weel as I do. 'Tis why I am here. I have watched ye toss and turn for o'er an hour."

"'Tis evident ye have no respect for a person's privacy either."

"Go to his bed, lassie. Ye ken that ye want to."

"Aye, I want nothing more than to become Ruari Kerr's whore for a night or two." She felt a chill on her shoulder and knew Crayton had touched her.

"Ye would ne'er be his whore," Crayton said. "Ye ken it and so does he."

She glared at him. "And just how would ye ken what Sir Ruari Kerr thinks? He doesnae see you and he certainly doesnae talk to you."

"I am a mon."

"Ye are a ghost and a twice-cursed interfering one as weel."

She put her pillow over her head even though she knew it could never shut Crayton out. He was saying all the things she kept thinking, and she wanted him to stop talking. Part of her wanted to throw all caution to the wind, climb into Ruari's bed, and thoroughly enjoy all the passion she knew he could give her. Another part of her told her to stay away, to hold tight to her virtue and honor. It had helped her stay well out of Ruari's long reach so that she could not be further tempted by his kisses. So far she was obeying the more sensible part of her, but doing so was causing her some sleepless nights. Even when she did go to sleep, she dreamed of all the things she was fighting so hard to deny herself.

"I am saying no more than your Aunt Neil says or your other aunts who are too cowardly to say it to your face," Crayton said.

"Are they all discussing me behind my back?" The thought of that dismayed Sorcha.

"They love you, lass. 'Tis the one thing about this clan that ofttimes astounds me. Ye all are quite fond of each other, e'en of that witless, reckless Dougal. Your kinswomen just wish ye to be happy. As do I. Truly. And I have some experience in such matters. I have seen many a lass at Dunweare pine for her laddie and many a mon caught tight in the throes of lust."

"Oh, aye—lust. I suspect seeing men caught up in their lust is no great trick. 'Tis now clear to me that most men suffer from that affliction. The very first Englishmon I have ever had dealings with proved that when he eyed me most lustfully. In truth, Sir Treacher's looks were so lustful, I felt dirty by the time he left." Sorcha screeched softly in surprise when suddenly Crayton's face loomed right in front of hers. "Stop that! I am accustomed to ghosts, but even I suffer a shock when a disembodied head floats right in front of my face." She frowned when she saw the tight expression of fury on his face.

Crayton ignored her. "Did ye say that this lustful Englishmon was named Treacher?"

"Aye, Sir Simon Treacher. He came to Dunweare to discuss my brother's ransom."

"Ye met with my murderer."

"Nay, Crayton. That is impossible. Even if the mon who murdered you and Elspeth lived a very long, full life, he would still be food for the worms by now."

"Then this mon must be his son, his blood. Ye *must* make him pay for his father's crimes."

"I suspect this mon is your murderer's grandson. This

mon was older than me, but a great deal younger than
my parents." She watched as Crayton paced, or so she
guessed from the back-and-forth movements of his head
and shoulders. "And although this mon seemed a low
sort of fellow, I dinnae believe in making anyone pay for
the crimes of his forefathers. He may be no relation to
your killer at all. He could just have the same name."

"Were his eyes like the cold steel of a dagger blade?"

"Weel, aye—"

"And was his voice as cold as the ice cracking o'er a
pond on a late winter's night?"

"Aye, but—"

"And I would wager that he had a long, narrow face
cut in sharp lines and thin, dull black hair."

Sorcha cursed softly. "Aye, so he is clearly a kinsmon
of the mon who killed you. I am sorry, Crayton, but I
still cannae extract blood for blood when he wasnae the
mon who committed the crime. And how would I explain how I learned of the crime? Am I to walk up to
him, tell him a ghost told me his forefather killed him,
and now he must die for the crime? I think I would
swiftly, and loudly, be decried as utterly mad."

"So, ye willnae help me gain the revenge—nay, the
justice—I have waited so long for?"

"I didnae say that. I but said I wouldnae kill a mon
simply because his father or his father's father committed a crime against you. There may yet be a good reason
to kill him. He is one of the men holding my brother,
and if anything has happened to Dougal, I will be seeking my own vengeance."

"Fair enough." Crayton studied her for a moment.
"So, are ye going to go to Sir Ruari's bed?"

"Ye are like a dog gnawing on a bone. Nay, I willnae
play the whore."

"Ah, then ye willnae care when ye find him gone in the morning."

"Gone?" Sorcha tensed as she sat straight up in bed. "What do ye mean, gone?"

"He and that lackwit of a cousin are creeping down the hill."

"Why didnae ye tell me this before?" she cried as she leapt out of bed.

"I have told ye now, havenae I? 'Tis good enough."

"How far have they gone?"

"Not verra far the last time I looked."

"Weel, why dinnae ye go and look again whilst I get dressed."

Sorcha muttered a curse after Crayton disappeared from the room. The playfulness of the spirits could often be highly irritating. Crayton knew she would be interested in Ruari's attempt to escape, but purposely withheld that information until he felt inclined to release it. Sometimes she dearly wished he was more solid so she could hit him. As she yanked on her clothes she prayed Crayton had not waited so long that Ruari and his cousin had successfully completed their escape. She cried out in surprise when Crayton's face suddenly appeared in front of her again.

"Will ye stop doing that? I shall be aged before my time," she growled.

Crayton ignored her complaints. "Ruari and the laddie will soon cross the moat on the southern side of Dunweare. None of the guards upon your walls has spotted them yet."

"If I can rouse Robert and his son quickly enough, we can slip through the bolt-hole and catch those two fools as they reach the other side of the moat. If they dinnae drown first, that is."

Sorcha threw on her cloak and rushed out the door. She cursed the dark every step of the way as she hurried out to the stables. Once inside she hollered up to the loft where Robert and his son made their home during the warmer months. It was a moment or two before a tousled Robert appeared at the top of a thick-runged ladder.

"Is there some trouble, lass?" he asked even as he buckled on his sword. "I heard no alarm."

"That fool Sir Ruari and his witless cousin Beatham are escaping," she replied, then paced until Robert and his son joined her. "Crayton says they are about to cross over the moat on the south side."

"We can go through the bolt-hole and be there in time to catch them."

"Aye, just as I thought, Robert. Fetch a good lantern, please. I cannae abide creeping through that dank tunnel in the dark."

"Dinnae worry, lass. We will fetch them back."

"I pray ye are right, Robert. Otherwise, Dougal's ransom is gone."

Ruari cursed softly as he crept toward the moat. One touch with his fingers was enough to tell him that the summer's heat had done very little to warm the water. His wounds were nearly healed, but the exertion needed to creep out of Dunweare had left them aching. He doubted that even a short swim in such icy waters would do them much good.

"We are almost free, Cousin," said Beatham as he crouched on the bank of the moat next to Ruari.

"Almost. Dinnae let your hopes rise so high they make you foolish, however. We could still be taken. Aye, anywhere 'twixt here and home."

"Once we are on the other side of this moat, we can run toward the wood and safety."

"Mayhap once we are inside the wood I will feel safer, but at this moment all I can see is a great deal of open ground and far too many chances of being seen."

"Are ye verra certain ye are weel enough to do this?" Beatham asked. "I ken that ye are a miraculously fast healer, Cousin, but it has been barely a fortnight since ye were gravely wounded."

"I am weel enough to flee this cursed place. Cease trying to use my injuries to return to Dunweare and Margaret Hay. Get in the water and try to cross it as silently as possible." Ruari gritted his teeth as he eased his own body into the cold water, feeling the chill bite deeply into his barely healed wounds.

"At least the water is clean," said Beatham through equally gritted teeth.

"How can ye tell that in the dark?"

"There is no smell to it."

Ruari took a deep breath and realized his cousin was right. Despite the cold, the tension in his body eased a little, and he knew he had been somewhat concerned about exactly what he might be swimming in. As soon as he touched the far bank, he hauled himself out of the water then turned to help his cousin up the embankment. Both of them were shivering badly, and Ruari prayed that the night air did not grow any cooler, or they could easily contract a deadly chill.

He was about to tell Beatham that they must move to the trees when a faint light fell over him from behind. Fury tightened his stomach as he realized what that light meant. They had failed.

"And just where did ye think ye were going?" asked a soft, sultry voice Ruari recognized with ease.

Sorcha shook her head as both men turned to look at her. She did not need the light from the lantern to show her how wet and cold they were. She could hear their teeth chattering.

"We felt we had abused your hospitality long enough, mistress," Ruari replied.

"How considerate ye are, sir. Howbeit, there is no need for you to creep off like thieves in the night. We are more than willing to accommodate you both until your kinsmen come to take ye home. Gentlemen," she called to the four armed men with her, including Robert and his son, "please escort our guests back to their chambers. We would not wish them to take a chill whilst in our care."

As he was led toward the imposing gates of Dunweare, two burly men flanking him, Ruari heard the sound of the drawbridge being lowered. He looked at Sorcha who walked just to his right and in front. "How did ye find us? I heard no outcry and saw no change at all in the activity upon the walls or in the cottages we slipped past."

"Not all our guards are visible," she replied and grinned when Robert and the other Dunweare men laughed softly.

"What do ye mean?" Ruari demanded.

"Crayton, my ghost, told me ye were creeping down the hillside."

"Ye wish me to believe my escape has been thwarted by a spirit?"

"I dinnae care if ye believe it or not. 'Tis the way of it."

Beatham nodded. "Margaret said—"

"Cousin," snapped Ruari, immediately silencing the youth. "Ye cannae mean to tell me that ye believe in all this nonsense?"

Sorcha smiled when, even in the dark, she could see the high color in Beatham's cheeks, and the way he nervously eyed her. "Ye shouldnae demand that the mon make such a definite statement of belief or disbelief, Sir Ruari. He fears to anger you by saying 'aye' and yet fears to offend me by saying 'nay.' Leave him the right to hold his opinion to himself."

Ruari was about to reply when the four Hay men stumbled over a rut in the dark. He immediately took advantage of their distraction. Slapping Beatham on the arm in order to get the youth to follow him, Ruari bolted for the wood. He did not have much confidence in his chances of escape, but hated to walk back into Dunweare with the meekness of a lamb. Only briefly did he fear that his and Beatham's lives were in danger. The Hays wanted them hale and alive, for they needed the ransom. He smiled when he heard the startled, angry cries of Sorcha and her men. There was some small pleasure to be found in making the Hays work hard for their prize.

The thick protection of the forest was just steps away when Ruari experienced a feeling he had endured only once before. A coldness swept through his already chilled body, and he grew completely disoriented. Dizzy and unsteady on his feet, he collapsed. He sternly refused to believe that, as Sorcha had told him once, he had walked through a ghost, but he heartily cursed the unseen entity anyway.

"Thank ye, Crayton," Sorcha said as she walked up to Ruari and watched Robert help the man to his feet. She smiled faintly at the barely visible form of Crayton. "I hadnae realized ye could come this far."

"If he had taken another few steps, I might not have been able to help." Crayton looked toward the wood. "I

can go in there. Aye, at times I am pulled there against
my wishes, but I dinnae go there of my own accord."

"'Tis the place of your tragedy?"

"Aye," he whispered and faded away.

"I thought Ruari collapsed because he was still weak
from his wounds," said Beatham as he and Ruari were
gently but firmly steered back toward Dunweare by
Robert and the other men. "Ye say it was your ghostie?"

"Utter nonsense," grumbled Ruari as he slowly regained his balance and walked more steadily.

"Then ye *are* unweel." Beatham quickly put a sup-
porting arm around Ruari.

Ruari shook off his cousin's light hold. "I am *not*
unweel. I wasnae felled by some insolent spirit, either,"
he snapped, glaring at Sorcha.

"Ye stumbled, then, did ye?" asked Sorcha, biting
back a smile caused by his stubborn refusal to believe
in Crayton.

"Aye, that will satisfy as an explanation."

"I am pleased to be able to give you some satisfaction."

Sorcha flushed beneath the sudden sharp look he
gave her. Even in the dark she could read in his expression what he was too polite to say before others. He was
not so reticent whenever they were alone, so it was easy
for her to guess at what he wanted to say. Although remaining at arm's length had saved her from the blinding
effect of his heated kisses, it had not halted the constant
seduction of his words. He knew she wanted him, and
he constantly prodded at that. She forced herself to
simply smile briefly and then concentrate on getting
him and Beatham secured inside Dunweare.

As they ushered the Kerrs toward their bedchambers,
Margaret suddenly approached them, and Sorcha sighed

with a mixture of annoyance and resignation. Her cousin wore a voluminous white nightrail, and her thick blond hair tumbled freely to her tiny waist. The spell-bound look upon Beatham's face warned Sorcha that the romance between the two was probably already beyond halting. The scowl on Ruari's face told her that he was no happier with the situation than she was.

"Where did ye go?" Margaret demanded of Beatham, making no effort to hide her anger or her hurt.

"Ruari and I tried to flee," Beatham replied in a weak voice. "'Tis our duty."

"Your duty is to worry me to death?"

"We were safe enough."

"Margaret," Sorcha said, halting the conversation before the two could reveal more than they might wish to before others. Although, she mused a little crossly, the romance was certainly no secret. "Why dinnae ye take Beatham back to his bedchamber and see that he is made dry and warm."

Margaret took Beatham by the arm and dragged him toward his bedchamber, softly scolding him every step of the way. Sorcha could not hear what Beatham murmured in reply, but his tone indicated that he was doing all he could to smooth down Margaret's ruffled feathers. He was certainly not sternly reminding her that his duty as a Kerr was to try to thwart the Hays' attempt to collect a hefty ransom on his head.

"I can take care of this fool from here, Robert," Sorcha said, grasping Ruari's arm and trying not to worry so much over the state of Margaret's heart. "I think our prisoners now realize the folly of any attempt to escape."

"Are ye sure ye dinnae need any help strapping this stallion down?" muttered Robert, eyeing Ruari with blatant distrust.

Sorcha inwardly grimaced when she saw the look on Robert's weathered face. Her problems with Ruari were clearly no secret despite all her attempts at denial. Although it was comforting to know she could depend upon Robert for support or defense, she wished he had remained blissfully ignorant of all that passed between her and Ruari. It was a little embarrassing to have so many people knowing her private business. It also meant that most people at Dunweare would undoubtedly know what decision she finally made about Ruari and when. She dearly loved the people of Dunweare, but at times like this, she would also dearly love a little more privacy.

"I believe I am capable of tethering him," she told Robert.

"Weel, first ye will let my son get him out of those wet clothes. His lordship isnae a badly wounded mon any longer. Go on, Iain." Robert nudged his son toward Ruari. "Take the fool into his bedchamber and make him dry and warm."

Ruari inwardly cursed as Iain took him into his bedchamber. He would unquestionably need assistance in shedding his wet clothes, but he had hoped that Sorcha would be the one to help him. She would not be able to stay out of reach if she had to assist him in undoing his sodden laces. He had looked forward to his first good chance in days of stealing another kiss, of stoking the fire that burned between them to such a height it finally robbed her of all reticence. Inwardly sighing, Ruari grudgingly accepted the help of a silent Iain.

He thought it odd that he could go so quickly from the hearty disappointment of a failed escape attempt to wondering how and when he could get Sorcha Hay back into his arms. It was increasingly evident that he did not really know what he wanted. One moment he was anxious to get as far away from Dunweare as possible, and the next he wanted to hold tightly to the very woman who made him a prisoner. Ruari wondered if the madness that was so rampant at Dunweare was beginning to infect him.

"We are all verra fond of wee Sorcha here," Iain abruptly announced as Ruari, dressed only in a clean, dry pair of braies, sprawled on his bed. "She has far more wit than her reckless brother."

"The woman talks to the air, and ye all coddle her madness," Ruari snapped.

"Simply because ye dinnae believe her doesnae make her mad. 'Tis such thinking that forced us to move here. Ye didnae think we *chose* to live in the midst of reivers and outcasts and so close to the cursed English, did ye?" Iain shrugged. "Many folk believe in angels and saints, plant rowan trees to ward off witches, and fear the devil and all his unseen minions, yet no one suggests that they are mad."

"The teachings of the church feed such beliefs. Howbeit, they dinnae speak of ghosts."

"Nay, but the church does speak of the soul and the spirit of a person. It doesnae matter. If ye dinnae believe, then there is little I can say to change your mind. I just wished to warn you that any hurt dealt to our Sorcha willnae set weel with any Hay."

"That much I *do* believe and could easily judge for myself." Ruari winced and smoothed his hand over the still-raw scar on his abdomen. "Mayhap ye could tell Lady Sorcha that I think I may have done my wounds some harm. " He met Iain's disgusted look with a smile and, after the youth left, waited tensely to see if Sorcha would respond to his ploy.

* * *

"He doesnae expect us to believe that, does he?" grumbled Robert when Iain repeated Ruari's complaint about his injuries. He scowled at Sorcha. "Ye arenae thinking of going in that room, are ye?"

Sorcha sighed and lightly rubbed at her temples as indecision began to make her head ache. "Robert, I love you dearly and I ken that ye only have my weel-being in mind when ye speak so bluntly. Howbeit, I am twenty now, Robert." She turned to look at him. "All of my life I have stepped so verra carefully, a close eye kept to duty. I dutifully learned all of my lessons and dutifully took on the burden of being the lady of Dunweare. For all of my admittedly few adult years I have dutifully tried to keep Dougal's recklessness from harming Dunweare. I help my aunts. I help my cousins. I help the people who depend upon the Hays and Dunweare. I could continue until your eyelids are weighted closed with boredom. Mayhap, Robert, I am past due a wee bit of recklessness myself."

"Aye, ye are," said Iain, grabbing his father by the arm and tugging him away.

Although Robert looked startled, then annoyed, he made no attempt to break free of Iain's hold and allowed his son to lead him away. Sorcha turned to stare at the door to Ruari's bedchamber. She took a deep breath to steady herself and reached for the door latch. Instinct told her that the moment she entered the room she would be making a decision.

Chapter Eight

Ruari sat up and smiled when Sorcha entered the room. He quickly recalled that he had made a complaint about his wounds so he winced and lightly rubbed his scar. Sorcha stood by the side of his bed, her hands on her slim, shapely hips. The look on her face told him that she was not fooled by his ploys. He felt his hopes rise, even though a small voice in his head struggled to recall him to the possibility that she could simply have come to confirm her own suspicions, not to fall into his arms.

"I think I may have pulled something," he murmured, trying to look pained, but knowing by the disgusted look on her face that he was failing miserably.

"Aye, ye try to pull my leg, or at least attempt to tug upon my sympathies," she grumbled even as she dutifully checked his wounds. "Ye still heal with an astounding speed." She gave a soft cry of surprise when he curled one strong arm about her waist and tugged her down on top of him. "Healing is clearly not all ye do with undo haste."

"Haste?" He wrapped his other arm around her, holding her just tightly enough to still her attempts to squirm free. "We have kenned each other for many weeks."

"Not so many that ye should feel so free to force your lewd attentions upon me."

"That was spoken with an almost believable piety and outrage."

"Yet ye apparently dinnae believe that I mean it."

He brushed light kisses over her softly flushed cheeks. "Not as deeply as ye would like me to think ye do." When the tension of resistance began to leave her slender body, he moved his hands to gently cup her face. "Ye could don a nun's garb and fair glow with the light of piety and innocence as ye intone poetic, heartrending words of denial, but it wouldnae change the fact that your passion matches mine."

His arrogance annoyed her almost as much as his feather-soft kisses enflamed her. The fact that he was right only annoyed her more. She could speak beautifully of what was right and proper and demand that he treat her as the wellborn virgin she was, but the words would be empty ones. She wanted to be held close to his large, strong body. She wanted his kisses and his touch. Her denials and demands to be released were born of the remnants of honor and pride, but behind them lurked hypocrisy.

In truth, honor, pride, and a sense of propriety had very little to do with her constant denials. Her nays were born of fear, a fear of being hurt. She wanted to taste the passion he offered, but knew that her heart could easily be torn apart. Sorcha was not confident that she had the strength to risk so much on what appeared to be an already lost cause—his love.

"I think ye forget who is the prisoner here, Sir Kerr," she said, hoping that reminding him of his humiliation would make him angry enough to push her away, thus relieving her of the need to make any weighty decisions.

"Oh, nay," he replied, touching a kiss to the hollow behind her ear, and smiling against her skin when she shivered. "And ye must ken that, somehow, someday, I will make ye pay for this. Howbeit, this flame we spark within each other is a thing apart from that. 'Tis a thing that makes us equals for it holds us both captive."

"'Tis also a thing ye could use to wreak your revenge against me." Just speaking of such a possibility aloud was enough to send chills down Sorcha's spine.

"Nay, never. As I have said, our passion is something apart from all else that exists between us. I am not a mon to use passion in such devious ways. Nor am I a mon to promise anything simply to have my way with a lass. I detest such games."

"I suspect ye dinnae need to make use of them either," she whispered as she stared into his rich green eyes, their color made all the more intriguing by the desire he made no attempt to hide.

"I would rather be celibate than entangle myself in such lies and ploys."

"Ah, so it isnae concern for a lass's feelings that keeps ye so honest, but a desire to protect yourself from troublesome women wailing loudly about broken promises and vows ye have neglected to honor."

"Ye dinnae have much faith in your fellow mon, do ye?"

"Why should I have much faith in a mon who tells me plainly that he means to seek revenge against me?"

"Because I *did* tell ye plainly."

That made a strange sense, Sorcha mused, even as she arched her head back to allow him free access to her vulnerable throat. She knew she wanted to believe him although he often said things she did not wish to hear. If she could trust in his word, it somehow made it more acceptable to become his lover. At least then she would only appear foolish for trying to capture a man who bluntly told her he only sought her passion, and not become the object of pity because she was seduced by flattery and false promises.

She struggled to keep her mind sharp enough to think straight, but it was increasingly difficult. Ruari's big hands moving slowly up and down her sides, his thumbs brushing the side curves of her breasts, made her thoughts cloudy. The only thing she was sure of was how much she wanted him. The only words she could hear clearly in her head were the words of advice given to her by others—"take all ye can now, take the chance now, or ye will be forever sorry."

"I shall delight in heartily thrashing my wayward brother when he returns," she muttered.

"What does your brother have to do with this?" Ruari teased at her lips with tiny, nibbling kisses.

"'Tis his fault that ye are here. If he hadnae gone to that battle and been captured by the English, ye would ne'er have been found by me."

It suddenly occurred to her that if she had not found him, he would be dead. It was a chilling thought. She could tell by the look that briefly darkened his fine eyes that he was well aware of this. She could also tell that it would not soften his need to seek revenge.

To try to win his love was clearly a lost hope. She should wrench herself free of his light hold, leave the room, and stay out of his reach until his kinsmen came to ransom him. A heavy sigh that held both pleasure and resignation escaped her as Ruari pressed a fuller kiss upon her mouth. She curled her fingers into his thick hair and pressed her lips against his, silently asking for one of the deep kisses that could set her blood on fire.

Knowing how dismal her chances were of finding a lover or a husband, she simply could not turn aside the delights he offered her. This could well be her only chance of tasting them.

"If ye mean to hold fast to your chastity, lass, ye had best flee the room now," he warned, his voice hoarse with desire.

Sorcha lifted her head to look at him, sitting up slightly on his body. The lines of his face had tautened, and his cheeks were lightly flushed. There was a dark compelling look in his eyes that pulled strongly at some need deep within her. She hopped off the bed, smiling to herself when he tensed, began to protest, and clearly bit back the words. He was being gallant, and it was costing him dearly. That gesture only strengthened her decision. She reached the door, latched it to insure there were no interruptions, then turned back to face him.

Ruari felt the frustration that had begun to knot his body swept away by a flood of searing desire. A simple "aye" would not have carried the power of her eloquent gesture. He slowly sat up as she tugged the leather tie from her hair and shook her thick chestnut waves loose around her slim shoulders. Ruari was sure that he had never ached so badly for a woman in his life. Nor had he ever seen anything so simply and quietly sensuous. It took all of his willpower not to leap from the bed, sweep her up into his arms, and toss her onto the bed. He wanted her to walk to him, to willingly enter his arms. He wanted there to be absolutely no doubt that she would take him as her lover.

He clenched his hands into tight fists as she walked toward him. Although he felt she was strong and sure of her decision, he did not wish to make any sudden moves that could cause her to falter. There was not much time left before he was ransomed and returned to Gartmhor, a few nights at best. He wanted to spend every one of those waning hours wrapped in the soft heat of her passion.

Fleetingly he thought about his claims that the trouble between them, due to her holding him as a prisoner for ransom, and their passion for each other were two separate things. That was not exactly the truth. Although his anger and need for revenge did not dim his passion for her, it did influence what may or may not develop between them beyond the desire pushing them into each other's arms. He did not envision himself wanting more from her than sweet passion, for Sorcha Hay was definitely not what he sought in a wife, but he knew that any emotional softening he might start to feel for her would come up hard against the anger, stung pride, and need for vengeance that so often knotted his innards.

Sorcha stopped by the edge of the bed, her legs almost touching his. Ruari realized she had misread his silence and lack of movement. There was a ghost of uncertainty in her dark eyes. He reached out and took her small hands in his.

"Your 'aye' was verra eloquent, lass, but are ye certain of it?" he was astonished to hear himself ask. "I offer ye only passion, no more."

"I ken it," she replied, blushing faintly. "Have I asked more of ye?"

"Nay, but most weelborn virgins would."

"Weel, Sir Kerr, I believe ye have been at Dunweare long enough to ken that I am not like most weelborn virgins." She smiled faintly when he laughed. "I am no child, either. I am twenty, far past marrying age in many minds. I believe I am of an age to ken what I want, what I am willing to risk and the price I may well pay for my actions. Aye, and I think I have the wit to ken it, too."

He tugged her closer. "Aye, sweeting, I sometimes think ye have the wit to ken more than ye ought to. Howbeit, I asked if ye were certain, despite all my instincts screaming at me to hold my tongue and grasp what ye offer, because there is no turning back once the deed is done. I do *not* wish to rouse myself from the sated stupor of heartily spent passion only to find an outraged maiden or her kinsmen demanding I do things I have ne'er promised to do. I am in no position to deal with all of that nonsense."

"Ah, I see. Ye fear ye may find yourself trapped, a prisoner of an arrangement ye cannae be ransomed out of."

Sorcha wished he would cease talking and get on with making love to her. His insinuation that she might try to trick him into marriage was insulting. The desire that had driven her to latch the door was being nibbled away by an increasing irritation. When his eyes narrowed and he lightly tightened his grip on her, she suspected he had guessed at her growing annoyance.

"Nay, I cannae believe ye capable of such cunning," he said as he pulled her into his arms and tugged her down onto the bed. "I think we have talked enough."

"Ye nearly talked too much."

He grinned, and Sorcha felt her heart skip in her chest. The man was irresistible when he smiled so freely. It made it easy to believe that they could be lovers, that their passion could remain separate from all else that stood between them. She desperately wanted that to be so. Although she had little hope that his passion could turn to a deep, abiding love for her, she wanted it to be honest and unfettered. She wanted no suspicions or resentments to cloud it.

Slowly, gently, he traced the fine lines of her small face with kisses as he unlaced her gown. Despite the heat flowing through her veins, Sorcha blushed faintly as he eased her gown off of her body and she lay in his arms wearing only her chemise. She fleetingly wished she had taken the time to put on more clothes before rushing off to thwart his escape. A few more articles of clothing would have given her passion time to become so strong that it would push aside all remnants of her modesty.

Ruari smoothed his hands over her slim arms. "Ye blush most prettily, m'lady."

"I should burn with the high color of modesty." She found talking difficult, her thoughts scattered by his touch as he caressed her side, his lightly callused fingers brushing the sides of her hips as he inched her chemise up her body.

"Nay, I want ye to burn with a far different emotion."

She was unable to answer for he covered her mouth with his. With a sigh of surrender, she opened her mouth at the first proddings of his tongue. So enflamed was she by the hungry, almost demanding, kiss, she barely noticed him finish removing her chemise. When her skin touched his, she shuddered, the heat of his flesh entering her veins with a dizzying swiftness. A flicker of awareness returned when he neatly turned so that she was swept beneath him. She slowly opened her eyes when she felt him staring at her. Her instinctive attempt to cover her nakedness was quickly halted as he gently but firmly grasped her by the wrists and pinned her arms to the bed.

"Did ye think we would do our loving in the darkness or with our eyes closed?" he asked, his voice thick and hoarse as he touched a kiss to the gentle swell of each small breast.

"Nay, but I didnae think I would be the only one who would be naked." The tartness she tried to put into her words was severely dimmed by the rich huskiness of her voice.

Ruari grinned, sat up straddling her body, and swiftly removed his braies. Sorcha knew he was studying her closely, but she was unconcerned. All of her attention was centered upon his fully exposed form. Although the sight of his erect manhood made her a little uneasy, she found him beautiful. His skin was smooth, dark, inviting. When she had seen his body before, he had been wounded and in need of her help. That had tempered her interest. Now, despite the raw scars decorating his skin, she looked her fill and allowed the desire she felt run freely through her. With an unsteady hand, she reached out and traced the scar on his abdomen with her fingers.

"Still rough and a poor sight, I fear," he murmured.

"I was just thinking that ye must have a mightily thick hide." She smiled a little as she finally met his heated gaze, and he briefly grinned back.

Ruari eased his body down on hers. She shuddered and felt him echo her trembling. Sorcha was just thinking that nothing had ever felt so fine when he cupped her breast in his hand and brushed his thumb over the hardened tip. She gasped from the strength of the pleasure that tore through her and clutched at his broad shoulders. He kissed her, and she readily matched the hunger he revealed. She threaded her fingers into his thick hair and tentatively met the thrust of his tongue with her own. The low, deep groan he gave swept away her uncertainty, and her kiss grew bolder.

He tore his mouth from hers, his breath coming hard and fast. Sorcha realized that she, too, was breathing as if she were running a hard race. She tilted her head back as he slid his mouth over her throat. The strength of her desire robbed her of all modesty and hesitancy.

When he touched a kiss to the tingling crest of her
breasts, she arched toward his mouth. A soft guttural cry
of delight escaped her as he lathed the hardened tips
with his tongue. When he began to suckle, she lost the
last vestiges of clear thought. Each pull of his mouth
tugged at an ache deep within her, drawing it to a height
that was nearly painful.

She smoothed her hands over his taut body, squirming beneath the increasingly intimate strokes of his
hands. He was muttering broken flatteries against her
skin as he kissed her midriff, then her stomach, but she
did not have the wit left to make sense of his words.
All she was aware of was how good his mouth, his
tongue, and his heated breath felt against her skin. The
sensations sweeping through her were only briefly
checked by shock when he slid his hand up her inner
thigh. She gasped, then shuddered, with the force of the
feelings his intimate touch invoked.

A soft kiss on the inside of each of her thighs was her
reward as she opened to his touch. He covered her stomach and legs with kisses as he stroked her until she
feared she would shake apart from the force of the
desire that had completely conquered her body and her
senses. When he replaced his hand with his lips, she
gave only one inarticulate cry of denial. He stopped her
from closing her legs against such a shocking intrusion
and, with but a few strokes of his tongue, stole away
all of her resistance.

Despite a faint, faraway voice within her head that
cried out in mortification and outrage, she soon greedily arched into his caress. She could not gather the clarity of mind to understand his words of encouragement
and praise, but the tone of his voice was enough to
foster her boldness. She tried to reach him to return

some of his caresses, but cried out in frustration when he proved to be beyond her grasp. Then suddenly he was there, leaving a trail of feverishly hot kisses up her body as he returned to her arms. She quickly took advantage of his nearness, wrapping her limbs around him and covering his strong throat with kisses.

"Sweet Mary, lass, there is more fire in ye than even I had guessed," he said in a thick, unsteady voice.

"Aye, I am so hot I fear I will soon catch afire and burn to a cinder right here on this bed." She took his face in her hands and kissed him, finding his kiss as feverish as her own.

"Weel, dinnae go up in flames yet, dearling," he said as he ended the kiss. "I want that fire to help us take the next step with as little pain and urgency as possible."

"I ken that there will be a little pain." She found speaking a difficult task and hoped her words were coherent, for she wished to reassure him. "Ye need not fear that I shall retreat from it."

Sorcha doubted that she had the will to retreat no matter how much it hurt. Her whole body cried out for the union still to come. Knowing that it would mean far more to her than it would for him was not even enough to make her hesitate.

"Good, for, by God's toenails, I am so in heat I fear I will be deaf to any nay ye give now," he muttered against the curve of her breast, "and I have no wish to become a rapist."

Her only reply was a soft moan of pleasure as he drew the hard tip of her breast into his mouth. For a moment she was only vaguely aware of his positioning himself to enter her. As he began to ease into her, all her thoughts and feelings centered upon the spot where their bodies were slowly being joined.

She wrapped her legs around his trim hips as she looked up at his taut face. Her eyes slowly closed as he filled her. A sudden, sharp, searing pain briefly dimmed her passion, and she gripped his broad shoulders so tightly she felt her nails cut into his skin. He grew still, gently stroking her body, as she grew accustomed to their oneness.

When her desire returned, Ruari still did not move. She glanced at his face. His eyes were closed, and he looked painfully strained. Cautiously she arched toward him, rippling with delight as his body sank deeper into hers.

A low, almost feral groan escaped Ruari, but Sorcha did not find it frightening. She released a soft cry of welcome as he began to move, wrapping her lithe body tightly around his in silent encouragement. His movements quickly grew fiercer, and she met and gladly equaled that increasing ferocity.

One small flicker of concern broke through the haze in her mind when the feelings sweeping through her began to grow frighteningly intense. Her passion proved too strong, easily pushing that fear aside as something within her seemed to break. She cried out Ruari's name as her release crashed over her. Part of her dazed mind loudly rejoiced when she heard him call out her name as he joined her in sweet oblivion. As he collapsed in her arms, Sorcha was surprised that she still had the strength to hold him close.

As the haze gradually cleared from her mind, Sorcha looked down at the man sprawled in her arms. He lifted his head from her breasts and smiled. She smiled back, but inwardly heaved a heavy sigh. She was in serious trouble.

The passion she and Ruari shared was heady and fulfilled every untutored dream she had ever indulged in.

She knew that was because, unlike Ruari, she gave more than her body when they made love. Her heart had been thoroughly captured by the dark-haired knight resting comfortably in her arms. She knew she would never fully regret becoming his lover no matter how short-lived the interlude, but she now knew she would pay dearly for it. She loved him and she suspected the devil would be needing a fine wool cloak in hell before Ruari returned her love.

Chapter Nine

After a long, languorous stretch, Ruari looked at the door and wondered when Sorcha would return to their bed. For two days they had spent every possible moment they could steal curled up in each other's arms and making love. His greed for her surprised and faintly alarmed him. He had thought that once he had thoroughly enjoyed her favors his interest in her would begin to fade. Instead it grew stronger, as did his need for the sweet passion they shared. The voice of caution in his head told him he should draw back, but he ignored it. He would return to Gartmhor soon, and that would cure him, especially if he began his search for an appropriate wife with more vigor than he had employed in the past. Once he had a woman in his bed every night, his unwise attraction to Sorcha Hay would wane. He might even find a passion to equal the one they shared, he mused, and stoutly ignored the scornful laugh that echoed in his head.

The door to the room opened, and Ruari sat up, tense and eager, only to flop back down with a curse when Beatham entered the room. "What do ye want?" he demanded and frowned when Beatham stood at the end of the bed and stared at him with a solemnity that looked odd on his boyishly pretty face.

"I believe someone needs to have a stern word with you, Cousin," Beatham said.

"Oh, aye? And ye think ye can do that?"

"There is no one else. True, I am but a lowly squire, and ye are my laird upon whom I am dependent. Howbeit, your actions affect all Kerrs, and thus I feel that gives me leave to voice my opinion of how ye are behaving."

"I should give ye a sound cuffing for your impudence."

Beatham ignored that and continued. "Sorcha Hay is a weelbred lady and was undoubtedly a virgin."

"Undoubtedly she *was*." Ruari crossed his arms behind his head and studied his young cousin, impressed by the youth's daring even though annoyed by the interference in his personal affairs.

"Ye should *not* have lured her into your bed. That was ungallant of you. 'Tis the act of a rogue."

"A rogue, am I? Ye do grow bold."

"Are ye going to wed her?"

"Nay. What a foolish question. The lass has taken us captive for ransom, speaks to the spirits, and has a crowd of kinswomen who are quite mad. Those arenae qualities I look for in a wife."

"Then why did ye bed her?"

"Because she makes me burn."

Beatham snorted with disgust. "At your age ye should have learned to temper that need."

"At my age?" Ruari sat up and glared at his young cousin. "Heed me, ye impudent whelp, I didnae *lure* that lass into my bed. She burns for me as hotly as I do for her and made her choice."

"Nay, she is a lady. Did ye promise her marriage or speak falsely of love?"

"Ye dinnae have the highest opinion of me, do ye, laddie?"

"Oh, aye, the highest. 'Tis just that I understand the games a mon will play to draw a lass to his bed."

"Weel, I dinnae play them. I never have. I told Sorcha exactly what I sought—the passion we couldnae hide— no more, no less. She kens that I willnae offer marriage or vows of love and that one day I will make her pay for taking us as prisoner for ransom."

"Yet she still came to your bed?" Beatham's voice was soft with shock.

"Aye—willingly, eagerly."

"This is hard to believe. Margaret always speaks so highly of her cousin." Beatham sighed and shook his head. "I am in difficulty now. Margaret will wish to ken what words passed between us, and I cannae tell her that her cousin is but a whore."

Ruari acted without thought. Even Beatham's cry of alarm did not penetrate the haze of rage clouding his mind. He bounded to his feet, grasped Beatham by the front of his jupon and backhanded the youth across the face. It was not until Beatham hit the floor, sprawling gracelessly at his feet, that Ruari began to realize what he was doing. He stared down at the wide-eyed young man as he took several deep breaths to cool his fury, his fists clenching and unclenching at his sides.

"That was wondrous strange," Beatham murmured as Ruari finally helped him to his feet.

"Aye, it was."

Very strange, Ruari thought to himself as he sighed and dragged his fingers through his hair. He moved to pour himself and Beatham some cider as he considered his actions. Why, when he had no plans to marry her or love her and even intended to exact some revenge, should an insult to Sorcha cause him such rage? A simple reprimand should have been enough. Such a strong reaction was disturbing. It hinted at a deeper entanglement than he wished to acknowledge or even wanted. As he handed Beatham a tankard of strong cider, Ruari decided it was indeed a very good thing he would be leaving soon.

"Sorcha Hay is no whore, Beatham," he said after a steadying drink of the hearty cider. "I believe the lass has carried the weight of Dunweare for so long she thinks much like a mon. 'Tis clear from the way she and Margaret can handle their weapons that they were taught many of a mon's ways."

"They need to be prepared to help defend Dunweare," Beatham said. "There are too few men here."

"Aye, verra few. 'Tis that which makes these women different. Ye cannae judge them as ye would judge a lady of court. These women arenae pampered, sheltered, and kept tied to their needlework. Sorcha considered the matter much as a mon would and made her decision. She kens the possible consequences of taking a lover and accepts them."

"I find this most confusing. How can ye bed a woman against who ye intend to seek revenge, and how can she bed you kenning your intentions?"

"Because we agreed that the passion we share should be a thing apart."

"But if the passion is so strong, why dinnae ye just wed her?"

"Can ye see Sorcha Hay at court? I will introduce her to our king, she will do her curtsy, and then begin to chatter to the spirit floating at his shoulder." He grinned when Beatham gave a reluctant laugh. "Nay, I must seek a wife who is suited to my position and may e'en enhance it. Ye carry the same burden," he added, grasping the moment to remind Beatham that Margaret Hay was no more suitable as a wife than Sorcha was.

All Ruari got in reply was a sulky muttered response, and Beatham quickly took his leave. A soft curse escaped Ruari as he refilled his tankard. Beatham was not making any attempt to restrain his feelings toward Margaret Hay. It would cause the youth heartbreak later, for Ruari knew he and Beatham's family could not ease their stand on the sort of marriage the boy had to make. Margaret had neither the money nor the standing Beatham needed in a wife. If he had to bow to the weight of his responsibilities, his young cousin could do the same, Ruari thought crossly then glared at the door and wondered where Sorcha was.

"Sorcha?" Neil called as she entered the kitchen.

Setting the bread on the tray she intended to take up to Ruari, Sorcha smiled tentatively over her shoulder at her aunt. Her chores had taken far more time than she had planned, even though several people had marveled at how swiftly she had worked. Now she was eager to get back to Ruari. Sorcha knew the time they could spend together was short, and she did not wish to waste one precious minute of it. She hoped Neil was not about to tell her that something required her immediate attention.

"Is everything all right?" she asked her aunt, frowning a little when the two kitchen maids scurried out of the room. "Now, where are they hurrying away to?"

"I waved them out of here," Neil replied as she sat down at the table. "Sit," she ordered, pointing to the rough bench in front of Sorcha, then nodded when her niece did as she was told. "I think we need to talk."

"Have ye been coerced into reprimanding me by the others?"

"Nay, no one wishes to reprimand you. We are just concerned. None of us wish to see ye get hurt."

"That is most kind, but ye ken, better than all others, that ye cannae shelter me from that."

"Aye, but none of us wished to sit silently by and then be tormented by the guilty thought that we may have been able to help." She grinned briefly when Sorcha laughed. "I would have felt the greatest guilt, for it was I who told ye to take a chance."

Sorcha reached across the work-worn table and patted Neil's clenched hand. "Nay, ye told me that I was free to make my decision without fear of recriminations. Aye, and ye told me your tale of a past love. I have the wit to realize that ye saw I was troubled and told me things only to help me make my decision. The decision was completely my own."

"Good, but did ye have enough of your wits about ye when ye were close to that rogue?"

"Not many, but enough. In truth, my decision was made whilst I was away from him. I didnae rush into his arms without a great deal of thought. Aye, 'tis probably a mistake for he doesnae offer me love or marriage, only passion, but 'tis a mistake I make with a full understanding of what I risk. 'Twill be a short taste of recklessness, and I suddenly felt I was due one."

"Aye, more than most, and ye are right. 'Twill be a short one. Mayhap shorter than ye thought for."

"What do ye mean?" Sorcha asked, her voice softened by a sudden stab of fear.

"One of our riders came in today, but an hour past. Sir

Kerr's people are riding this way with his ransom in hand." Neil took Sorcha's hand in hers when she suddenly paled. "They will be here on the morrow."

"So soon," Sorcha whispered and shuddered, knowing that she had just heard the death knell for the small hope of making Ruari love her that she had nurtured. "Mayhap if I had come to a decision sooner," she murmured.

"What?"

"Nothing, Aunt. I dinnae ken why I am so shocked that the Kerrs will arrive for I kenned that they must. And I dinnae think more time would help me anyway."

"Are ye certain he feels only passion for you?"

"Who can be certain how a mon feels or thinks? I ken only what he said and I ken that he does desire me as much as I do him. Beyond that?" She shrugged.

"Did ye plan to make him love you?"

"Nay, not truly. I had but the tiniest of hopes. Mayhap it was bigger than I thought for the dashing of it has certainly caused me a sharp pain."

"Mayhap ye should end this now. I can tend to him until his kinsmen come."

"Nay, what sense does that make? I have already forfeited my maidenhead and have spent the better part of two days in his arms. To stand back now gains me nothing, not even a lessening of the pain I shall feel when he rides away." She stood up and picked up Ruari's meal tray. "Nay, I want this last night with him. If my heart is to survive on memories, I intend to give it as many as possible."

Ruari tensed as the door opened, then smiled as Sorcha stepped in with a heavily ladened tray. He quickly relieved her of the weight, setting it on a table by the bed as she shut and latched the door. It surprised him to be so pleased to see her. It also irritated him a little. He had had a plan concerning Sorcha—a clear, precise, sensible plan—and it was not working out as trouble-free as he wished it to.

A man should be able to enjoy a woman and walk away carefree, perhaps carrying a few pleasant memories but no more. Hundreds had done so. He himself had done so a few times. Something about Sorcha Hay made it complicated. He turned to look at her, resentment gnawing at him, and she shyly smiled. Inwardly laughing at his own vagaries, he felt his annoyance melt away. He walked over to her, caught her up in his arms and gently tossed her onto the bed, lolling on top of her. She neatly wriggled out from beneath him.

"Come here, wench," he said, and reached for her.

Sorcha danced free of his grasp. "Calling me 'wench' is no way to lure me to your bed." She edged back near to the bed, poured him a tankard of sweet mead, and curtsied as she served it to him. "Ye shouldnae allow your food and drink to set too long. 'Twill steal its flavor."

"The only flavor I hunger for is yours."

He laughed when she blushed, then sat up to help himself to the bread, fruit, and cold meats she had brought him. "Sit with me, dearling. Ye havenae eaten already, have ye?"

"Nay." She sat down on the bed, and he set the tray between them, plumping up the pillows behind them. "I fear 'tis poor fare tonight. Our cook fell ill."

"I pray 'twas not from her own cooking."

She grinned briefly. "Nay, 'tis but a chill from the slow change of the seasons."

As they ate, he studied her. She seemed quieter, almost sad, and he realized he missed her easy smile, her tart remarks, her spirit. Ruari reluctantly admitted to himself that he wanted to cheer her, to chase away whatever had darkened her mood.

"Has some ill befallen Dunweare?" he asked as he set the empty tray aside and took her into his arms.

"Nay, why would ye ask?"

"Because ye seem somewhat solemn."

Sorcha grimaced and leaned against his chest, trying to find some comfort in the strong, steady beat of his heart. She had hoped to hide or overcome her sadness. It was clear that she had failed to do either. When she told him about the imminent arrival of his kinsmen, he would undoubtedly guess that she was troubled by his leaving, and she would prefer to keep that weakness a secret. That was now impossible for she had no other news to impart, none that would explain away her mood, and she was too poor a liar. Cursing silently, she decided to just tell the truth and get it done with.

"Your kinsmen will be here on the morrow," she said and felt him tense. She waited a little breathlessly to see what would happen next and eyed him warily when he grasped her by the chin and turned her face up to his.

"Then this will be our last night together," he said.

"Aye." She frowned as she searched his expression for some hint of what he was feeling or thinking, and found none. "Ye will be ransomed and may return to Gartmhor." Even the reminder that he was a prisoner for ransom did not produce a flicker of expression she could understand. "Weel, do ye have naught to say?"

"All this talk is wasting what little time we have left." He began to unbraid her thick hair. "So, 'tis my leave-taking that makes ye sad."

"I dinnae ken why ye should think so."

"Ah, so 'tis just concern for your old ailing cook that puts the shadows in your eyes."

"Aye, 'tis that."

She did not like the crooked, arrogant grin he wore and decided it was time to distract him. If he kept teasing and questioning her, she feared she would reveal far too much. He did not want her love, and she had no intention of allowing him to guess the state of her emotions. She would not bare her soul just to stroke his male pride and vanity. Passion was all he sought, and it was all she would freely give. She knew it was also the perfect way to distract him.

Smiling invitingly, she pulled free of his hold enough to unlace his shirt, teasingly kissing each newly revealed patch of skin. Beneath her hands she could feel his heartbeat quicken. She fleetingly wished she had more experience, knew more about pleasing a man. It was the last night she would ever spend in his arms, and she dearly wished to make it one he would never forget. As she tossed his shirt aside and slowly removed his hose, she decided that, although she might not be able to give Ruari all he liked or wanted, she would certainly try.

Ruari held himself still, despite his rapidly growing passion. He wanted to see just how daring Sorcha Hay would be. There was an odd look on her face, a strange mix of determined, impish, and sensual, and he ached to see just where those feelings would lead her.

She sat up, straddling his body, and began to unlace her gown. Ruari's breath grew so uneven and swift it was almost uncomfortable as she slowly shed her clothes. He knew she was an innocent, that the only experience she had had with a man was in his arms, yet he was sure he had never seen, nor would see again, a woman shed her clothes with such sweet invitation and sensuality. He clenched his hands so tightly to keep from touching her that he could feel his nails lightly scoring his palms. He could not fully suppress a groan when she shed the last of her clothes. When she bent to kiss him, he finally reached for her, unable to resist any longer. Her kiss was bold and hungry, firing his blood. It took all his willpower to let her go when she ended the kiss, but he was heartily glad he did. Sorcha edged her way down his throat and chest, caressing him every inch of the way with her hands, her lips, her tongue, even her lithe, silken body. He shuddered as she teased his thighs with kisses and slowly removed his braies.

Her thick hair brushed back and forth over his groin as she kissed and stroked his legs, and Ruari found that almost painfully tantalizing. When she touched a kiss to his aching manhood, he cried out, startling her. He quickly stopped her retreat, threading his fingers through her hair and gently holding her in place as she intimately caressed him. Silently, with subtle movements of his body, he requested she take that last step. A hoarse, unsteady cry of delight escaped him as she enclosed him in the warmth of her mouth.

Gritting his teeth until his jaw ached, Ruari fought to control his raging desire. He wanted to enjoy the exquisite sensations she was gifting him with for as long as possible. Too soon he had to bow to the need screaming within him. He grasped her under the arms and pulled her up his body, trembling at the look of sensuality flushing her small face and darkening her eyes.

Sorcha neatly eluded his attempt to take control of their lovemaking. She found that leading their intimate dance was a rich, heady experience and she was loath to give it up. He was short of breath, a faint trembling rippled through his strong body, his face was flushed, and its lines were taut from the strength of his passion. She knew she had caused that and the knowledge was intoxicating. He had barely touched her, but her own passion was running as hot and fast as his.

Smiling and brushing a kiss over his mouth, she slowly joined their bodies. The control she had so jealously clung to abruptly vanished as he filled her. He grasped her by the hips, but she did not need his direction. Lost in the depth of blind need, she took them to the height they both ached for, their cries of release blending perfectly.

It was several moments after she had collapsed in his arms before her senses returned enough for her to consider all she had just done. She felt no tension in the man she sprawled on top of, no hesitation in the languid movement of his hands over her hair and body. That did not completely quell her growing uneasiness, however. Men were strange creatures, liking such passionate interludes but condemning the women who indulged in them. She was still struggling to garner the courage to look at him, when he grasped her by the chin and turned her face up to his, touching a kiss to the tip of her nose. There was not a hint of reproach or disgust in the sweet smile he gave her.

"Ah, lass, ye could easily send a mon tumbling into madness," he said in a quiet reverent voice.

"Weel, I wouldst prefer ye sane." She knew it was foolish, but before she could halt the words she asked, "So ye were pleased?" She grimaced when he laughed, but then he kissed away her embarrassment, holding her close as he turned, placing her beneath him. "A foolish question?"

"Aye, verra foolish." He began to cover her slim neck with slow tantalizing kisses.

She felt the first hint of his renewed desire twitch against her leg. "Dinnae ye need to rest?"

"There is no time."

He looked at her and saw the hint of sadness return to her eyes again. It did not really surprise him to feel a pang of regret as well, not after such all-encompassing pleasure. And he was beginning to accept that Sorcha Hay was capable of stirring some very inconvenient feelings inside of him. He also knew that tomorrow when the ransom was handed to her, he would leave without hesitation, and his anger would return. Now, however, he did not wish to think about that. He wanted to revel in the sweetness of her passion. He wanted to soak himself in the feel and scent of her.

"Sweet, bonnie Sorcha," he said in a low voice as he nibbled on her full bottom lip. "Ye are going to be verra tired come the dawn." When she slowly smiled, he kissed her with a hunger he made no attempt to hide and tried not to remember that this would be the last time.

Chapter Ten

Sorcha stared down at Ruari as she silently tugged on her clothes. He was sprawled on his back sound asleep, and she heartily wished she could join him. Her eyes were itchy and swollen with exhaustion, and her body ached from the long night of lovemaking they had so greedily indulged in. She knew she had to slip away before he awoke, however. Sorcha did not want the matter of his ransoming to steal any of the pleasure they had found in the night.

As quietly as she could she slipped out the door. When she turned to make her way to the great hall to break her fast, she came face-to-face with Margaret. Clasping a hand over her mouth, she stifled her sharp cry of surprise over being so unexpectedly confronted. She grabbed Margaret by the arm and dragged her away from Ruari's door.

"Ye frightened me half to death," Sorcha scolded when they were several feet away from the bedchamber.

"Why are ye being so secretive?" Margaret asked, sullenly yanking free of Sorcha.

"I didnae wish to waken him."

"Why not? He is leaving today."

There was a deep note of anger and resentment

behind Margaret's words, and Sorcha inwardly winced. She had not given much thought to her cousin. Ruari was not the only one who would leave Dunweare today. Despite everyone's attempt to warn and counsel Margaret, the girl had continued her romance with Beatham Kerr. Sorcha knew that Margaret, and undoubtedly Beatham as well, had thought that somehow their love would conquer all, that some good fortune would come their way and stop their separation. Her own heart sore from the impending loss of Ruari, Sorcha was not really in the mood to comfort Margaret.

"Aye. We kenned this day would come. It hasnae been kept some dark secret." She started down the narrow stone steps toward the great hall.

"Ye ken verra weel how I feel about Beatham and how he feels about me. How can ye send him away?" Margaret demanded as she closely followed Sorcha. "Why did ye not devise a new plan?"

"A new plan? Such as what? Ransom only Ruari and continue to hold Beatham captive? Think, girl. We would then set ourselves squarely against the Kerrs for we would be imprisoning one of their own. 'Tis the sort of idiocy that breeds long and bloody feuds."

"Beatham wouldnae be a prisoner. He would be with me."

"His clan wouldnae understand that. They probably wouldnae care. They would clamor at our walls for his return and what would ye have us reply? I am sorry, kind sirs, but my cousin Margaret wants to keep him."

"There is no need for ye to make me sound the fool."

Sorcha stopped when they reached the foot of the stairs and sighed. She hated to even discuss the matter. She wanted to harden her heart, clear her mind, and get through Ruari's leaving with as much cool dignity as she could muster. It was impossible to simply shrug Margaret aside, however, and it could even prove dangerous. There was no surety that her emotional cousin would do what must be done. Margaret had to be reminded of all that was at risk.

"I am sorry I was unkind," she said. "I need all of my strength to endure this day with some semblance of calm and dignity. Do ye think I wish Ruari to leave?"

"Oh. Nay . . . of course not. Mayhap—"

Sorcha held up her hand to halt her cousin's words. "Nay, no more plots or arguments or possibilities to consider. There are none which will work. We have made a bargain with the Kerrs. We must now honor it."

"Then let us put an end to this wretched game. I dinnae wish the Kerrs to be our enemies. I dinnae wish Beatham to go."

"Do ye really wish to hold him at the cost of someone's life, at the cost of Dougal's life?" When Margaret paled, Sorcha knew her cousin had been fully recalled to the vital importance of returning their prisoners, and she gave the girl a comforting squeeze on the arm. "Beatham and Ruari wouldnae even be here if we didnae need the money their ransoming will bring us. If we dinnae pay the English for Dougal as agreed, he will be killed. If we try to hold Beatham here and only release Ruari for the coin we need, we will anger the Kerrs and they will fight us. More lives lost—on both sides."

"I should have heeded everyone's warnings," Margaret whispered, her eyes aglow with tears.

"And I should have kept a tighter rein on my emotions as well. Howbeit, one cannae always dictate to one's heart. Now, we must endure this loss as countless numbers of women have done before us."

"I hope I can be as good at enduring as ye are and I

shall *never* speak to Dougal again." Margaret's vow ended in a wail, and the girl ran back up the stairs.

" 'Tis a pity. They are weel-suited," said Neil as she stepped up beside Sorcha and watched her other niece run away.

"Aye, perfectly, although such a pair would require a great deal of watching over."

Neil laughed then grew serious as she studied Sorcha. "And how are ye, child?"

"Dinnae fear. I willnae die of this wound."

"Ye may wish ye could from time to time."

"I ken it, but 'twill heal. All I worry about is if I have the strength to get through this day without making a fool of myself, with my pride unbruised by any revelation of what I truly feel."

"And are ye certain the mon wishes that? Might he not wish more from you than passion?"

"He made it most clear, Aunt, and showed no hint of changing his mind." She smiled, an expression weighted with sadness, and winked at Neil. "Howbeit, I do believe I have left a deep and lasting mark upon his memory. Aye, Sir Ruari Kerr will remember his stay at Dunweare for a verra long time."

Ruari stared out the narrow window, his gaze fixed upon the small stretch of land beyond the gates that he could see without hanging precariously out the opening. It was now midday, and he was eager to see his men. He had woken up in an empty bed and immediately fallen into the foulest mood he had suffered in a long time. Now he just wanted to leave Dunweare, to put it and its strange little lady far, far behind him.

The click of the door opening drew his attention. He

cursed when he realized he was tense, eager, and hopeful for one last moment alone with Sorcha. Beatham cautiously entered the room, and Ruari cursed again, irritated by the sharp pang of disappointment he felt.

"I was told to wait in here with you," Beatham said in a quiet, nervous voice as he warily eyed the dark expression on his cousin's face. "A rider came in to report that our men are only an hour's distance from here, mayhap less."

"Good. Then we will soon leave this cursed place." Ruari poured himself a tankard of tart cider and took a long drink, but it did little to sweeten his mood.

"Ye speak verra cruelly about this place considering that ye spent the last three nights curled up in bed with its lady."

"Which was the only good thing about this whole wretched business. Mayhap too good," he added in a quiet voice and ignored Beatham's sharp look.

"I, myself, would verra much prefer to stay."

"That comes as no surprise. Sorcha Hay willnae allow it. She needs the ransom ye will bring her."

"Do ye believe that she really needs it now?" Beatham helped himself to some cider when Ruari returned to the small window to glare out toward the road winding up to the heavy gates of Dunweare.

"I believe *she* is convinced that she does. Howbeit, I dinnae think it is right that my pockets should be emptied to bring Dougal Hay back to his keep. He doesnae sound a verra good laird anyway."

"Good or not, he is their laird. Our people didnae hesitate to buy ye back, and Sorcha cannae hesitate to buy her brother back. Duty demands she do all in her power to try."

"'Tis nae her trying that galls me, but her success,"

Ruari admitted with blatant reluctance. "Weel, I will see that she pays dearly for this."

"Do ye forget that Margaret and Sorcha also saved our lives?"

"Nay, so that will indeed temper the means of revenge I use, but it willnae stop me from seeking some form of vengeance."

"Are ye sure ye havenae already extracted your revenge? By taking her into your bed and using her for three nights then casting her aside, ye have sadly blackened her good name."

"I told you. What passed between Sorcha and me in that bed has naught to do with all else that has gone between us. Mayhap ye can forget we were held for ransom, but I cannae. The coin she will use to buy her foolish brother back is mine, and I intend to get it back."

Beatham shook his head and sat down on the bed. "I still dinnae understand why ye cannae be more forgiving. Sorcha only does what she must, she and Margaret saved our lives, and ye willnae be left poor and starving after this ransom is paid."

"Nay, I willnae be left poor and starving, but I cannae forgive being bartered by a wee lass of but twenty years and I cannae abide my hard-wrung coin being spent on that idiot of a brother of hers."

Ruari moved to stand in front of a sullen-faced Beatham and continued, "I ken why ye take it upon yourself to argue with me. Ye wish to soften my heart so that I will bless a union between ye and Margaret."

"We love each other and wish to be married. What wrong is there in that?"

"No wrong, I suspect, but 'tis remarkably stupid and ill thought out. And I am not the only one ye need to pull to your side. In truth, I am the easiest one to turn.

Your family will stand firm against such a marriage, and so they should. Ye have no money or lands nor does Margaret. What would ye live upon—the air? Hope? Love?" he concluded with a sneer. "Such things willnae fill your bellies or those of your bairns. Try to think for once in your blessed life, lad. Cast aside all else that has recently passed between the Hays and the Kerrs, and 'twould still be a verra unsuitable match."

"I *will* have Margaret."

"Have her, then, just dinnae marry her." Ruari shook his head. "I wash my hands of the matter. I dinnae wish to hear any more about it. Marry your precious Margaret, but dinnae come crawling to me when ye and your wee poor family are left crouching in some hovel, dressed inadequately in naught but rags, and havenae eaten for so long ye have forgotten what food e'en looks like."

He shook his head when he saw that Beatham's expression had only grown sulkier. Not wishing to discuss the matter any further, he refilled his tankard and returned to staring out of the window. To his relief, Beatham did not utter a word.

It would be pleasant to be able to choose a mate freely, but it was not something men of their birth could afford. One had to consider alliances, lands, and money. A laird had far too many responsibilities, too many mouths to feed and men to arm. Beatham's father's holding was tiny and poor, barely more than a crumbling towerhouse on a rocky knoll. It needed a good marriage if it was to survive. In all honesty, Ruari also wanted the lad to marry well so that he no longer needed to support Beatham and his family.

Beatham's talk of marrying for love or simply by choice also grated on an already exposed nerve. Ruari had forestalled his own marriage and the begetting of heirs for far longer than he should have. He knew the dull, unemotional business of such a matter was what held him back. He would dearly like to marry where and when he chose, but duty dictated otherwise.

When the thought of marriage filled his mind with a strong image and the heated memory of Sorcha, he cursed. He met the sight of his men approaching a moment later with relief. His stay in Dunweare had clearly disordered his mind, and the sooner he fled it the better.

Sorcha stared up at the huge man on the mottled gray stallion. He appeared to be a vast assortment of reds— his brilliant hair a shade lighter than his full beard, and the freckles liberally sprinkled over his wide face a shade darker than his beard. His jupon and hose were a dull brownish red, and she idly mused that he needed someone to choose a different color for him. She breathed an inward sigh of relief when he dismounted. Although he was still big, a head or more taller than Ruari, at least he did not cause her to tilt her head back quite so far.

"I am Rosse, nearest cousin to Ruari Kerr and the mon who guards his back," he announced in a deep rich voice as he bowed slightly before her.

"Sir Ruari's back wasnae guarded when I found him." She decided that something else Rosse should not do was blush.

"I was still recovering from a wound when my laird rode to Otterburn and had to send an underling. He was unhorsed in battle and, although he didnae flee, he did forget his laird in the heat of victory."

"Weel, I hope he has the sense to hide for a wee while when his laird returns, as Sir Kerr is verra displeased with all of this." She was sure she caught the flash of a smile beneath his large beard as she curtsied slightly. "I am Lady Sorcha Hay."

"I have heard great tales of you, m'lady. It takes a mighty foe to fell the laird of Gartmhor."

Sorcha did not need to hear the snickers of Rosse's men or see the way Rosse kept his gaze fixed on a point behind her to know that Ruari and Beatham were there. She had sensed Ruari's presence the moment he had stepped out of the keep. The way the hairs on the nape of her neck stood on end told her he was staring at her, and instinct told her it was not a kindly look. When he stepped up beside her, it did not surprise her to see by his expression that all his anger had returned. She felt the cold touch of shattered hopes freeze her heart, but struggled to hide the pain. There would be no forgiveness from Ruari Kerr.

"Is the business done, then?" he demanded of Rosse.

"I havenae given your mighty captor the ransom yet, m'laird," Rosse replied as he held a heavy sack out to Sorcha.

"'Ware, Rosse," growled Ruari. "I am not in the sweetest of humors."

Sorcha smiled faintly as she took the sack, idly weighing it in her hands. She knew Rosse but teased his cousin, and at another time and place she might have seen the humor in it. Now, however, there was nothing funny about it. Rosse was feeding Ruari's anger and resentment, picking at Ruari's injured pride until it was a deep wound. With every jest the chasm widened between her and Ruari, and her hopes shriveled.

"Dinnae ye wish to count it?" Ruari snapped, glaring at her,

"Nay, I am sure I can trust Sir Rosse," she replied with a false sweetness, deciding that, since all hope of

any further pleasant dealings with Ruari were lost, there
was no need to bow to his spite.

"What of my arms—my sword, scabbard, and shield?"

"As spoils of war, they are rightfully mine," she reminded him even as she signaled to Iain. "Howbeit, I
have all I want right here." She jingled the sack as Iain
gave Ruari and Beatham their weapons. "'Tis coin I
need to bring my brother home, not swords."

As he buckled on his sword, Ruari muttered, "I begin
to think ye would serve Dunweare better if ye just kept
the coin and let your witless brother look after his own
head." Before Sorcha could reply to that insult to
Dougal, Ruari's attention was fixed upon Beatham who
was attempting to steal a tender farewell from Margaret.
"We are leaving *now*, lad."

"Ah, that bonnie youth has e'er had a way with the
lasses," Rosse said as he signaled one of his men to
bring up the horses for Beatham and Ruari,

"Weel, this was an ill-advised flirtation, but then a
great deal of what happened here was ill advised," Ruari
added with a sharp glance at Sorcha.

That stung, then angered Sorcha. There was no need
for him to insult her before he left. He would not do so
if it had been a man who had held him for ransom. The
anger and resentment would still ferment in his heart,
but he would treat a man with dignity.

"Aye, ye are right. Ye may leave now, Sir Kerr, although
your men are welcome to abide here awhile to quench
their thirst and fill their bellies. Ye, howbeit, have had
more than your share of Dunweare's hospitality."

She could tell by his narrow-eyed look that he did not
like the implication of her words. It was foolish of him
to believe the subtle hint that it was not fully passion
that had put her in his bed, but she knew men could be

easily confused about a woman's reasons for bedding them. Sorcha felt it would do the arrogant Sir Kerr some good to suffer a few doubts. She was a little shocked at the idea that suddenly entered her head, but her pain and anger drove her.

"Who can say, mayhap your wee efforts will replenish some of the monly stock of Dunweare," she added, leaning close to him so that no one could hear her. She could tell by the way his eyes widened, the green flaring brilliantly with the light of fury that he understood.

"Do ye try to say ye have used me for a stud?" he hissed.

"I dinnae *try* to say it. I just did. Quite plainly, I thought." She found his rage curious for he declared he was interested only in her passion so how she made use of that should matter little to him. "Why do ye linger, Sir Kerr? Ye have made it verra clear for weeks that ye were anxious to be released. I release you. Go."

"Ye have *not* heard the last of this, Sorcha."

"If ye return to Dunweare 'twill undoubtedly only be as a prisoner again, and then I shall ransom ye for a hefty profit. 'Tis costly to tend after your tough hide."

"There will be payment extracted all right, m'lady, but 'twill be ye who pay it, and be assured ye will pay dearly indeed. Beatham," he yelled even as he mounted his horse.

Sorcha watched Beatham hurry to mount his horse. A soft sob echoed behind her, and she heard someone running back into the keep. She knew Margaret had reached the limit of her strength. As Sorcha watched the Kerrs ride away, she knew it was none too soon as she, too, was finding the strength to be calm and dignified an increasingly elusive thing. She wanted Ruari's last sight of her to be that of a woman who could hold to the bargain of giving and taking passion only, no more. Another moment or two and she was certain he would have been able to see the pain that was tearing away at her insides. She gave a start when she felt someone's arm encircle her shoulders, and looked up to see it was Neil.

"How are ye faring, lass?" Neil asked quietly.

"I will survive, Aunt." She looked out the gates at the disappearing horsemen of Gartmhor. "At least, I will if I stay verra far away from Sir Ruari Kerr."

"Threatened you, did he? Dinnae take it to heart, love. He was just angry."

"Oh, aye, he was that, but I believe he means his threat. If I ever see that mon again I believe I will ignore the dictates of my heart and run, swiftly, in the other direction."

Ruari ground his teeth as he tried to control his temper. The jests of his men soon grew too much to bear, however. A little sullenly he decided it was time they were reminded of the fact that he was their laird.

"Enough," he bellowed and was pleased when his men immediately grew quiet, sensing that they had pushed him hard enough. A little of his pleasure in exerting his authority faded when he turned to look at Rosse, who rode by his side, and caught the glint of amusement in the man's dark eyes. "And what do ye find worth grinning about?"

"Ye. Have ye spent all these weeks at Dunweare acting as if ye have a thistle in your braies?" Rosse asked. "Nay, ye couldnae have or that wee doe-eyed lassie would have been giving us a chest of gold to take ye away. She did seem to grow angry after ye appeared. Until then she was a sweet lass for all she gently reprimanded me for not protecting your back." He studied Ruari for a moment. "Ye threatened her, didnae ye."

"Ye seem mightily concerned about a lass who has cleared out our money chest."

"Nay, not nearly, although that whisper of a mon, Malcolm, clucked like a broody hen o'er every coin we counted out. From what I hear, the lass is burdened with a high fool of a brother, and this is but one more thing she has been forced to do to save his wretched hide. She dealt fairly with us."

"Mayhap, but she took my money, and in the beginning there was deception, for she played my rescuer, lulling my suspicions. Weel, she will pay for those crimes. I dinnae ken when or how, but I will get my money back and mayhap teach the wretched girl not to play at a mon's games."

Chapter Eleven

"We will be fine, Robert," Sorcha assured the scowling armorer as she mounted her horse.

She adjusted the reins in her hands as she tried to steady herself for what lay ahead. Two painfully long days had passed since Ruari had ridden out of her life, and she heartily welcomed the chance to do something besides think of him. The serious business of ransoming Dougal from his English captors was the perfect distraction. It would require every ounce of her concentration and skill to accomplish it without trouble. She wished Robert would cease to fret over her and allow her to get on with it.

"I dinnae like sending ye to those English swine," Robert said. "Aye, and especially within reach of that narrow-faced Sir Treacher. Ye watch him closely, lass. Verra closely. I dinnae trust him to follow the rules. I believe honor is a complete stranger to him."

"I agree with you, Robert. That mon is a slinking cur, and, from what Crayton tells me, he comes from a verra long line of curs. 'Twas his ancestor who butchered

Crayton and his lover, Elspeth. Have no fear, old friend, I shall keep a keen watch on that English adder."

"As will I," vowed Neil from her post at Sorcha's side. "And, Robert, see if ye can do something to cheer our Margaret. The lass has been weeping for two days. If she doesnae stop soon she will flood her eyeballs right out of her wee empty head." Neil nudged her horse into a trot and rode out of the gates of Dunweare.

After exchanging a brief grin with Robert, Sorcha followed her aunt. The sound of the four heavily armed men riding behind her quickly eased what trepidation she felt. She had never done anything of such grave importance before, and the responsibility of it all frightened her far more than facing their lifelong enemies, the English. It was only with great reluctance that the English had accepted her as the only one of a high-enough birth and position within the clan to be the negotiator. She did not wish to do anything to add to the scorn she knew they already felt. In fact, she wanted to be so impressive she banished that scorn forever.

"This will be good for you," Neil said as she maneuvered her large white gelding to ride at Sorcha's side.

It was hard not to smile at Neil. The woman was dressed like a man, but her femininity was easy to see from her long, thick red braid to the full curves that shaped her padded jupon and mail. Neil Hay would be a sight the English did not soon forget.

"Actually, Aunt Neil, I was just thinking that it will be somewhat of an ordeal for me," Sorcha replied. "Ye could tell by the way Sir Treacher acted that the English consider dealing with a woman the height of idiocy. I dearly wish to show them that I can dabble in a mon's business with all the skill, wit, and courage of any mon."

"Ye can do that, lass. Of course, there will be some

ye will never convince, but I shouldnae concern myself about what those English dogs think. Nay, I but meant that 'twill be good for you as it gives ye something verra important to deal with. Ye need that to stop ye from dwelling upon Sir Ruari Kerr."

"I havenae been dwelling on that mon."

"Oh, aye, ye have. S'truth, ye havenae been as foolishly weepy as Margaret, who weeps buckets all the day, but ye *do* dwell on the mon. Not that I fault ye. He was a fine figure of a mon. Aye, verra fine. If a lass is going to lose her head over a laddie, there be one to do it with."

Sorcha smiled faintly. "Aye, I would say so. Weel, mayhap I do dwell on the oaf, but it has been only two days since he rode away. And, ye need not fear that I thrash myself o'er what I could have done or should have done. I took a toss of the dice and I lost. 'Tis Margaret I grieve for."

"That wee fool does enough grieving on her own to sate an army of widows."

"True, she does carry on a wee bit too much, but she lost more than I did—far more. Beatham returned her feelings. He was a sweet, beautiful lad who truly loved her and would have willingly, eagerly married her. Instead he is now at Gartmhor, and it does appear that there is no hope of a match there. Nay, I too wish she would cease her wailing, but I do understand her grief. I also feel guilty for I believe I stole away whatever faint chance she may have had."

"Ye?" Neil shook her head. "Nay, 'tis that arrogant Sir Ruari who stands between Margaret and the mon she wants. He is too stubborn and prideful to forgive and forget."

"True, but he still might have eventually forgotten or, at least, forgiven Margaret. Howbeit, when Ruari was leaving, he was in an ill mood and said things that angered me. I fear I said a few things in return, things that will insure he remains angry for a very long time." Sorcha grimaced and told her aunt what she said to Ruari just before he rode out of Dunweare.

Neil stared at her niece in wide-eyed shock before asking in a voice weakened by disbelief, "Ye told that mon ye were using him for stud?"

"Aye, I fear I did."

"'Tis no wonder he looked to be breathing fire when he rode away."

Sorcha nodded. "He didnae look that angry even when he discovered he wasnae rescued but captured." She smiled when her aunt started to laugh. "'Tis curious, but he appeared to be highly insulted."

"Of course he was. Ye were supposed to be in his arms because ye were blinded by passion for him. Now he isnae sure that was why ye were there. Mayhap ye just chose him as ye would any stallion. Men use women as little more than breeders of their seed time and time again, but they detest being used in the same way.

"Aye, lass, I would say ye have made him verra angry indeed," Neil continued, "but I wouldnae blame myself for Margaret's loss in any way. 'Twill not only be Sir Ruari's anger that halts that marriage, but the boy's own close family. They will want him to make a marriage that gains them more than a pretty, witless child like Margaret."

"Oh, of course. I had not really given that much consideration. Ah, weel, her grief will ease soon. All we can do is pray that this love was *not* the one no other can equal."

"Was that how it was for you?"

It was, but Sorcha was not going to admit it, not when

she had spent the last two days denying it to herself. "That is something I would rather not think or talk about."

"Understood. Weel, lassie, let us prod these horses to a wee bit more speed. Dougal will be anxiously awaiting us."

"And I eagerly await the chance to have a word or two with my reckless, thoughtless brother," Sorcha muttered as she prodded her horse into a slightly faster gait.

"The Sassenach camp is just ahead," announced Ronald, the largest and eldest of Sorcha's guards, as he rode up to her, returning from a brief scouting foray.

Sorcha straightened her shoulders and tried to shake the weariness caused by almost two full days of travel. "I think we will stop here for just a moment or two, Ronald. I want to tidy myself. The English ken how long it would take us to ride here from Dunweare, and it may work to my advantage to ride in looking as neat as possible. If naught else, 'twill give me a wee bit more spine if I dinnae look as if I have spent two days in the saddle."

"Aye," he agreed. " 'Tis always good to present yourself as best ye can."

With Neil's help, Sorcha found a sheltered spot to clear off the dust of travel. She changed into a clean gown and tidied her hair as best as she could without washing it. After a moment's hesitation she donned her weapons. It might well impress the English if she rode in unarmed, as most women would be, but it was also dangerous to ride into the heart of the enemy's camp without some protection. She took a long steadying drink of the hearty cider Neil offered her.

"We can wait a moment or two more, lass, if ye feel ye need it," Neil said.

"Nay." Sorcha glanced up at the darkening sky. "Now that fall is here, the days grow shorter. I wish us to be several miles away from the English when night falls."

"Wise indeed. Most of these ransom exchanges proceed smoothly, honor upheld on both sides, but one must ever be prepared for treachery."

Treachery was the first word that came to mind when they rode into the English camp a half hour later and Sorcha espied Sir Simon Treacher. She had forgotten how reptilian the man looked. When he nudged his way through the gathered Englishmen to grasp her reins, she inwardly shivered. He held out his hand to help her dismount, and she reluctantly accepted. Now was not the time to deliver an insult. Although, she thought with a hint of pique, no one would have noticed as all eyes were on Neil.

A tall gray-haired man dragged Dougal forward. Sorcha studied her brother, who was five years her senior but too often acted like a beardless youth. He was tall and slender, almost pretty with his finely drawn features, smooth skin, and reddish-blond hair. She wondered idly if that was why he was always so eager to take up his sword. It was one way to indisputably prove his manhood. There was a slightly beseeching look in his golden brown eyes, but she was in no mood to bend to it.

"Did you bring the sum agreed upon, m'lady?" the tall man asked.

"Aye." She held up the sack of coins. "Who am I delivering it to?" she asked and was pleased to see the man flush slightly at the reminder that he had lacked the manners to introduce himself.

He bowed slightly before taking the bag of money. "Lord Matthew Selkirk, at your service, Lady Hay. As you can see, your brother is hale."

"Aye." Although his fine clothes were badly tattered, she mused. "His arms?"

"My man has just delivered them to your . . ." he hesitated as he glanced at Neil.

"My aunt, Neil Hay." She had to bite back a smile when she saw how hard he struggled not to say anything that could be construed as an insult.

"You are welcome to quench your thirst and rest your horse," he added finally as he handed the ransom to a thin, balding man to count.

"Nay, m'lord, but I thank ye for your hospitality. 'Tis a long, hard ride back to Dunweare, and we must make the best use of what little there is left of the day."

It was several more minutes before Dougal was given his horse. Sorcha intended to let him know just how dearly it cost them to get not only him back, but also his horse and arms. Feeling the chill of Simon Treacher's unblinking stare boring into her back, Sorcha quickly mounted. With a brief word of farewell to his lordship, she led her small group out of the English camp. She felt she had dimmed a little of their scorn, but was heartily glad to get away from them.

"Where did ye get all that money?" asked Dougal as he rode up beside her.

Sorcha found some satisfaction in the shocked look on his face when she told him exactly how she had gotten the funds needed to rescue him. It was probably a faint chance, but he might just be shocked into some semblance of responsibility. No woman should be

forced into such a situation. That was the province of
the laird. She knew her brother was not completely
without a sense of duty, and perhaps this incident might
finally shame him into doing what he was supposed to.

"How much of Sir Kerr's ransom do ye have left?" he
asked.

"None. I asked only what was needed to buy your
freedom."

"The mon has heavy pockets. Ye could have gained
us a small fortune." He leaned away a little when she
glared at him.

"Aye, we may well have if we had not had to ransom
your worthless hide."

"'Tis all right, Sorcha. Ye did weel. I meant no insult."

"Ye were right, m'lady," said Ronald as he rode up
beside them. "That mon follows us."

"How many men?"

"I was unable to see. More than we have, however."

Dougal pulled his sword. "So, there is treachery
afoot. Weel, we shall make them pay dearly for it."

"Will ye put that away?" Sorcha snapped and was a
little surprised when her wide-eyed brother quickly
obeyed her.

"Would ye have us run from the Sassenachs with our
tails tucked between our legs?"

"Aye, if we must. Dougal, we are but five men and
two women. Ronald says there are more English than
us, and I dinnae think they plan to sweetly escort us
back to Dunweare. I didnae do all of this just to have ye
killed but moments after ye have been freed."

"Ye kenned this would happen."

"I suspected it. I fear Sir Simon Treacher feels somewhat lustful toward me." The look of surprise on

Dougal's face irritated her. "Ye need not take my word on it. Ye can ask any of the others here."

"Nay, nay, I believe you. It grows dark. 'Twill not be easy to run away from these men."

"The darkness will hinder them as weel."

"And soon we will be on lands we ken better than they do," added Robert.

"What do ye think, Aunt?" Dougal asked Neil.

"I think ye are an idiot." She ignored his glare and the snickers of the men. "I believe we had best start on our dash to safety. I dinnae believe that mon will trail us too deeply into Scotland. He probably only has a small part of his force of men."

"I will trail the fool and let ye ken the moment he turns back," said Ronald, riding away before anyone could thank him.

Before Dougal could further argue the course of action the rest of them had decided upon, Sorcha edged up next to Neil, and they both kneed their mounts into an easy gallop. She heard Dougal curse softly and follow them and the other three Dunweare men. It was undoubtedly going to be a long night, and, after two full days in the saddle, Sorcha was dreading it.

It was dark when Ronald appeared to tell them that Simon and his men had made camp. Dougal did not protest when the rest of them decided to keep moving, even if it meant walking their weary horses most of the way. When dawn began to lighten the sky, they finally stopped to rest for a while. Sorcha echoed the groans of exhaustion the others released as they gathered around a small, sheltered campfire.

"This mon seems most determined to get you," said Dougal as he sat beside Sorcha, took a long drink from the wineskin being passed around, and handed it to her.

"He is," replied Neil, seated on the other side of Sorcha. "Ye would be certain of it if ye had seen him ogle her whilst we negotiated your ransom."

"This cannae be approved of by Lord Selkirk. That mon is one to honor the traditions of ransoming," Dougal said, scowling into the surrounding wood. "Weel, once ye are back in Dunweare, Sorcha, ye will be safe."

"I should like to think so," she murmured.

"But ye dinnae believe it?"

"This chase has made me uneasy. The mon breaks all the rules to pursue me. Aye, he will probably turn back this time, but that doesnae mean he has given up."

"Nay," agreed Neil. "This was an unthinking leap at the prey he seeks. We slipped free of his grasp, and now he will sit back and carefully plot his next move. Another thing we have in our favor is that winter creeps ever closer. Mayhap a long, cold stay in whatever keep he haunts will cool the snake's ardor."

"Dinnae ye think ye make too much of this?" asked Dougal. "Treacher would risk a lot to come into Scotland after Sorcha. It makes *no sense*. There must be women in England he can seek out to cool his ardor."

"Ye have ne'er been stricken with a great passion, lad. That is why ye cannae understand."

"I am no innocent bairn, Aunt."

"I didnae say ye were untried, fool. I just said ye havenae kenned the sort of blinding lust that makes ye act unwisely. 'Tis for the best. Ye act quite unwisely enough without it."

Sorcha inwardly sighed as Neil and Dougal proceeded to argue, Neil insulting Dougal and he angrily defending himself. It was an old game. They loved each other dearly, but Neil wanted Dougal to be the responsible laird of Dunweare he was not ready to be, and

Dougal felt the need to violently defend his ideas and actions.

She found her thoughts drifting to Ruari and inwardly sighed. It was just her luck that the slinking Simon Treacher was the one who lusted after her so much he would chase her down into enemy territory while the man she wanted raced back to Gartmhor as fast as his horse could carry him, never to return. She had barely looked at Treacher, and certainly not in an inviting way, and he was running after her like a stag scenting a doe in season, while she had made passionate love to Ruari for three long nights, and he set her aside without a thought. Fate had a very cruel sense of humor, she decided.

As she helped herself to some of the bread and cheese being passed around, she realized that a goodly part of her sadness came from the fact that she and Ruari had parted in anger with her delivering insults and him hurling out threats. She had wanted his memories of her to be sweet ones, maybe even sweet enough to pull him back to her. It was doubtful he would remember her very sweetly now.

"Stop it," whispered Neil, nudging her hard enough to nearly cause her to lose her balance.

Sorcha quickly looked for Dougal, only to see that he had gotten so angry he had walked away. "Stop what?" she asked her aunt and could tell by Neil's disgusted look that her act of confused innocence was not working.

"Cease brooding o'er that mon. I ken 'tis hard for he hasnae even been gone a week yet, but the quicker ye fight the urge to brood, the quicker the pain eases."

"Aye, it probably does. I wasnae really brooding. I was but wondering why a mon I want no part of chases me, and the one I do want runs away. It doesnae seem quite fair."

"Nay, it doesnae, but if one expected things always to be fair, one would be constantly disappointed." She smiled when Sorcha laughed. "Ye need not fear that Dougal will learn of what passed between ye and Sir Ruari."

"A lot of people ken what happened—most all of Dunweare, I suspect."

"Aye, but they will say nothing. Trust me in this, lass. Aye, Dougal may come to suspect that something happened, but unless ye tell him the full tale, he will ne'er hear it from us."

"I am grateful, and yet it somehow doesnae feel right to keep secrets from Dougal. He is my brother, but more important, for all his faults, he is my laird." When Neil opened her mouth to argue, Sorcha held up her hand. "'Tis best if secrecy is maintained howsomever. Dougal can have a hot temper and act without thinking. There is enough trouble between the Hays and the Kerrs. I certainly caused my share of it. We dinnae need Dougal adding to it."

"Sweet Mary, nay. That lad has a true skill for making good things bad, and bad things worse." Neil winked at Sorcha. "For all that, 'tis good to see the fool alive and weel."

"Aye, that it is. 'Twould be even better if this taught him some much needed caution, but I have learned the hard lesson of hoping for something one cannae have."

Neil draped her arm over Sorcha's shoulders, briefly hugged her, and kissed the top of her head. "Dinnae completely lose the ability to hope, lass. That could leave you with a cold, empty heart. Now, look there, Ronald returns."

Sorcha frowned when she saw the serious look upon Ronald's rough features as he crouched beside her. "Are they still following us?" She spared one brief glance for Dougal as he joined them.

"Nay. They have only just roused themselves from a heavy sleep and they will return to England. The mon has some verra poor scouts with him. They passed within reach of me time and time again, but told Sir Treacher we had all disappeared and they could find no sign of us."

"So he has given up." Sorcha started to breathe a sigh of relief only to have it catch in her throat when Ronald shook his head.

"He simply returns to England. The mon is near to frothing at the mouth because ye have slipped out of his reach. He was cursing and threatening all his men with dire punishments for their failure. He means to seek ye out in the spring, lass, with more men and better skilled ones, too."

"Weel, spring is many months away. There is more than enough time for the mon to change his mind." Sorcha could tell by the expressions on everyone's faces that they did not believe it any more than she did.

Chapter Twelve

"Snow. Good," Rosse grumbled as he stepped into the great hall at Gartmhor and shook the icy damp from his clothes.

Ruari looked up from the tankard of wine he had been morosely staring into. It was now late December, over three months since he had ridden away from Dunweare and Sorcha Hay. The more difficult he found it to forget her, the angrier he got. Rosse's terse announcement that winter had well and truly arrived in all its cold misery did not improve his dark mood at all, nor did he see anything good about it.

"Since when have ye liked the snow?" he demanded as Rosse sprawled in the seat beside him at the head table and helped himself to some wine.

"Since it means an end to the constant marching in and out of tittering, blushing, weak, and witless maids ye think ye wish to wed. At least now I can have a wee respite from watching the foolish lasses struggle to catch your eye when ye arenae interested in them and ne'er will be."

"I need to marry. I need to breed an heir."

"Ye dinnae *need* any of these children ye have

inspected and weel ye ken it. Not one of these courtly bred bairns are really what ye want or need. Ye are just too stubborn to admit it was a poorly conceived plan or to let go of your anger and poor wee bruised pride."

Rosse was right, and that only annoyed Ruari more. He had planned his life carefully, right down to the sort of wife he needed, and he did not like the way it was failing so miserably. Rosse should be trying to help him instead of ridiculing him.

"I suppose ye would smile and forgive being taken for a fool, taken captive, and then ransomed."

"If 'twas done by a lass as bonnie as Sorcha Hay— aye."

"Mayhap 'tis past time ye heard a few hard truths about that bonnie lass," Ruari said.

"I dinnae think there is much ye can say that would prove bad about such a sweet-faced lass. The bonniest brown eyes I have seen in many a year. Mayhap ever."

"Weel, aye, she does have verra fine eyes," Ruari admitted. He would never admit to anyone that those eyes were what he had searched for in the long procession of possible wives that had wended its way through Gartmhor in the past few months. "I would ne'er try to claim that Sorcha Hay isnae bonnie, verra bonnie indeed. If 'twas only a pretty face I sought in a wife, she would be admirably suited. Howbeit, everything else about her and her family is completely *un*suitable."

Ruari proceeded to tell Rosse everything about the Hays, about Effie and her strange fancies, and all the aunts with their vagaries. He told him about the angry spirits, the curse they claimed to suffer under, and Sorcha's belief that she could see and speak to the spirits of ones who had died. Almost word for word he repeated Sorcha's wild explanations for the things she did and the odd things he had seen and heard. Ruari made it very clear that he did not believe any of it, but he was unsettled when he did not see the same disbelief reflected in Rosse's expression.

"Ye dinnae believe all this foolishness? Do ye?" he finally demanded.

Rosse shrugged. "A lot of people believe in such things. Aye, 'tis a wee bit odd that so many in one family believe, but such unity might make me look closer."

"And just how do ye think such ideas will be seen in court which, like it or not, I must deal with?"

"Probably with a lot less trouble than ye think. Even if ye still do not believe the lass's tales, ye came to accept *her* belief in them. Ye ceased to think she was a madwoman, didnae ye?"

"Not completely," he replied and wondered if he sounded as sullen to Rosse as he did to himself. "If Gartmhor is to continue to grow and prosper, I must wed with an eye to money, land, and position. Aye, a lass like Sorcha is weelborn, but her clan has little or no power. She has no money and no lands. There is also a verra poor history amongst the Hays of producing sons."

"If she produces daughters like that strapping red-headed aunt of hers, it willnae matter." Rosse met Ruari's glare with a crooked smile, but then grew serious. "Weel, I still think ye are blinded in your search for a wife. Ye dinnae need the faint-hearted, lack-witted females ye have been courting either. They could hurt Gartmhor as weel, mayhap more than a poor, dowerless lass who speaks to spirits."

"I dinnae ken why we are discussing her as if she is one of my choices for a wife," snapped Ruari.

He refilled his tankard and took a long drink to ease his anger. It did not help to lighten his mood to realize that he liked the idea of Sorcha as his wife. It was tempting, far too tempting.

"Sorcha Hay suits ye better than the others ye have looked o'er. Aye, and ye want her," Rosse said.

"Carnally, aye," Ruari agreed. "That isnae a good reason to marry a lass."

"As good as any of the ones ye list."

"This is a waste of words and time. Sorcha Hay could meet every one of my requirements for a wife, and I still wouldnae wed her. She held me for ransom and emptied Gartmhor's coffers of a goodly sum of money. She allowed me to believe I was being rescued, then informed me at the gates of Dunweare that I was a prisoner."

"That sounds a clever lass to me. She and her cousin couldnae fight you."

He was right, but Ruari was not about to admit it. "Let us just say I can forgive and forget her treachery and the strange beliefs she holds, even the way she talks to the air. It would make no difference. She wouldnae have me."

"The lass shared your bed. Why wouldnae she wed a mon she took as her lover?"

Ruari wished he had not confided that to Rosse. He knew it was why the man kept pinching at him about Sorcha. In one drunken moment of weepy confession about a lost and much-missed passion, he had given Rosse a good-sized club to use against him. Now, to get the man to stop worrying the subject of Sorcha, he was going to have to confess something he found both painful and embarrassing. His life had never been so complicated or emotionally trying, and he freely blamed Sorcha for the unpleasant changes.

"She doesnae want me for a lover or a husband," he finally said.

"I havenae formed that opinion from all ye have told me."

"I didnae tell ye everything, although 'tis clear I told ye far too much. When I was leaving, she made it verra clear that she just used me for stud."

"What?" Rosse asked, his shock and confusion clear in his voice.

"She said, and these are her exact words, 'Who can say, mayhap your wee efforts will replenish some of the monly stock of Dunweare.'" Rosse said nothing, just stared at him, so Ruari continued. "I asked her plainly if she was trying to say she had used me for stud. Her reply was: 'I dinna *try* to say it. I just did. Quite plainly, I thought.'"

Ruari frowned when an odd choking noise escaped Rosse. The man looked away then stared down at the table. Ruari suddenly noticed that the man's broad shoulders were shaking, and he gaped at his closest friend.

"Are ye laughing?" Ruari demanded, outrage roughening his voice.

"Aye." Rosse choked out then roared with laughter, no longer able to hide it.

It was difficult for Ruari to suppress the strong urge to strike his friend, but he knew it would solve nothing nor did the man really deserve it. That the man he considered as close to him as a brother would laugh so heartily at an insult to him was disconcerting and a little painful. He had expected sympathy and instead he got hilarity. When Rosse's laughter faded to chuckles and he wiped the tears from his eyes, Ruari glared at him.

"I am pleased to have been able to provide you with such enjoyment," he said, his voice cool as he struggled with a sense of betrayal.

"Come, Ruari, ye didnae really take the lass's words to heart, did ye?" Rosse asked in astonishment.

"And how else should I take them?"

"As angry words spat out to respond to some unkind thing ye said. Think. What did ye say just before Sorcha implied that ye were no more than some convenient stallion?"

Ruari thought over the entire conversation and felt the first flickerings of unease. "Weel, I may have spoken unkindly."

Rosse made a sharp noise of disgust. "*What* did ye say?"

"I may have indicated that our time together was, weel, ill advised."

"Verra weel said, Cousin. I suspect ye made it verra clear indeed. Sweet Mary, what did ye expect a lass with pride to do? Thank ye sweetly for stealing her maidenhead then spitting on such a gift?"

"Ye dinnae understand. Aye, we were lovers, but—" Ruari stopped as he struggled to explain, only to discover he did not really have the words. "Sorcha and I didnae and cannae follow the rules most lovers follow."

"That is plain to see," Rosse shook his head. "I have been talking to ye as if ye had the wit to ken what was right beneath your nose, but I begin to doubt that ye do."

"And so now ye feel free to insult me, too? First my lover, then ye and that fool Beatham. Weel, now that winter is here at least that morose boy willnae be lurking at every turn casting reproachful looks my way." When Rosse coughed nervously, Ruari tensed. "Beatham returned home, didnae he?"

"Nay, I fear not. He still refuses to speak to his parents because they still refuse to accept Margaret as his wife. So, he lingers here."

"Someone ought to have a long, stern talk with that boy. I cannae, for he refuses to speak with me. He just glares accusingly."

"I am surprised at the steadfastness of the lad. Ye have to admire it. He at least kens exactly what he wants."

Ruari slammed his tankard down on the heavy oak table and stood up. "I grow weary of this conversation. Ye carp at me like some old woman. I will do what I must for Gartmhor and I *will* make that Hay wench pay for playing a soldier's game."

Tossing off the last of his drink, Ruari strode out of the great hall. He would never admit it to Rosse, but he was also glad that winter had put an end to his search for a wife. None of the girls he had met had pleased him in the slightest. He knew he was comparing each one in looks and spirit to Sorcha which annoyed him. He simply needed more time to forget the three glorious nights they had shared. It was not surprising that such a sweet, strong passion would linger in his mind. Once he had the time to shake free of that memory's grip, he would be able to choose a wife. As he strode to the small, private chamber where the ever-diligent Malcolm kept the records of Gartmhor, Ruari cursed Sorcha Hay. He hoped she was having as difficult a time shaking free of his memory as he was of hers.

Sorcha caught sight of a scowling Dougal seated at the head table as she entered the great hall. She briefly considered making an escape, then squared her shoulders and walked to her seat on his right. In the more than three months since Ruari had left her, she had become adept at avoiding her brother. It was time to stop being such a coward.

"Have ye decided to bless me with your presence, then?" Dougal asked, eyeing Sorcha with a mixture of sullen anger and sharp curiosity.

"Ye seem to be accusing me of avoiding you," Sorcha said as she filled her trencher with the savory roasted beef and vegetables. "I dinnae ken where ye get such ideas." She ignored Dougal's scornful laugh as the small page filled her tankard with cider.

"Mayhap my suspicions are bred of the certainty that everyone at Dunweare is keeping something secret from me."

"Nay. What could they possibly wish to hide from their laird?"

"The truth about what happened whilst the Kerrs abided here."

"The only truth about that is that they were held here for several weeks, a ransom was paid for them, and they returned to Gartmhor. What more could there be?" She jumped slightly when Dougal slammed his tankard down on the thick wooden table.

"A great deal more, which has put a sadness in your eyes I have ne'er seen there before and which has turned the cheerful Margaret into a pale, sniffling shadow. Although Margaret hasnae the keenest wits, she used to be pleasant company. Now one dreads the few times she ventures out of her bedchamber for she casts a damp pall o'er everything around her."

Sorcha used the chewing of a thick piece of bread to consider her reply. Dougal had quickly suspected something had occurred between her, Margaret, and the Kerrs, and he had become determined to ferret out the truth. She decided that perhaps giving him a little of the truth would make him back away. The first snow of winter had begun to fall, and Sorcha did not enjoy the thought of being sequestered inside the keep with a forcefully curious Dougal.

"I fear Margaret became quite enamored of young Beatham Kerr."

"Were they lovers?" Dougal demanded, his intention of seeking redress for such an insult to his kinswoman evident in his voice.

"Nay, but if matters were different, there could have been a match there. Beatham clearly returned her feelings. Howbeit, the Kerrs would not want any marriage with a clan that took their laird prisoner, and Beatham is as poor and as landless as Margaret."

"Ah, aye, that would be a poor match. It willnae be easy, but both need to find a mate with at least some coin and land. 'Tis a pity. If Margaret had a full purse and even a small holding, we could wed her to Beatham to secure a peace with the Kerrs. It would make all sides happy. Howbeit, she has no dowry at all, and we dinnae have the means to give her one." He studied Sorcha for a moment. "And did ye lose your heart to Sir Ruari Kerr? Is that why your humor has grown darker?"

"Are ye saying that I am no longer pleasant company?"

"I dinnae see ye long enough to know, and dinnae try to divert me by feigning insult."

"If my mood has been dark, I humbly apologize. I found the ransoming of men to be a distasteful business. Mayhap, too, having two handsome, weelborn gentlemen at hand made me too keenly aware of how few marriageable men there are about here and how little chance there is that I shall ever marry."

Dougal flushed and murmured, "Ye would make some mon a verra good wife."

"A verra good but verra poor and landless wife. I thought I had accepted my lot, but it seems I had not.

Now I will do so. Dinnae look so guilty, Dougal. Ye didnae leave us so poor. Our coffers were emptied whilst ye were still in the womb."

"I ken it, but I havenae replenished what was lost either." He sighed and ran his fingers through his thick hair. "I thought the way to gain coin was to go to battle. Many men gain land, money, and power upon the battlefield, but it hasnae happened to me."

"If ye consider how many men go to battle and how often they do so, it makes the number of men who actually profit from it look verra small indeed. Aye, and most of them are close friends or kin to the mon with the highest standing."

She could tell by the still look upon Dougal's face that he had never considered that fact. It was somewhat comforting to know that his constant rush to battle had not been solely a headlong grasp for honor, that he had actually been trying to recoup the lost fortunes of Dunweare. Sorcha now hoped that he would see what a poor gamble that had been.

"Weel, it looks like ye may have knocked some sense into the fool's head," came Crayton's voice so abruptly and so close to her ear, Sorcha jumped.

Taking a deep breath to steady herself, Sorcha looked over her shoulder. Crayton was visible only to the waist, and it looked as if he was leaning on the back of Dougal's chair. "Ye will turn my hair white ere I am five-and-twenty."

Crayton ignored her complaint and rested his hand on Dougal's shoulder, grinning when the man shuddered and jerked away. "The men in your clan ne'er get the gift, do they?"

"Nay, and dinnae tease him."

"'Tis that cursed Crayton, isnae it?" said Dougal, glaring over his shoulder.

"Aye," replied Sorcha, and she gave Crayton a reprimanding glare. "And he *will* leave you in peace so that ye can enjoy the rest of your meal."

"Thank ye." Dougal spared one last glare behind him and returned to the business of eating.

"Ye seem to take delight in spoiling my fun," grumbled Crayton. "The lad deserves a wee bit of tormenting. Mayhap, if he is made unhappy enough, he will pause to think now and again."

Since Dougal was sitting right next to her, Sorcha did not think she could reply to that insult, so asked, "Why are ye here? Ye rarely come into the great hall when a meal is served."

"And why should I? To stare at all I hunger for and cannae eat? I always had a fondness for cider," he said with a longing look at her tankard.

"If ye dinnae like to be here then why have ye appeared? Are ye dawdling in giving me some important news again? I often have this nightmare that ye ken someone is stalking me, plotting to murder me, yet dinnae think to mention it until my head rests atop the killer's spear."

"I wouldnae let anyone stick your head upon a spear."

Sorcha frowned when she realized he had not said he would try to halt her murder. "Crayton, what do ye want?"

"Did ye ken that someone spies upon Dunweare?"

"I have heard nothing." She nudged Dougal. "Has anyone reported that someone has been watching Dunweare?" she asked him.

"Nay. Why? Does that fool ghost say he has seen something?"

"I would be cautious about who I call a fool if I were

ye." Crayton glared at Dougal and started to swing at him only to be halted by an equally fierce glare from Sorcha.

"Where is the spy?" she asked. "I need more than the fact that ye ken there is someone watching us."

"The mon was set in the highest of the high trees just beyond the fields," replied Crayton. "He is one of the Sassenach Treacher's dogs."

"How do ye ken that?"

"The trappings on his horse, the clothes the mon wore, and he happened to heartily curse one Simon Treacher as he struggled to perch himself in the trees."

As Sorcha relayed that information to Dougal, she felt a chill of fear slip down her spine. It was an ominous sign that Simon Treacher would set a spy on them. When Dougal called for a man to go with him to find the spy, Crayton shook his head, and Sorcha told her brother to wait until she had extracted the whole tale from Crayton.

"Do ye see the trouble ye cause by not telling us everything as quickly as possible? Now, why shouldnae Dougal go and hunt the mon down?"

"Because the mon has probably limped all the way back to England by now."

Sorcha lightly massaged her temples as she fought the urge to scream. "Do ye think ye could tell me this tale in one telling, start to end?"

"I saw the mon in the wood. 'Twas one of those times when I was drawn there, ye ken. I recognized him as Treacher swine and decided to watch him. He climbed a tree which gave him a fine sight of Dunweare. Mayhap ye should thin those trees out, lass."

"Crayton," she snapped, "how did the mon get from sitting in a tree peering at us to limping back to England?"

"Ah, weel, I think he did himself a serious injury to his leg when he fell out of the tree."

She sighed, resigned to the fact that Crayton simply could not relate news in a clear, unbroken manner. "Did ye push him?"

"Nay, but I did afright him some. Ye ken weel that I can make my presence known e'en if the fool hasnae the gift to see me."

"Ye do ken that it might have been more helpful if we could have talked to him?"

"Aye, but I couldnae help myself. He was a Treacher mon."

"I understand. I dinnae suppose that, whilst ye were terrifying the mon, he happened to let slip why he was sent to spy on us?"

"As he dragged himself after his fleeing horse—"

"Ye afrighted his horse, too?"

"Aye. Why should the mon return to England in comfort? Although he may have caught the beast by now. He said only one thing, many times and in many colorful ways."

"And this one thing he said?" she prodded when Crayton fell silent.

"That no wee Scottish whore is worth this trouble. His words, lass. Not mine."

"I ken it."

She related the whole tale to Dougal, who decided he and a few men should at least check to be certain the man was gone. Crayton slipped away with them, unable to resist even a small chance to frighten Treacher's man one more time. Sorcha refilled her tankard and fought the beginning of a severe headache.

Her life had been relatively calm until she had found Ruari Kerr on that battlefield. The worst of her trials had been sorting out the difficulties her feckless relatives stumbled into. Now she had fallen in love and lost it, held a man for ransom, dealt with the English, lost her maidenhead, and had inspired some ferret-faced Sassenach to hunt her. It was all Ruari's fault, she decided crossly. When and if she ever saw the man again, she still planned to run away, but only after she gave him a sound and very painful punch in the mouth.

Chapter Thirteen

"There ye are," cried Dougal, hurrying over to where Sorcha worked to ready the kitchen garden for the spring planting.

Sorcha stood up, rubbing at the small of her back as she greeted him with a smile. Over the winter he had matured, and they had grown closer. He still acted before he thought, but he was increasingly willing to listen to advice. She prayed those changes were real and not simply the lulling effects of a long, cold winter.

She briefly glanced up at the spring sky, finding it unusually clear and bright for early April, and smiled to herself. A dull ache of emptiness seemed to have permanently lodged itself in her heart, yet even that sorely bruised part of her could not fully resist the uplifting effects of spring. Sorcha could almost envision herself living a happy life without Sir Ruari Kerr at her side. Shaking free of her musings, she centered her attention upon Dougal before he could notice and question her distraction.

"Is there something I can help ye with, brother?" she asked as she wiped her dirty hands on her apron.

"Nay, ye do more than your share of work as it is. I have come to ask if ye wish to go to the market fair in Dunbum today. If we leave soon we need spend but one night upon the road."

"Oh, I should greatly enjoy that, but do ye think it will be safe?"

"Unless Crayton has been keeping secrets from us, no one has caught sight of a Treacher mon for nearly a month. 'Twill be safe, lass. I will be there as will Robert, Iain, Aunts Neil, Bethia, Grizel, and Eirie and several weel-armed soldiers. And the market will be crowded. No Englishmon would dare venture close to it. I wondered if ye could convince Margaret to go with us. It might cheer her."

Sorcha was not sure of that, but nodded. "I will try to coax her. What of young Effie? She loves such market fairs."

"Aye, but I told her she would have to forgo this one. The spirits are still troublesome."

"I dinnae think they would follow her."

Dougal shrugged. "I couldnae find anyone who could say for certain so I decided 'twas best not to risk it. I have promised her a visit to a fair as soon as the trouble ends."

Although she felt badly for young Euphemia, Sorcha did not argue with Dougal's decision. He was right. They could not risk Effie's spirits starting their nonsense at a crowded fair.

She took only a moment to clean the dirt from her hands and discard her apron before searching out Margaret. It did not really surprise her to find her cousin draped on her bed, staring morosely at her ceiling, but she was distressed by the sight. Margaret was proving obstinate in her melancholy mood. Nothing seemed to cheer the girl, and no one had been able to talk her out of it. Sorcha knew Margaret would not greet the idea of going to a fair with any enthusiasm, but she was determined to drag the girl along. If nothing else, Margaret needed to get some fresh air.

"Ye are a sorry sight," she told Margaret as she sat down on the edge of the bed. "Ye will certainly make yourself unweel if ye continue on like this."

"How can ye be so happy?" Margaret asked, staring at Sorcha in sad-eyed curiosity. "I thought ye loved Ruari."

"Aye, I did, more fool I. And I am not exactly happy. 'Tis simply that I refuse to be brought to my knees by a mon. One doesnae have to die of love."

"One cannae. I have tried."

"Margaret!"

"Oh, dinnae look so concerned. I dinnae think it can be done. My first thought was to just let myself slip into death, but I am too healthy and I kept feeling hungry so I would eat. 'Tis clear that one cannae waste away if one eats."

Although it upset her that Margaret had even considered dying, Sorcha found her cousin's complaints about her failure amusing and had to bite back a smile. "Nay, I believe one is supposed to starve."

"Weel, I cannae do that because I cannae *not* eat. Hunger isnae a verra nice feeling. I cannae just sleep my way into death because I keep waking up. And then, of course, I eat again. I even considered going to a nunnery, but I couldnae. They dress so poorly, live in such dank places, and eat poor food as weel. I have failed at all the things 'tis said a heartbroken lass does. In truth, I think I didnae try verra hard. Then I begin to wonder if I truly love Beatham."

"Of course ye do, and he would never fault you for surviving the parting forced upon you." She patted

Margaret's shoulder in a gesture of sympathy. "Since I am certain he is still verra much alive, your pining away would only make him feel terrible."

"I have begun to think so, too."

"Good. Now, I have come to drag ye along to a fair."

Margaret sat up and frowned at Sorcha. "Ye cannae expect me to go and be frivolous when my heart is crushed, can ye?"

"I dinnae expect ye to dance through the town, singing and flirting—nay. Howbeit, I insist ye leave this room, something ye have rarely done all winter. Cloistering yourself in here willnae mend your heart or bring Beatham back."

"Neither will going to a fair."

"Nay, but at least ye will be getting on with the business of living instead of huddling in here wondering why ye cannae die."

It took a lot more arguing than Sorcha felt was reasonable, but she finally convinced Margaret to go to the fair. The girl was not going to be good company, Sorcha decided as she hurried to ready herself for the journey, but some time away from Dunweare could only be good for the girl.

Patting her hair to make sure her braid was tidy and secure, Sorcha started out of her bedchamber only to come face-to-face with a very solemn Euphemia. She prayed the child was not going to try to play upon her sympathies in order to go to the fair.

"I am sorry ye cannae come with us today, Effie, but there will be other fairs," she said.

"Aye, I ken it. I didnae come here to argue Dougal's decision. I think *ye* ought not to go, Sorcha." Euphemia grasped Sorcha by the sleeve to stress her warning.

"I would agree to stay and keep ye company, although

I think there is plenty about, but I have convinced Margaret to go. I really think I should accompany her."

"Nay, ye dinnae understand. Something told me to tell you not to go."

"Have ye had some vision? Ye wondered if ye were to gain some gift. Mayhap it is the sight."

"I havenae had a vision really." Euphemia lightly bit her lower lip as she struggled to say what she was compelled to say more clearly. "I just ken that ye will only find trouble at the fair, and mayhap ye shouldnae go."

"There has been no sign of the English, and we have no enemies amongst the Scots who usually attend this fair. Ye say trouble. Do ye mean danger? Do ye sense that my life is in danger?" Sorcha wished she had the skill to help Euphemia understand her premonitions so that she could relay them more exactly.

For a moment Euphemia frowned in thought then shook her head. "Nay, your life isnae in danger. I just sense, weel"—she shrugged—"trouble."

"Weel, I thank ye for the warning and I shall keep a close watch, but that really isnae enough to make me stay behind. I have to go or Margaret willnae go, and I think this fair will lift her spirits."

"Oh, aye, a day at the fair will make Margaret verra happy," Euphemia declared and strode away.

Sorcha sincerely began to doubt Euphemia's prediction when, as they all gathered in the bailey, Margaret arrived looking as if she were being dragged to the funeral of someone she had heartily disliked. Margaret was clearly not going to cooperate with everyone's efforts to cheer her.

"There walks a black cloud," murmured Neil as she mounted her horse and edged up next to Sorcha who sat astride a dappled mare.

"At least she is out of that room," Sorcha said as she checked to be sure her panniers were secured.

"True, although she acts as if she goes along with us under threat of torture."

"That was the next thing I was about to try." Sorcha smiled faintly when Neil laughed, and they nudged their horses to follow Dougal as he rode out of the gates.

"I ne'er thought she would remain so upset."

"Ye thought her love a passing fancy?"

"Aye. Margaret has never shown much hint of stubbornness or even steadfastness. I didnae think her heart would remain broken for so many months. She and Beatham were more weel matched than even I guessed."

"That assumes that Beatham suffers as she does."

"True. I cannae say why, but I am inclined to believe that he does. Mayhap that feeling is born of her unexpected faithfulness. If she can remain so firmly in love, why cannae he?"

"Aye, why cannae he indeed." Sorcha sighed and glanced toward Margaret who rode in a cart with her aunts. "I dinnae expect her to be cured by this trip, but mayhap 'twill prove to be a step toward putting the worst of her grief behind her."

"As ye have done?" Neil asked quietly, watching Sorcha closely as she waited for a reply.

"Aye, as I have." Sorcha could tell by Neil's frown that her aunt did not completely believe her. "As I told Margaret, I cannae say I am happy but I am sure that I will survive. At times, such as on a day as bonny as this one, I can almost believe that one day I might actually find another mon to love. Of course, I then recall how scarce men are about Dunweare."

Neil chuckled and nodded. "As scarce as udders on a bull. 'Tis good to hear ye talk so, lass. That is a true sign of a healing heart." She winked. "And who can tell, mayhap the market fair will be aswarm with men."

Sorcha smiled and nodded, joining in the play as Neil proceeded to conjure up visions of a veritable army of rich unwed men prowling Dunburn in search of women to marry. She realized it was her kinsmen who had saved her from slipping into a true blackness of spirit after Ruari left. It would be they who would help her finally banish Ruari's ghost from her heart and mind. Laughing at Neil's foolishness, Sorcha decided she was going to do her best to enjoy the fair thoroughly and thus take one step closer to being completely free of Ruari Kerr.

"That boy will come to the fair if I must tie him to his horse," snapped Ruari as he paced the bailey. "Fetch the idiot down here," he ordered one of his men.

Ruari slapped his leather gauntlets against his leg as he watched the man run back into the keep. The April sun felt warm and pleasing after the long cold winter, and Ruari decided it was Beatham's fault he was not enjoying it more. Despite the youth's continued refusal to speak to him or his own parents, Ruari had begun to try to pull Beatham out of his black mood. Nothing he did helped and he grew more irritated with each failure.

"Mayhap we should just leave the boy," suggested Rosse, moving to Ruari's side after kissing his everpregnant wife Annie farewell.

"Nay. This has gone on long enough. He had done little more all winter than lie on his bed and sigh mournfully. His only respite from that was to follow me about, glaring at me accusingly. He needs something to distract him. The lad could have any lass he wanted despite his poor and nearly landless state. Mayhap a trip to the fair with all its bonnie flirtatious lasses will remind him of that and show him the foolishness of languishing."

"We ne'er attend this fair as it is a long, hard ride from here. It seems a far distance to travel just to pull Beatham free of his melancholy. Aye, especially when I dinnae really think it will work. Only one thing that lad wants—Margaret Hay."

"Weel, he cannae have her, and 'tis past time he understood that. And we arenae going solely to cheer that fool. Malcolm believes there may be a new source of trade there." Ruari looked toward where the too-thin Malcolm sat awkwardly on the oldest, gentlest mare in Gartmhor's stables. "Ye ken weel that the poor mon is terrified of horses and that it takes a great deal to prompt him to climb on the back of one."

"He should ride in the cart."

"I suggested it, but he does have his pride. He would be shamed by riding with the women." Ruari noticed Beatham striding out of the keep. "Finally. We have delayed our journey long enough."

Rosse studied Beatham as the youth mounted his horse. "He doesnae wish to go. I wouldnae have thought the laddie's pretty face could twist into so black an expression."

"He means to try to dampen all our spirits, but he willnae succeed," Ruari vowed as he mounted his horse. "Malcolm has assured me that I will find a way to fill my coffers at this fair, and even Beatham's sulky face cannae dim the pleasure that will bring me."

Dougal reined in his mount at the top of a small rise and looked toward the busy town, then turned to smile at Sorcha who reined in at his side. "It looks to be even bigger than last year." He glanced toward the cart Margaret rode in as it meandered along the rutted road to town. "There must be something at such a fair that will put a smile on Margaret's face."

"It would seem so. Howbeit, dinnae take it to heart if her spirits dinnae improve much at all," Sorcha said. "Margaret is determined in her melancholy."

"S'truth, I dinnae ken why I think I can cheer her when all of ye women have failed to do so, and ye understand this far better than I do."

"Understanding it doesnae mean we ken how to cure it. I fear Margaret is the only one who can heal her heart. The rest of us can only help as needed."

"Love is clearly a troublesome business," Dougal muttered as he nudged his horse forward. "I believe I shall do my best to avoid it."

Following him down the rise, Sorcha wished it was that simple. To her cost she had discovered how independent a heart can be, deaf to all good sense and discipline. Men did seem to have a tighter rein on their emotions, but she suspected a lot of them found their hearts very hard to control. She hoped that her brother did not have to endure too much pain when he discovered that.

The noise of the fair struck Sorcha first as they stabled their horses at the edge of town. It was clearly going to be a boisterous as well as a busy fair. As she walked over to Margaret she noticed that even that heartsore girl could not resist looking toward the sound of laughter and sellers crying attention to their wares.

"I think I had best stay with my sisters," said Neil even as the other women walked toward the stalls of goods for sale that filled the streets.

"Go on. I will stay with Margaret." Sorcha smiled

faintly as Neil strode after her sisters, cursing them for their impetuousness. She hooked her arm through Margaret's. "Shall we see if there is any cloth worth spending our meager coin on?"

"Weel, I suppose a new gown would be nice," Margaret said as she allowed Sorcha to drag her into town.

"Aye, I suspect the walls of your bedchamber would loudly cheer a change."

"Ye need not ridicule me. I cannae help being sad."

"I ken it, and 'twas not ridicule. I but tease you. Ye must ken that no one wishes to see ye so sad and listless. Can ye not have a wee bit of concern for us? Just try to enjoy today. Think of it as a favor for Dougal as he truly hoped this fair would cheer you."

Margaret stared at her feet for a moment then nodded. "Aye, ye are right. In truth, I should be soundly scolded. I have given little thought to how others might feel. I have been naught but a pall of misery all winter, and that has been most unfair to all of you." She took Sorcha by the hand and tugged her toward an eye-catching display of colorful bolts of cloth. "We can begin by choosing some material for new gowns. Despite my heavy heart, I truly do wish a new one."

"I am pleased to hear ye say so. Howbeit, we must be frugal in our choices."

"That is one matter in which I am most knowledgeable." She glanced over her shoulder toward the inn and saw Dougal and the other men. "Should not at least one of the men keep a watch on us?"

"I am sure they are being watchful," Sorcha replied, a strong touch of doubt in her voice as she observed the men ogling the buxom maid pouring their ale. "We have never been in danger here, nor do I recall any tales of some ill fate befalling a kinsmon while at this fair."

"Aye, so let us leave them to their fun. I am being foolish, seeing shadows and dangers where there are none."

"Mayhap not. Euphemia warned of trouble ere we left for the fair."

"Did ye tell Dougal?"

"Nay. She said our lives werenae in danger, just that there would be some trouble."

"Weel, trouble can be many things, and if there is no real threat to our lives, I cannae see fretting o'er such a warning. We shall just keep a closer watch."

"I hope Euphemia soon gains the skill to be more exact in her warnings. 'Twould be helpful to ken exactly what we must watch for."

"Do ye think she has the sight?" Margaret produced the ghost of a smile for a minstrel as he strolled by, pausing only long enough to nod a bow her way.

"If she does, then today shall be quite pleasant for you."

"For me? How so?"

"Euphemia says that ye will be verra happy indeed by the end of the day."

"I am not sure how that could possibly be true, but 'twill be interesting to see if she is right."

Sorcha was not sure either for, although it was possible Margaret would grow a little less morose, she could not see that one day at a fair would sweep away all of her sadness. She did wish she knew exactly what sort of trouble lurked at the fair, however. It made her uneasy to know that something could go wrong, yet not know when or where. A moment later she shrugged and decided it did not matter, as all of her attention was drawn to the beautiful materials Margaret was spreading out for her approval. After all, if anything threatened them, Dougal was just a short distance away.

"Look there, laddie, a tavern," said Ruari, trying to ignore the fact that Beatham was still sullen and silent. "I would certainly enjoy an ale after such a long, dusty ride." He grasped his young cousin by the arm and started to drag him toward the tavern. "There will probably be a bonnie wench or two to please our eyes as we quench our thirst."

"I dinnae think the lad is paying ye much heed," Rosse murmured as he kept pace on Ruari's other side. "'Tis much akin to talking to yourself, I should think."

"'Tis like banging my head against a wall. Howbeit, he isnae the only one who can be stubborn."

"Nay, ye have proven to be most persistent from time to time. Not always when ye are right, either." Rosse met Ruari's glare with a brief smile.

"And what would ye do with a fool who has sulked for a sixmonth or more?"

"Let him sulk if it makes him happy."

Ruari's reply got wedged in his throat as he looked toward the tavern again. Hissing an order for both men to be quiet, he pushed Rosse and yanked Beatham behind a cluttered stall where a woman was selling yards of fine lace. He peered through the delicate banners of lace and cursed, a second look confirming his first suspicion of whom he had seen.

"The Hays are here," he said and held tightly to Beatham's arm when the young man started to move. "I didnae say your lover was here. 'Tis her idiot of a laird I see. In front of the tavern stands Sir Dougal Hay."

"A handsome lad," said Rosse and shrugged when

Ruari looked at him as if he was the basest of traitors. "'Tis the truth."

"That handsome lad is quaffing down ale he probably bought with my hard-won coin."

"Nay, all that money went to ransom him," protested Beatham as he feverishly looked over the crowds, searching for one particular person.

"Ah, so the fool hasnae completely lost the use of his voice," Ruari said, then turned to Rosse. "If he is here, then others from his clan may weel be, too."

"Ye are thinking of kidnapping one of the Hays, arenae ye?" Rosse shook his head. "Ye cannae just grab a Hay in the midst of a fair."

"Nay? Why not?"

"Our men are scattered all about," he began to protest.

"And they will gather quickly if we give the battle cry, or hide until they are sure they can slip away safely."

"Margaret," Beatham whispered and bolted from their hiding place before Ruari could stop him.

Ruari looked in the direction Beatham was headed and slowly smiled. His gaze fixed not upon the fulsome Margaret, but on the slim dark-haired woman walking beside her. "Malcolm was right," he said to Rosse. "This fair will indeed provide me with the means to refill my coffers." Ignoring Rosse's muttered protests, Ruari hurried after Beatham.

Chapter Fourteen

"Margaret!"

Sorcha cried out softly, scrambling to catch her balance as Margaret abruptly broke free of her grasp and spun around to look behind them. "Be careful," she snapped, but knew Margaret was oblivious to her protest.

"Beatham," Margaret whispered and pressed her tightly clasped hands to her chest.

As quickly as she could, Sorcha grabbed Margaret firmly by the arm, halting her cousin's tentative step toward the one calling out her name. It did not surprise Sorcha to see Beatham waving frantically as he pushed his way through the crowds. A quick look toward the tavern revealed that Dougal and his men were oblivious to this impending disaster. She could not see her aunts in the milling crowd of people either. When she looked back toward Beatham she cursed long and viciously. The man striding along the path Beatham was clearing was the very last man she wanted to see.

"Come along, Margaret, we must get away." She yanked Margaret after her as she hurried through the crowd, but Margaret fought to break free. "Will ye cease fighting me? We must either reach Dougal or find a place to hide."

"But 'tis Beatham."

"Aye, 'tis Beatham, and close on his heels is Sir Ruari Kerr. Do ye think that mon is seeking us out to tell us how much he has missed us?"

"Weel, nay, but I must see Beatham."

"Ye will some time soon, I am sure. Howbeit, today is *not* that time."

She shoved Margaret in front of her then herded the girl through the crowd. To her dismay, once the crowd cleared a little, she found that Beatham, Ruari, and his man were between her and the tavern where Dougal was. She still could not see her Aunt Neil either. Grabbing Margaret, who had started toward Beatham again, Sorcha decided they had to hide.

"Mayhap we should just call for help," Margaret suggested as Sorcha pulled her through the crowded street in a dizzyingly erratic fashion.

"If none of our kinsmen have heard that idiot bellowing your name, how do ye think they will hear us?" Sorcha ducked behind the draped cart of a man selling breads and savory cakes.

"Beatham isnae an idiot. Oh, Sorcha, let me go to him. This is what Euphemia meant. She knew the fair would make me verra happy because I would see Beatham."

"Aye, but dinnae forget that she also said there would be trouble, and the trouble is the hulking black-haired knight following hard on Beatham's heels."

"What can he do to us? Arenae there laws that protect people attending a fair?"

"Mayhap not laws, but custom certainly dictates that he leave us be. Howbeit, he swore he would make the

Hays pay for ransoming him, and I am certain revenge is why he is chasing us down. I just wish I kenned what he plans to do with us if he catches us."

"Beatham willnae let him harm us."

"Nay, and I truly dinnae believe Ruari would harm us anyway. Howbeit, there are a lot of other things he could do. Why, he could kidnap us for ransom, and where would that leave us?"

"I would be with Beatham."

"How wonderful for ye. Being with your beloved could cost Dunweare far more than it can spare, and what of me? How do ye think my poor bruised heart will fare if I am thrust into the hold of a mon who wants only passion from me?"

"Oh," Margaret whispered. "'Twould be terrible for you."

"Aye, that it would." Sorcha touched a finger to her lips and, nudging Margaret in front of her, crawled beneath the cart. "Now, hush, Cousin. They draw near."

Sorcha was relieved when Margaret grew silent and still at her side. She fully understood how difficult it was for Margaret to ignore Beatham's calls. Despite knowing that Ruari was eager for revenge, it was very difficult for Sorcha to hide from him. Just beneath her strong instinct for survival was an equally strong instinct to run to the man she had foolishly fallen in love with, if only to see if the passion they had shared still lingered as strongly in him as it did in her.

She tensed as she caught sight of three pairs of soft rawhide boots poking beneath the edge of the drape. Although the man whose cart they crouched beneath had no idea why they were hiding from three well-dressed knights, he decided to take the side of the women. He denied having seen them. What made Sorcha uneasy was the clear disbelief she could detect in Ruari's rich voice.

A moment later she saw a gauntleted hand grasp the edge of the cloth and knew they would be discovered. Sorcha cursed and, still crouched low, ran out from under the cart, catching Ruari at the knees. The sharp blow sent him falling backward. Unbalanced by her attack, Sorcha almost fell on top of him. Margaret grabbed her by the arm and yanked her to her feet. Without a word she and Margaret began to run.

"Get them," bellowed Ruari as a laughing Rosse helped him to his feet.

"I dinnae ken why Margaret is running away from me," Beatham said, looking crestfallen as two of Ruari's men who had joined in the chase hurried after Margaret and Sorcha.

"Mayhap the lass isnae as witless as I thought," grumbled Ruari as he brushed himself off, glaring at the people who were laughing.

"Ye shouldnae speak so unkindly of my beloved," Beatham snapped, and he rejoined the chase.

"I wish ye would heed me, old friend," Rosse said as he followed Ruari.

"Ye fret o'er nothing."

"Nothing? Ye are about to kidnap a weelborn lass—"

"Two weelborn lasses."

"From a market fair," Rosse continued through gritted teeth. "Ye may not be breaking any written law— I cannae say for certain if one exists—but ye *are* breaking custom. This will offend a great many people. It may e'en raise an outcry that reaches the king's ear."

"It may weel do that. Howbeit, any outcry made will quickly be reduced to a few sullen mutterings when I tell my tale and explain why I felt the need to bend custom."

"*Bend* custom? Ye have broken it so blatantly they will hear the cracking of it in London. Many people may not see what the lasses did as the great crime ye think it is."

"Any mon with pride in his name would find it a bitter root to chew on, and weel ye ken it. There they are," he cried and struggled to move more quickly through the crowd.

Ruari understood Rosse's concerns, but had no intention of heeding them. It was possible that kidnapping Margaret and Sorcha from a fair would cause some outcry, but he felt confident he could rise above the small scandal. He was, after all, not intending to harm them in any way or force them into marriage. He simply wanted his money back. From what he could see, he and Dougal Hay were the highest-ranking men there. He was not going to make the business a public concern, and instinct told him Dougal would also want it to remain a private matter; so Rosse's concerns did not carry the weight they might have under other circumstances. So strong was his need for some retribution, he doubted that even the certainty of being dragged before his king to make some excuse for his crime would deter him. The opportunity to gain the revenge he had thought of for months had walked into his hands, and he fully intended to grasp it.

"Sorcha, he is getting closer," whispered Margaret.

The tone of her cousin's voice assured Sorcha that it was not Beatham who was nipping at their heels. She searched frantically for a new place to hide or some ally to turn to for help, but saw none. The only thing that was clear was that Ruari's men were alert enough to see what their laird was doing and had joined him.

As she turned into a narrow lane between two houses she saw a small woodpile and raced toward it. She grabbed a thick log and spun around just in time to see Ruari reach out for her. Cursing him, she swung, the log connecting soundly with his shoulder and sending him crashing into the side of one of the houses. She threw the log toward the men who had followed Ruari into the lane, and they scrambled back despite Ruari's bellowed commands to grab her. With Margaret close behind her, Sorcha raced out the other end of the lane.

"I dinnae think I can keep running like this," Margaret said, her breathlessness evident in her voice. "Are we near the inn where Dougal is?"

"I fear I dinnae ken where we are now." Glancing behind her, Sorcha cursed when she saw Ruari and his men come out of the lane. "We need to find someplace to hide so that we can catch our breath, or they will surely catch us."

"'Tis curious, but Beatham has disappeared."

Sorcha did not reply for she considered that a good thing. Any time Margaret set eyes on Beatham she seemed to lose what few wits she had. They were only steps ahead of Ruari and his men. Any delay would ensure their capture.

Just as Sorcha began to think exhaustion would bring about their defeat, she turned a corner and saw a place to hide. Grabbing a panting Margaret by the arm, she yanked her cousin into a small shed tucked up next to a tiny thatched roofed cottage. The small wattle-and-daub building was dark which would aid them. She shoved Margaret into a pile of loose hay and dove in after her. For several moments they crouched there, trying to catch their breath as quietly as possible. As their breathless exhaustion began to ease, Sorcha grew sharply aware of the discomfort and sour smell of their hiding place. She could tell by the soft noises Margaret was making that her cousin was finding it even more distasteful than she was.

"We are going to smell like a dung heap," muttered Margaret, squirming around in a vain attempt to get comfortable.

"Mayhap we will smell foul enough that Ruari will-nae wish to set hands on us. Now hush, Cousin. Ruari and his men werenae far behind us. They could be near at hand even now."

"There is no fear that they will be able to sniff us out e'en if they had the best hounds in all of Scotland."

"Will ye hush!" Sorcha tensed as she heard a footfall. "Someone is in here."

She huddled next to Margaret, lightly touching her cousin until she found where her mouth was. It would be foolish to expect her cousin to remain completely silent for very long, and Sorcha wanted to be prepared to stop any ill-advised attempt to speak.

"I am certain they are in here," came a voice Sorcha easily recognized as Ruari's.

"Weel, just in case this is one of those rare times ye are wrong, I sent a few men down the lane to look around."

Sorcha bit the inside of her cheek to stop a surprised laugh over the heavy sarcasm she heard in the other man's voice. She resented the revelation, but finally conceded that the fact that one of his men felt so at ease with his laird he could tease him, said something very good about Ruari himself. At the moment, huddled in straw that stuck into her painfully and smelled as bad as anything she had smelled in a very long time, she did not want to know that there was anything good about the man who had forced her to hide there.

"Ye arenae being verra helpful, Rosse," snapped

Ruari. "Instead of complaining, ye could help me look for the wenches."

"How much help do ye need? This hovel is so tiny I couldnae e'en lie down in it."

A rustle at the edge of the pile of hay made Sorcha's heart skip. Margaret inhaled, and, afraid her cousin was about to make a sound, Sorcha clamped her hand over Margaret's mouth. She silently cursed the dry crackle of hay her tiny movement made. In her mind she could see Ruari tensing with alertness, his head cocked like a hound that has caught the scent of its prey.

It did not startle her at all when, a moment later, the thin layer of hay that covered them was swept away, and the dim light revealed Ruari's grinning face. Sorcha could not believe that she once considered that smile attractive. It appeared to have an unpleasantly wolfish cast to it now.

"How fitting," he drawled as he grabbed her by the arm. "Hays in the hay."

She was not sure which was worse, losing or Ruari's gloating. She seriously considered drawing her sword or dagger and inflicting enough pain on the man to lessen his arrogance. As he yanked her to her feet, Sorcha decided that, although she was unable to hurt him, she simply could not accept defeat so meekly. She balled up one fist and, as he set her on her feet, she punched him square on the jaw so hard she felt the force of it ripple back to her shoulder.

To her utter surprise, Ruari howled and released her. She grabbed Margaret by the hand even as the girl rose to her feet and raced out of the shed. Rosse made no attempt to stop them as he struggled to stop laughing and help a loudly cursing Ruari.

"I cannae believe ye hit him," cried Margaret, casting

a terrified glance over her shoulder at a shouting Ruari who stumbled out of the shed to resume the chase.

"Better that than wiping that accursed grin off his face with my sword."

Sorcha was not terribly surprised when a moment later she rounded a corner and discovered she had not really escaped. They had managed to run right through town to the far edge, as far from Dougal as possible. Standing in front of her were several of Ruari's men with the horses saddled and ready. She could hear Ruari running up behind her. A glance to her right revealed Beatham and two more men closing in on her. To her left was a fast running river. She spat out a curse when Ruari grabbed her from behind, one of his men moving quickly to take away her sword and dagger. An instant later Beatham wrapped his arms around an unresisting Margaret, although Sorcha noticed that the youth rather quickly eased his hold on her as soon as she, too, was disarmed.

"Ye stink, woman," Ruari said, setting Sorcha down, but keeping an almost painfully tight grip on her arm.

"Weel, if ye release me, I will rush to bathe as I shouldnae wish to offend your delicate sensibilities," she retorted and kicked at him, but he neatly eluded her foot.

"We had to hide in a muck heap," Margaret explained to Beatham.

"How horrible for you, dearling," murmured Beatham.

Just as Sorcha opened her mouth to make a scathing remark, a fierce war cry rent the air. She laughed and looked in the direction it came from. Racing toward them, her skirts hiked up above her knees and her sword upraised, was Neil. Although Sorcha suspected her aunt was still too far away to help, and singlehandedly not

powerful enough even if she reached them in time, she
was an inspiring sight.

"Get the women on the horses," Ruari ordered even
as he scooped Sorcha up under one arm.

"Why run? 'Tis just one woman," complained one
man as he swung himself up into the saddle.

"Aye, but she willnae let us take the lasses without a
fight, and that woman can fight as weel as any mon. I
have no wish to hurt her."

Sorcha cursed Ruari's foresight in picking her up so
that she faced backward. Her fists could not cause him
as much pain in such a position, but she pummeled away
at him anyway. A vicious curse escaped her, as well as
most of the breath in her body, when he tossed her over
his saddle, quickly mounting and holding her in place.
He was going to carry her to Gartmhor like a sack of
grain. Sorcha swore that, if she survived, she was going
to do her best to make his life miserable.

As Ruari turned his mount and prepared to kick it into
a gallop, he noticed that Malcolm was not moving. The
man stood agape, reins in hand, staring at Neil who was
closing in fast. For one brief moment, he thought his
cleric was frozen in fear, then realized the look on Malcolm's long thin face was of a man smitten. He cursed.

"Rosse, grab that fool Malcolm. He has lost his wits,"
he ordered.

Rosse bent down, grabbed the thin Malcolm under
one arm and flung him over the saddle in front of him.
He slapped Malcolm's horse on the rump, prompting it
to run after the others, then spurred his own horse into
a gallop. Confident that all of his men were racing
safely toward Gartmhor, Ruari kicked his mount to a
gallop just as Neil reached him. He cursed as she swung

MY LADY CAPTOR   193

her sword, cutting through his hose and lightly scoring his thigh.

"Come back here and fight like a mon, ye thieving bastard," Neil screamed after the retreating horsemen.

"Go and tell Dougal," yelled Sorcha and yelped when Ruari smacked her on the backside.

"We will be halfway to Gartmhor ere your halfwit of a brother can saddle his horse," Ruari taunted her.

"Dougal will kill you."

"Dougal willnae have the time for such bravado. He will be too busy trying to get the coin to pay me for you. I believe ye can guess how much ransom I intend to ask for."

Sorcha used what little breath she had to curse him, his manhood, and his ancestors. Ruari surprised himself by laughing. For the first time in months he felt fully alive. He attributed the feeling to a thrilling chase and a satisfying victory, obstinately ignoring the voice in his head that mocked him for denying the truth—that it was the tiny, cursing woman flung over his saddle who made him feel so good. He would get his money back, he had salved his bruised pride, and mayhap he could enjoy the passion he had once shared with Sorcha. That was enough to make any man's spirits soar.

Neil cursed and raced back through town toward the inn where she had last seen Dougal. She was furious that she had failed to help Sorcha, but even more furious that Dougal had been too busy swilling ale and ogling barmaids to notice that his sister was being kidnapped. When she reached the inn, she saw him seated on a bench, a buxom maid settled on his lap. Cursing her nephew as the greatest fool in all of Scotland, she strode over to him and yanked the woman off his lap.

"Aunt, what ails you?" protested Dougal, his complaint ending abruptly as he noticed the disheveled state she was in. "Is something wrong?"

"So, the lad finally sees something besides the ample breasts of a whore." When Dougal's men started to laugh and the tavern maid began to protest, Neil glared them all into silence.

"There is no need to start hurling insults."

"Nay? Tell me, when did ye last see your sister or Margaret?" The way he looked around almost frantically then paled only softened Neil's fury a little.

"What has happened to them?"

"Ruari Kerr has them and is right now riding hard and fast for the safety of Gartmhor."

Dougal ordered his men to saddle their horses then asked Neil, "How far ahead of us are they?"

"I would wager my sword that they are too far ahead for ye to catch them."

He cursed and slammed his fist down on the filthy table, sending his tankard of ale skittering to the floor. "Has the mon no honor? An unspoken truce exists at these fairs."

"Aye, but this isnae the first time it has been broken nor will it be the last."

"He means to demand a ransom, doesnae he?"

Neil nodded and sighed. "He will probably ask the return of the ransom we got for him."

"I cannae gather that sort of money."

"I dinnae believe he will be inclined to negotiate, lad."

"Then we shall have to do our best to snatch the lasses back," he said as the men returned with the horses and he swung up into his saddle. "Take a room at the inn, and I shall return as soon as I can."

Neil sighed as she watched her nephew and his men ride away. Dougal would be back and, sadly, without Sorcha and Margaret. The Hays could no longer afford the fine, swift mounts the Kerrs rode. Pursuit was fruitless, but it would ease whatever guilt Dougal felt.

She resheathed her sword and smoothed down her skirts before setting out in search of her sisters whom she had abruptly deserted when she had caught sight of Beatham. Although she was confident that no physical harm would come to her nieces, she was concerned. Margaret would now fall even more in love with Beatham, if such a thing were possible, and would be devastated anew when they would be forced to part. Sorcha would now have to spend time in close proximity to a man she loved who did not love her. It was an abysmal situation, and Neil cursed men and their pride. While Dougal and Ruari concerned themselves over ransoms and money, Sorcha and Margaret would be forced to pay the highest price of all.

Chapter Fifteen

A soft, vicious curse escaped Sorcha as she eased herself out of the saddle. Only after miles of hard riding had she been set upright in the saddle but soon endured hours more. She did not believe there was one part of her body that was not bruised and aching. When Ruari dragged her over to a tree and pushed her to sit under it, she had to bite her tongue to keep from cursing him. It only seemed to amuse him, and she found that amusement harder to tolerate than anything else he had done.

As he tended to his horse, she looked at Margaret. Beatham was lovingly tending to the girl's needs, a painfully marked contrast to the way Ruari was treating her. It also caused Sorcha to feel her first pang of real concern. Margaret had finally begun to shake free of the melancholy she had suffered when Beatham had returned to Gartmhor. Being reunited with the youth and being so tenderly reassured of his undying love could well be the worst thing that could happen to Margaret, for nothing had really changed. Margaret and Beatham might be a perfect match, but they could never marry.

A timid cough drew her attention, and Sorcha looked

up to find one of Ruari's men standing before her. He was an odd little man, a good head shorter than the rest of the Kerrs, reed-thin in every way from his narrow features to his almost wispy brown hair. This could not be one of Ruari's men-at-arms. Sorcha doubted the man could even lift a battle sword let alone wield it skillfully.

"M'lady Hay, I am Malcolm Kerr, first cousin to Ruari and cleric at Gartmhor." He bowed.

Sorcha found it a little amusing that the man's voice was as thin as he was, and it held the slightest tremor, revealing his nervousness. "Ye will understand if I cannae bring myself to say that I am pleased to meet ye."

"Oh, aye, m'lady. I but wished to ask ye a question."

When he hesitated, wringing his long-fingered bony hands, she prompted, "Your question is?"

"I was wondering who the woman was who tried to rescue ye."

"Ah, her. 'Twas my aunt, Neil Hay."

"Neil," he said in a tone of reverence. "A good, strong, proud name."

"Er, aye. Her father had hoped to have a son," she murmured, a little startled by Malcolm's unusual reaction to her aunt's name.

"Is she wed or promised?"

There was such anxiety behind the question, Sorcha suddenly realized what prompted the man's interest. She struggled to control her expression, hiding her surprise and budding amusement. The idea that this little man was enamored of Neil was enough to make her bite back a smile, especially when she recalled what the man's first and only sight of Neil had been.

"Nay," she replied. "My aunt is without husband or lover."

Before Malcolm could say anything else, Ruari

joined them, slapping the little man on the back and then quickly steadying him when he almost fell. "Ye were right, Malcolm," he said, grinning at Sorcha. "This trip to the fair was verra profitable indeed."

"Oh, weel, I really hadnae considered this," Malcolm said in a small voice, looking pleadingly at Sorcha. "Truly. This kidnapping wasnae my idea."

"Ye arenae going to scold me about this, too, are ye?" Ruari frowned at the nervously shifting Malcolm. "I have had to abide Rosse's fretting since I first espied Sorcha and I have had my fill of it. She is the reason our money chest is so empty and she will be the means to refill it."

"I would ne'er scold ye, Ruari. Ye usually ken what ye are doing. Um, I will fetch Lady Sorcha some food and water, shall I?" He hurried away without waiting for an answer.

Ruari watched his cousin leave then looked at Sorcha. "Ye werenae trying to sweeten the poor lad so that he would help you, were ye?"

"Dinnae be a bigger idiot than ye already are," she snapped. "The mon was just inquiring about my Aunt Neil. I believe he may be taken with her."

He shook his head. "I noticed that. He almost got himself captured or, worse, impaled on that sword she was waving around."

"Aunt Neil would never have killed an unarmed man."

"Ye can ne'er trust a woman wielding a sword."

"I dinnae ken why ye try so hard to anger me. 'Twould be hard for me to become any angrier. 'Twould please me greatly if this outrage, this blatant disregard for custom, has ye decried far and wide as the outlaw ye are." Even as she said it, Sorcha realized that, despite her fury, she would never wish him to suffer such a dire penalty.

"Outlaw?" gasped Malcolm as he arrived with food and enough water for Sorcha to tidy herself. "Is there a chance that ye could be cried an outlaw, Ruari?"

"Nay. Dinnae fret, Malcolm. The lass but spits out her anger. She cannae stomach defeat weel, and it sours her," said Ruari.

"Ye are what sours me." She briefly smiled her gratitude at Malcolm before he scurried back to the others who were seated around a sheltered campfire. "Am I to be allowed no privacy to wash away the muck and the dust of travel?" she asked, glaring at Ruari.

"Ye may step around the tree, but dinnae forget I am near at hand, and I have verra keen hearing."

As she stepped behind the thick, knotted trunk of the tree, she only briefly considered trying to escape. She was not sure where she was or how to get back to either the town or Dunweare itself. After the long day of trying to escape Ruari, followed by a hard ride, she was also too exhausted. Sorcha doubted she would get very far at all before she lacked the strength to go another step. Neither could she run and leave Margaret behind even though she knew her cousin would not only be safe, but also quite happy.

It was difficult to get very clean with the meager washing supplies Malcolm had given her, but she did her best. Removing even a little of the dirt and odor on her skin and clothes was better than doing nothing at all. She ached to indulge in a long, hot bath and decided she would demand one the moment she reached Gartmhor. She would demand that Ruari give her the same comforts she had provided for him.

Except one, she suddenly thought. If Ruari thought

she would climb back into his bed for the time she would be his captive, he would have to think again. That would surely mark her as no better than a whore. This time, before she allowed him to touch her, she would have more from him than sweet words of desire. At Dunweare she had believed she would only have a few days with him and then would never see him again. That had all changed now, and he would find that the rules for sharing her bed had changed as well.

Still feeling dirty, but at least somewhat refreshed, she stepped back out from behind the tree and sat down to eat the food Malcolm had brought her. "Am I to be kept away from the others, then?" she asked, finally meeting his steady gaze.

"For a wee while, aye," he replied as he sat down facing her. "I think it best if ye dinnae talk to your cousin until ye are both secured behind the walls of Gartmhor."

"Ye dinnae think Beatham is enough of a manacle to hold Margaret?" She nodded toward where the young couple sat close together, whispering and smiling at each other.

"Mayhap, but ye made her run from him before. 'Tis clear ye ken a way to make the lass consider duty to her clan o'er her heart's desire." He frowned toward the lovers. "Of course, 'twill be difficult to pull them apart again, but it must be done. Unless, of course, Margaret has gained both land and fortune o'er the winter."

"Aye, it fell from the sky at Michaelmas."

"Tsk, still a sharp tongue."

"If ye dinnae wish to hear it, dinnae ask such foolish questions." She took a long drink from the wineskin Malcolm had left with her. "Margaret will be heartbroken yet again, and that will only add to my brother's fury."

"I am all atremble."

"Arrogant bastard. Dougal verra nearly caught ye several times today." She could not fully suppress the pride she felt over the hard, skillful chase Dougal had accomplished.

"Being nearly caught isnae quite good enough, is it? For all his efforts I still hold ye and Margaret, and he must limp back to Dunweare to await my ransom demands."

"And there will be an act of complete senselessness. I told ye we were poor. Did ye think I lied? Aye, perhaps ye did. Weel, ye will soon discover that demanding ransom for a Hay of Dunweare is like asking the sky to turn royal purple."

Ruari stood up and idly brushed himself off. He found that her words irritated him and he suspected it was because he was beginning to really believe her talk of being poor. Although he would never admit it to her, Dougal had put up a masterful chase. He had lost because he lacked the right horses. His mounts were sturdy animals, but not the sort a knight with any coin weighting his pocket would ride. If it did prove impossible for Dougal to raise the ransom he intended to demand, he would be confronted with a difficult problem. Shrugging off his sudden doubt and hesitation, he decided he would face that particular quandary when and if it arose.

"I will set Rosse to guard ye while I eat," he said, catching Rosse's eye and waving the man over. "Dinnae try any of your cunning female tricks on him."

Sorcha fought the urge to toss her plate after him as he walked away. The grin on Rosse's face as he sat down across from her told her he had guessed her inclinations. She smiled faintly and returned to her meal. It struck her as a little odd that she did not find Rosse's amusement irritating at all, while Ruari's set her teeth on edge.

'Tis because Ruari was so cursed arrogant, she mused, glaring his way. His blatant gloating did little to improve her mood either. She heartily wished there were some way Dougal could gather the ransom in but hours and get her out of Gartmhor, for she was certain that a long stay with an openly victorious Ruari was going to be extremely hard to stomach. A quick look toward Beatham and Margaret warned her that Ruari's arrogance was not all she would find difficult.

She sighed as she set her empty plate down. Ahead of her lay an extremely trying time, and complaining about it would not help. She decided it would be wise to use the time before she got to Gartmhor to prepare herself for the trials yet to come. As she leaned back against the tree and let her exhaustion take control, she prayed that Dougal had returned safely to Dunweare.

Neil stood up as she espied the weary horsemen ride back into town. She had settled her sisters in their bedchamber, then taken up her post just outside the inn. Sleep would have been impossible as she needed to know if Dougal had succeeded. She also needed to know he was safe. The dejected way he slumped in his saddle told her he had failed to rescue Sorcha, but she was not surprised. For the moment, it was enough that Dougal and his men had returned unharmed.

"I fail miserably at everything I try to do," said Dougal in a heavy tone as he dismounted and allowed his men to lead away the exhausted horses.

Prepared for such black humor Neil urged him to a seat and poured him a tankard of ale from the jug she had kept ready. "Ye did your best," she assured him as she sat down next to him.

"If I had done my best, they never would have been taken."

"Mayhap not today, but at some other time or place. I believe Sir Ruari has planned this little act of revenge for a long time. We should have paid his threats more heed."

"He threatened to do this? Why wasnae I told about that?"

"Because we all felt his anger would ease, that he would forget all he threatened. It has been months, plenty of time for the heat of anger to cool."

"Ye keep saying he was angry. He could hurt Sorcha and Margaret."

"Never," Neil said firmly, and realized she wholeheartedly believed her assurances.

"Not even if I cannae raise the ransom he will demand?"

"Nay, not even then. If naught else, he owes them his life and he kens it."

"If he kens that, then why has he done this? 'Tis an odd way to show his gratitude."

"Weel, he was furious about the money. The mon heartily resented his coin entering our pockets. He wants his money back."

"I can understand that. What concerns me is what he will do when he finally kens that I cannae give it back, that I dinnae have it and have no way to raise it."

Neil patted him on the back in a silent gesture of sympathy. "Trust me, laddie. That mon will ne'er hurt our lasses. Now, I should like to be the one who deals with him."

"Ye? Why should ye wish to go? 'Twill mean a great

deal of hard riding between Gartmhor and Dunweare," he warned her.

"I ken it, but I want to go. I ken the mon, ye dinnae. He kens me. I dinnae mean to give ye an insult, but because your sister had to save your hide, he doesnae hold the highest opinion of ye." She watched anger tighten Dougal's fine features. "No one else faults you. Weel, not much."

Dougal laughed, a dry, bitter sound. "Ye are ofttimes a little too painfully honest."

"Mayhap. And ye are ofttimes a little too hot-blooded. That would not help the lasses."

"Nay, it wouldnae. All right, ye may deal with the Kerrs in my stead. Howbeit, ye will make it verra clear that, if any harm comes to my sister or my cousin, I will hunt the mon down and take great pleasure in killing him."

"Ye will have to move fast or I will surely steal that privilege."

Sorcha winced and decided she could easily grow to hate horses. Although she had slept soundly for several hours when they had made camp, it had not been enough to banish her bone-weariness completely. When Ruari pointed out Gartmhor in the distance, Sorcha almost welcomed the sight, for it meant she would be able to get off the saddle she had ridden for two days.

Her first sight of Gartmhor made her uneasy. It was a huge, thick-walled keep on a rocky hill. Although it did not look as impregnable as Dunweare, it certainly looked as if escape would be difficult, if not impossible.

As they rode through the thick iron-studded gates of Gartmhor, Sorcha shivered. She prayed that was not some sort of premonition. One thing she had not been

concerned about was that she and Margaret were in any
sort of physical danger. She did not wish to be proven
wrong.

"Weel, what do ye think of Gartmhor?" Ruari asked
when they halted in the inner bailey and he moved to
help her dismount.

She could hear the pride in his voice and wished she
could see some glaring problem with his keep, but there
did not appear to be one. Wriggling free of his light
hold, she looked around. Everywhere were signs of
Ruari's wealth, from the large number of well-armed
men to the clothes everyone wore, and Sorcha felt her
anger return. He was going to make poor Dougal work
frantically and worry himself sick trying to gather
money Ruari did not really need.

"I can see how destitute ye were made by the ransom
we took from you," she said, glaring at him, thinking
that Dougal might have been right to say she should
have demanded more.

"Simply because I have money doesnae mean I must
sweetly accept others helping themselves to it. 'Tis
mine. I worked hard for it."

"Aye, ye look worn to the bone by your many labors."
She knew it was not really fair to make his wealth sound
like a crime, but she was too angry to care about fairness.

He grabbed her by the arm and dragged her toward
the keep. "I will show ye to your chambers—"

"My prison."

He ignored her and continued, "—Where ye can have
the bath ye so sorely need."

"Please, kind sir, accept my deepest regrets if I have
offended your large nose. I fear I had no time to properly ready myself for my abduction."

"Ye do sorely try a mon's temper, lass."

Before she could reply, they were stopped by a plump, gray-haired woman. Sorcha frowned when the woman glanced nervously toward her and hesitated to speak. The way the woman looked toward the closed doors of the great hall several times was also curious. Sorcha began to feel uneasy.

"Come, Mistress Duncan, ye have ne'er been afraid to speak before," said Ruari.

"We have guests, m'lord," she replied, wringing her hands.

"Ah, weel, see that they are fed and made comfortable. I will deal with them in a little while." Ruari took a step toward the narrow stone stairway and frowned when Mistress Duncan abruptly grabbed his arm, stopping him. "Is there more?"

"The guests are Sir Brodie, his lady wife, and their daughter Anne. They are here to discuss the possibilities of a match between ye and the lass," she reminded him when he continued to frown in confusion.

Sorcha felt her anger abruptly interrupted as a chill ran through her veins. While she had been struggling to overcome the pain of loving and losing him, Ruari had been inspecting all the local wellborn maidens to find a wife. Despite his little speech to her of seeking only passion and not wishing any emotional entanglements, he clearly had every intention of marrying someone.

A sense of deep insult began to swell up inside of her. It was not a wife he objected to, but her as a wife. She was good enough to bed, but not to wed. Sorcha suspected the unseen Anne Brodie met all the usual requirements being well-bred, well-mannered, and possessing the appropriate lands, money, and powerful kinsmen. Suddenly she was desperate to be alone.

"I believe ye were showing me to my chambers,

m' lord," she said, and was not surprised to hear a distinct chill in her voice. Her emotions were too strong, too confusing, to be given free rein, so she suppressed them all and became icy but dignified. "I ache to have a bath."

Ruari hastily ordered Mistress Duncan to see that baths were readied for Sorcha and Margaret, then led Sorcha up the stairs. He felt uneasy, almost embarrassed, and he was not sure why. He had not lied or seduced Sorcha with false promises. She also had to be fully aware of her unsuitability as a wife.

Despite all that sound reasoning, he still felt an uncomfortable pinch of guilt and a strong urge to explain himself. That irritated him; yet, as he stopped before the door of the bedchamber he had chosen for her, he found that he could not visit that irritation upon her. There was a remote coldness in her eyes he had never encountered before. He ached to banish it, to see the life return to her fine eyes, but he did not know how.

"Your bath will soon be prepared, and I shall have the women find ye some clean clothes."

"How kind. Now, if ye will excuse me, I am verra tired."

She stepped into the room and shut the door with a sharp click. Ruari sighed and headed down to the great hall to greet the visitors he had no wish to see. He had entertained a lot of hopes, and they had all been abruptly, painfully dashed by a sharply closed door.

Chapter Sixteen

A heavy sigh escaped Sorcha as she stared up at the ceiling of her bedchamber. One full day had passed since her arrival at Gartmhor, and she had only seen Mistress Duncan and one timid maid. She had repeatedly refused to see Ruari each time he had come knocking. Margaret was obviously well occupied with Beatham, and Sorcha knew it might be days before her cousin even realized that she had not seen anything of her.

The worst of her shock over the news that Ruari was seeking a wife had begun to fade after the first few hours. Since then she had battled her way through hurt, fury, and insult. At the moment she was not sure what she felt except for a strange, numbing sense of defeat. It was not a feeling she was very fond of.

"Sweet Jesu, ye are the saddest-looking lassie I have seen in many a year."

Sorcha tensed as that deep rich voice echoed in her mind. She knew what it meant, but was not sure she wanted to look around to see who had decided to haunt her now. Ruari had never believed in her spirits back at Dunweare. She really did not want him to discover that she was conversing with one at Gartmhor. After valiantly struggling and failing to ignore the presence she could strongly sense in the room, she looked around.

At the foot of the huge carved bed she was sprawled on floated a nearly complete apparition of a man. He was tall, raven-haired, and very handsome. Sorcha was sure that she was facing one of Ruari's late kinsmen. She sighed again for she would have preferred someone a little less close to the disbelieving Ruari. He would certainly ridicule her if she claimed she was communicating with one of his dead relatives.

"I dinnae suppose ye can go and talk to someone else," she said. "I really do have more than enough trouble on my plate."

"There is no one here who can see or speak to me," the man replied, a strong hint of melancholy in his voice. "I have been roaming these cursed halls for nearly ten years trying to catch someone's eye. Ye are the first person who has acknowledged me."

Deciding that she almost preferred to speak to a spirit than to be left alone with her tormenting thoughts, Sorcha sat up. "And who are ye?"

"Sir Ivor Kerr." He made a sweeping bow, the short cape on his shoulders giving the movement an added grace. "I am uncle to the current laird."

"Ye do have the look of a kinsman of his."

"Ye dinnae make that sound like much of a compliment."

"Just now I dinnae consider it one." She poured herself a small drink of sweet cider from the ewer Mistress Duncan had placed upon the table by her bed. "And how is it that ye died before ye were ready?"

"How did ye ken that I wasnae ready to meet my maker?" he asked as he neared the side of the bed.

"I have yet to meet a spirit who was prepared. I suppose ye were cruelly murdered."

"Ye have dealt with this many times before, have-nae ye?"

"Aye, Sir Ivor. Many times."

He began to pace the room. "Weel, I will confess that I had a weakness for the lasses. There was one verra bonny lass here called Mary. Ah, me, we had many a fine tussle beneath the sheets and sometimes we didnae e'en trouble ourselves with a bed."

"I really dinnae care to hear all the sordid details."

"They arenae that sordid. Howbeit, one night her husband stumbled upon us. I had no wish to hurt the fool, so we struggled round and round the west tower room. Mary began to fear that I would kill her husband or that he would kill me, and she joined the fray. In the ensuing melee, I was struck a mighty blow to the head. They feared they would hang for my murder and tried to hide their deed. I was soaked in ale and tossed out the window. It was believed that I was in my cups, stumbled, and fell to my death."

Sorcha almost smiled at the high note of insult that colored the conclusion of his tale. It was the disgrace of people thinking he had died such an ignominious death that troubled his spirit. The man clearly had as much stubborn pride as his nephew.

"So ye wish to make them pay for their crime?" she asked, feeling confident that he was not really seeking revenge as Crayton was.

"Weel, nay, not truly, although I wasnae much pleased to discover that the cost of a few tosses with a faithless lass was my verra life. Nay, I just want them to admit what they did, to clear my name."

"Ye consider being killed by accident by an enraged husband clearing your name?"

"'Tis far better than to be thought a drunken fool who would stumble out of a window in the verra castle he was born and raised in."

"I am not certain if I can be of much help to you, but I will consider the matter. Ye see, I am no guest, but a prisoner for ransom."

"I did overhear a few people speaking of that. Is that why ye are so sad?"

"Some of the reason." She gave the man a brief, circumspect explanation of what had passed between herself and Ruari.

Ivor nodded. "So ye and the lad became lovers."

"I never said that."

"Ye didnae have to. I ken my nephew. He wouldnae be able to resist wooing you. Aye, and there is something in the way ye speak my nephew's name. Ye have some strong feelings for the lad, and he is being a fool."

"That last opinion I can heartily agree with." She flopped back down on the bed, turning onto her side so that she could watch Ivor. "As he woos me, he searches the countryside for a woman he believes will be a proper wife." When Ivor spat a curse, her eyes widened slightly.

"Is that young fool still indulging in that fruitless quest?" demanded Ivor.

"He was doing this when ye were alive?"

"Oh, aye. The boy has gotten some idea in his empty head that he, as a mon of some wealth, power, and position, needs a very particular kind of wife. He is verra exacting in his requirements. What he needs is a strong wife with skill and wit, yet he looks o'er gigglers, weepers, and swooners."

Sorcha realized that she had discovered a very good source for information about Ruari, and at the moment the spirit was being most cooperative. Although she was not certain how knowing more about Ruari would help her or if it would be any use at all, she smiled at the talkative ghost. Somewhere in Ivor Kerr's memories might well be the clue she needed to reach a solution to the trouble between her and Ruari.

"The evening meal will soon be laid out in the great hall," Mistress Duncan announced as she poked her head around the edge of the door.

"Good," Sorcha replied and tried not to smile at the way the woman gaped over this abrupt change of mood. "I am feeling verra hungry." She took one last look at the pale blue gown she wore and walked out of the bedchamber, gently nudging Mistress Duncan out of the way. "I believe Sir Ruari's guests are still at Gartmhor?"

"Aye, m'lady. They have been told that ye and Lady Margaret are not guests, yet not prisoners, that ye stay here until a small disagreement is sorted out betwixt our laird and your brother."

"A small disagreement, hmm?" Sorcha laughed softly, then, to soothe a worried-looking Mistress Duncan, said, "Dinnae fret, I will play your laird's game."

Mistress Duncan left her at the outside of the closed doors of the great hall. Sorcha took a moment to restore her wavering courage. Ivor had been a flood of interesting information yet had not really given her anything she considered a revelation, something that had immediately revealed what she must do to either find the strength to give up on Ruari or to make him immediately see that they were a perfect match. What she had learned, however, was that Ruari was a man worth fighting for. She did not intend to demean herself or forfeit all of her pride, but she was now determined to do her utmost to win his love.

That determination wavered a little as she stepped into the great hall, for her first sight of Ruari since he had escorted her to her chamber was that of his head bent close to Anne Brodie's. Inwardly stiffening her spine, she strode to the seat to his left, pausing only to nod a brief greeting to her cousin Margaret. One of her strategies for winning Ruari was to show him that he did not really wish to marry one of the weak, simpering ladies of the court he was so assiduously courting.

As she took her seat, he finally glanced her way, and she gave him a bright smile. The look of wary uncertainty that crossed his handsome face almost made her laugh. She had unsettled him, and that could only work in her favor.

"I am pleased that ye have recovered enough from your journey here to join us," he murmured and quickly introduced her to the Brodies.

"Aye, I am much improved although my stomach is still bruised from being tossed o'er the horse like a sack of grain." She saw the color tinting his high-boned cheeks and felt a small flicker of satisfaction.

"We need not belabor the Brodies with our private troubles," Ruari said as he filled her tankard with a strong mead.

"Nay, of course not."

She met his glare with a calm look and then began to fill her plate with the help of the small pages swarming around the head table. Her remark had not been so much to test his temper as to gain some hint of what sort of young woman Anne Brodie was. It did not take long for

Sorcha to see that the somewhat plain but well-shaped Anne was a very timid woman and that she found a man like Ruari very intimidating. That was something Sorcha knew she could make good use of.

As the meal progressed, Sorcha stoked Ruari's impressive temper with sharp, whispered asides and more subtle remarks when others could overhear her. As Ruari's temper grew easier to see, Anne Brodie grew more and more quiet, her hazel eyes rounder and her glances toward Ruari more fearful. When she saw that Anne would soon be leaving the table to seek her bedchamber, Sorcha thanked Ruari for a fine meal and excused herself. Just as she had expected him to, Ruari quickly followed her.

"Just what game are ye playing now?" he demanded the moment the door closed behind them.

"Game?" she asked, looking at him with the most innocent face she could muster.

"Ye have missed no chance to insult me and refer to your abduction, although ye were always careful to make such references difficult for others to understand fully."

"But of course ye are so clever that ye understood all of them."

"As ye intended me to." He grabbed her by the arm and shook her slightly. "Ye had best tread warily, lass. I willnae abide ye interfering in this."

"By this do ye refer to your trotting before ye every unwed maid ye can find?"

"Curse ye. There is no need to make that sound as if I go awhoring. I seek a wife suitable to my position. 'Tis something every mon must do."

"Ivor told me ye would try to explain your actions in that way."

She waited patiently for the import of her words to

settle fully in Ruari's mind. It was perhaps unfair of
her to use her gift as the tinder to ignite a fire under
Ruari, but it was the one thing she knew would make
him lose his control. He might have convinced himself
to accept such things at Dunweare, but she was certain
he would refuse to allow it at Gartmhor. She could see
Anne Brodie peering out of the door and wanted the girl
to see Ruari's temper in all its glory.

"Oh, nay. Nay!" he shouted, grasping Sorcha by the
shoulders and vigorously shaking her. "Ye will *not* indulge in that foolishness at Gartmhor."

A little dazed, Sorcha did not have to feign her un-
steadiness when he stopped shaking her. She brushed a
stray lock of hair off her face and looked at him. Subtly,
she glanced at Anne and caught a satisfying look of
terror in the girl's face.

"'Tis not something ye can command away, Sir
Ruari."

"'Ware, Sorcha. If I must I will lock ye in the dark-
est hole I can find until ye come to your senses."

Sorcha knew it was an empty threat, but the complete
loss of color in Anne's round cheeks told her the girl did
not. The girl disappeared for a moment when Ruari
cursed and moved to return to the great hall. Sorcha pre-
tended to smooth out her hair and gown as she waited
for Anne Brodie to slip out of the room. A few moments
after Ruari returned to the great hall, Anne Brodie fled
it so swiftly she barely caught herself before careening
into Sorcha.

"Greetings, Lady Brodie," Sorcha said, giving the
girl what she hoped was a very shaky smile.

"Are ye all right, m'lady?" Anne Brodie asked.

"Aye. Did ye think something was wrong?"

"I watched ye and Sir Ruari argue." She shivered. "Does he often get so angry?"

"Oh, he wasnae that angry. I have seen him in far worse tempers."

"Worse?" Anne whispered, the very thought of such a thing clearly terrifying her.

Sorcha continued as if she were oblivious to the woman's fear. "Oh, aye. This was but a mild reprimand. I have seen him nearly kill a mon for serving a vegetable that wasnae done just to his liking. Nay, this was but a wee fit."

"He threatened to throw ye in the dungeon."

"Aye, but they arenae as bad as ye think," she assured her, implying that she had been put there before. "When ye are married ye will soon learn what to say and do to keep his temper even."

"I shall ne'er marry that mon," Anne vowed.

"I thought your parents wished the match to be made."

"Aye, but they willnae force it upon me. I will speak to them tonight ere they go to sleep. I wish to be away from this place come the morrow. There is a kindly older mon in Sterling who has expressed an interest in me. I should try to flee here as weel, Lady Sorcha. If that was but a mild display of Sir Ruari's temper, your life could be in danger."

Sorcha thanked her kindly for her advice and concern and watched the girl hurry up the steps to the bedchamber she had been given. A small part of Sorcha tried to make her feel guilty, but she shook it away. She loved Ruari. Anne Brodie did not. That made her ploys and games seem a great deal less distasteful. In the end, even if Ruari did not choose her, it was best if he found a wife he could care for and one who would care for him in return.

Just as she started up the stairs to go to her chamber, Margaret and Beatham slipped out of the great hall. She watched with a pang of jealousy as the couple whispered and laughed while, arm in arm, they strolled out into the moonlit bailey. Although she found the young lovers a little too earnest and sweet, Sorcha was envious. That shared love was what she ached for. She heartily wished she had not chosen a man as difficult to catch as Ruari Kerr. It was going to take a lot of work, if not a small miracle, to make him look at her with anything more than lust.

When she entered her bedchamber she caught a fleeting glimpse of her newest spiritual companion and decided it might be wise if she waited a little while before undressing. From all Ivor had told her, she was not sure she could trust him to be gentleman enough to allow her some privacy. As the man had told her himself, he had a weakness for the lasses.

"I ken ye are in here, Ivor Kerr. If ye wish to have some help in exposing your murderers and finding the peace ye want, I think ye had best abide by a few rules." She smiled grimly as he slowly became visible.

"Ye gave my stubborn nephew a fine turn tonight, lass. That timid girl is already packing her things," Ivor said, grinning at her.

"I doubt she will be the last one I must deal with."

"Sadly true. Did ye espy that whore Mary I told ye about?"

"Nay, but I was busy trying to sort out my own troubles. Now, ye will listen to my rules and ye had best obey them or ye can begin your search anew for someone who can help ye."

It was late before she felt confident that Ivor understood her wishes and would honor them. Just as she crawled into bed, looking forward to a much-needed night's sleep, Ruari walked into the room. He was obviously still angry, and, after watching him walk all around the room looking at everything, she realized he was looking for Ivor.

"Your uncle isnae here now. I will be sure to tell him ye were looking for him," she drawled. "Now, I would greatly appreciate if all uninvited guests would leave me in peace so that I may sleep." She tensed when Ruari strode to her bedside but she met his glare with outward calm.

"Ye will speak to no one about your delusion that ye are speaking with my Uncle Ivor. The mon was an embarrassment and is better left buried."

"I havenae dug the mon up. I but speak to his restless spirit."

"Enough," he snapped and he grasped her chin in his hand. "Mayhap the long winter without a mon to warm your bed has left ye even more inclined to pull them out of the air."

It took all the willpower she could muster, but Sorcha successfully subdued the very strong urge to hit him. "Your arrogance is only excelled by your ignorance and stubbornness. I am willing to keep these visitations a secret, but ye have neither the right nor the power to tell me to cease to believe. Now, as I told ye, I am tired."

"I ken that ye are playing some game with me, Sorcha Hay, and mark my words, I will discover what it is."

She winced as he slammed the door on his way out. The very last thing she wanted him to do was to discover what her plans were. That could easily expose how she felt about him, and she had no intention of doing that until she could be certain of some return.

As she settled herself more comfortably in her bed she knew the other thing she would have to make a decision about was whether or not to allow Ruari back into her bed. He had been speaking in anger, trying to frighten her with threats and cause her to become complacent, but in that brief moment as he had bent over her in the bed, she had caught a hint of the passion they had once shared shining in his fine eyes. Soon he would try to draw her back into his bed, and she wanted to have already made up her mind before he began his seduction, for this time she would not be sharing his bed with the stalwart acceptance of it being only for a short time. If she returned to Ruari's arms, she intended to do everything in her power to stay there.

Chapter Seventeen

"I cannae believe it. That is the third lass to flee this place in less than a week's time," muttered Ruari as he and Rosse stood on the walls on Gartmhor and watched yet another prospective bride hurry home. "I am certain that Sorcha Hay has a hand in this yet I cannae catch her doing anything. One moment the girl and her kinsmen are smilingly discussing a possible match, and the next they are all riding swiftly away as if the devil himself haunts these halls."

"Weel, some folk felt your Uncle Ivor was, if not the devil himself, certainly one of his minions." Rosse eyed his friend warily when Ruari indulged in a short but colorful rant of curses.

"My uncle Ivor is *not* floating about these halls!"

"A lot of people have long suspected that he was haunting the place."

"And now they listen avidly to a strange wee lass from Dunweare."

"Weel, nay. She hasnae said anything, not unless she is asked directly."

"'Tis bad enough. I told her to keep her belief that she is talking to that old fool a deep secret."

"And ye expect her to bow, smile sweetly, and do just as ye command? I should think ye would ken her better than that as ye have known her better and longer than any of us." Rosse held up his hand to halt Ruari's beginning arguments. "I havenae said that I believe old Ivor is floating about and telling tales to Sorcha. Howbeit, I cannae bring myself to decry the lass as a liar and madwoman either."

"And far worse than all of that, I think she has become devious," Ruari grumbled as he pointed toward the rapidly disappearing guests. "She is doing this. I am as certain of that as I am that ye are standing next to me."

"And why should she trouble herself to muddle in your plans? Ye made it plain that ye are not considering her as a bride, and she has refused to become your lover again."

"She hasnae refused."

"Ye arenae in her bed."

"I havenae tried to get there. There was such a coldness in the woman when she arrived, I felt it would be fruitless to even try. I have no wish to beat my head against a locked door." A strong urge to kick the twice-cursed door down mayhap, he mused, but he was not about to confess that to Rosse.

Rosse shook his head and started down the narrow stairs to the bailey. "Ye want her, but ye insult her and show her how truly unacceptable she is, and then ye complain that she doesnae want you. Mayhap, my friend, 'tisnae Sorcha who is chasing away these possible brides."

"Are ye saying that I am unattractive to them? Ye jest.

I am young, healthy, have a fat purse and a fine keep. What more could any of these lasses want?"

"Someone who will treat them as something a little more important than his chair."

Once down on the solid dirt of the bailey, Ruari spun around and glared at his lifelong friend. "Do I ask for your advice in this matter? Nay. I do this for Gartmhor."

"Nay." Rosse shook his head. "I begin to think ye do this for yourself. Ye want Sorcha Hay. Ye are so eaten up with wanting that it has made ye sour of temper and verra short of sight. I think ye now cling to your plan for a certain sort of wife with a certain sort of dowry so that ye cannae e'en look at Sorcha as a possible mate. After all, if she doesnae meet all these qualifications ye have set, then ye couldnae possibly wed her and so ye will be safe."

"Safe? What do ye mean?"

"I mean just what I said—safe. Safe from thinking and feeling. I believe Sorcha Hay affected more than what dangles between your legs, and ye fight that as hard as ye have ever fought an Englishmon. I dinnae ken why and, mayhap there is no real reason, but ye are afraid of the emotions she stirs up inside of ye."

"That is utter codswallop," Ruari snapped.

Rosse shrugged. "I didnae expect ye to heed what I say as ye clearly cannae even heed what your own heart tells you. I but pray that ye try to open your eyes ere it is too late to mend things, or one day ye shall awake to find that ye have the wife, the son, the power, and the heavy purse, but that there is a deep gnawing hunger inside of you that isnae satisfied and will never be fed." He turned and left before Ruari could even think of a reply.

Cursing softly to himself, Ruari returned to the great hall. He was beginning to resent the constant advice and criticism he was belabored with. How could anyone know what he thought and felt, even Rosse whom he had known since birth?

He struggled to dismiss Rosse's words as he sat down to try to finish the meal his prospective bride's abrupt flight had interrupted. No matter how hard he tried to shut the words out, they continued to echo in his mind, forcing him to examine them closely. He did not like the idea that some small, brown-eyed lass could frighten him and he wanted to find the perfect rebuttal to Rosse's claim. Try as he would, however, nothing came to mind except for a vague acceptance of his friend's idea which he struggled mightily to suppress.

With a heavy sigh that was a mixture of resignation and fury, he leaned his elbows on the table and thrust his fingers through his hair. Sorcha Hay was everything that was opposite of what he had always been taught was the perfect lady. She and her family would bring whatever husband she managed to snare a lifetime of trouble and upset. Her passion, however, was perfection. He had finally admitted that he would never find its like in another woman's arms. It was certainly a strong argument in her favor.

On the side of the scales that weighed in against her was a great deal to contend with. She was poor, she had no lands, she could fight like a man, and she insisted on talking to ghosts. He was working to add to that list when he heard a soft footfall and looked up to see the bane of his existence, Sorcha Hay, looking at him with undisguised curiosity. He idly admitted that another thing in her favor was that pair of fine brown eyes.

She stood before him in a borrowed gray gown that was a little too big and too long. Her hair was loosely tied with a black leather thong, a few thick waves of it falling over her shoulder to drape over her chest. She was small yet beautiful, and every part of his body ached for her. He did not know whether to laugh or curse. There was a very good chance that Rosse was right, but Ruari had no idea of what he should do about it or even if he should try.

Sorcha resisted the urge to shift from foot to foot under his steady gaze. There was the oddest look in his eyes, a mixture of anger and amusement as well as a strong hint of accusation. She wondered nervously if he had guessed that she was the one sending all his little brides running for the hills. She had not really considered the consequences of being caught out in her game. It would be hard to make any sort of reasonable explanation without exposing a great deal about the state of her heart.

"Where are your guests?" she asked, deciding to take the direct approach.

"As before, the lass suddenly took fright and fled for her home as fast as she could."

"Oh, how odd," she murmured as she sat down and helped herself to some cider.

"Very odd, considering that each one of them had expressed a keen interest in a match. What is even odder is that I actually wondered if ye might have something to do with that." He leaned back in his chair and sipped at his wine.

"Me? What could I possibly have to do with your skittish brides?"

"Nothing, I suppose."

"Exactly, nothing. Even if I was to talk to them, what could I possibly say that would make them run away from you, from a marriage many a lass would work verra hard to secure?"

"Quite true. What could ye say? 'Twas but a passing

thought." He stretched out in his chair. "And how does life at Gartmhor treat you?"

"Quite weel, thank ye kindly. One cannae call me a guest, yet I am treated with all the courtesy usually offered one. There is one question—is there a maid here called Mary?"

"Near half the women in Scotland and England are called Mary."

"I ken it. I thought ye might have only one, but that would be far too lucky."

"Why do ye ask?" He frowned and sat up straighter when she looked guilty then tried too hard to keep her face averted. "It doesnae have anything to do with spirits, does it?" he demanded.

"Ye told me never to speak of it," she reminded him.

"Everyone else at Gartmhor is, so ye may as weel forget that I gave ye that order."

"'Tis forgotten." She tore off a piece of bread from a thick loaf and carefully spread some honey on it.

"Ah, so it is the ghost. Why would my Uncle Ivor be interested in a maid called Mary?" He heard a soft cry and looked in the far corner of the room to see a maid almost hiding. "What do ye want, Mary?"

"I want nothing, m'lord. I was sent to clean and I am just waiting for ye to finish."

"Mayhap ye could wait somewhere else, please?"

Sorcha watched the maid hurry out of the room and began to think that fate had revealed the Mary she had been searching for. The woman matched Ivor's description, although he had been talking of a much younger Mary, but the fear lurking in the woman's eyes made Sorcha suspicious.

"Ye are staring at that poor maid verra hard, lass," Ruari said. "Aye, she is named Mary, but if ye are acting upon something ye think Ivor told you, I canna believe she would be involved. A verra timid lass who couldna have had anything to do with Ivor, she is almost dotingly faithful to her husband David."

Aye, now, Sorcha mused. She suspected that there was no stronger bond that could exist between two people than the knowledge that they had shared in the death of a man, even if they had not truly meant to kill him. The Mary Ivor spoke about had also had a husband named David. There were too many coincidences, and she decided that at the very first opportunity she had she would corner the skittish Mary.

"Of course she couldnae have. Your uncle is a most lively and outspoken sort of mon, not the kind of mon a woman like that would ever deal with," she finally agreed.

"I dinnae feel as if ye mean that wholeheartedly, lass. Now dinnae go troubling Mary. She is a good hard worker."

"Of course. Have ye heard from my kinsmen yet?"

"Nay, but I expect to verra shortly." He stared at her when she just nodded. "Weel, arenae ye going to tell me that I waste my time and yours? That the Hays dinnae have the coin I am asking for and probably cannae get it?"

"I have told ye that a hundred times. Telling ye another hundred times is but a waste of precious breath. I am not in favor of beating a dead horse. And ye will soon see the truth of all I have said for yourself."

"If ye are saying that I willnae be paid—"

"Aye, that is exactly what I am saying. Ye cannae get coins out of an empty purse."

"But your brother's purse wasnae empty last summer. It was heavily weighted with my coin. I only ask for what is mine."

"Ye are an unpleasantly obstinate mon, Sir Ruari Kerr."

"That is an insult I have heard so often it but rolls off my back."

Sorcha was struggling to think of one he could not shrug aside so easily when Rosse entered the hall and said, "Someone from Dunweare is approaching."

"Oh, how nice," Sorcha cried and started to get to her feet only to have Ruari quickly yank her back down onto her seat. "Ye arenae even going to let me see my family?"

"I believe it would be verra unwise to let ye get within yards of another member of the Hay clan. Whene'er more than one of ye get together there is trouble." He waved his old friend closer. "Would ye please escort our guest to her chambers?"

Sorcha spared one final glare for Ruari before Rosse led her out of the great hall. She did not know what plots she could possibly devise in one brief meeting with her kinsman while inside the thick walls of Gartmhor, but it annoyed her that he was not going to allow her the slim opportunity to try. Now she would have to use the unreliable Ivor as a spy to find out what transpired between Ruari and her kinsman. The first thing she was anxious to discover was which one of her clan had been sent as a mediator. She smiled sweetly at Rosse as he nudged her into her bedchamber, wondered idly why that expression seemed to make the men of Gartmhor so nervous as she shut the door and then called out for Ivor. It was going to be rather enjoyable to use a ghost Ruari refused to believe in to ferret out all the little secrets he tried to keep from her.

Ruari hid his surprise when Neil strode into the great hall. He had not really expected to deal with a woman. It would temper his enjoyment, for a deeply rooted sense of the courtesy due a woman meant he could not gloat as much as he had anticipated.

As Neil was seated and served a tankard of mead, Malcolm slipped into the room, his long, bony hands clutching his papers. It amused Ruari to watch the lovesick look on the little man's face as he stared at Neil so intently he stumbled several times on his way to his seat at Ruari's side. Ruari did not think Malcolm could have picked a woman more completely different from him if he had tried. He began to feel badly for his cousin, for he did not really like the idea that the man would suffer for his infatuation.

"Lady Neil Hay, this is my cleric and cousin, Malcolm Kerr," Ruari introduced, watching as Malcolm thrust out his unsteady hand and had it firmly shaken by Neil. "He is here because he takes care of all of Gartmhor's business and monies."

"Weel, this is a waste of his time," Neil said. "There is no chance that ye can get any money out of the Hays. Aye, mayhap my witless nephew can buy ye an ale or two at a tavern, but he cannae raise much more than that."

"That is verra poor negotiating, m'lady," Ruari said. "I hold your nieces. Ye should at least ask what I want ere ye tell me ye cannae give it to me."

"I ken exactly what ye want. Ye want your own ransom returned in full. Weel, the only way ye are going to get that is to go and take it back from the English."

Malcolm cleared his throat, but nervousness still made his voice higher than usual. "Are ye saying that the Hays are destitute?"

"Aye, 'tis exactly what I am saying, little mon," Neil replied then looked at Ruari. "And this oaf kens it as weel as any mon."

"I only have the word of the Hays," said Ruari.

"'Tis as trustworthy as your own."

Neil finished her drink and looked for the ewer to refill her tankard. Malcolm scrambled to his feet and nearly upended the ewer in his efforts to be the one to serve her. She smiled her thanks, eyeing him a little warily, and Ruari almost laughed.

The humorous interlude was not enough to soothe his rising temper completely, however. Everyone steadfastly said that he would not be able to get his money back, that the Hays did not have it and could not raise it. He was starting to believe it, but that left him in a very precarious position. How could he call a halt to this and return the Hays women without taking any money for them, but still salvage his pride? He could not see a way to do that, which irritated him. He had backed himself into a tight corner, and it was going to take a lot of wriggling to get out of it without looking like a complete fool. For now, until he could think of some solution, he would act as if he did not really believe their claims of poverty or as if he did not care.

"Ye will tell Dougal Hay that he can have his sister and cousin back when he returns the money he took as my ransom. That is my offer for their lives, and I willnae bend on it."

"Then play out your fool's game if ye must. I have the strength to ride 'twixt here and home a hundred times if need be." She slowly stood up. "Now, I should like to see my nieces."

"I fear I cannae allow that. Ye forget, m'lady, I spent several weeks in Dunweare. I soon learned the risk of allowing a few Hays to put their heads together, especially the women."

"Ye had best not hurt those lasses, Ruari Kerr. I think

ye ken that it isnae an empty threat when I tell ye I will hunt ye down and gut ye like a pig if any harm comes to my nieces."

"Oh, I ken the value of your threats, Neil Hay. And ye can trust in my word that I shall not hurt a hair on either lass's head."

"And mayhap ye could show a wee bit of concern for more than keeping them hale. I dinnae just refer to bodily harm when I talk of hurting them." She nodded when he frowned, clearly understanding her. "Dinnae fear. I will-nae fault ye for what happens 'twixt Margaret and Bea-tham. I cannae expect ye to control that foolishness better than we did, and we did a right poor job of it. Nay, 'tis my Sorcha ye had best tread carefully with, laddie. Verra carefully indeed."

"I think ye worry unduly, m'lady. Sorcha can take care of herself."

"Oh, aye, but dinnae go thinking she is stronger than she is. Now, I had best begin the journey back to Dun-weare. I dinnae like to spend too many nights sleeping on the hard ground."

Malcolm stood up so fast he tipped over the small stool he had been perched on. "Allow me to escort ye to your mount, m'lady." He moved to her side and crooked his bone-thin arm for her to hook hers through.

Ruari's eyes widened with surprise when he caught the ghost of a smile curling Neil's full lips. She feigned a curtsy and slipped her arm through Malcolm's. Ruari's astonishment increased tenfold when he saw a faint af-fectionate look in Neil's eyes as she gazed down at the top of Malcolm's head. He murmured a farewell as the woman left, too stunned to say more. He was still mulling over the incident in disbelief when Rosse joined him, sprawling in the seat to his left and helping himself to some mead.

"Did she leave?" he finally asked.

"Aye. Did ye ken that she came alone?" Rosse asked.

"Nay. That seems a dangerous thing to do."

"So thought our Malcolm, and he insisted that, at least while she rode over Gartmhor lands, she would have a small escort."

"Malcolm took it upon himself to order my men to ride with her?"

"He ordered one to go along and appointed himself as her second guard." Rosse grinned when Ruari stared at him in open-mouthed surprise for a full minute before laughing heartily.

Sorcha tapped her foot in a gesture of impatience as she waited for Ivor to stop laughing. She was not sure what he found so funny as he had not completed a full sentence before he had begun to laugh. From what she had gathered, his amusement had something to do with her Aunt Neil and Malcolm, Ruari's timid cleric.

"Ah, lass, ye should have seen it," Ivor said at last, his voice hoarse from laughter.

"I wasnae allowed to. That is why I sent ye to the great hall. I am waiting for ye to tell me what happened."

"I was telling ye."

"Nay, ye said something about my aunt being a glorious woman, then about Malcolm being a lovesick oaf, and then ye laughed. That doesnae tell me verra much at all."

Ivor held his hands out as if he were fending her off. "Dinnae get angry, lass. I will tell ye every word that passed between your aunt and my stubborn nephew."

To Sorcha's relief, Ivor proved better able to tell a story from start to end than Crayton ever had. When he told her about Neil and Malcolm, she could understand his being diverted. It was certainly something she would like to know more about, but that would have to wait until she could talk to Neil, and she suspected Ruari would hold firm to his decision to keep her from her kinsmen during her stay at Gartmhor.

"So, the fool continues to ask for coin my clan does-nae have," she murmured as she sat on the bed, fixing her mind firmly on the matter of her ransoming.

"He cannae do much else, lass," Ivor said as he floated closer to the edge of the big bed. "He has taken ye and your cousin for ransom. He cannae just say he is sorry, he misunderstood, and give ye back."

"Mayhap not, but he has to believe by now that the Hays cannae give him back his money, so why does he insist upon it?"

"I think he bides his time until he can think of a way to wriggle out of this and still keep his mighty pride intact. The mon cannae chance looking a fool."

"He has already lost that battle." She smiled faintly when Ivor laughed. "I think I saw the Mary ye talked about. She is older, of course, but she looks much like ye described. She also grew verra skittish when I told Ruari ye had asked about a Mary."

"And she is wed to a mon named David?"

"Aye, devotedly, says Ruari. That could be because they are bonded by guilt. I must catch her alone, and that will take time for she is terrified of me."

"Be wary, lass. If they truly believe ye are speaking to my spirit, they may become dangerous. They murdered me."

"Oh, I dinnae believe it was murder and I dinnae think

ye really do either. Ye are just angry that they didnae think of a more honorable explanation for your death."

"Aye, true enough. They could have thought of a tale that didnae leave my kinsmen thinking I was naught but an embarrassment."

"Be easy, Ivor," she said, sensing the pain and despair that had washed over him. "I will clear your name. Weel, as much as I can."

"I ken it, lass, and I shall ne'er be able to repay ye for such a deed, but ye ken the depth of my gratitude. And one way I can do so is to keep ye warned of all that is afoot in this keep. Ye had best be readied for a visit from my nephew."

She frowned. "Why would he seek me out?" She decided she did not particularly like the lecherous smile that crossed Ivor's face. "Ah, so he hopes to seduce me into warming his bed while I am here."

Ivor grew serious. "I think it may be more than that. I have been following the lad about, ye ken. Rosse has been talking sense to the fool, and I think he may weel have begun to heed his friend's words."

"What do ye mean?"

"Just dinnae be too quick to toss the oaf out on his backside."

Before she could press Ivor for more of an explanation, he disappeared. She thought over his vague advice and tried not to let her hopes rise. Ivor was better than Crayton at being clear and understandable, but he could still be annoyingly subtle as well. It sounded as if he were saying Ruari might finally be seeing her as more than an object of his passion, but she did not dare trust in that interpretation. Too much was at stake—her heart and her happiness. If Ruari used her and cast her aside this time, it could easily be a wound she would never recover from.

* * *

Ruari stared at the door to Sorcha's bedchamber. He did not like the sense of nervousness that had afflicted him as he had approached her room. The way she could make him feel uncertain was not something he enjoyed. It was, however, more proof that Rosse could be right, that he was running away from the things Sorcha could make him feel. It was that hint of cowardice that drove him to confront her. Neither could he bear to think that his own fears might make him destroy his own happiness. Taking a deep breath to steady himself, he rapped at her door.

As he heard her soft footsteps approach the thick door he tried to think of what he would say to her. He could not tell her that he was there to try to sort out the confusing knot of feelings that twisted his insides. He did not, however, want to give her the impression he had come in search of a good rutting and no more. Not only was that an insult he had no wish to deliver, but also it could push her away from him at a time when he might want to pull her closer.

He had always been confident with women, knowing what to say and do to please them. None of those things would work with Sorcha, and he had to admit that was because he did not want to play flirtatious games with her. He liked the honesty of their relationship even if it was mostly one of anger and insults at the moment. When she opened the door and eyed him warily, Ruari decided that now was the time for complete honesty even if it was only to confess that he was confused about what he felt and wanted. He just prayed that she was equally as honest and that what truths she confessed were ones he wanted to hear.

Chapter Eighteen

"M'lord," Sorcha murmured as she allowed Ruari to step into her bedchamber. "And what causes ye to honor me with your presence?"

"I thought ye might wish to hear what passed between your kinswoman and myself," he replied, watching as she hesitated a moment then shut the door.

"'Tis kind of ye to consider my interest, but I have already had a report on the meeting. Ye willnae like to hear it, but your Uncle Ivor was there."

"Sorcha," he said with a strong hint of irritation in his voice, "I have come here intending to seek some form of peace between us. I dinnae think ye help matters by talking of spirits." He shook his head, briefly paced the room, and then turned to stare at her. "God's teeth, lass, if ye must speak to a spirit at Gartmhor, couldnae ye choose one the rest of us might actually miss or want to talk to? Did ye have to pick a drunkard who fell out of a window, his braies fluttering down after him?"

Even as Ruari spoke his last word, a strong, icy cold wind swept through the room. It slammed into his back hard enough to make him sway, then, as abruptly as it had begun, it stopped. He strenuously fought the urge to look around for his uncle and instead stared at the narrow arrow slit that was Sorcha's only window.

"It seems the weather is about to take a turn for the worse," he murmured and turned back to Sorcha in time to catch her rolling her eyes as she smoothed out her windtousled hair.

"'Tis common at Gartmhor for a wee gale to slip in a tiny window and swirl about the bedchamber, is it?" she drawled.

"And what would ye have me believe?"

"Ye insulted Ivor, and 'tis clear that he is close enough to hear you. Being a ghost, he cannae strike ye down for such an insult so he must show his displeasure in other ways."

"If the mon's spirit is here, he must be hardened to the insults by now. The mon's ignominious death is often the subject of jests."

He jumped slightly when the lid to the heavy clothes chest beneath the window suddenly banged shut despite the lack of any wind in the room. Ruari began to feel uneasy. Sorcha's strong belief in her spirits had clearly infected him enough that he found it difficult to simply shrug off such strange occurrences. He moved to the table by the bed and poured himself a tankard of cider, taking a long drink before he faced Sorcha. She was watching him closely as if she knew exactly what he was thinking.

"A few clever tricks arenae going to change my mind," he said firmly. "Now, I have come here to discuss the matter of the ransom, not my old fool of an uncle." A stool that had stood in the corner of the room suddenly tipped over and rolled across the floor. "He was always an ill-tempered bastard as weel," he muttered and was not surprised when a cold gust of wind blew through the room again.

"Mayhap we should not mention him anymore," Sorcha murmured, wondering if Ruari knew that he had just spoken and acted as a man who was starting to believe. "'Tis clear that ye have put him in a foul mood. Tell me about my aunt and Malcolm. I was told that your cleric is interested in Neil."

"Interested?" Ruari laughed and shook his head. "The mon is so besotted he falls o'er his own feet. He has never been verra graceful, but when your aunt was near, he was in danger of hurting himself."

"Oh, dear." She had to bite back a laugh at the image Ruari painted with his words.

"Aye, oh dear. Howbeit, at first I had to bite my tongue to keep from laughing and mayhap hurting the mon's feelings, but as your aunt left, I began to wonder." He paused as he thought over what he had seen.

"Began to wonder about what?" she pressed when he said no more.

"Weel, I am no real judge of such things, but it did look as if she may be interested in him. She smiled at the mon, and there was almost a tender look in her eyes. 'Twould be a strange match. I cannae think of two people more completely different than Malcolm and your Aunt Neil."

"'Tis true that they would make a strange sight, but mayhap they are aware of something we could never see. My aunt has little love for men who try to catch her interest, yet clearly, she accepted Malcolm's attempts to woo her."

Ruari sat down on the bed and studied her. Just watching her as she moved across the room to pour herself a tankard of cider was enough to make his loins tighten painfully with need. He knew, however, that he could not draw her into his arms this time unless he offered more than passion. She had made no demands of him, but instinct told him she would continue to refuse him if he only sought a bedwarmer for a few nights or the duration of her stay.

"And what does it take to woo you, Sorcha Hay?" he asked in a quiet voice, deciding to take the most direct route to what he craved.

"More than a fire in the blood and a fine pair of eyes," she answered, turning to look at him. She was tense, sensing that he was planning to talk to her more openly than he had ever done before, and she was no longer certain of how much she should demand or how much she was willing to be patient about.

"Do ye expect vows of undying love and promises of marriage?" he asked, unable to keep all of the sarcasm out of his voice.

"I expect to be treated as more than an enjoyable tussle in the sheets."

"Oh, ye have always been more than that, lassie. Always."

"Why are ye asking me these things?"

"Mayhap I wish to ken the road I must walk to get back into your bed."

"Ye cannae expect me to lie down each night with a mon who is vigorously looking for a wife all the day long." She walked closer to him, wanting to see each shift of his expression as he answered.

"It seems I have come to the end of my list for the moment. The last bride I was to consider left as abruptly as the two before her." He eyed Sorcha speculatively. "Are ye sure ye had naught to do with that?"

One thing Sorcha was sure of was that it would be a

very long time, if ever, before she confessed to sending his little brides running for the safety of home. "Now, why should I wish to so disrupt your search for a wife?"

"I was rather hoping ye would say it was because ye didnae want me to choose any of them."

"That would give your vanity a fine stroking, would-nae it?"

"It would also help me decide what to say next." He grimaced. "Mayhap I should just spit out what is in my head and heart."

"That would certainly simplify matters. We could spend many an hour choking out one hint at a time, our questions wary and our answers vague."

"Verra true. I cannae read your mind, and ye cannae read mine." He frowned a little and looked at her. "Ye cannae do that, can ye?"

Sorcha laughed and shook her head. "Nay, of course not."

"Weel, at the moment it probably wouldnae matter if ye could, for the thoughts whirling about in my head arenae even allowing me to read them clearly. There is only one thing I am verra sure of, and nothing changes it—I want you in my bed." He briefly grinned. "Or me in yours. Or most anywhere else."

"I believe I understand," she said before he could go on. "And I want you. I dinnae believe I have e'er made a secret of that. When ye were at Dunweare and I thought we would part and ne'er set eyes on each other again, the passion was enough. I didnae want to lose the chance to taste something I kenned would be verra fine. Weel, I have tasted it and, even though I still hunger for it, I can be a wee bit more discerning now. I need not sell myself so cheaply."

"Not even to replenish the monly stock of Dunweare?"

he said, then inwardly cursed the touch of sullenness in his voice.

Unable to suppress it, Sorcha giggled, but a glare from Ruari cut it short. "Ye didnae believe that, did ye? 'Twould be somewhat of an insult to me if ye did."

"I certainly didnae consider it flattery to be told I was being used for stud."

"Ye deserved it for calling what we had shared ill advised. It doesnae sound so terrible when I say it, but ye made it sound as if it was a horrible crime ye would regret for the rest of your days."

Ruari grimaced and thrust his fingers through his hair. "So, there were angry words exchanged. I didnae mean mine any more than ye did yours. Let us cry pax."

"Fair enough. That isnae enough though, my fine knight."

"'Tis the ransoming?"

"I should like to consider that a matter between ye and Dougal. Aye, even when I was the one holding you for ransom. It has always concerned Dougal. Nay, as ye said we should the last time, let us consider this ransoming business a thing apart. I have already made it clear what I think of this twist in the game. I have no need or wish to say more."

"Nor do I." Ruari did not add that he wished he could also forget about it all. "So what do ye want?"

"More than passion. I cannae be much more specific. I willnae demand that ye tell me things ye dinnae truly feel and I willnae drag ye into a marriage ye dinnae want. Nevertheless, I want more than the fact that your braies grow tighter when I am about." She smiled faintly when he was surprised into a brief laugh.

Ruari stared at her for one long moment. There was no sign of cunning in her fine eyes, no hint that she was

not saying exactly what she felt. She would not demand
more of him than he was willing to give or try to entrap
him, dragging him before a priest when it was the very
last place he wanted to be. He suddenly knew that he
could deal with Sorcha with the same straightforward-
ness he used with his friends and kinsmen. She was
simply asking a slightly higher price for her passion
and, although she had not yet offered more for his, he
knew instinctively that there was more. It was why she
was so hesitant to become his lover again.

"Weel, lass, there is more. I cannae put a name to it,
but 'tis there. Ye have haunted me consistently since I
left Dunweare. I looked for your bonnie eyes and your
wit and spirit in each one of the lasses I inspected." He
reached out, gently caught hold of her slim hips, and
drew her closer. "At times I fear that made me verra
angry with you."

She smiled and lightly ran her fingers through his
thick hair. "Aye, there were times when I heartily cursed
you as weel."

Sorcha was amazed that he could not hear her heart
racing. He was not saying much, but it was far more than
she had hoped for. She had reached him. The seed she
had planted at Dunweare might still be a tender sapling,
but she now had a chance to make it grow strong. Every
word he said told her that she had a foothold in his heart,
and she intended to make good use of that.

It was not, however, enough to make her bare her soul
and tell him of her love for him. She was not sure just
how much she should reveal. He had asked nothing from
her, and she suspected that was because he had already
guessed that she felt far more than passion for him, that
those feelings made her hesitant to become his lover
again. Sorcha decided that she would match whatever

revelations she made to his. Whatever he gave her she would return in equal measure. If he wanted more, he would have to give more.

"Although I fought the admission, I have long kenned that it was something deeper than passion we shared. If 'twas no more than passion, sweet as it was, I would have been able to find a salve for the ache I have carried around like a battle scar. Instead I lie alone in my bed and have done since Dunweare, because I know, have always known, that none could feed the hunger gnawing at my innards except you."

"Are ye saying that ye have been celibate since leaving my bed?"

"Weel, aye, although I thought I worded it more prettily."

"Oh, aye, 'twas verra pretty." She grinned down at him, wondering if he knew how much that information meant to her.

"Um, I assume ye have also been alone?"

"Nay, there has been a veritable horde of men in my room." She bit back a laugh when she saw the dark look upon his face. "Idiot. Of course I have."

"Ye should be careful what ye jest about, dearling. There are some things a mon just cannae find amusing." When she just smiled and made no attempt to wriggle free of his hold, he asked, "So, have I given ye what ye wanted?"

"Weel, aye, but"—she leaned forward and touched a kiss to his lips—"I think ye still have a great deal of work ahead of ye."

He began to slowly untie the thong and free her hair for his caress. "A great deal of work, ye say?"

"Oh, aye. It could easily take most of the night."

"I was rather considering spending all of the night at my work."

"And I was allowing ye time to rest."

Ruari laughed and flopped backward onto the bed. Her hair fell forward, and he wriggled his face through it, taking several deep breaths, savoring the feel and smell of it. He wanted to tear her gown off and bury himself deep inside her, but he also wanted to move slowly so that he could more fully enjoy her return. As he unlaced her gown, he prayed that he could accomplish something between the two.

He kissed her hungrily as he helped her slip out of her clothes. The moment she was naked, he paused to drink in the sight of her lithe frame as he yanked off his own clothes. When their flesh met for the first time in months, he finally conceded that he had missed her more than he could ever put into words.

With one graceful turn he arranged them lengthwise on the big bed with Sorcha lying beneath him. Reverently he kissed and caressed his way down her body, leaving no silken inch untouched. The way she squirmed beneath him, the soft noises of pleasure she made, and the touch of her hands all enflamed him almost past control.

When she cried out for him, her body trembling with need, he slowly eased himself inside of her. He shuddered beneath the force of the pleasure that tore through him. A sense of coming home, of being exactly where he had always belonged, swept over him as she curled herself around him. Groaning her name, he began to move, swiftly driving them both to the blinding culmination of their passion. As he collapsed in her arms he savored the musical way their names blended as they both cried out from the power of their releases. They were in perfect harmony and he prayed that nothing would happen to sever that bond.

Sorcha stretched and looked at the man sprawled on his stomach by her side. Dawn's light was just inching into the room. The night had passed too quickly, she mused as she traced Ruari's spine with her fingers. The reunion of their bodies had been sweet and hot, and she hated to think it would end. She knew they could still savor the pleasure of their lovemaking at any time, but the fact that they had come to a new understanding before falling into each other's arms after a long separation had added something she could neither describe nor name.

Idly smoothing her hand over his taut buttocks, she smiled as he shifted beneath her caress, passion slowly pulling him from his sleep. Her whole body ached, but it was a good feeling, and she wanted to add to it. She leaned down and marked the line of his backbone with warm, lingering kisses, smiling against his skin when he murmured her name.

He turned onto his back and tried to pull her into his arms, but she neatly eluded his grasp. The sounds he made as she inched her way down his long frame were an odd mixture of pleasure and protest over the fact that he could not really return her caresses. When she touched a kiss to the tip of his erection, he ceased to protest his inability to participate fully in the lovemaking, thrusting his fingers into her hair and subtly directing her intimate kisses.

A hoarse cry escaped Ruari, and he grabbed her beneath the arms, pulling her up his body. She laughed softly, her voice husky and low, as she eased their bodies together. For a moment she straddled him, making no move to continue the lovemaking, and taking enormous pleasure in the feeling of his body filling hers. When he tightly grasped her by the hips and moved her, she gave him no argument, swiftly retaking control as she took them both to the sweet oblivion they had sought almost continuously through the night.

She stretched languorously and made no effort to hide herself as Ruari cleaned them both off. When he returned to the bed and took her into his arms, she curled up against him contentedly. She did not yet have all she wanted, but everything he had done and said during the night gave her more hope than she had had in many months.

"I shall be staggering about Gartmhor all day today, too weary to do my work," Ruari said as he brushed a kiss over the top of her head.

She grimaced as she realized that his men would all know why he was heavy-eyed yet not ill-tempered. "I hope your men arenae too free with their jests and teasings. I dinnae wish to spend my day trying fruitlessly to hide my blushes."

"They shall probably wish to bury ye in praise and gifts for they have had to suffer beneath the yoke of my ill temper for too many months."

"Ah, I see. Celibacy doesnae make ye feel cheerful and pious."

Ruari chuckled and shook his head. "Nay. I snarl like a vicious dog at everyone and everything."

"I shall confess that I wasnae the sweetest of company either."

Just as Ruari was about to reply, Sorcha gasped softly and yanked the covers over her, clutching them tightly beneath her chin. She was acting as if someone had just walked into the room, but he could see no one. Then his sleepy and sated mind cleared enough for him to realize what she was doing. She thought one of her spirits was in the room. He was surprised when he did not immediately grow annoyed and demand she cease to play that game. Instead he looked around, seeing nothing.

"Is one of your spirits in the room?" he asked as he tucked his arm around her sheet-wrapped body and drew her close to his side.

"I fear Ivor has come to visit," she replied. "I thought ye agreed that ye would respect my privacy," she said to Ivor who was little more than a dim shadow in the far corner of the room.

"I have just arrived," Ivor said as he neared the foot of the bed and frowned at Ruari. "I hope the lad didnae seduce ye back into his bed."

"Nay, he didnae, and I dinnae ken why ye are looking so angry and suspicious. Ye were the one who said I should listen to him."

"Ah, so he has confessed to loving you, has he?"

"Weel, nay, not exactly. That is none of your concern anyway. Now, I believe I had a stern talk with ye about infringing upon my privacy. Could ye please leave now?"

"I dinnae ken why ye are acting so shocked. Ye have covered your nakedness."

"Aye, but I am in bed with a mon," she said, failing to completely subdue her blushes. "I dinnae want ye seeing that."

"Such modesty." He held up his hand when she opened her mouth to speak. "Dinnae scold me, I shall leave. Ye had best put some clothes on anyway, lass."

"Why? 'Tis barely dawn."

"A few of Ruari's men are headed to rouse him. When they dinnae find him in his own bedchamber, I dinnae think it will take them long to ken where he is."

"Will ye leave, ye old lecher," Ruari called out, a little

irritated with lying next to Sorcha as she talked with another man. "Did he go?" he asked after a moment.

"Aye, he has disappeared," she answered as she slipped free of Ruari's light grip and got up to dress herself.

"If he is gone, why are ye out of bed and dressing? There is no work ye must hie to."

"Nay, but Ivor says a few of your men will soon come here looking for ye."

Ruari was up and in his braies before he realized what he had done. He had yelled at a ghost. He had ordered from the room something he could neither hear nor see. A soft curse escaped him as he continued to dress and wondered just when he had begun to believe Sorcha's claims that she could hear and see the spirits that haunted too many keeps.

He had no chance to complain about how Sorcha was making him believe in things he had no proof of and would not wish to confront even if they did exist. A moment later, a loud rapping sounded at the door, and he jumped. Ruari did not wish such proof of all he was denying. Ivor had said his men were coming and, hearing Rosse call to him through the door, Ruari felt himself edge a little closer to belief.

"M'lord," called Rosse. "I think ye had best come with us for a moment."

"Why?" Ruari demanded the moment he opened the door.

"We caught a few Hays creeping into the inner bailey last night," Rosse explained, nodding to Sorcha in greeting when she crept up behind Ruari.

"My kinsmen are here?" she asked. "Ye havenae hurt them, have ye?"

"Nay, although there were a few knocks and bruises as they were caught."

"And how did they get so close?" Ruari asked, frowning at Rosse. "They should have been seen ere they got inside the gates."

"Aye, but I fear the men on the walls, myself included, were diverted by a wee lady wailing at our gates. She cried that she had lost her children and she needed the hounds and the keen eyes of the men of Gartmhor to find them. It may have worked except that we were troubled by the fact that we had never seen this woman before. Our hesitation as we tried to decide what to do was almost enough."

"Did ye happen to learn who the woman was?" asked Sorcha.

"I believe someone called her Eirie. A few of the Hays did slip free, and they called out to her as they disappeared into the dark. I was most surprised at how quickly the lady disappeared with them."

"What did ye do with the ones ye did catch?" asked Ruari as he finished lacing up his jupon.

"We have secured them in the dungeons," replied Rosse.

"The dungeons?" Sorcha cried.

"Dinnae fret, dearling," Ruari said quietly, and he kissed the tip of her nose. "I will keep them there but one day and a night then send them back where they came from with a message for your brother."

"May I visit with the prisoners?"

"Nay. I still believe that placing two Hays together means only trouble for the one foolish enough to allow it. Ye stay here, lass. I shall not be gone long. I but need to get the fools to understand that they will be free if they swear to forget trying to capture ye back."

"It may not be easy to get them to do that."

"Be at ease. I swear to ye, they willnae be left in that dank, dark place for verra long."

Sorcha sighed as she closed the door behind Ruari and Rosse. She was tired, but she did not feel inclined to crawl back into her now-empty bed. A little smile curling her lips, she decided what she needed to do was wash and have a very large meal, for the night of love-making had left her very hungry.

Just as she finished braiding her hair and deciding that it was not too early to seek out something hearty to break her fast with, another knock came at the door. Her eyes widened when she opened it, and a very agitated Mary walked in. A little warily, Sorcha closed the door and watched the older woman pace the room for a moment before sharply turning to confront her.

"Ye have been talking with Ivor, havenae ye?" Mary said, twisting her hands convulsively in front of her apron.

"Aye, I have seen and spoken with the mon's spirit," Sorcha replied.

"Oh, sweet merciful God," Mary moaned and sat down on the bed, burying her face in her hands. "He wishes us to hang for our crimes."

"Nay, he doesnae." When Mary looked at her with blatant disbelief, Sorcha walked over to the woman and gently clasped her shoulder. "Rest easy. Ivor doesnae want anyone dead."

"Then why is he haunting this place? I can sometimes feel him, ye ken. I am certain that he watches me."

"He but seeks someone to tell the truth. Ye didnae give him a verra respectable death."

"If I tell the truth I will be hanged, and so will my husband. I cannae tell anyone that my husband and I murdered the laird's uncle. If I must keep what happened that night a secret for the rest of my life, I will, for at least I will still be alive and not be cold in my grave with hemp burns on my neck."

"It wasnae murder. Did ye or your husband plan to kill Sir Ivor?"

"Weel, nay, but he is dead, and his death was caused by our fighting with him that night."

"Nay, it was brought about by his sleeping with another mon's wife." She smiled gently when Mary blushed. "Neither ye nor your husband will be hanged for what was no more than a tragic accident."

"If that is what Ivor believes, why is he haunting this place?"

"This is where he died, and what troubles his spirit so that it cannae find rest is that everyone speaks of him with scorn and laughter. He was obviously a proud man, and having folk think he was so drunk he would stumble out of a window is more than he can bear. I would guess that it was your enraged husband who tossed Ivor's braies out the window after his body."

"Aye, David did that. Are ye sure we willnae hang? This has tormented me for years, and I should dearly like to seek absolution."

Sorcha frowned. "Ye mean ye havenae even sought absolution from the priest?"

"Nay," replied Mary, "for he is a Kerr and would tell someone."

"Weel, now ye are going to tell someone instead of continuing to fret. Why not think of poor Ivor if ye need some more backbone to face Ruari? Think of how he has suffered, rooted here when he wishes to finish his journey. Think of how tormented he has been kenning that his whole clan is embarrassed over his death and that that scorn is born of a lie." She took Mary by the hand and dragged her out of the room. "Ye are going to speak to Ruari right now."

Mary did not drag her feet too much as she allowed Sorcha to lead her toward the small room next to the great hall where Ruari and Malcolm spent hours going over the books and trying to find ways to improve Ruari's fortunes. Sorcha had been a little piqued when Ruari had not returned, but word had reached her that Malcolm had demanded some of Ruari's time to sort through the books.

"I should speak to my husband first," Mary protested weakly as Sorcha opened the door and tried to yank her into the room.

"Nay, for he will quickly try to stop you, and I grow weary of doing Ivor's business when I have enough problems of my own to ponder."

"Sorcha," Ruari murmured as he and Malcolm stood up out of courtesy to greet the two women. "Is there something wrong?"

"Nay, not truly. Howbeit, this shaking woman has something she must tell you. She has kept this secret in her heart for years. 'Tis past time that everyone knew the truth about that rogue Ivor."

After a stuttering beginning, the whole sordid tale began to pour out of Mary. Sorcha slipped away as Ruari sent for Mary's husband. She paused only to get a whispered assurance from Ruari that the couple would not be hanged for the death, although they would have to suffer some retribution for their lies and the blackening of Ivor's name. Now all she had to do was let Ivor know that he could seek peace at last.

Once she was back in her bedchamber, Sorcha sat on the bed and looked around the room. She could not see Ivor but she knew he was near. It was not easy to let her spirits go for they were her friends and she missed them when they were no longer around, but she knew it would be cruel to hold him.

"I ken ye are here, Ivor. I ken ye were here when Mary came to confess."

"I didnae hear her say she would confess to anyone else," Ivor said, still too dim for her to see, but his voice came from near the window.

"Weel, she has already confessed to Ruari. They were calling for her husband when I left."

"What did my nephew have to say?"

"He was angry that they had let your name be so blackened and that they had held to that lie for so long. Ye are now in a better standing although I believe he still sees it as a senseless loss of a kinsmon."

"Oh, aye, I found it most senseless as weel. 'Tis done, then."

"Aye, 'tis done," she assured him. "Go, Ivor."

"I am somewhat afraid of where I am going to go."

"Ye have done a penance by being forced to linger here. I should think ye will be quite happy once ye let go."

"And ye are certain she willnae hang?"

"Verra certain. Ruari himself said so."

A long moment of silence passed, and she began to think he had quietly left when a soft voice whispered near her ear, "Thank ye, lass. And dinnae let that nephew of mine escape. Ye are what he needs and what he wants."

Sorcha prayed he was right. She sat quietly on her bed for almost an hour before she accepted the fact that Ivor had left her. A heavy sigh escaped her just as Ruari walked into the room. There was such a dark look on his face that she began to fear that he had changed his mind and decided to hang the couple.

"What have ye decided about Mary and David?"

He sat down beside her and took one of her small hands between his. "I havenae thought of a good punishment for their lies, but I will. Howbeit, David's tale of what happened that night was much the same as Mary's so I feel they are telling the truth."

"Oh, aye, their story matches Ivor's as weel."

"Have ye told Ivor that we all ken the truth now?"

"Aye, I told him. He is gone now."

Ruari frowned. "Gone where?"

"I fear I cannae answer that. I dinnae really ken what happens."

"Ye will miss him?"

"Aye, as I miss all of my spirits when they leave."

Pulling her into his arms, Ruari fell back onto the bed and grinned into her startled face. "Then I feel it is my duty to ease your mind of all such despair."

She slid her arms around his neck and smiled back at him. "Never let it be said that Sorcha Hay did anything to impede Sir Ruari Kerr's sense of duty."

A soft sigh of pleasure escaped her as he kissed her. When he held her like that and tenderly kissed her, she found it easy to believe that she could win his heart. She just prayed that she was not deluding herself. Cupping Ruari's face in her hands, she returned his fierce kiss and decided that the best and most welcome way to end the torment of her thoughts was to savor the passion she and Ruari shared.

Chapter Nineteen

"More Hays?" Ruari grumbled and scowled at Sorcha when she giggled.

For the past week her family had made themselves a complete nuisance, and Sorcha loved them dearly for it. She wished she was allowed to meet with some of them, for she would like to tell them to stop trying so hard to rescue her and Margaret, but then suspected it would make little difference. They all knew that Ruari and Beatham would never harm her or her cousin. The sole purpose of these consistent troublesome forays onto Gartmhor land was an attempt to snatch her and Margaret back to Dunweare so that no ransom had to be paid. It had been five days since she had become Ruari's lover again, and her kinsmen had made nearly an equal number of attempts to retrieve her and Margaret. Sorcha was a little astonished at their perseverance.

"How near did they get this time?" Ruari asked, frowning when Rosse grimaced.

"The kitchen maid found them tiptoeing through the herb garden," Rosse replied.

"They nearly got within the keep itself? What

distraction could they have used this time to make ye all so careless in your watch?"

"A lass. A wee, bonny lass. She had long fair hair that swirled about with each breath of the wind, as did her white loose gown." Rosse shook his head. "An angel, she was. E'en I was quite enthralled. She stood before our gates, arms outstretched, and kept us all keenly interested with a wild tale about being taken by the fairy folk, of how she had escaped and now needed our help to find her kinsmen."

"She sounds like Euphemia," Sorcha said, shocked that such a young girl would be used, yet unable to deny that she was the perfect diversion.

"I begin to think that your entire clan is skipping about my lands," drawled Ruari, then he turned his attention back to Rosse. "Ye didnae capture this lass, did ye?"

"Weel—nay. The kitchen maid sent out an alarm, and we rushed to answer it. The lass fled into the wood."

"Of course. The Hay women have proven to be curiously elusive all week. How do these fools keep getting inside the walls?"

"They climb them."

"Climb them?"

"Aye. It appears that most of Dunweare can climb even the smoothest rock. They climb like cats."

"Aye, we are all good climbers," Sorcha said, Ruari's sharp look quickly wiping away her grin. She sat quietly as Ruari and Rosse discussed the captured men until Ruari gave an order he had given many times in the last week. "I cannae understand where all these people are coming from," she said as Rosse left the great hall to put the latest two captives in the dungeon for a day and a night before releasing them. "Dunweare shall be emptied."

"I think these are the same men we captured two days ago and then released."

"But ye made them swear they wouldnae try again. I canna believe a Hay would break his word."

"Someone has given them a very clever vow to placate me with. I think they are assuring me that they willnae try to rescue ye and Margaret again, but it seems what they really say is they willnae try to rescue ye that way again. I must needs come up with a vow that doesnae give them a way to circle 'round it."

Although she bit the inside of her cheek to try to stop herself, Sorcha finally gave in to the urge to laugh. "I suspect Neil devised that wee trick of words. She has always been clever in that way. She will be coming here for the third time in another day or two. Could I not at least wave to her from the door ere I am locked away?"

"I will consider it. Now, 'tis a fine day, and I thought ye may have an urge to see something other than the walls of my keep. Would ye like to take a ride across my lands?"

"Oh, aye, I would. When?"

"As soon as ye can be ready."

She hastily finished the honey-coated bread she had been eating and raced off to her bedchamber. She did not have many gowns, and most of them were too large, but she decided to change into the blue one with the neatly embroidered sleeves. If any of Ruari's people were about to catch a glimpse of her, she wanted to make sure she looked her best, or as close to that as she could get in a borrowed gown.

As she dressed she hesitated only a moment before buckling on her sword and slipping her dagger into her boot. Ruari had finally agreed to let her have her weapons when she swore that she would not use them to escape or to help her kinsmen rescue her. She thought about the last five days with Ruari. He had lost a great deal of his reserve and, although he had not said the three words she ached to hear, she was more confident that he did care for her. He did not hide his tenderness or his appreciation. He was freer with his compliments, and there was no doubt in her mind that they were sincere ones. There had been no more visits from prospective brides and their families either.

What troubled her the most was that there was no talk of the future, of what would happen when and if she and Margaret were allowed to return to Dunweare. She knew Ruari had not yet found a way to end the ransoming without getting his money yet with his pride intact. Nevertheless, if he intended there to be a future for them, he should at least be alluding to it by now.

Margaret's future was also still uncertain, yet the girl and Beatham carried on as if they would get all that they desired. Beatham's family was furious that Margaret was at Gartmhor, and Ruari was constantly receiving angry missives and trying to reconcile the family. Neither side would bend, Beatham would not give up Margaret, and his family refused to condone any marriage. Something Malcolm had let slip made Sorcha think Ruari was struggling to come up with some compromise, but that first he had to get Beatham's family to be willing to even consider one.

Sorcha shook her head as she hurried out to the stables to meet with Ruari. The only ones who seemed to be content and hopeful were Neil and Malcolm. To everyone's astonishment, there was a definite romance budding there. In Neil's and Malcolm's case, the only ones who had to decide what they should or could do were Neil and Malcolm. Neil being the seventh daughter of a poor laird and Malcolm being a poor relation of

Ruari's gave the couple a freedom none of the rest of them really enjoyed.

As she walked into the stable she saw Ruari jovially arguing with several of his men, and studied him for a moment. When she looked at him, she sometimes wondered if she was reaching far too high, thus dooming herself to a very hard fall. Ruari was not only as handsome as any woman could wish for, but healthy and strong, wealthy and possessing some of the most fertile lands in the area. He could have any woman he wanted. At times it seemed preposterous that she thought she could win his heart.

She quickly shook away that assault of self-doubt. There was a lot she could offer a man. The only thing she felt went against her in a way it would be hard to overcome was her family's dismal record of producing sons. There were a great many male Kerrs about, however, close and distant cousins of Ruari. His name was not in danger of dying out as hers was. If she could win his heart, he might be able to accept that he had only daughters; he might be willing to gamble that she was one of the few Hay women who could produce a son.

"There ye are, dearling," he said, extending his hand to her and smiling as she walked over and placed her hand in his, then glanced at the sword she wore. "Do ye think ye will need that?"

"I cannae feel safe riding out alone without some weapon on me."

"I fear we cannae ride out alone. My men stand firm. We will have a small guard."

"Verra wise of them." She winked at him. "After all, someone may try to kidnap you." She smiled when the men laughed, realizing that her having taken Ruari for ransom was no longer considered a crime, even by Ruari.

"Where is Rosse?" she asked as she looked around and saw no sign of the huge red-haired man. "Is he not the one who watches your back?"

"Aye, but his wife is verra near her time, and he likes to stay close at hand when one of his bairns is to be born. Since I am not riding out to battle, there is no need to demand that he join us."

"Of course not," she agreed as he helped her mount the sturdy brown mare he had chosen for her. "So, we shall be a group of a dozen," she murmured as she watched the other men mount with Ruari.

Ruari chuckled as they rode out into the bailey. "Not the private little trot I had envisioned, but 'tis the time of the year when raiding is a real danger, and I would rather there were men to protect you than lose ye to the English because I wanted a wee bit of privacy."

"I think I would prefer that as weel. I have met with the English and have no desire to do so again." She shivered slightly as talk of the English made her think of Simon Treacher, a man she thought she had successfully banished from her mind.

"Was there trouble when ye went to ransom Dougal?" Ruari asked when he saw the shadow that abruptly clouded her expression, a shadow he knew was not cast by the gates they rode through.

After a moment of consideration, Sorcha decided there was no harm in telling him about Simon Treacher. Even though she could not believe the man was still a threat or that he could find her at Gartmhor, it could also prove helpful. She watched the expressions on Ruari's face with interest as she told him the trouble she had had with the Englishman. Ruari was furious, the extent of his anger quite possibly a mark of the strength of his feelings for her. After all, he would not find the fact that another man had looked at her lustfully so infuriating if he did not care about her.

"Why do ye think the mon is no longer pursuing ye?" he asked, his voice tight with an anger he struggled to control.

"The spies he sent to Dunweare disappeared. We assumed he stopped sending them because his lustful interests had turned elsewhere," she replied.

"Or mayhap he just sent better ones, ones ye and Crayton didnae see."

A thrill of fear went through her along with one of pure joy. She dreaded the thought that Simon Treacher could still be hungering for her, but she was elated at the way Ruari spoke of Crayton as if he was real. There were more and more such slips of the tongue on his part, revealing that slowly, ever so slowly, he was beginning to believe. She had never demanded that he believe in all the same things she did, but a touch of belief would certainly make her life easier if she was going to spend it with him. Knowing it would be unwise to point out what he had just done, she centered her thoughts on the possibility that there was still a lustful Englishman on her trail.

"If there had been any sign of Simon at Dunweare, Neil would have mentioned it and told you to tell me," she said.

"Lass, both sides of the border teem with spies and men highly skilled in ferreting out any sort of information one wishes to gather. I can tell ye almost to a head how many cattle Lord Selkirk has in England. I suspect he can tell ye much the same about me. There are few secrets."

"That is rather alarming news."

He briefly smiled at her reaction. "'Tis the way of it

when two countries sit side by side and have fought each other since long before the first Graeme leapt over that Roman wall. Every soldier kens that it is best to learn all ye can about his enemy. 'Tis one of the first lessons a warrior learns. Nay, trust me in this, if Simon Treacher still wants ye, if another poor lass hasnae caught his eye, he kens what ye are doing and where ye are."

"Then why did we catch so many of his spies or send them fleeing back to England?"

"Arrogance on his part, I think. He simply didnae believe he had to use his best men to keep watch on one tiny Scottish lady from a poor border clan."

"Oh. I would appreciate it if ye would tell my aunt about this when she comes again. Dunweare needs to ken that it might have a traitor or a spy close at hand."

Ruari nodded then reached over to pat her hand. "Ye are safe, lass. Even if he kens that ye are here at Gartmhor, there has yet to be an Englishmon who could take this place."

Sorcha wished she felt as confident as he sounded. Gartmhor may well have never been taken by the English, but Simon did not have to assault the keep to get his hands on her. The man could simply skulk around Gartmhor waiting for her to venture out.

Like now, she suddenly thought and nervously looked around. Despite her efforts to shake the thought from her mind, Sorcha could not dispel the notion that this ride over Gartmhor lands was ill-advised. The further away from the keep she rode, the more uneasy she grew, but she hesitated to tell Ruari to turn back. He could easily think that his talk about clever spies had frightened her or, worse, believe she was saying that he and his men were incapable of protecting her. That was not an insult she wished to deliver.

She took a deep breath to steady herself and smiled at Ruari as he pointed out the cattle grazing on a hill-side. Gartmhor had good grazing land as well, and she was almost envious. The rocky land covered thinly in scrub and moss that encircled Dunweare could not support many cows, sheep, or goats. There had been some very lean winters at Dunweare, something she suspected Gartmhor and its people saw only rarely.

It was more than her lack of a dowry that separated her and Ruari. Every aspect of his life, from the food on his table to the number of well-armed men on Gartmhor's high walls, enhanced their differences. Sorcha began to find the constant signs of Ruari's wealth very depressing. Despite the near equality of their births, it was painfully clear that Ruari would have to step down to marry her. She was not all that confident that she had given him enough reason to do that.

"Ye have been graced with verra fine and fertile lands, Ruari Kerr," she murmured as they paused by a small rivulet so that the horses could drink.

"Aye, I have been weel blessed," he agreed, dismounting and helping her do the same.

Sorcha tried to listen as he told her of his plans for Gartmhor, all the ways he planned to fill his purse as well as improve the lives of his people, but it was impossible. She kept looking at the trees. They were in a clearing, but only yards from them the trees began to thicken until she was unable to see into their depths. She was not sure why the trees held such an allure, but she was certain that their attraction was not due to their great beauty. Fear knotted her insides, not admiration. There was something out there, something that meant only harm to her and Ruari. All too aware that Ruari was slow to believe in what he could not see, she continued to stare into the shadowy forests, her eyes beginning to sting from the strain as she searched desperately for some sign, some warning signal, Ruari would heed.

"The woman can see us," warned Thomas, hesitating in his advance and looking to Simon for instructions.

Simon Treacher paused and stared through the thick trees toward the prize he had worked so hard to claim. Sorcha Hay was indeed staring intently in his direction, her lovely face slightly marred by a frown of deep concentration. He waited tensely for a warning cry to escape her full lips.

"Nay, she does not see us," he finally said, inching forward and signaling his men to do the same.

"She will soon."

"Then it will be too late."

"Aye, for us."

"If you are too great a coward to face a few Scots, Thomas, you may remount and ride back to England." Simon nodded when Thomas flushed, tightened his jaw, and continued to move. "And all of you are to remember that the woman is not to be harmed and that Sir Kerr is mine." He stared back at his small army, glaring at them until they all nodded. "I intend to make him pay dearly for taking what is mine."

"Ye dinnae seem to be paying me much heed, lass," Ruari murmured, frowning at Sorcha's distraction as he took her by the arm. "Mayhap this will catch your interest. 'Tis important to me that ye learn about my lands, my people, and my plans for them both," he said in a quiet, serious voice, watching her intently for a moment before tugging her toward the trees.

"Nay," Sorcha cried, fighting his pull. She inwardly cursed the whims of fate for she knew Ruari was about to speak of the future, quite possibly a shared future, but she could not let the desires of her heart outweigh her common sense. Something was very wrong, and she had to get him to heed her warning. "We must leave this place."

"Sorcha, what is wrong?" he asked, stopping to grasp her gently by the shoulders as he became aware of her agitation.

"We must leave here—now." She glanced toward the forest. "We must get far away from those accursed trees."

"There is something about the trees that afrights ye?"

"Nay!" She pulled free of his light hold, grasped him by the arms and dearly wished he was smaller so that she could shake him until his teeth rattled. "There is no time to argue this. Call it a woman's whim—tell your men I have lost my wits or that the sun has disordered my poor wee female brain. I dinnae care! Just tell everyone to mount and hie back to Gartmhor." The faint jingle of a horse's harness reached her ears, and she cursed, spinning round to stare at the woods. "Too late."

Ruari looked toward the wood in time to see the first horseman emerge from the dappled shadows that had hidden him, and he cursed. "Sassenach bastards."

He knew there was no time to mount and meet the enemy on horseback. Pulling Sorcha along, he raced back to his men, bellowing orders each step of the way. They all grabbed their helmets and shields from their horses then slapped the animals into a gallop straight toward the swiftly advancing Englishmen. In the instant of extra time the resultant confusion gained them, Ruari and his men ran to a more open piece of land and formed a tight circle. Despite Sorcha's protests that she could fight with them, he pushed her into the center of the protective circle.

"Stay there, lass," he ordered her. "I need both mind and heart set on one thing now—fighting these dogs. I cannae do that if I think ye are in their reach. Now they must climb o'er me to get to you."

Sorcha had no time to reply as the first onslaught swept over them. With their shields and long swords, Ruari and his men pushed aside the Englishmen's charge. A few loud curses from the men of Gartmhor told her that it had cost them a few drops of blood, but none of the men faltered or fell as the English reined in and turned to charge again.

The second charge cost the English two men who were unhorsed and killed by the Scots. One of Ruari's men fell to his knees, knocked senseless by the blow of a flail, but he was quickly helped to his feet by the men flanking him. He wiped the blood from his eyes and, after swaying a little, stood firm.

She was astonished when the English regrouped for a third charge. It was a poor choice of tactics. In two assaults they had not successfully broken Ruari's circle yet had lost two of their men. Despite the fact that they numbered close to thirty compared to Ruari's mere dozen, it was still an unacceptable loss. It did not show much hope of being successful either, for the horses shied as they drew near the tight group of shielded Scots, and not every one of the Englishmen could strike at the same time.

Another two Englishmen fell when they charged, Ruari's men unhorsing them and breaking the circle only long enough to deliver the death stroke. In the one brief moment when one of the English horsemen paused to try fruitlessly to cut down one of Ruari's men, Sorcha recognized her enemy. Sir Simon Treacher had found her. At the moment it was not particularly comforting to discover that Ruari was right when he spoke of how thoroughly the Scots and English could spy upon each other.

"'Tis Simon Treacher," she yelled. "Ye were right, Ruari. The mon does have good spies."

"I imagine it pained ye some to say that, dearling," Ruari called back even as he parried a blow aimed at his head.

Before Sorcha could demand to know how he could jest at such a time, the English struck a telling blow. It had cost them four men, but they finally reduced Ruari's numbers to eleven. One of the Scots screamed as an English sword cut deep into the flesh of his sword arm. He was quickly pushed inside of the circle, his companions closing ranks around him.

A quick look told Sorcha that the man would probably live, but he could no longer hold his place in the circle. She tore off a length of her petticoat and hurriedly bound the wound to stop the bleeding, then stared at the man. He was thickly muscular, yet smaller than most of Ruari's men. A quick glance toward their enemy revealed that they were dismounting. It was not going to be easy to fend off nearly twice their number when they were all on an equal footing. Ignoring the man's protests, she grabbed his light helmet, stuck it on her head, and then took his shield. Although the shield was heavier than she had anticipated, she knew she could hold it as long as was necessary, and she slipped her arm through the straps on the back. After taking a deep breath to steady herself, she nudged her way into the circle next to Ruari and braced herself for both the ensuing attack and his certain protest.

"Get back inside the circle, ye fool lass," Ruari yelled after staring at her in shock.

"Nay, 'tis my enemy ye are fighting," she said as she drew her sword.

"Ye cannae fight grown men hefting a shield that is nearly as big as ye are."

"'Tisnae that big, and even if it is, then it just means that more of me is protected."

"Lass, this enemy doesnae wish to hurt ye. He wants ye verra much alive. Ye need not put yourself in harm's way."

"Better in harm's way than being pulled into his cold arms." She met Ruari's intent gaze for a moment then sighed with relief when he nodded.

"Just dinnae die before me," he ordered her in a gruff voice.

"I shall do mÿ best to see that neither of us dies."

She readied herself to meet the advancing enemy and was surprised that, despite the danger they faced, Ruari's words caused her heart to skip with joy and hope. Telling her not to fall first might sound a foolish command to others, but the way Ruari said it was what pleased her. The gruffness in his voice had not been that of command, but of deep emotion. Ruari did care for her, she was certain of it. As the first clash of English and Scottish swords echoed in the small clearing, she prayed that they would both survive Simon Treacher's attack so that she could find out just how much Ruari did care.

Chapter Twenty

"Hold," cried Dougal, waving his small group of ten men, two women, and one slender girl to an abrupt halt. "Did ye hear that?"

"Hear what?" demanded Neil as she stepped up beside him, tugging her weary horse behind her.

"It sounds like swords clashing, like steel against steel." He took a few more steps, crouching slightly as he listened intently. "Aye, 'tis fighting. Straight ahead of us."

Neil cursed softly when Dougal hurried forward, heading toward the sound with a complete disregard for the noise he was making and what danger he might be heedlessly running toward. She signaled to the others to keep pace, but to be quieter, then hurried to catch her nephew. When she grabbed him by the arm, stopping him short, she ignored the glare he sent her.

"Will ye but think a moment?" she scolded him. "Ye dinnae ken what ye are running into the midst of, who is fighting and who is winning. Can ye approach with a wee bit more caution, please?"

"Oh, aye, of course. I but feared that Sorcha might be

in trouble. After all, that is the very direction in which we saw her and Sir Kerr ride."

"She could verra weel be in trouble, but ye willnae help her much if ye stumble into the hands of her enemies, will ye?"

"Nay, ye are right." He frowned and sent her a half-annoyed, half-amused look. "'Twould be nice if ye werenae right quite so often, Aunt. It sore bruises a mon's vanity."

"Yours could weel afford a chip or two knocked out of it."

Neil smiled faintly when Dougal ignored her and started to move ahead silently. The sounds of a battle grew more distinctive with each step they took. When the battle finally came into view, she cursed and crouched next to Dougal.

"'Tis that English bastard Sir Simon Treacher," whispered Dougal. "He has found Sorcha. How did the cursed mon discover that she was here? I have done my best to keep this whole matter strictly between the Kerrs and the Hays."

"Ye ken as weel as I do that both sides of the border fairly teem with spies and traitors. There could have been eyes on Sorcha for months, even near enough at hand to see what happened at the fair."

"Aye, I ken it." He rubbed his chin, his expression thoughtful as he watched the Kerrs fight an English force twice in number.

"Weel, let us go and give them some help." Neil glared at Dougal when he grabbed her by the arm, stopping her advance. "What foolishness is this?"

"We could wait here and let the English fight the Kerrs for us."

"Ye would squat here and let Sassenach dogs kill Scots before our verra eyes?"

"I have no wish to risk my life for a Kerr."

"And what of our Sorcha?"

"Sir Simon doesnae want her injured."

"She is in the midst of the fighting. What Treacher wants could be easily forgotten in the heat of battle. And what do we do if she survives after all the Kerrs are slaughtered?"

"Take her from the English."

"Chase them down on these horses?" She nodded when he flushed slightly and scowled. "The English may also still outnumber us when they are done with the Kerrs. If we go and aid Sir Ruari now, we will number nearly as many as the English and we will have the advantage of catching the motherless swine between us and the Kerrs. 'Tis too good an advantage to toss aside just because ye have no love for the Kerrs."

Neil ignored Dougal's curses as she wrenched free of his hold. She ordered the wide-eyed Euphemia and Eirie to take the horses and hide, then drew her sword. The sound of the rest of their small group doing the same steadied her. She stood up and, after securing her skirts above her knees so that they would not hinder her, she raced toward the English, the Hay war cry upon her lips. At her heels raced Dougal and their small group of warriors.

Sorcha nearly faltered in parrying the thrusting sword of an Englishman as a familiar cry rent the air. Against her back she felt Ruari start with surprise as well. They had ended up back to back as the battle had slowly deteriorated into a melee with Ruari's men doing all they could to save their own lives or at least make the English pay dearly before they died. As more of Ruari's men fell, her hope for their survival had grown thinner. With Neil's war cry still ringing in the air, Sorcha felt a renewed strength surge through her aching arms.

"'Tis my aunt to our rescue," Sorcha cried, enjoying the brief respite from fighting as the English struggled to overcome their shock and confusion when they saw this unplanned-for threat rapidly advancing on them.

"Aye, and your brother. I thank God that He has sent us aid, for we are in sore need of it, but I dearly wish He had chosen others to be our saviors."

Not quite sure what he meant, Sorcha defended her clansmen. "They are all good fighters."

"Oh, aye, I have no doubt that we shall now send the English scurrying for home. 'Tis the confrontation that must come after the victory I would cheerfully have avoided."

She cursed as she finally understood what he was talking about. There would certainly be trouble once the fighting was over. Sorcha had the sinking feeling that what *she* wanted and needed was not going to be the first consideration of either her brother or her lover when the two men came face-to-face at last. It would not be a good time for her to try to assert herself either. As she watched her brother quickly dispatch an Englishman, Sorcha shared Ruari's mixed feelings of gratitude and apprehension.

Before she could say anything to Ruari, Simon Treacher elbowed his way through his fighting and fleeing men. Occasionally he paused to threaten or push his retreating men back into the fray, but it was useless. A rout was in the making. Even as Simon reached out toward her with one gauntleted hand, Ruari grabbed her by the arm and nearly flung her behind him. She decided to stay where he had placed her, but kept her sword at the ready.

"You will pay a high price for taking what is mine," Simon said as he confronted Ruari.

"Yours?" Sorcha cried, but both men ignored her.

"She was never yours, Treacher," Ruari replied. "Ye but saw her, and with the sick greed suffered by so many Sassenachs, ye decided to take her."

"Such righteousness from the man who kidnapped her from a fair," Simon drawled as he and Ruari began to warily circle each other, carefully studying each other's strength. "You are no more than a base reiver, Kerr."

"Aye? Then what are ye who ride into another mon's country to steal his women?"

Sorcha barely nodded to Neil and her brother as they each grabbed her by an arm and tugged her a little farther away from Ruari and Simon. A small part of her acknowledged the fact that the English had been successfully routed, those who were not dead or so badly wounded they could not mount their horses, fleeing the field and callously leaving their lord to his fate. She dared not take her full attention from Ruari. When the two men finally clashed swords, she was startled by the sound, then tensely watched each parry and thrust. Neil lightly rested her arm around Sorcha's shoulders, and she was thankful for the silent and subtle support.

The fight between Ruari and Simon dragged on for what felt like hours to Sorcha. The two men were well matched in skill and strength despite Simon's much thinner build. Although she did not like actively wishing for someone's death, even Simon Treacher's, Sorcha almost sagged with relief when the Englishman began to show signs of weakening. Ruari was still strong, still calm, and his movements still held a deadly grace. He now possessed a clear advantage.

When Ruari finally delivered the death stroke to Simon, piercing the Englishman's heart with one swift thrust of his sword, Sorcha felt no sense of victory, just relief. Only in the heat of battle when her own life was clearly in jeopardy could she push aside the horror of taking a man's life. She moved to go to Ruari as he turned to face her, only to be caught up hard by Dougal's tight grip on her arm.

As she started to protest, she caught sight of Neil's frown and the slight shake of her aunt's head. The woman's message was clear—do not argue now. It was hard, but Sorcha decided she would bow to the woman's proven wisdom. She tried to relay her disappointment in the look she gave Ruari, and the crooked smile he gave her made her sure she had succeeded. There was so much more she wanted to say and do, but now was not the time. Judging by the tension in the Hay men and what remained of Ruari's group, Sorcha knew that speaking too freely could make matters far worse than they already were.

"I looked o'er your men, Sir Ruari," Neil said, breaking the tight silence. "I fear two are dead, one may yet die, and nearly half the rest are wounded, although I dinnae believe they risk dying if they are treated weel."

"They will be. Thank ye, Neil," he said, severing his steady gaze at Dougal only briefly to glance her way and nod his gratitude. "We had best get them back to Gartmhor as soon as possible." He reached for Sorcha, but was not really surprised when Dougal, his sword still bloodied from the battle, yanked Sorcha even farther away from him. "I believe ye have my prisoner."

Sorcha glanced at Neil who responded by rolling her eyes heavenward. She was somewhat glad that she was not the only one who thought that was a particularly stupid thing for Ruari to say. A brief, painful tightening of Dougal's hand on her arm told her that he had responded to Ruari's brash statement with a sudden surge of anger. That had to be no surprise to Ruari. What puzzled her was why Ruari would try to enrage Dougal instead of placating him. She decided it had to be something only a man could really understand. She simply could not believe that Ruari would purposely act in a way that would force Dougal, through pride or anger, to take her away.

"And I believe I have just saved your worthless hide, though it galled me to do so," said Dougal.

The Kerrs who had the strength to do so grumbled threateningly, and the Hays bristled back. Nearly every man had his hand on his sword. Neil was right. She could not step into the middle of such intense male posturing. When she did have the opportunity to speak to Ruari again, she intended to give him a sound scolding about indulging in such nonsense.

"I was considering the ransoming a thing apart from this," Ruari said.

"Ye do that a lot," Sorcha murmured, earning a glare from both men.

"It cannae be a thing apart," snapped Dougal. "I wouldnae have e'en been here if ye hadnae stolen my sister from the fair. Nor would Simon have tracked her down here."

"Nay, he would have come for her at Dunweare."

"We would have been able to protect her. Aye, and we wouldnae have been fool enough to take her outside the walls where that cursed Englishmon could get her."

"Dougal," Sorcha protested. "To be fair to Ruari, he didnae ken about Sir Simon until I told him only a few hours ago."

Both men glared at her again, clearly annoyed at her

interruptions. She was about to tell them they were both idiots when suddenly her Aunt Neil grabbed her and yanked her completely away from the men. Sorcha looked at the woman, considering her the worst of all traitors, as Ruari and Dougal returned to their argument with no one attempting to talk sense to them.

"They need their heads banged together," she muttered as she fruitlessly tried to wriggle free of her aunt's iron grip.

"Aye, they do, but it will do no good now," Neil advised, looking around at the men and shaking her head. "This is a particular sort of male stupidity that needs to be treated carefully, lass. Ye will only make matters worse if ye reveal to them what fools they are or even that ye think they are being foolish. Especially while they are all still seething with the bloodlust of battle. Nay, lass, as hard as it is to do so, leave this be."

"But I shall be taken back to Dunweare."

"Aye, as will Margaret and I. That cannae be stopped, but we can correct this idiocy there, when tempers have cooled."

"He was beginning to care for me. I cannae leave now."

"Ye must. And I believe that black-haired knight has cared for ye for a long time. 'Tis sometimes difficult for a mon to ken such things, to understand his own heart. Ye willnae be leaving him by your own choice, so if he has begun to recognize what he feels, such emotions cannae be destroyed because ye leave him for a wee while."

A part of Sorcha knew that Neil was right. If Ruari had begun to care for her, it would not die simply because her brother dragged her home. A greater part of her, however, was terrified of leaving Gartmhor just when it appeared that she was starting to inch her way into his heart. Then she recalled that she would not be the only one torn from her lover if Dougal and Ruari remained near swordpoint.

"Oh, poor Margaret," she murmured then looked at Neil. "And you as weel."

"'Tis Margaret I worry over. We shall have to endure more of that cursed weeping and melancholy."

"True." Sorcha frowned for a moment as she thought over the whole problem and still saw no quick and easy solution except for Neil. "Howbeit, ye dinnae need to leave Malcolm if ye wish to stay with him." She still did not understand that romance, but knew she could not discuss it now.

"I do. My wee mon will wait for me. I cannae settle to that when ye and Margaret cannae settle as weel."

Sorcha was about to argue what appeared to be a needless self-sacrifice when a faint change of tone in Ruari's and Dougal's bickering drew her attention. The anger and tension were still there, but Ruari was suddenly less combative. An instant later, she knew why.

"Ye owe me a debt of blood, Kerr," Dougal said. "Many times over, for ye and your men were surely doomed. That more than pays the ransom for my sister and my cousin and the two men ye caught this morning."

Ruari nodded. "Then consider the ransom paid. Take your cousin and your men, but leave Sorcha here with me."

"Ye ask me to leave my sister, my own flesh and blood, here to play the whore for ye?"

"Nay, as my wife."

Those three words pounded in Sorcha's mind as she struggled to believe what she had just heard. Everyone was looking at Ruari in surprise, but she knew that none of them felt as stunned as she did. Dougal's shock slowly turned to a cold rage, and Sorcha started toward Ruari. She was confused, unsure of what emotion lurked behind Ruari's abrupt proposal, but she was sure that if she did not get to him before Dougal could react, all chance to find out might be gone. A sharp curse escaped her when Dougal ordered two of his men to grab her and she was unable to elude them. Ignoring her curses, insults, and struggles, they dragged her toward a horse.

"Tie her on there if ye have to," Dougal ordered, and then he looked at Ruari. "I want no Kerr as kinsman. Ye owe me a debt of blood, Ruari Kerr, and we both ken that such a debt cannae be scorned. I dinnae want ye within ten miles of my sister. Send my cousin home with my two men," he snapped then turned sharply and strode toward the horses they had taken from the English.

"One last thing," Ruari said, following Dougal.

Dougal stopped, turning with his hand on his sword. "We have no more to say to each other."

"I have but one thing to say to Sorcha." He ignored Dougal's threatening pose and called to Sorcha. "What of Crayton?"

She abruptly stilled her struggles and looked at him. "I will tell him that his enemy is dead."

"That may not be enough. Take the Englishmon's body with ye. Then Crayton will have no doubts and can finally seek his rest as my uncle did."

Sorcha nodded, briefly silenced by the strength of the emotions tearing through her. Ruari might not fully believe in spirits and all the rest, but he had finally and fully accepted her belief in them. She unthinkingly took a step toward him, only to have her guards renew their efforts to get her on the back of a horse.

The men struggled a long time before they finally flung her over the saddle. What reluctance they had felt over treating her so roughly vanished, wiped away by all of the bruises and insults she had inflicted upon them. She lifted her head to see Ruari just standing there, silently watching Dougal take her away. The only sign that he was distressed by it was the way his hands clenched and unclenched at his sides and the cold, remote expression upon his face, a look she knew he assumed when he wanted to hide something. Since this could well be the last time she saw him, she wished he would give her some hint of what he felt. She would have liked to have known that she was not the only one who was being torn asunder inside.

Ruari watched the Hays leave until even the dust from their horses could not be seen. He shuddered as the tension eased from his body. The moment it was gone he wished it back, for now he was too conscious of the intense pain gnawing at his insides. As he watched Sorcha being taken away, he realized something he wished he had remained blissfully ignorant of—he loved her.

He spat a curse and turned to help his men prepare to return to Gartmhor. If revealing how much he needed Sorcha at the very moment she was taken from him was some form of punishment, Ruari felt it far outweighed his crimes. Bound by a debt of blood, the only way he could get Sorcha was for Dougal to unbend, but Ruari doubted that the angry young man would do that. What tortured Ruari the most was the knowledge that he had had numerous chances to understand what he felt for Sorcha, to love her and wed her, but he had wasted all of them.

There was very little left to take from the English.

The Hays had picked the enemy clean and taken the few prisoners caught with them. Ruari struggled to fix his thoughts on his men, many of whom would need his help to get home. It allowed him to subdue the turmoil in his mind and heart for a time, as did the need to deliver the sad news to the widows of the men who had died once he reached Gartmhor.

Weary and heartsore, he wanted to go to his bedchamber, but Beatham's parents waited to meet with him in the great hall. He knew they had not seen their son, for the youth had sequestered himself in his room after Margaret had been taken from Gartmhor, kicking and screaming, by her kinsmen. Beatham's parents arrived after the Hays had left. As Ruari stepped up to the head table, he became aware of their shocked stares and tersely explained why he was in such a disordered state as he filled his tankard with strong wine.

"We were hoping ye could persuade Beatham to speak with us," said Lilith, Beatham's delicate, fair-haired mother. "We have decided to concede to his wishes."

"I fear your surrender comes too late. 'Tis clearly a common affliction amongst the Kerrs," Ruari added in a distracted tone.

"I dinnae understand."

"There will be no marriages between the Hays and the Kerrs. Sir Dougal Hay has sworn it."

"Then the lad will speak to us again, for 'tis no longer our fault he cannae wed the lass."

"He thinks differently."

It took a long time to convince Beatham's parents that they would not be able to enjoy a reunion with their obstinate son just yet. When they left to rest before beginning their journey home, Ruari sank into his high-backed oak chair, sighed, and refilled his tankard. He was not sure he was pleased when Rosse arrived. Yet again he had to explain what had happened. Each retelling stirred up the painful feelings on which he struggled to keep a tight rein. Rosse also looked prepared to discuss the matter thoroughly.

"Ye were a wee bit slow to see the truth," Rosse said when Ruari finished his tale, including relating the painful revelations he had endured.

"Aye. I suppose ye will claim ye saw it ere I did," drawled Ruari.

"'Tis often easier for one who watches the couple involved to see such things ere the couple does."

"Weel, it matters not who sees it or saw it, for 'tis a truth that is now utterly useless."

"Mayhap."

"'Tis a debt of blood I speak of, Rosse. I cannae go against Dougal Hay's wishes. For Sorcha I would be willing to taint my honor, but to do anything against Dougal Hay now would leave me with no honor at all. I would be an outcast, as would Sorcha if she wed me. Nay, my only hope is that Dougal's fury fades and he begins to realize that I am a good match for his sister and Dunweare. I see that as a verra faint hope."

"Ye must not forget the lass," Rosse said. "She is clever. She may think of a way to untie this knot."

Ruari felt the tiniest flicker of hope cut through the gloom encompassing his heart. He knew Sorcha would understand why he could not act. What he could not be completely sure of was if she would want to try to solve the impasse between their clans. They had never spoken openly about their feelings. Not only could he not be certain of how deep her feelings ran, but she had to be uncertain about his as well. She might even doubt that he would welcome her if she did find a way to return to him.

"'Tis a verra thick knot, Rosse," he murmured. "And 'tis not only Dougal Hay who helped tie it."

Sorcha grimaced as they rode into Dunweare, people gathering around to see the prizes brought back from the battle. Dougal had not kept her tied to the saddle long, but he had kept a very close watch on her. Margaret had joined them, weeping vociferously, and although the noise she made had grown fainter, it had not ceased. She and Neil had spent the long journey telling Dougal what an idiot he was, demanding that he change his mind about the Kerrs, and even occasionally trying to coax him to their side. Nothing had worked, and Sorcha was so frustrated that all the grinding of her teeth she had done had left them aching badly.

Her first instinct had been to get free of Dougal and race back to Ruari's arms, but with Neil's help she had seen the error of that plan. Ruari was caught tightly in a debt of blood. He would lose all honor and standing at court if he broke it, and that would not only hurt him, but also Gartmhor and all of his people. The only solution was to get Dougal to back down and agree to their marriage, but after arguing the matter all the way from Gartmhor, Sorcha saw very little chance of that happening.

As she dismounted she caught the shimmer of a figure in the shadows near the gates. Even though he was not very distinct, she knew it was Crayton. There was some small comfort to be had in the knowledge that she could now give Crayton the peace he had sought for so long. It was the one good thing that had come out of that tumultuous day by the creek at Gartmhor.

"Crayton, your enemy is dead," she announced.

"Are ye certain? Ye said he must be dead of old age by now," came Crayton's voice in her head.

"Aye, the one who actually murdered ye is long dead, but will it not satisfy your need if one of his blood has been cut down by a Scottish sword?"

"A Hay sword?"

"Nay, but it was the arrival of the Hays upon the battlefield that brought about his death, and"—she lowered her voice so that the people near at hand could not hear—"the mon who killed him is the lover of a Hay."

"Good enough. 'Tis odd, I trust in your word, but—"

She held up her hand to stop his fumbling explanation. "Dinnae fear that ye will insult me, my dear friend. Ye have waited too long for this day. 'Tis not enough just to be told." She walked to the litter that held Simon Treacher's body. "Ye must be shown." She lifted up the blanket.

The shadow that was Crayton grew more distinct as he looked over the body. By the time she dropped the blanket back over the dead man, Crayton was almost completely visible. She felt a deep sadness, for she knew he would leave her now. She was happy for him, yet would truly miss him.

"Crayton," called a sweet female voice.

Sorcha started slightly and looked around. She noticed that Crayton was staring into the distance, and she tried to see what had caused the intense look of joy upon his face. Slowly a light appeared, growing wider and brighter until she caught the glimpse of a pretty young woman in its depths. The woman smiled at Crayton and held out her hand.

"Elspeth," Crayton whispered, and the depth of emotion in his voice made Sorcha shiver.

When Crayton turned her way, a hint of fear and reluctance briefly dimming the elation on his face, Sorcha
smiled. "I shall miss ye. Go, Crayton. She waits for ye
and she has waited a verra long time. Ye are done here."

She wrapped her arms around herself as he moved
toward the woman. For one short moment, she felt the
chill of his leaving. Alongside it was a deep warmth,
and Sorcha knew she was being touched by the joy and
emotion Crayton felt as he took his Elspeth's hand. The
couple embraced and, in the blink of an eye, were gone.

A heavy sigh escaped Sorcha. She was tired and,
when Dougal approached her, she glared at him. He was
the reason she was alone, but she was determined that
he would not succeed in keeping her and Ruari apart. If
she could not change his mind she would find another
way. If Elspeth and Crayton could be reunited after
being separated by death itself, then there had to be a
way to salve honor and pride on both sides and also
have Ruari.

Chapter Twenty-One

"Nay, never, and that is my final decision," bellowed Dougal.

Sorcha cursed and glared at her obstinate brother as he strode out of the great hall. Two long, contentious weeks had passed since she had been dragged back to Dunweare, and Dougal still refused to bend. She was beginning to feel afraid despite Aunt Neil's constant assurances that if Ruari had cared for her, he would still care for her no matter how long it took her to get back to him. Neil and Margaret had the added security of open declarations of love from their men. All Sorcha had was passion, a certain look, a few promising words and hints, and that blunt, un-adorned statement that she would be his wife if Dougal allowed her to stay. She could not even be certain if he would still hold to that now that he had had time to think about it.

"Dougal can be such an idiot," she grumbled and poured herself a tankard of cider.

"Aye," agreed a soft voice at her shoulder.

A soft cry of surprise escaped Sorcha, and she turned to frown at Euphemia who now stood at her side. The girl was too quiet, constantly startling people. Little Effie was also not quite so little anymore, her slim figure noticeably becoming more and more womanly each day. The petulance was gone from her pretty face as well.

"Ye will age me before my time," she said, smiling crookedly at the girl.

"Sorry, Cousin. I but agreed with ye that Dougal can be an idiot. If naught else, he should pause to think about what an excellent match ye and Ruari Kerr would make, for the Kerrs have money and fine, rich lands."

"The sort of mon few Hay women find."

"Exactly. The sort of mon who could truly help Dunweare shake off its lingering poverty."

"Weel, Dougal isnae going to change his mind." Sorcha scowled, drumming her fingers on the heavy wooden table. "I have rarely seen him this furious or this determined. 'Tis good that he has finally gained that sort of strength. I just wish he hadnae chosen this particular time to behave in this way. My head aches from banging it against his stubbornness for a fortnight." She smiled faintly when Euphemia giggled.

"Aunt Neil says she is glad that he is finally acting the laird, but she wishes he would have a wee turn of recklessness again. She says it might give ye something ye can use to change his mind."

"Aye, it might, but I fear our Dougal has finally decided to become a mon."

"'Twould appear so, but it matters not. That wouldnae solve this trouble anyway."

There was an odd tone to Euphemia's sweet voice, and Sorcha looked closely at the girl. There was a faint glitter in Effie's big blue eyes that she had begun to recognize. If the girl had not had a premonition, she had certainly had a strong feeling about something. Sorcha was almost afraid to ask. What would she do if Euphemia told her that there was no hope for her and Ruari?

"Have ye had a dream?" she asked, unable to hide her fear and reluctance.

"I dinnae have dreams or visions—at least, not yet. I just ken things. Something in my head and heart tells me how things will be or how they must be done."

"And ye have had one of these—er—messages?"

"I think so. I am still verra uncertain, ye understand, and I cannae explain what I feel so that someone might help me."

"Just tell me what the message was, then, and I will see if I can decide what it means."

"'Twas just a wee one. Ye must give the power back to Ruari."

"What power?" Sorcha asked.

Euphemia shrugged. "I dinnae ken. Whenever I think of ye, Neil, Margaret, and the Kerrs, that one sentence slips into my mind. Ye must give the power back to Ruari."

For nearly an hour they fretted over the words, but found no answers. Euphemia was still too young, and Sorcha decided she was too tired. As she gently sent Euphemia to help with the children, Sorcha silently cursed the fates. They kindly gave Euphemia a useful gift, only to make the warnings and messages they sent so obscure that they were almost impossible to understand. She finished her drink and decided she had best return to her own chores, welcoming the chance to stop brooding. As she strode out of the keep and went to weed the herb garden, she prayed that if she did not have some brilliant plan by the week's end, Ruari would.

* * *

"Ruari?" Malcolm called softly as he timidly entered the laird of Gartmhor's bedchamber.

For a brief moment Ruari stared at his cousin, wondering idly how the little man could be so calm and diligent when he may well have lost all chance to marry Neil Hay. He sat up in his chair. Slouching there by the slender window, staring morosely in the direction of Dunweare and trying to drink himself into a dull stupor was proving to be a trial. He decided he would welcome some diversion even if it was one of Malcolm's long explanations of some new way to put more money in his purse.

"Sit, Malcolm." He waved his cousin toward a seat on the other side of the small table he had set a decanter and tankards on. "Wine?"

"Oh, nay. It takes verra little to make me confused, and I need a clear head," Malcolm replied as he sat down and put some papers on the table. "M'lord, I believe I have found something that may end the disapproval for a marriage between Beatham and Margaret Hay."

"Malcolm, the only way for Beatham and Margaret to be wed now is for Margaret's brother to allow it. Ye do recall that Dougal vowed that no Hay would ever wed a Kerr?"

"Aye, I recall. How could I not recall it? It cost me verra dearly."

"Of course. Forgive my surliness. Howbeit, if ye ken that, why have ye come to me with this?"

"I hold out hope that my Neil or her niece, who is a verra clever lass, will think of a way to solve that problem. If naught else, 'tis their kinsmon who must be dealt with, and they ken the mon better than anyone else does. Nay, what I have discovered may ease the trouble that will come after Sir Dougal is convinced that he should ease his stance against us. What has been the only real objection to a marriage between Beatham and Margaret?"

"Neither of them possesses a farthing or a shearer's hovel to live in."

"Exactly. Ye can change that. Your Uncle Ivor left ye a peel tower less than a day's ride south of here. 'Tis small, with equally as small but good land, and the mon who tends it for you is aged and childless."

"And would probably welcome a rest and a lad to train to take his place," finished Ruari. "Aye, that will do perfectly, Malcolm. 'Tisnae much, but 'tis gain enough for those two bairns and enough to please both families." His pleasure in the solution was brief, for he was quickly recalled to the insurmountable problem that had to be solved before Malcolm's efforts could help the young lovers. "Let us hope ye can present them with this bounty before they are too old to care."

"I will, Cousin."

Ruari wished he could share his cousin's optimism, but he found it hard. Even the morose Beatham had more hope for the future than he did. Both men seemed to think Neil or Sorcha would devise some plan that would solve their problem. Even though he heartily agreed with their opinion that Sorcha was clever, Ruari could not believe that she could think of an answer when he could not. He had thought about nothing else in the long, lonely fortnight since Sorcha had been taken away, yet did not have even the beginning of a plan.

He stared at the tankard in his hand. He knew there were no answers in the heady wine, but it did help to ease the pain of loss. It also helped him to sleep without being tormented by memories that left him aching. He knew that a great deal of his pain was caused by the knowledge that it was self-inflicted, that his own pride and arrogance had led to his loss. And Malcolm's, he thought, and smiled faintly at his cousin.

"I am sorry, Malcolm. Ye could be with Neil now if not for me," Ruari said.

"Oh, I could be with my Neil now despite ye, but she said she needed to be at Dunweare with her nieces. They need her help now. More than I need her."

"She could be trapped at Dunweare for a verra long time."

"Nay, she, Margaret, and Sorcha will return soon."

"I pray ye are right, Cousin." Ruari looked at the wine he held and thought of how often he was reaching for it now. "Aye, I dearly hope ye are right."

"I have it," Sorcha cried as she burst into her Aunt Neil's bedchamber, startling her aunt and Margaret. "I am glad ye are here, Margaret. This concerns ye as weel."

Sorcha could barely contain her happiness. She sat on the bed beside Margaret, glancing briefly at the cloth the two women had spread out between them on the bed, clearly trying to plan Margaret's new gown. At any other time, she would be interested and offer to help, but she had more important matters on her mind. In the midst of clearing weeds from the herb garden she had suddenly understood Euphemia's message, understood it clearly and begun to form a plan. She had not even paused to clean the dirt from her hands and gown as she had raced to find Neil.

"Exactly what do ye have?" asked Neil, frowning as she looked Sorcha over carefully. "Except a great deal of muck which ye are getting on my bed."

"Euphemia has had a message," she explained, ignoring her aunt's complaint.

"She has told ye how we can get back to Gartmhor and our men?" asked Margaret.

"Weel, nay. Euphemia doesnae have visions," Sorcha said. "I have begun to call them messages and warnings. They can require some thought to ken what is really being said."

"So what did our little Effie say?" asked Neil, callously pushing aside the soft blue material as she sat down more comfortably on the bed.

"She told me that I must put the power back in Ruari's hands," Sorcha replied, not surprised when the other two women frowned in confusion.

"Curse it, what does that mean?"

"I found it most confusing at first so I went to work in the herb garden. 'Twas easy to see that it was one of her more intricate messages. For a while I thought it was beyond my reach, but suddenly I could see it all so clearly. 'Tis so simple."

"Ye must give the power back to Ruari," Neil muttered then shook her head. "I cannae see it. What power can ye give the mon? He has a lot now."

"Ruari has a lot of power at Gartmhor. That isnae the power Euphemia's message referred to. We have to give Ruari back the power he lost that day he killed Sir Simon Treacher. Until the moment when Dougal rode to Ruari's rescue, the two of them could deal as equals. When Dougal saved Ruari and his men from certain death, he took that away. Dougal bound Ruari in a debt of blood so tightly that the mon can do nothing. He is now powerless."

"I ken that everyone keeps saying that, but I dinnae really understand," said Margaret. "'Twas only right that Dougal save Ruari and his men. Why should we all suffer for Dougal doing as he should? How can there be such a heavy debt when Dougal couldnae act in any other way?"

"True. 'Twould seem that it should be a favor that needs no repayment," agreed Sorcha. "Howbeit, confusing as they may be to us, men of battle have rules and customs they must follow. Dougal saved Ruari's life and the lives of his men. Aye, he could do nothing else, but 'tis still a debt. So, when Dougal says that no Hay will wed a Kerr, Ruari is bound by this blood debt to bow to that wish. To do otherwise would be to stain his honor so deeply there would be no washing it clean again. That would lead to the loss of a great deal more— power, his place in court, mayhap even his wealth. He has to do nothing, absolutely nothing, to bring us back to Gartmhor."

"So how can we get back?"

"We have to take the first step. We have to do something that Ruari must act upon or risk looking a complete fool. A Hay has to be the one to break the bond first."

"And how do ye plan to do that?" Neil asked.

"We are going to kidnap a Kerr," Sorcha said and smiled at the shock on the two women's faces.

"This is your idea of simple?"

"Aye. Cannae ye see it? We would begin the game all o'er again. If we take a Kerr for ransom then we all return to where we started."

"Nay, then we begin that nonsense again. Ruari will have to pay a ransom—"

"Nay, he willnae, for we will allow ourselves to be caught."

Sorcha did not appreciate the way Neil was looking at her, as if she had gone mad. Poor Margaret just looked confused. It had all seemed so simple to her. It was the perfect way to give the power back to Ruari.

They would grab the first Kerr they could, be captured while committing the crime, and then Dougal would be forced to deal with Ruari again.

"Ye are utterly mad," muttered Neil. "Mad as it is, however, it could weel work."

"As I see it, the verra worst that can happen is that we will fail, Dougal will discover our plans, and he will be furious with us."

"He is already furious with us for pestering him about changing his mind," said Margaret.

"Exactly," agreed Sorcha. "So the worst that can happen is that nothing changes."

"But how do we get hold of a Kerr?" asked Neil.

"That is the one weakness in my plan," Sorcha admitted.

"Only one?"

Sorcha ignored that. "All I can think of is that we must lurk about Gartmhor until one rides by."

She waited patiently while Neil laughed. It was a fairly large weakness in her plan, so she could understand her aunt's amusement. It was the only plan anyone had devised in a fortnight of hard, continuous plotting, so despite its flimsiness, she felt sure that Neil would agree to it.

"'Tis one of the worst plans I have ever heard," Neil said, her voice hoarse and unsteady from laughter. "Howbeit, ye are quite correct about one thing. If we fail all we need to suffer is Dougal being even more furious with us than he is now. I am certainly willing to risk that."

"Because ye ken that, if I succeed, I will have indeed put the power back into Ruari's hands."

"Aye. We will need more than the three of us, however."

"I ken it. I thought ye might choose a few of the older men besides Robert."

"Nay, ye cannae take Robert. Ye cannae take any of the older men who were here to pledge themselves to your father and then carry that pledge to Dougal when he became the laird. For all they may wish to help you and feel that Dougal is being unreasonable, ye would be forcing them to break an oath they have abided by for most of their lives. I will find a few of the younger men, ones who havenae become knights or are still young enough to be forgiven or to have it considered an error in judgment. All I ask is that ye give Dougal one more chance."

Sorcha argued that request for a quite a while, but finally gave in to her aunt's desire. They needed a little time to gather their small group of kidnappers anyway. She had to reach deep within herself for the patience, however. No matter what approach or argument had been used, Dougal would not be swayed, and now that she had a plan, she wanted to act upon it. In her opinion, trying to talk to Dougal again was simply a waste of precious time.

Her teeth so tightly clenched that her jaw hurt, Sorcha scowled at her brother. She had come to the great hall to break her fast with him, only to find him in a particularly foul mood. Yesterday afternoon Neil had adamantly insisted that she talk to Dougal one more time, yet she noticed that her aunt and Margaret were nowhere to be seen. She had been left completely alone to try to talk some sense into an already ill-tempered Dougal.

"Dougal, we need to have a talk," she said, not surprised when he hissed a curse and glared at her.

"Ye have done nothing but talk since ye were brought back to Dunweare."

"Aye, and ye havenae even tried to listen. I dinnae think I have been able to complete more than one full sentence ere ye start bellowing and then leave."

To her astonishment, he said nothing, just stared at her for several minutes with a look of concentration on his face. Some of the anger eased out of his expression. He looked ready to listen to her, but she did not let her hopes rise too high. Listening to her did not mean he would agree with her.

"I ken what ye are going to say," he finally argued in his defense.

"Aye, there is a good chance ye do, yet that doesnae mean ye shouldnae do me the courtesy of listening to it anyway," she said.

"Weel, then, say it and be done with it."

"If that is how ye mean to act, then I need not pretty the words up. It is wrong of you to keep me, Neil, and Margaret from the men we love and who want us."

"'Tis my right as your laird to decide who ye can and cannae marry."

"The Hays havenae been that strict since long before our father's father's time."

"They havenae had the good reasons I do to be that strict. The Hays arenae going to be connected by blood and marriage to the Kerrs."

"Not even if such a connection is what your own sister, aunt, and cousin all want, more than anything they have ever wanted before?"

"Nay. Ye are all still verra young. Ye will soon cure yourselves of this love ye claim to feel. Ruari Kerr has humiliated the Hays. I cannae act as if that means nothing to us."

She took a deep breath and decided to try one of the best arguments they had, one they had not yet been able to use to its fullest potential, for Dougal had refused to listen. It was clear that talking about the love she had for Ruari was not going to move him. Dougal had never been in love. He simply could not understand what it felt like as was indicated by his foolish talk of curing oneself of it as if it was some irritating sore one could spread a little salve on.

"There will never be a better opportunity for the Hays to gain through a marriage. We are poor and dowerless as well as landless. Tying our clan to the Kerrs will gain us a lot of what our forefathers lost. Through the Kerrs the Hays could gain a better position at court, and certainly we could improve our fortunes. Do ye really want Dunweare to keep filling up with women who cannae find husbands because they lack any dowry or with widows left too poor to live on their own?" She could tell by the sudden upward twitch of one of his eyebrows that that had caught his interest. "If naught else, a connection to the Kerrs will offer all these females cluttering up Dunweare a wider field of men to pluck a husband out of."

"Oh, ye are good, Sister, I will grant ye that," he murmured as he shoved his empty trencher aside. "Ye ken exactly what to say to catch my interest. Weel, it doesnae matter. Do ye think me too stupid to ken that in lands, power, and coin the Kerrs would make a perfect match for any of the women in my household? I have thought of that, and the gains dinnae outweigh what is lost by bowing to a mon who has made a fool of me and given the Hays of Dunweare a grave insult when he brazenly took ye from the fair."

"Weel, ye are a fool," she snapped, unable to constrain her temper. "Ye didnae need Ruari Kerr to show anyone that."

"Ye sorely try my temper, woman," he yelled as he leapt to his feet. "I will hear no more of the Kerrs in this household. The next person to even whisper that name will pay dearly for it."

She cursed as he strode out of the room. He had listened to her, but, as she had suspected, he had no intention of letting anything she said change his mind. It had been a complete waste of time as well as emotionally draining. She did not really like to be at such odds with her brother. In the past, for all his weaknesses, they had been close. Now she felt as if a great wall had been erected between them. They could not even share a meal without rancor. Despite that, she knew she would do her best to get back to Ruari. She could only pray that the reunion with the man she loved would not cost her the love of her brother.

"I am not one who likes to say I told ye so," began Sorcha when she met with Neil in her bedchamber a few hours later.

"But ye will anyway," said Neil as she sat down on Sorcha's bed, Margaret sitting beside her. "I wasnae verra hopeful myself, but I felt it our duty to give the lad one more chance. Now I can go against his wishes without much guilt, for he has shown that he will not bend even enough to consider the feelings of three women in his family. Did the fool really say we can cure ourselves of this love?"

Sorcha grimaced and nodded. "I cannae really fault him too much for that idiocy, for he has never been in love. How can he realize or even begin to understand what it means or how we feel?"

"Aye, and he is a mon. They arenae the wisest creatures

when it comes to matters of the heart. Weel, he will soon learn just how serious we are, although I am surprised that the melancholy and copious tears havenae made him see sense."

"He probably thinks it is just some female malady," muttered Margaret.

"We havenae raised that laddie right," said Neil and exchanged a quick grin with Sorcha.

"Did ye gather a few men to go with us?" Sorcha asked, eager to get on with enacting her plan, for the more she considered it, the more she felt sure it was the perfect solution to their problems.

"Iain and a few of the younger men. They see it as an adventure and are young enough to still be a little romantic. We really only need them for added protection on the journey to Gartmhor and mayhap to help us subdue whatever Kerr we may be able to grab. Iain feels it is a mad plan with more holes than a beggar's shirt, but oddly enough, I think he found that made it all the more tempting."

"And they are fairly sure that they dinnae face any real danger."

"Aye, that too. 'Tis a game, and they are eager enough to play it. Curious to see what results, too."

"So, when do we ride for Gartmhor?"

"We will try to slip out tonight. Iain and three of the lads will claim they are going on a short hunt later this afternoon. Then ye, Margaret, I, and the other three lads will ride out about an hour later."

"And what are we supposed to be doing?" asked Margaret.

"Searching for herbs to replenish the medicinal supplies," replied Neil. "There are a few which are best collected in the afternoon, and few of the men will ken what to ask or if we tell the truth."

"And once we are away from Dunweare we meet with the others and ride for Gartmhor," finished Sorcha.

"When it grows dark and we dinnae return, they will worry about us," said Margaret. "That seems unkind."

"What Dougal is doing to us is unkind."

"And Dougal has the wit to guess what we are up to," Neil said, interrupting what could easily become an argument between the soft-hearted Margaret and the infuriated Sorcha. "As soon as he realizes exactly who is missing he will ken that we are trying to get to Gartmhor. If he doesnae, Robert will. I wouldnae be surprised if that mon already kens what we are planning."

"Iain wouldnae tell him," said Sorcha.

"Nay," agreed Neil. "He doesnae have to."

"True. Robert has always had a keen nose for whatever trouble a Hay is getting into. He wouldnae stop us, though, would he?"

"Nay. The mon thinks Dougal is behaving like a stubborn fool. He doesnae agree at all with the stance Dougal has taken although he has admitted to admiring the way the lad has stood his ground. 'Tis not something Dougal has done often."

"True. I will admit to a verra rare moment of being proud. I just wish he had chosen something else to develop his backbone on. 'Tis just like Dougal to finally be what everyone has wanted him to be, but at the wrong time and over the wrong thing." She laughed softly with Neil and Margaret. "The only thing I worry about," she added in a softer, more serious tone, "is that I may weel anger him beyond redemption. I should hate to see such a rift open up between us."

Neil caught her hand up in hers and gave it a gentle,

comforting squeeze. "That willnae happen, lass. Dougal's blood can run hot, but he isnae one to cast aside his own sister simply because she doesnae do what he wants her to."

"I hope ye are right because, although I fear such a thing happening, I cannae turn back."

"None of us can, dearling. Now, we had best go and collect what we may need for the journey to Gartmhor. It cannae be much and must be carefully hidden in the guise of tools needed to hunt medicinal plants."

Sorcha nodded, and, as soon as Margaret and Neil left, she began to pack a small bag. It was not going to be a pleasant journey, for only the most vital things could be taken. If they rode out with too much on their saddles they would immediately raise suspicion and might not even get through the gates. Dougal was always alert for something suspicious, always worried that they might try to run back to Gartmhor. Although he had not kept them all locked in their rooms or confined within the walls, he did watch them closely. Whatever they took had to look like far too little to make a long journey with. As she set her bag aside, Sorcha decided she would go and be sure that Margaret really understood what was meant by packing lightly.

Sorcha saw Iain and his friends waiting a few yards away and glanced behind her. Dunweare was almost completely out of sight. They had gotten away, and the chances were good that they had all of the few hours of daylight remaining to travel before anyone at Dunweare became suspicious. That would be enough to give them a good lead over Dougal when he rode out in pursuit of them as she fully expected him to do.

"This has begun successfully," she said to her aunt as Neil rode up beside her.

"This was the easiest part," Neil said.

"Ye arenae going to be the voice of doom at every turning, are ye?"

"Nay, just the voice of caution. One doesnae want to become too confident of success for then one becomes careless."

"I intend to be verra careful. This is the most important hunt I have e'er been on. I also ken that, if this fails, it will become more and more difficult to get away from Dunweare. Dougal may just lock us all in the dungeons as he has threatened several times during the past fortnight."

"If he thinks that will stop us or silence us, he is verra much mistaken."

"Aye," agreed Iain as he rode up on the other side of Sorcha and watched the careful way the women rode. "I shouldnae worry about noise as ye ride. If this plan works out to be as mad as it sounds, Dougal will be hearing the laughter from the walls of Gartmhor all the way into the garderobes at Dunweare."

Chapter Twenty-Two

"Mayhap this isnae the wisest plan I have ever had," Sorcha muttered as she peered through the trees toward the high, thick, and very imposing walls of Gartmhor.

Neil patted her niece's slim back. "Margaret and I find it most clever. Dinnae we, Margaret?" she asked her other niece who crouched on her left side.

"Aye, verra clever," agreed Margaret. "Although I am not certain how it works."

"I am not so certain I do either. And, 'twas foolish to ask ye two if ye like it. Margaret wants Beatham, and ye want Malcolm, dinnae ye, Aunt Neil?" Sorcha frowned as she thought of the bone-thin, timid Malcolm and looked at her aunt. "Are ye sure ye want that mon?"

"I ken that he is a mere wisp of a mon from his thin brown hair to his bony wee feet, but he does have one verra big thing in his favor," Neil replied.

"And what is that?"

"The mon fairly worships the ground I flatten beneath me big feet." Neil grinned when Margaret and Sorcha giggled, but then she grew serious. "Lass, I have loved a mon with a face and form any woman would yearn for, and I discovered what an empty shell such a bonnie mon can be. Aye, wee Malcolm might have eyes that are somewhat beady and lacking in color, but when ye look in them ye see life and honesty. True, he trembles o'er the sight of his own shadow, but I have no doubt at all that he would give his life to save mine. And, he may not speak words that can set a lass's heart to fluttering or have a deep rich voice that warms a woman's blood, but when that wee mon stutters out a bit of flattery or a pledge, I ken without one single doubt that 'tis heartfelt. He will love me, lasses. He will honor me, he will never leave me, and, tiny as he is, he will give me the bairns I ache for."

"I think that is an accolade any mon would be honored to accept."

"And, of course, he does sorely need someone to fight for him." She exchanged a grin with Sorcha. "So what do we do now, lass?"

"I hope we hurry and do something," muttered Iain as he inched up next to Sorcha. "My father is certain to throttle me for this, and I would like to have accomplished something ere I meet my fate."

Sorcha laughed softly and clapped the youth on the back. "Your father kens exactly where we are and what we are doing. I would wager Bansith on it."

"Did ye tell him?"

"Nay, no one has to tell Robert what games we Hays are playing. He always seems to ken exactly what we are about. The moment he discovers that we are missing, and who in particular is gone, he will ken where we are. He would have helped us, I am certain of it, except that he cannae be seen to go against Dougal's wishes."

"All that doesnae mean that he willnae be feeling strongly inclined to have a sharp word or two with me." Iain frowned toward Gartmhor. "So, what do we do now?"

"We wait until we see someone we can capture," Sorcha answered.

"That is all?"

"Weel, we also pray that someone meanders by ere Dougal can arrive to drag us all back to Dunweare." She shrugged. "Aye, 'tis a verra weak plan. Strong in its reasoning, but verra risky to carry out. If we fail to capture anyone this time, we can only pray that we will have another opportunity and mayhap another until we can grasp hold of a Kerr."

"And then be caught," said Iain, cursing softly and shaking his head. "I must have been mad to agree to this." He quickly held up his hand to halt the protest Sorcha began to make. "I but mutter complaints. They shouldnae be heeded. I just wish this plan could have been more carefully thought out."

"There isnae much else we can do, I fear. We have no way of kenning when or where a Kerr will be, so that we may capture him or her." She sighed and scowled at the huge iron-studded gates of Gartmhor. "I couldnae get a Kerr to help me either. To save his honor Ruari must *not* do anything or be suspected of having a hand in this. The only way to end the vow he made to Dougal is for me, or any Hay, to return the advantage to Ruari."

"Here, look there," Neil cried softly, poking Sorcha in the arm to get her attention. "Someone prepares to ride out."

"Aye, I see him." Sorcha tensed. "They are trying to stop him," she muttered as she watched several men struggle to turn the horseman back.

"'Tis Beatham," said Margaret, moving forward so abruptly that Neil grabbed her by the arm and yanked her back. "Oh, sorry. I forgot that we must remain hidden."

"Do try to recall that we dinnae wish to be discovered

until *after* we have a prisoner," said Sorcha. "Curse it. He is riding out and coming this way, but he has two armed men with him."

"We couldnae expect such a wealthy clan to allow its chieftain's family to wander about unguarded." Neil shrugged. "Nay, especially not when we have only recently reminded them of the perils of doing so."

Sorcha whispered a curse and tried to think of a way to capture Beatham without causing anyone to get hurt. The men with Beatham looked ready and able to fend off any attack. If they perceived any threat, they would immediately meet it with force. She could not risk any of her companions on the slim chance that Beatham's guards would recognize him before they tried to kill him.

Him, she mused, lingering over the word. Ruari's men would certainly see any man as a threat, but they would hesitate to strike at a woman too quickly. She slowly turned and looked at Margaret. Beatham had a proven skill at recognizing his beloved from quite a distance away. No matter how hard she thought about it, she could see no way that she would be putting Margaret in any real danger.

"I think I have an idea," she murmured.

Neil followed her look and slowly smiled. "Aye, and I think it might work."

"Why are ye staring at me?" Margaret asked warily.

"Ye are going to help us capture Beatham," Sorcha replied.

"Me? What do ye expect me to do? Charge him and knock him off his horse?"

"Being in love has made her quite impudent," drawled Neil.

Ignoring her aunt, Sorcha explained, "Margaret, we all ken that Beatham has verra keen eyes when 'tis ye he is looking at. Ye are a fairly swift runner so, I thought, why dinnae ye run ahead of the men—"

"They are on horseback!"

"Aye, but they arenae going verra fast. Now, I want ye to stay within the cover of the trees. 'Twill do us no good if they see ye ere we want them to. Once ye are a goodly distance in front of them ye are to dash out and allow yourself to be seen."

"But then I will be captured."

"Nay, for we shall all be close at hand, near enough to help yet not so near that they see us when and if they see you. Now, ye can use your own judgment when ye finally step out and let them see you. Ye can wave or swoon or whatever pleases ye. 'Tis here that I am depending on something else ye and Beatham seem much inclined to do, and that is how, when ye see each other, ye call each other's name and run into each other's arms."

Margaret frowned. "There is no need to make it sound foolish. We are in love."

"I dinnae mean to sound as if I belittle that, I dinnae. Aye, and now it could prove verra useful."

"Aye," agreed Neil. "Once Beatham sees you, he will call to you and try to reach you. That will hold the attention of his two guards and allow us to encircle them."

"Now, Margaret, there is one difficult thing ye must do," continued Sorcha. "If Beatham reaches you ere we can reach him and his men, ye are to pull your sword and take him captive."

"Pull my sword on Beatham?" Margaret whispered in shock.

"I am not asking ye to take his head from his shoulders, just to hold your sword on him and make his guards hesitate to act. Aye, they may doubt that ye are any threat, but they willnae dare to act too quickly if ye are waving a sword about. Do ye understand all of this?"

"I think so. I am to run ahead of them then get in front of them so that they are watching me and the rest of ye can grab them."

"Exactly. Go on then. Remember, stay out of sight until ye choose to show yourself and try to keep your wits about you when ye finally see Beatham. Just keep reminding yourself that, after this, there is a better chance of making the marriage ye want whilst there is none now." Margaret nodded and Sorcha briefly squeezed her arm in a gesture of good luck. "Go on then. Run your fastest."

As soon as Margaret left, Sorcha turned to the others. "Now, we willnae have verra much time after she shows herself, so keep alert. And ye are to do your best to let one or both of Beatham's guards escape. After all, this plan fails if no one kens we have kidnapped Beatham or if Dougal finds us first."

Everyone nodded, and she signaled them to move forward. She was impressed by the silent way they moved. At times she was tempted to glance back to be sure her companions were still with her, but she kept her gaze fixed upon Beatham and the trail she had to carefully wind her way along.

The moment Margaret staggered out into the open, Sorcha and her group hurried closer. As predicted, Beatham recognized Margaret almost immediately. He cried out her name and started toward her. The full attention of his guards was then on trying to stop him from racing headlong into a trap. They never saw the trap being closed behind them.

As they raced toward the three Kerr men, Sorcha realized that her little group was too successful, their surprise too complete. If one of Beatham's guards did not act soon, all three men would be captured, and no one would be able to warn the people of Gartmhor. When she was just a few steps too far away to stop the older, larger Kerr man from fleeing, she screamed out the Hay battle cry.

The older man cursed aloud in surprise. With but a few quick glances toward Beatham and the other guard, and then the advancing Hays, he made the judgment she hoped he would. He turned his horse and galloped back toward Gartmhor. As they closed in on Beatham, the young man guarding him prepared to defend him then frowned in confusion as he recognized Sorcha and Neil. His battle stance immediately grew lax.

"What goes on here?" demanded Beatham as Neil took his and the guard's weapons. "Why are ye disarming me and Artur? We arenae your enemies."

"Be at ease, dearling," Margaret said as she smoothed her hand down Beatham's arm. "Sorcha has devised a plan that may help us be together."

"Ye arenae going to kidnap me again, are ye?" Beatham asked Sorcha.

"Only for a wee while," Sorcha replied as she looked toward Gartmhor and watched the guard disappear into the castle. "How long does it take your cousin Ruari to mount and ride when an alarm has been raised?"

"Only a few moments." Beatham frowned even as he slipped his arm around Margaret's shoulders and held her close. "At times he and his men have not e'en taken a moment to saddle their mounts."

"Good. 'Tis always wise to be at the ready. Iain, will ye and Gordon fetch our mounts, please? We will amble this way until ye can catch up with us," she said as she pointed southward.

"Ye dinnae have your horses with ye?" asked Beatham as Iain and Gordon strolled away. "How could ye expect to escape with me and Artur?" His eyes slowly widened as an expression of revelation spread over his face. "Ye dinnae want to escape."

"Beatham, my dear boy, why would we go to the great trouble of kidnapping ye if we then allowed ourselves to be caught in the deed?" She winked at her Aunt Neil when a look of utter confusion returned to the youth's handsome face. "Now, we shall walk a wee bit faster. We wouldnae wish to appear to be too easy prey." She smiled at Beatham when he cursed softly, gently begged Margaret's pardon, and dragged his fingers through his hair.

"M'lord, there is trouble!"

Ruari looked up from the papers Malcolm had spread out before him as George, one of his more skilled men-at-arms, burst into the great hall. The man's agitation indicated that something of grave importance had happened. Although he would never wish anyone any harm, Ruari found the news almost welcome. He desperately needed the diversion of a battle or a chase to turn his mind from constant thoughts of Sorcha, if only for a brief time.

"Are the English raiding our lands again?' he demanded.

"Nay, 'tis the Hays," George replied and, filling a tankard with ale, started to drink, only to have Ruari snatch the heady drink out of his hands.

"Did ye say that there are Hays upon Gartmhor lands?" Ruari struggled to control his rising hopes, but his mind quickly became crowded with possibilities.

"Aye, Ladies Sorcha, Margaret, and Neil. They had

but a handful of men with them." George shook his head. "Margaret stumbled out in front of us, and of course Beatham raced blindly toward her."

"Of course," murmured Ruari, beginning to get an idea of Sorcha's plan, yet not daring to believe that she could have found the solution to their problem. "They used her as bait."

"That they did, and she proved a powerful lure for the lad. Artur and I didnae ken what was about and tried to stop the lad. Just as we drew close enough to turn him from his headlong charge toward the lass, the others rushed up behind us." He frowned and rubbed his hand over his beard-roughened chin. "'Tis most strange, but Artur and I didnae see the others and probably would-nae have if the wee Lady Sorcha hadnae suddenly screamed the Hay war cry."

"Which allowed ye to avoid being captured, and thus ye could ride here to tell me all that has happened."

George nodded then took a long drink of ale when a grinning Ruari released his hold upon the tankard. A moment later, George cursed and slammed the nearly empty tankard down on the long table. "'Twas no trap or abduction, but some game the lasses are playing with us?"

"There is a verra good chance of that, although I may weel be letting high hopes cloud my good judgment." Ruari clapped his stocky man-at-arms on the back. "Come, we will climb upon the walls, and ye can show me where this abduction took place."

As he and George ascended to the walls of Gartmhor, Ruari noticed that most of the men on guard there were looking south. There was no tense air of alertness or danger, simply confusion and curiosity. When Ruari looked in the same direction, he understood what had his men talking amongst themselves and neglecting their duties to some extent. Beatham's and Artur's kidnappers were meandering along the open fields as if they were simple travelers admiring the countryside and enjoying a rare sunny day. When their horses were brought to them, they mounted as if they had no pressing need to go anywhere. Ruari started to laugh when it became obvious that several members of the party kept looking back toward Gartmhor.

"They should have been miles away by now," murmured George.

"Aye," agreed Rosse as he stepped up on the other side of Ruari and looked toward the Hays. "If they dawdle much longer they may as weel run this way."

"'Tis probably all they willnae do," said Ruari.

"Are we going to give chase?"

"Let us stand firm for a wee while. I am interested in what they will do if they think we arenae going to come and retrieve Beatham."

"Those fools arenae doing anything," complained Neil, glaring toward Gartmhor as she mounted her horse.

"They must do something," protested Sorcha as she, too, mounted her little pony Bansith. "They ken that we have Beatham and they cannae wish to play this game out until money must change hands."

"Nay, Ruari would certainly not allow that, and my wee Malcolm would grow quite melancholy if he was forced to make note of another large deficit." She turned her mount to face Gartmhor. "Mayhap they but need someone to spit in their eyes."

"Ye arenae going over there, are ye?" Sorcha asked, but

Neil had already spurred her mount toward Gartmhor. "Now Ruari will truly think that the Hays are all mad."

"Weel, this wasnae going to be a true kidnapping anyway," said Iain as he edged his horse up next to hers. "And I can understand her annoyance. If we have gone to all this trouble to snatch up a Kerr and then be captured ourselves, Sir Kerr could at least have the courtesy to follow our rules." He grinned when Sorcha began to laugh.

"Oh, aye, Ruari will surely claim this as proof that we have all lost our wits."

"'Tis my Neil," cried Malcolm.

Ruari turned to see his cleric on the high walls of Gartmhor and found that almost as startling as Neil's rapid approach. Everyone knew that Malcolm was terrified of even the smallest of heights. The man was as white as the finest linen, and he trembled visibly as he edged nearer. It could well develop that loving Neil Hay finally gave Malcolm some of the backbone he had always lacked. Ruari shook his head and turned back to watching Neil just in time to see her rein in at the base of the walls just below him.

"Malcolm," she yelled, lifting herself slightly off her saddle, "is that ye up there?"

"Aye, my beloved," Malcolm replied, swaying a little as he looked down at her.

"Weel, get off of there, ye fool, ere ye swoon and break your neck." She grinned up at him. "If your witless laird will move his puny legs and do as he ought, ye will be seeing me soon."

"I will be waiting in the bailey." Malcolm started

down the steps to the ground, and one of the men hurried over to lend him a hand.

"Ye have come to hurl insults at me, have ye, Neil?" Ruari asked, fighting the urge to laugh again.

"'Tis clear that ye need to be given a wee push," she replied. "Or do ye wish to give us more of your precious coin?"

"Oh, nay, nay. Dinnae play the game too earnestly, however, as we were all on a hunt yestereve, and our horses are weary." He laughed when she waved and rode back to the group from Dunweare.

"This is madness," muttered George as he and Rosse followed Ruari down the narrow steps to the bailey.

"Nay, 'tis quite clever," said Rosse, chuckling and shaking his head. "Ruari vowed to stay far away from Sorcha Hay. 'Twas a debt of blood. He couldnae break it. Howbeit, 'tis no longer binding now, for the Hays themselves have broken it. By taking Beatham and Artur, they have freed Ruari of his troublesome vow. No one would expect a man to sit idly by and allow his kinsmon to be stolen and ransomed."

"Now Dougal must come to me," Ruari said with a satisfaction he could not hide.

"Did ye accomplish anything?" Sorcha asked Neil when her aunt reined in at her side.

"Aye," Neil replied as she closely watched the heavy gates of Gartmhor and smiled when nearly a dozen men raced through them, riding straight for their little group. "I suppose we ought to make them chase us for a wee bit."

"'Twill make it less of a jest, although I am not sure that is possible any longer."

Sorcha spurred Bansith into a gallop knowing

full well that her little pony could not outrun even the smallest and oldest of Ruari's horses. The rest of her group, mounted on beasts that were a little swifter, quickly drew out ahead of her. She just smiled and shrugged when Ruari reached her side, leaned over, and grabbed the reins from her hands. As his men continued past them to gather up the rest of the Hays, he brushed a kiss across her mouth.

"Welcome home, lass," Ruari whispered.

"Dougal shall be verra angry," she said in a quiet voice.

"Oh, aye," agreed Ruari, "and I hope ye will forgive me if I find some enjoyment in all of this."

"Ye are forgiven, for I fear I will feel a little of that myself. Dougal has become nearly as stubborn as ye are." She winked at him.

Ruari laughed, swept her from her saddle, and set her in front of him. "Shall we wait for the others?" he asked in a husky voice as he enclosed her in his arms.

There was a glint in his eyes Sorcha recognized with ease, and her desire swiftly rose to meet it. She curled her arms around his waist and kissed his throat, savoring the soft murmur of pleasure that escaped him. "I believe they can find their own way back to Gartmhor. So, we dinnae have much time before Dougal arrives."

"Then we had best cease talking. I can think of far better things to do with my mouth."

"Oh, aye. So can I."

As he nudged his horse into a gallop, Sorcha prayed that Dougal had an unusual amount of difficulty guessing what she had done and in finding his way to Gartmhor.

Chapter Twenty-Three

Ruari stretched and smiled down at the woman he held in his arms. He had no idea what had happened to the others after Sorcha and he had raced back within the walls of Gartmhor and he did not care. Beatham and Margaret were undoubtedly staring into each other's eyes and murmuring nonsense at each other. He was not sure he wanted to think about what Neil and her little man were doing. Dougal would soon be at the gates of Gartmhor, and he would have to rouse himself to deal with that. For the moment he refused to think about what he faced or what anyone else was doing. He simply wished to savor the pleasure of having Sorcha back in his arms.

She raised herself up on her elbows and smiled at him. "I was a wee bit worried that ye wouldnae welcome me back, but I think ye have done a verra fine job of it, Sir Kerr."

"And I intend to welcome ye a few more times ere your troublesome brother comes pounding on my gates."

Sorcha grimaced. "I pray he isnae going to be too furious and unreasonable."

"Oh, he will be furious, but he isnae completely

without wits. He has to see how weel this solves the
whole problem. I wouldnae like it either if I were in his
boots, but he only suffers a small loss, and there is much
to gain if he concedes."

"What does he gain?"

"Ye will make a fine marriage."

"Oh, with whom?" she asked and laughed when he
scowled at her.

"I dinnae think I make such a poor choice of husband."

"Nay, although there were all those brides who fled
from ye as if ye were the devil himself come to drag
them down into hell."

He eyed her suspiciously. "Are ye about to confess to
having a hand in that?"

"Me?" she asked with an overdone innocence.

"Aye, ye."

Sorcha could tell from the glitter of amusement in his
eyes that she would suffer no penalties for her interference. It was probably time to confess to what she had
done. He was going to marry her, and although the
thought of how he had searched for a wife still nettled
her a little, she could see the amusing side of what had
happened.

"Oh, weel, I suppose one ought to start one's marriage with a clean soul. Aye, I sent them running
from ye."

"I was sure ye did, but I could ne'er figure out how."
He turned so that she was sprawled beneath him, but
the scowl he tried to give her quickly turned to a grin as
he saw the laughter in her lovely eyes. "What did ye do
to them?"

"Most anything I could think of." She laughed along
with him. "I mostly watched them to see if they were

nervous, for ye are an imposing mon and ye werenae in the sweetest of tempers at that time. Most were easily afrightened by your temper,"

"Oh-ho! So that is why ye were always stirring up my anger."

"Most of the time. There were times when ye had angered me, and I felt I must pay ye back in kind. There was only one lass who needed a bit more persuasion, and the reasons why arenae so flattering to you."

"Dinnae try to soothe my poor vanity. I had no illusions as to why most of those lasses were allowing themselves to be picked over like ripe fruit. I am a good match."

"True, although ye need not sound so proud of that. This one lass was verra eager to share in all that makes ye such a good match—especially your coin and your position in court. I needed to do a little extra to make her leave. Ivor gave me a hand with that one."

"My Uncle Ivor assisted you? He was never the helpful kind."

Sorcha briefly grinned and nodded, "I ken it, but he thought this would be fun. I am not sure what he did, but I could tell that he had thoroughly enjoyed himself. Weel, that lass may have coveted your purse and position, but she didnae wish to abide where there were ghosts."

He laughed and held her close, nuzzling her neck until she giggled. "I should make ye pay dearly for interfering in my life, but I can only thank ye for saving me from making a verra poor decision. Rosse tried to tell me I was wrong in what I thought and was trying to do, but I didnae wish to heed his opinion."

"Weel, ye had held to that plan for a verra long time. 'Tis not easy to see that something ye have set your mind to is not the wisest thing to do."

"And marrying ye is the wisest thing for me to do?" he said, smiling at her to assure her that he was teasing.

"Of course." She sighed and became serious for a moment. "I had decided even before I began the game in earnest that even if ye did not choose to marry me, I couldnae let ye marry those others. They were all so wrong for ye, and ye were not looking closely at the lass who came with the dowry and breeding."

He thought that over for a moment and finally nodded. "Nay. In truth, I forgot their faces the moment they rode away. That is how little they lingered in my mind."

"There. I saved ye from spending the rest of your life asking people who that woman at the head of the table is."

"Wretch."

She slid her hands down to his hips and winked at him. She knew there were a lot of questions she should ask, such as exactly why he wanted to marry her. It was easy to push them all aside. There was no promise that he would answer her questions in the way she wanted him to, and she wanted nothing to spoil the pleasure and passion of their reunion.

Sorcha also knew that she did not wish to chance Ruari answering in a way that would make her hesitate to marry him. She could ride along on her hopes and happiness for now and face the consequences of that blindness later. Even if he did not love her as she loved him, she was confident that he had some feelings for her. That would be enough. She could spend their years together continuing to try to gain his heart. The frightening thought that she might never succeed in that goal was pushed aside. It was even more frightening to think of the years ahead spent alone, Ruari forever out of her reach. It was better to have a little than nothing at all.

"Do ye realize that ye have never asked me to marry you? Ye just told Dougal and now just informed me," she said and smiled at his surprise.

"I am a fool. I had intended to ask ye properly when we returned from our ride, but the arrival of Simon Treacher and then of your brother rather spoiled my plans." He touched a soft, warm kiss to her mouth and asked solemnly, "Will ye marry me, Sorcha Hay?"

"Aye, Sir Kerr, I would be most honored to wed you."

She gave herself over to his fierce kiss. His response to her acceptance was hopeful. This was not to be a cold arrangement. Ruari truly wanted to marry her, penniless and landless though she was. He had seen his other choices and decided that he wanted to spend his days with her. She tried to convince herself that that was enough.

Dougal cursed and shifted in his saddle, wiping the dust from his brow with his sleeve. He acknowledged Robert when the man rode up beside him with a curt nod of his head. It had been a long, hard ride from Dunweare and now Gartmhor was in sight. They had failed to catch Sorcha and her little band of traitors. Dougal heartily cursed that failure, for he suffered all the ill effects of a harried journey but had gained nothing for the trouble.

"I cannae believe Sorcha would betray me like this," he muttered.

"The lass hasnae betrayed you," snapped Robert. "I grow weary of hearing ye speak of the lass and her companions as if they have just sold ye to the English or crept into your bedchambers and cut your throat so that they could take what little ye possess."

"Ye just say that because one of her companions is your son."

"Nay, I say it because ye condemn them for a heinous crime when the most they have done is disobey your orders."

"They are supposed to obey their laird."

"Aye, and they will, if ye give them reasonable commands." Robert shook his head and, unhooking his waterskin from the pommel of his saddle, had a long drink before offering it to a scowling Dougal. "Ye made it impossible for them to do anything else but disobey ye."

"Am I to expect everyone to obey or disobey as they see fit? 'Twill be naught but chaos at Dunweare."

"Ye made a decision without any regard to the feelings of three women in your care, women who have done verra weel by ye in the past. Remember who ransomed ye. They also spent two long weeks trying to talk to ye and let ye ken how they felt, but ye refused to heed them."

"I carefully explained why they couldnae marry a Kerr. They refused to heed me." Dougal scowled toward Gartmhor. "They chose their lovers over me."

"Ye forced them to it. I dinna ken what to say to ye, lad. Ye take this far too much to heart yet seem unable to understand the hearts of the women in your household. They love these Kerr men. They love ye. None of them wished to be forced to make a choice between ye or their lovers, but ye allowed them no compromise."

"There was no compromise to be found. To join my family to Ruari Kerr's after all he had done would make me look the fool. Worse than that, it makes me look the sort of mon who would swallow his pride and honor for the sake of making good marriages for his womenfolk."

"Ah, is that the burr in your braies, then?"

"Nay, not completely. I just dinnae understand why they

couldnae do as I ask. There are many men in Scotland. They could find other lovers."

Robert cursed and shook his head. "Ye need to fall in love, lad. 'Tis clear that there are a great many lessons in life ye have failed to learn. Aye, some women could shrug aside one lover and soon find another. Not these women. In truth, of all the Hay women I have kenned in my long time at Dunweare, I have kenned none who could be so easy in their affections."

Dougal frowned, handed Robert back his waterskin, and looked toward Gartmhor again. Robert was right about one thing; he did not understand love. He did not understand why his usually cheerful Aunt Neil and his sister had lost so much of their spirit. He certainly did not understand why Margaret had wept so often. The other women in his household had begun to look at him as if he were the worst sort of heartless beast. Standing firm on his decision had been an extremely tiring position to hold.

"Weel, we cannae sit here staring at the hulking lump of stone for the rest of what little remains of the day," Dougal grumbled. "Let us go and see what price that arrogant bastard Ruari Kerr will claim for the stupidity of my kinswomen."

Robert cursed softly, but quickly followed Dougal as the young laird rode toward the high walls of Gartmhor. "Just try to keep a rein on your temper, Dougal Hay. Ye cannae help matters if ye ride in there demanding things as if ye are the king of Scotland."

"All I intend to demand is that the bastard gives me back the women he has stolen from me—again."

Ruari brought Sorcha a full tankard of cider and sat on the edge of his huge bed. He watched her as she drank and wondered yet again how she had come to be the only woman he wanted. She was so different from all of the other ladies he had considered, yet she was definitely the one he desired and needed. She might never give him a son, she did not offer him a handsome dowry, and her home was full of the largest collection of strange people he had ever had the misfortune to know, yet he was content to marry her. He just wished she would give him more than an agreement to marry him.

Love, with all its turmoil, was what he wanted. He loved her and he desperately wanted her to love him back. He could not be completely satisfied with just her passion and whatever meager scraps of emotion she felt inclined to serve him. One way to discover exactly what she did feel was to ask her outright, but he found that he was a coward. He was not happy not knowing, but he dreaded hearing her say she did not love him, only cared for him and enjoyed his loving.

"Ye are staring at me verra hard," Sorcha murmured as she finished her drink and set the tankard on the table by the bed.

"I am but trying to make myself believe ye are really here," he replied.

"Climb into this bed, my fine knight, and ye will soon see that I am verra much here." She laughed when he scrambled in beside her. "Now, there is an eagerness any lass can appreciate. Howbeit, I was thinking that if we are to be wed, mayhap we should practice a touch of celibacy."

"After I have spent two long weeks without ye in my bed? I think not."

"Not even to make our wedding night a wee bit special?" She ran her feet up and down his calves, enjoying the feel of the hard mucles and light coating of hair beneath the soles of her feet.

"I plan to have our wedding but moments after we pry a blessing out of your obstinate brother, so our wedding night will be a little special. It will still sing with the greed of a long absence."

"If we keep feeding our greed at the pace we are now, we may be too exhausted to feed it some more on our wedding night."

He wrapped his arms around her, rolling so that she was lightly pinned beneath him, and kissed her. "'Twill take many a day for that to happen to me. Howbeit, if ye are not up to the challenge—"

She laughed as he cocked his left eyebrow in a silent gesture that dared her to accept the gauntlet he had just tossed down. Sorcha cupped his face in her hands and kissed him, slowly, deeply, and hungrily. The way his breathing increased revealed how she could stir his passion. It was a heady knowledge, but she now knew it could never serve as a replacement for the love she craved. For all of its delight and mind-clouding strength, she always felt a hint of sad unfulfillment when the passion faded. She feared that that hint of dissatisfaction would grow over the years, but had no idea of how she could dispel it without Ruari's love.

"Ruari," she murmured, stretching with pleasure beneath his stroking hands. "Ye do ken that I may ne'er be able to give you sons."

She wondered why she was about to list all that was wrong with selecting her as a wife. Something compelled her to reiterate everything that made her such a poor choice of wife. It was a moment before she realized that she wanted to hear Ruari say in a clear voice how he truly regarded each one of the reasons he had first refused to even consider her as a wife. She needed to be sure that he felt no hesitation and had no regrets.

He smoothed his hand over her forehead, brushing aside a few stray wisps of hair. "I willnae say that I dinnae want a son. Every mon wants a son. Howbeit, if God chooses to give us only daughters, I willnae grieve o'er it. There are a lot of Kerrs about. I have a veritable horde of male cousins. I hold no fear that my name will fade from the rolls."

"I have no money." Her voice shook faintly as he dampened the pulse point in her neck with gentle but heated kisses.

"I have enough, and ye have shown a true skill at gathering some coin when ye need it." He grinned at her when she gave a soft cry of false outrage, swatted him on the arm, and then laughed.

"I have no lands." She arched toward his mouth as he idly lathed the tips of her breasts.

"I dinnae need any more land. I have so much I can give Beatham a piece and never miss it."

"Ye are giving Beatham some land?" she asked, surprise briefly cutting through her own concerns and the haze of passion that was invading her mind.

Before Ruari could tell her what he had done to ease the marriage of Beatham and Margaret, a loud rapping sounded at the door. "Go away," he bellowed then grinned when Sorcha giggled.

"Weel, I am willing to leave ye be," Rosse said, his voice surprisingly clear despite the thickness of the door, as he yelled back, "but there is a laddie kicking at your gates who willnae be, especially if he kens what ye are doing in there."

"'Tis Dougal," cried Sorcha. "He is here much sooner than I thought he would be."

"What is his temper?" Ruari asked.

"I think he would chew his way through the gates if he could," replied Rosse.

"Oh, dear," murmured Sorcha. "I can see that the journey here didnae soothe his anger."

After admiring her small, firm breasts, the tips hard and inviting, Ruari sighed with regret that he could not immediately answer that invitation. "He willnae take you home this time, dearling." He patted her on the hip then got up and started to dress. "It may be a highly contentious meeting and persuading him to agree to our marriage and the others may take a long time, but he *will* agree."

"Ye sound so certain of that." She hopped out of bed and began to dress.

"I am. This time I hold ye secure within these walls. All he can do is bellow and demand that I give ye back. When he tires of that or his voice wanes, we will sit down and talk sense to the youth."

"What do I do about the lad?" asked Rosse.

"Disarm him and take him and one mon of his choosing into the great hall. I will meet with him there. If he starts chewing on the table, throw some cold water on him."

He could hear Rosse's laughter slowly fade as the man walked away. Ruari regretted the fact that Dougal Hay was so furious. It meant that it could take a long time to get the man to give his blessings to the marriages, and those blessings might well be given only grudgingly. That would hurt Sorcha, Ruari was certain of it. Praying that he could get what he wanted without causing any rift between the siblings, Ruari turned to Sorcha who was just finishing a light braiding of her hair.

"Ye dinnae have to face him if ye dinnae wish to," he said.

"Nay, I will go. I went against his wishes, disobeyed him, and I cannae hide away like a bairn." She shook her head as Ruari took her by the hand and started to lead her down to the great hall. "I dinnae want this trouble between us, but I cannae give him what he demands. That would leave me, Neil, and Margaret all terribly unhappy."

"I dinnae think I, Malcolm, or Beatham would be too pleased either. Dinnae fret, dearling. I dinnae ken your brother verra weel, but I can see that, although he is hot of temper and stubborn, he is not without wit. We but need to have him cool the fire of anger in his head and heart and he will see that these marriages can only benefit both clans, especially a marriage between ye and me."

As they entered the great hall, Sorcha had to fight the urge to bolt. Dougal was pacing back and forth in front of the head table, a scowling Robert keeping a close guard. The moment Dougal saw her, he started toward her only to be grabbed by the arm by Robert and brought to an abrupt halt. Sorcha realized that Robert had not been guarding Dougal, but guarding against Dougal doing anything foolish. As she and Ruari walked to the head table, Robert dragged Dougal to a seat placed opposite Ruari's big chair. Sorcha caught a glimpse of Margaret clinging to Beatham in a far corner of the great hall and Neil leaning against a wall with a nervous Malcolm by her side just before Ruari showed her to her seat at his side.

It was uncomfortable to sit under Dougal's glare as wine, cider, and a light repast were set out. That Ruari was acting as if he entertained willing, amiable guests was clearly irritating Dougal. Sorcha suspected that Ruari was goading Dougal in some subtle way. She did not think that was the way to gain some amiable settlement between the Hays and the Kerrs, but she could not really fault Ruari for doing it. Dougal had made life miserable for everyone for a fortnight and he did deserve some tormenting. After a few moments of Dougal being politely asked if he wished wine or cider, butter or honey, Sorcha noticed that her brother began to lose the tight rage that had driven him to race to Gartmhor. More and more he began to look simply impatient.

"Will ye cease this game?" Dougal snapped after taking a long swallow of wine. "I have been riding for nearly two days and I am in no temper to tolerate these pleasantries."

"Ye must have left only a few hours after we did," Sorcha said in surprise.

"Aye, I almost did as ye so clearly planned—waited until dark ere I wondered where ye had gone," Dougal replied. "'Twas just luck and a few remarks which were made—such as why ye were collecting herbs when we already had a large supply—which made me realize that ye might be riding here. I was still too late to catch ye for ye had taken all of the best horses. Howbeit, now ye can put your backside in the saddle again and ride back to Dunweare with me."

"Nay, I cannae. I willnae," she said, her tone of voice calm yet firm.

"Before this continues, there is something ye need to hear, Sir Dougal," Ruari said. "I didnae kidnap these women, and they didnae just ride into Gartmhor. They and their companions attempted to kidnap my cousin Beatham and Artur, one of my younger men-at-arms. We captured them as they attempted to flee with their prisoners."

Sorcha could not tell what Dougal was thinking for his expression of shock hid any other emotions he might be feeling. Robert was staring down at the table, his broad shoulders shaking faintly, and she was sure he was laughing. Ruari had the courtesy not to smile or be too cocksure, but there was a strong gleam of amusement in his eyes as he carefully watched Dougal and waited for the younger man's reaction.

"Ye tried to kidnap Beatham?" Dougal asked, his voice hoarse with shock as he looked at Sorcha. "What were ye thinking? That ye could just bring him home and keep him for Margaret?"

"Nay, of course not," replied Sorcha. "In truth, we hadnae planned on getting hold of Beatham. He just happened to be the first one to ride out of Gartmhor."

She sat quietly beneath his steady stare. When the expression on his face began to slowly change from shock to confusion and finally to understanding, she felt a sense of guilt and nervousness creep through her, making her shift in her seat. When Dougal chose to use it, he had an extremely keen wit. She just wished he had not chosen to use it now.

"'Twas all a plot," Dougal finally said, his tone one of amazement with a strong hint of annoyance. "Ye never truly meant to kidnap anyone; ye just intended to be *caught* kidnapping someone."

"Why should I wish to do that?" she asked, inwardly cursing the hint of timidity in her voice.

"Ye are far too clever for a lass," he muttered, shaking his head. "'Tis a blessing that ye havenae the heart to use that wit to practice deceit or dishonesty. Why would ye play such a game? What do ye gain by being caught in the act of committing such a crime?"

"Euphemia said that I must put the power back into Ruari's hands if I wished to solve the difficulties that have kept us at each other's throats for a fortnight." She took a deep breath to steady herself and continued, "Both of ye men were bound by your own pride." She ignored Ruari's and Dougal's mumbled protests. "Pride, anger, and the strict rules of honor. I dinnae think anyone gave much consideration to what I felt or wanted or Margaret or Neil. Aye, or even Beatham and Malcolm. Ruari sat at Gartmhor bound by the rules of honor and ye, my dear brother, let pride bind you in mind and heart and I decided I had had quite enough of it all. So, I devised this plan which allows Ruari to act without bruising his honor and ye to cease clinging to an unreasonable dictate which made no one happy."

"It also allows me to ask a ransom," said Ruari, smiling when Sorcha and Dougal stared at him.

"Actually, that wasnae part of my plan," Sorcha whispered, not sure what Ruari was doing.

"Weel, dearling, ye cannae be allowed to decide everything. Ye could become quite vain." Before Sorcha could reply to that impudence, Ruari looked at Dougal. "For their ransom I ask your blessings for the marriages of Margaret and Beatham, Neil and Malcolm, and, of course, Sorcha and myself."

For a moment Dougal stared from one couple to another, then he began to laugh. He held up his tankard as if he was about to make a toast and said, "That is no ransom, my friend, but a wondrous gift to me. Take them, make the lasses all Kerrs, and may God help ye."

Chapter Twenty-Four

"Are ye having second thoughts?"

Sorcha frowned at her brother as he stood next to her at the far end of Gartmhor's small stone chapel. She was not sure she had forgiven him for the insulting way he had handed her, Neil, and Margaret over to Ruari and his kinsmen with the words *"and may God help you."* The ensuing hilarity of all the men had only added to her irritation. For the week that had passed since that day, Dougal had been sweet, jovial, and unapologetic. She glanced toward the front of the church where Ruari stood by the altar talking quietly with the priest and wondered just how honestly she should answer Dougal's question.

"Nay, not truly," she finally replied, nervously smoothing down the skirts of her embroidered blue gown. "I want to marry Ruari."

"Ye love him?"

"Aye, I do."

"As he loves you?"

She shrugged. "He wants to marry me."

"Do ye mean to tell me that ye have put us all through

this turmoil and ye arnae even certain that the mon loves ye?"

A quick glance at his face revealed that he was more surprised than irritated, and she gave him a crooked smile. "They say that love isnae needed to make a strong union. And Ruari must feel something for me, or he wouldnae take me for his wife. He gains naught by doing so, and there is no one who would ever force him to do it."

"True." Dougal frowned and lightly rubbed his chin. "Do ye ken what I think ye ought to do?"

"Nay, but ye are going to tell me even if I say I dinnae wish to hear it, arenae ye?"

"Aye. Ye should tell him how ye feel."

"Dougal, I dinnae see why I should bare my soul when I have no assurances that Ruari will do the same. And, there are some men who dinnae wish to be burdened with such declarations of emotion."

"True. Some men find such sentiments an uneccessary thing, even an irritation. There are also men who would truly appreciate learning that the lass they have taken as their wife is in love with them, even if they dinnae feel such a depth of emotion themselves. And, of course, there is always the chance that he cannae speak of love until he is quite sure it is returned."

Sorcha stared at her brother for a full minute before whispering, "Oh."

"Aye, oh. Ye being such a clever lass, I am surprised ye didnae consider that possibility," Dougal drawled, then grinned when she glared at him. "Someone must go first and, fair or not, it will probably be ye who must do so."

She cursed softly for she knew he was right. "I must overcome my fears because he willnae overcome his, is that it?"

"Aye. Ye see, he can probably muddle along quite happily enough, even though ye never speak of love, but I think ye will find it most painful to go through the years and ne'er hear him speak of it."

"Mayhap, but I think I shall need some more time to gain the courage I need."

"Then consider this—if ye speak of love tonight and he doesnae return it, ye could say that ye were caught up in the strong emotion of the weddings. He will believe that and set the incident aside. 'Tis the only time ye could use such an excuse and have it work for ye."

Before she could discuss the matter any further, Ruari waved to her to join him before the priest at the altar. As Margaret and Neil stepped up beside Beatham and Malcolm, Sorcha gave Dougal a brief kiss upon the cheek, then walked up to take hold of Ruari's extended hand.

He smiled at her, and she smiled back, even though her heart was suddenly in her throat. What was she thinking of? Ruari looked every inch the strong, wealthy laird in his finely embroidered black jupon. What could she possibly offer a man like that?

As the six of them knelt before the priest who began the service, Sorcha peeked at her aunt and cousin. Both women looked radiant and calm, confident in the love of their men. As they repeated their vows they exchanged tender glances with their husbands. Sorcha fought back an attack of jealousy and centered her attention on the priest. The little chapel was filled to overflowing with Hays and Kerrs, and she wanted none of them to guess that she was feeling anything but that same confidence and joy.

* * *

The wedding feast in the great hall had been going on for several hours when Sorcha saw Beatham and Margaret sneak away. On the morrow the young couple would leave for their new home, the peel tower Ruari had so generously gifted them with. Neil and Malcolm would travel to Dunweare, staying there long enough to see if Malcolm could help Dunweare enrich itself, before returning to a small cottage on the edge of the village outside of Gartmhor. Sorcha realized that after tonight she would truly be alone with her new husband and she felt a small chill of fear. Since the day she had first seen Ruari, she had had one or more of her family always close at hand. Now she would be completely alone with Ruari, with a man she loved deeply but who might not love her at all. Sorcha knew that it was the closeness of her family that had kept her from dwelling too long on this issue. What would she do without their words of comfort or encouragement or their ability to distract her from feeling sorry for herself?

Neil approached her, and Sorcha knew that her aunt and her new husband would soon slip away as well. Her aunt easily brushed aside the occasional ribald remark tossed her way, grinning and responding with ones equally risqué. Sorcha hoped that she could be as sanguine when she and Ruari had to leave the great hall. She exchanged a brief kiss on the cheek with her aunt and smiled at the woman.

"I hope ye are happy, Aunt Neil," Sorcha said quietly.

"Aye," replied Neil. "Verra happy. Ye should try to be happy as weel," she added in a soft voice so that Ruari, who was laughing and joking with Rosse, could not overhear.

"I am verra happy, too," she answered in an equally

soft voice and frowned when Neil made a sharp noise of disbelief. "I am."

"Somewhere deep in your heart ye may be, but what I saw in your eyes as I walked over here was fear and sadness. Dinnae look so concerned, child. Ye hide it weel. Lass, ye have a good mon there."

"I ken it."

"And mayhap ye would ken a few more things if ye would just put aside pride and fear and talk to the mon. Mayhap the only reason ye dinnae ken how he feels about ye is because he waits to learn how ye feel about him."

"That is what Dougal said."

"It seems the lad may finally be using what wit he has beneath all that bonnie hair." Neil grinned when Sorcha giggled, but she quickly grew serious again. "Tell Ruari what lies in your heart, lass. Aye, there is a risk, but there can also be great reward."

Sorcha watched her aunt stride away. She had to smile when Neil grabbed Malcolm by the hand and dragged him from the great hall inspiring a lot of laughter and many a colorful remark. Malcolm beamed, something he had been doing a great deal of since the marriage ceremony, his pride in having Neil as his wife steeling him against all embarrassment.

"There goes a couple all of Scotland will wonder at," murmured Ruari as he took Sorcha's hand in his and brushed a kiss over her knuckles. "We should retire soon ourselves."

She nodded, flushing slightly beneath the heat of his gaze. Despite his protests and complaints, she had stayed out of his bed until they were married. She had not liked the idea of climbing out of his bed in the morning, getting married, and then climbing back into his bed. It would have made the marriage ceremony and their exchange of vows feel like little more than one extra duty they needed to perform. She wanted to have at least some hint of anticipation on her wedding night. She was pleased, however, that the fact that they had been lovers had made a bedding ceremony a pointless gesture and so she would not have to endure that.

"I dinnae suppose the guests will be sweet and courteous and allow us to slip away in peace and quiet," she said, inwardly grimacing at the thought of all the colorful remarks she would have to suffer.

"Nay, I dinnae suppose they will. Shall we run this gauntlet now?"

"Aye," she muttered as he stood up and tugged her to her feet causing everyone to look their way. "I dinnae suppose we could just run all the way to our bedchamber."

"Why not?"

Sorcha cried out in shock and surprise when Ruari picked her up and flung her over his shoulder. She could hear the roars of laughter from their kinsmen and guests as well as several bellowed crudities as he ran, but she was too concerned about the way she was bouncing around on his shoulder to care. He was halfway up the stairs to their room before she gathered the voice to complain and was able to pound her fists against his broad back a few times to get his attention. He only slowed his pace a little, however.

When he strode into their bedchamber and dropped her onto the bed, she could not scold him right away because she needed to catch her breath. A moment later she noticed that she was lying on rose petals that had been sprinkled freely over the bed, and she cried out in delight. She sat up, picked up a handful and started to smile up at Ruari only to gape, the rose petals fluttering from her hand. In the short time since he had dropped her onto the bed, he had shed all of his clothes.

She stared at him as he began to tug off her clothing, jokingly chiding her for being so slow. He was tall, strong, and breath-stealingly handsome, she decided. He had a number of battle scars, but they did not really mar the taut smoothness of his dark skin. She thought about his qualities, his humor, skill in battle, and concern for all the people of Gartmhor as well as his pride, arrogance, and temper, and she decided that he was perfectly imperfect. When he tossed aside the last of her wedding clothes and settled his long, hard body on top of hers, she wrapped her limbs around him and smiled.

"Ye havenae said a word," Ruari murmured against her cheek as he trailed soft, gentle kisses over her flushed face. "Ye have just stared at me and now smile. It causes me to wonder just what ye may be thinking."

"Are ye wondering?" she asked idly as she smoothed her hands down his sides.

"Aye, I am. Ye have an odd air about you. Just what are ye thinking about?"

"I was merely pondering how verra much I love ye," she replied in a voice barely above a whisper. "Probably far more than is wise."

She began to wonder if she had erred when he tensed in her arms. A gleam she could not understand flared in his fine green eyes and the lines of his face tautened. Just as she opened her mouth to try to explain away her abrupt declaration of love, he gave her a fierce kiss. His lovemaking proceeded with an equal ferocity, and Sorcha quickly realized that, whatever had produced the confusing expressions upon his face, he was neither angry nor disgusted. Her last clear thought as she succumbed to the passion he stirred within her was that, even if Ruari did not yet return her love, he clearly appreciated the fact that she was in love with him. It was a start.

Ruari cautiously eyed the small, slender Sorcha as he settled her lax body more comfortably in his arms. She looked exhausted, and there were a few reddish marks on her body as a result of his uncontrolled lovemaking. He felt a pang of embarrassment and, if he had hurt her in any way, he knew he would feel the keen bite of shame. When she had softly spoken of her love for him, he had not been able to think straight. All he had known was that he needed to make love to her, to be one with her. Hearing those words had given him such intense pleasure he had lost all restraint on his passion.

Although he dreaded her reply, he finally asked, "Are ye all right? Did I hurt ye, dearling?"

Sorcha half opened her eyes, stretched languorously, and smiled. "Nay. I can see, howsoever, that it may not be wise to let ye sleep too long alone. 'Tis clear that ye can store aside a mighty appetite."

He grinned and kissed the tip of her nose. "It wasnae being alone in my bed for three weeks with but one afternoon of loving to feed the hunger that made me just act like some crazed mon."

"It wasnae?" She idly smoothed her hands over his broad back.

"Nay. 'Twas what ye said before I lost all restraint."

When she just stared at him for a moment, saying nothing, he began to grow uneasy. Since the moment he had realized that he loved her, he had ached to hear her say that she returned his feelings. He started to fear that he had misheard her, that she had not just confessed to loving him.

"What did I say?" she asked, stroking his abdomen.

Her look was suspiciously innocent and Ruari began to think that she was playing a game with him. For a moment he considered lying about what he had heard, especially since his confidence about the exact words was now shaken, but then he decided it was time to take some risks. Sorcha had taken one when she had become his lover. He inwardly cursed, deciding that love was a troublesome, complicated, and irritating emotion.

He cleared his throat, watching her through narrowed eyes, as he replied, "Ye said, '*I love ye. Probably more than is wise.*'"

"I said that?"

"Sorcha."

She bit back a grin. Ruari looked both irritated and uncertain. It was a strange mixture of expressions. His confession that his wild lovemaking had been inspired by her declaration of love gave her hope as did his continuing intense interest in how she felt about him. He had to feel some depth of emotion for her if the state of her heart was of such importance to him.

"Aye, I did say that and I was right—'tis not wise." She released a soft cry of surprise when he held her close, almost too tightly. "Those words become risky to say," she murmured when he eased his hold a little. "First ye ravish me then ye try to squeeze all the breath from my body."

"I ask your pardon. 'Tis just that I find your words of love verra moving."

"Why?" She watched him closely, not sure what a discussion would gain her, yet feeling compelled to have one.

"Why? 'Tis a strange question. Why would any mon wish to hear that he is loved?"

"To feed his pride. To ken that more than passion and vows mumbled before a priest binds his wife to his side." She shrugged. "There are a lot of reasons. I am pleased that ye dinnae find it awkward or feel it is a burden ye dinnae wish to trouble yourself with." She found it interesting that he should look so stunned.

"If ye think like that, why did ye even say it?"

"I felt it was something ye ought to be told although I have held my tongue for many a month now. After Dougal and Neil spoke to me, I realized that keeping such feelings to myself and fearing how ye may accept them was a far worse torment than I could suffer if I just spoke my heart and finally learned what ye thought of it."

Ruari rolled onto his back, rubbed his temples for a moment, then turned his head to look at her. "Ye are the most peculiar lass."

"Am I?" She turned on her side, propped her head up on one hand, and casually trailed her fingers up and down his chest. "Why am I peculiar?"

"Ye mean aside from the fact that ye see and speak to ghosts?"

"Aye, aside from that."

"Ye make this confession from the heart, tell me how verra much ye love me, and then act as if ye have done little more than remark upon the quality of the wine. Ye ask nothing of me."

"Ye asked nothing of me save for passion. 'Tisnae your concern if my heart chose to give ye more than that. And of what use is an emotion if it isnae given freely, undemanded and unfettered? If I have made ye feel guilty or the like, I am sorry. That wasnae my intention."

He combed his fingers through her long dark hair. "I dinnae feel guilty, only surprised. I have done nothing to earn your love."

"True." She giggled when he sent her a mock scowl, then grew serious, bending to give him a tender kiss. "I dinnae believe one can earn love either. One can do all that is possible to make a person fall in love with her and never succeed. I fear love is a verra unruly emotion."

"Aye, verra unruly," he agreed in a soft, husky voice. "'Tis why most men try so verra hard not to fall in love. 'Tis also seen by many men as a weakness."

"Is it?"

She spoke in a voice that was barely a whisper, a sudden tension tightening her throat. There was a soft look in his eyes, a look that bespoke a deep emotion. He talked of all men, but she felt sure he spoke only of himself. She tried to slow the sudden rapid pace of her heart, to scold herself for letting her hopes leap at every hint of feeling from Ruari, but she could not still the heady anticipation that was making breathing difficult.

"Aye. No mon wishes his heart and soul held tightly by another." He pulled her into his arms, then turned so that they rested on their sides, face-to-face. "Once that happens, a mon can fear that he will be ruled by the woman's whims. Ah, and then there is the gnawing uncertainty. He has succumbed to love's tight hold, but has she? Should he tell her what he feels? Will she then see him as a hapless fool?"

With every word he spoke he caressed her, slowly moving his hands over her body as he touched gentle kisses to her face, neck, and lips. Passion began to cloud her mind, even though she struggled against it. She wanted to hear every word he said, clearly and loudly. When he cocked her leg over his hip and slid his hand between her thighs, she knew she had already lost that struggle. Her body grew weak and hot with a building desire. Her passion was not concerned with what Ruari was saying, only with how he was making her feel.

"If ye wish me to think about what ye say, ye should-nae be doing that," she said, her voice so thick and husky she barely recognized it as her own.

"Mayhap I dinnae really wish you to think too much or to hear my words too clearly." He slowly joined their bodies.

It took her a moment to cease gasping from the strength of the pleasure that swept over her and find the ability to ask him, "If ye dinnae really wish me to hear it or think about it, then why are ye even saying it?"

"It needs to be said. I need to say it." Holding her tightly against him, he began to move, stroking her intimately with every thrust of his body. "Mayhap I am also somewhat of a coward," he whispered as he touched his lips to hers. "Mayhap I use the passion which so often blinds us to shield myself as I bare my soul."

"Ye plan to bare your soul?" she whispered against his mouth.

"Aye, and 'tis no easy thing for a mon."

He said nothing else for a long time, just kissed her, a long, slow kiss, the strokes of his tongue within her mouth matching those of his body within hers. Sorcha's passion was running so hot and wild she was not sure she could put enough coherent words together to form the questions she needed to ask him. Just as she felt her body tighten almost painfully, her release but a heartbeat away, she felt Ruari's mouth at her ear.

"I love ye, Sorcha," he whispered.

Those three words acted upon her body like the most intimate of caresses. Ruari's breath warmed her ear as he spoke and sent the final wave of passion ripping through her body. She called out his name as she wrapped her body tightly around his, trying to pull him even deeper inside of her, her body shuddering with the intensity of her release. Just as she lost all capacity to think, she heard Ruari call to her as he joined her in passion's sweetest moment.

It was difficult to know how long a time had passed before Sorcha found herself clear-headed enough to think about what Ruari had said and done. She looked at the man sprawled across her body. He lazily moved his hand up and down her side, and she briefly wondered how long it would be before that idle stroking renewed her passion. She smiled faintly when she admitted to herself that, at times, she was positively insatiable.

He had said the words she had hungered for for so long. Sorcha was certain of it. When she recalled how reluctant she had been to speak her heart, she could easily understand why he had waited until she was nearly blind and deaf from desire before whispering the words. What she was not sure of was if he now intended to pretend that the incident had never happened or that that would be the only time he would speak those sweet words to her. He was certainly acting very reticent, neither speaking to her nor looking at her. She decided that if she could talk openly about such things, then he could as well. Sorcha gave him a sharp poke in his ribs, smiling when he cursed and looked at her in confusion.

"Such games ye play, Sir Kerr," she murmured.

He grinned. "They are fun, arenae they? Let me but regain my strength, and I will show ye a few more."

"I wasnae talking about the loving games, rogue. I was referring to the clever way ye waited to speak your heart until I was so frenzied with passion—"

"Frenzied, were ye?"

She ignored his interruption and continued, "—that

your heart wasnae the part of ye I was most concerned with." She grinned when he laughed, but quickly grew serious again. "I fear ye will have to speak more boldly, my fine knight. I have spent too many tormented months loving ye and fearing that I would never have your love in return. I cannae count the times I grew almost maudlin as I wondered how I could be so foolish as to believe that ye could ever love me."

"And why shouldnae I love ye?"

"Many reasons. Dinnae forget that at first ye believed that I was quite mad."

"A little mad," he murmured and briefly grinned. "As are all of your kinsmen and women." He traced the fine lines of her small face with his fingertips. "There are a great many reasons why I love ye and why I was a fool to try so hard not to love ye. Ye have strength, spirit, and beauty. Aye, ye have the finest brown eyes in all of Scotland." He kissed her cheek when she blushed.

"Ye remind me of the heather that can dress even the most barren of our hills in soft color," he continued. "Ye are wild and beautiful, delicate in appearance but as hardy as that flower. Ye have no dowry, no lands and ye talk to spirits. Aye, and even though Ivor has left us, I suspect ye will find a few more ghosts in the years ahead of us. It doesnae matter. Ye are what I want. Aye, ye are what I need."

"I need ye as weel, Ruari Kerr," she said quietly, curling her arms around his neck and gently kissing him.

"And when did ye ken that I was the mon ye needed? When were ye sure that ye loved me?"

"I suspected it for a long while, but I was so certain we could never be wed that I fought it. I fought the love growing inside of me as hard and as fruitlessly as I fought the passion ye stirred within me. I could no longer deny either the first night I came to your bed. The moment our bodies became one, I was certain that I loved ye."

Ruari brushed his lips over her forehead. "I wish it had been as easy for me."

"Ye are a trained warrior. Ye were a better fighter." Sorcha echoed his chuckle.

"There was also the matter of my precise plan for a wife. I was loath to give that up no matter how often Rosse advised me to do so." He smoothed a few wisps of hair from her face. "There was also the anger I felt, an anger born of my bruised pride."

"It doesnae matter. Aye, some of the obstacles in our way were ones of our own making, but we have overcome them. Now we only need to tend our love carefully so that it will still be strong when we are weak with age."

Ruari claimed her body with his and began to cover her face with small, warm kisses. "Say it loud and clear, loving. I find I have a deep hunger for the words."

"I love ye, Ruari Kerr."

"As I love ye, Sorcha, my wife. And although, as a mon of battle, I ken little or nothing of nurturing, I believe I will find no difficulty in coveting and caring for this bounty we share."

"And I shall be right there at your side to help as, along with whatever children we are blessed with, this love is our greatest treasure." She heartily welcomed and returned his tender kisses. "I wish Crayton and Ivor were still about so that I could tell them of this. They were both verra concerned about what the future held for us."

"I am certain that they know. Now, I have plans in mind that dinnae include a lot of talking, especially about your spirits. In truth, I have rather enjoyed the absence of them and pray that it continues for a long while."

Sorcha wrapped her body around his when he kissed her again and decided that now was not the time to tell him about the sad-eyed young woman who had flickered into view at the priest's side to watch the wedding with a mournful face. This time his passion was the force behind his kiss, and his hunger was easy to sense. She could think of no better way to enhance the sweet words of love they had spoken to each other than to make love. With both of their hearts and minds freed of fear and doubt, she knew it would be one of those moments of intimacy and passion they would both cherish and remember for the long years ahead.

Epilogue

Sorcha smiled at the young maid who had helped her wash and dress in a clean nightrail. As she eased her aching body beneath the now-clean linen on the bed, she looked at the two women bedded down in the room with her. Neil calmly reclined in a bed on her right, looking as if she would regain her strength before an hour had passed. To her left was Margaret who was fine, but looked exhausted and still a little shocked by the mess and the lack of privacy she had just endured. Shifting a little in her bed, Sorcha looked at the three tightly swaddled babies sleeping peacefully in their cradles.

Ruari had thought that they were all mad or suffering from some strange whim that often afflicts a woman with child. Nevertheless, he had done everything she had asked, insuring that a room was prepared where the three of them could give birth together just as Euphemia had instructed but weeks after the weddings. What neither she nor her aunt nor her cousin had yet told their husbands was the rest of Euphemia's prediction—that they would each give their husbands seven strong sons. That promise of ending the Hays' apparent inability to produce male

children was enough to make her, Neil, and Margaret
adamant about following every small detail of Euphemia's
sparingly worded, but very welcome prophecy.

She smiled when she heard the voices of their men.
They were impatient to see their wives and their newborn children. Sorcha knew that that impatience had
been strengthened by the lack of information they had
gleaned from the women slipping in and out of the
birthing room. They could not know that every woman
tending the birth had been threatened with some very
alarming retributions if they told the men anything, especially that they had had sons.

"Ye had best let the fools in," Neil said, draping her
thick bright braid over her shoulder, and waving the last
of the maids toward the door. "Smile, lass," she ordered
Margaret. "Ye shall put a bad fright into poor Beatham
if he sees ye looking so wan."

"I feel wan. Why shouldnae I look it?" grumbled Margaret, but she sat up against the pillows and tried to look
cheerful. "I dinnae think I am quite so happy about Euphemia's prophecy now. I dinnae think I can abide going
through this six more times."

"Weel, that would only give ye the seven sons Effie
predicted," Sorcha said. "Ye may have a daughter or two
as weel."

Sorcha and Neil were laughing heartily over the horrified look that had crossed Margaret's face when Ruari,
Beatham, and Malcolm cautiously entered the room.
Sorcha's full attention became centered upon Ruari as
he walked to her bedside, studied her intently for a
moment, then kissed her. She ruefully admitted to herself that she liked the way he had come to her first,
assuring himself that she had survived the ordeal un-

scathed, before he even asked after the child he had
been so eager for.

"Your bairn lies in the middle cradle," she said, smiling and watching him closely as he picked up the child
and sat down on the edge of her bed.

"She has black hair," he murmured, smiling proudly
as he set the child on the bed and carefully unwrapped
the swaddling.

Out of the corner of her eye, Sorcha could see Beatham and Malcolm doing the same, but her own husband held her attention tightly. She did not want to miss
the expression on his face. She grinned as he pulled
aside the last of the wrappings and saw that the child
was a boy. He gaped, and she heard his whisper of surprise echoed by the others.

"I have a son," he said, his voice hoarse as he finally
looked at her.

"Aye. I hope ye are pleased." She laughed at his
disgusted look then frowned when he began to look uncertain.

"Sorcha, ye ken that I would have welcomed any
child—" he began.

She placed her fingers over his lips to stop his words.
"Ye need not beg my pardon for your delight in having
a son. I have no doubt in my heart and mind that ye
would have loved a daughter as weel. Enjoy the happiness ye feel over being given the son every mon wants
and dinnae fear that I shall see something wrong or
hurtful in it."

As soon as he resettled the baby back in his little
cradle, Ruari gently took Sorcha into his arms and kissed
her with a tenderness that brought tears to her eyes. The
quiet in the room told her that Beatham and Malcolm had
been equally moved. A quick glance toward the cradles

revealed that Caroline, the sad-eyed English girl she had first seen at her wedding, was standing guard over the babes, and Sorcha inwardly smiled. She knew her child would be well-protected until Caroline finally found the peace she searched the halls of Gartmhor for.

"She is here, isnae she?" Ruari whispered, glancing around the room.

"Aye. Caroline watches over our child."

Ruari sighed then grinned. "I love ye, Sorcha, my wild sprig of heather. Aye, spirits and all."

"And I love ye, my fine green-eyed knight. Aye, and I shall love ye until all the light in my soul finally flickers out."

"Good, for if your love wanes after I answer God's call, ye can be sure that I will come back to haunt ye."

"My love will ne'er fade," she whispered, then grinned. "God forbid that ye should leave this earth ere I do, but perchance ye do, please—come and haunt me. I will be waiting for ye."

Ruari laughed and kissed her again. "Thank ye for my son, wife," he said in a deep voice thick with emotion. "A woman can give a mon no greater a gift of love, and I humbly accept it, vowing to cherish the child as I will always cherish his mother."

Sorcha relaxed against his broad chest, his tender words easing the lingering pain of childbirth. Later she would tell Ruari that he would have a great deal to cherish in the future, that he could expect to see six more sons.

SHE SAVES HIS LIFE . . .

For Chloe Wherlocke, it all begins with a vision—
a glimpse into the future that foretells a terrible plot
against Lord Julian Kenwood and his newborn son.
Chloe's psychic gift allows her to save the child from
certain death, but the earl remains in grave peril . . .

BUT WHEN HE STEALS HER HEART . . .

Julian Kenwood knows someone is trying to kill
him and he suspects his scheming wife and her lover
are behind the plot. But Julian is shocked when
Chloe, a captivating, dark-haired stranger, warns him
that sinister forces are indeed at hand—and exposes
a devastating secret that changes his life forever . . .

WILL SHE RESIST—OR SURRENDER?

As Chloe reveals her plan to save Julian, neither can
deny the attraction that grows each moment they're
together. Chloe knows the highborn earl could never
love her as she loves him. But when danger strikes
closer than ever, Chloe must risk everything—
or lose Julian forever . . .

**Please turn the page for an exciting sneak peek of
Hannah Howell's
IF HE'S WICKED,
now on sale!**

Prologue

England—fall 1785

"Damn it, Tom, the woman is dying."

Tom scowled down at the pale woman lying so still on the tiny bed. "She is still breathing."

"Barely."

"Just worn thin from birthing is all, Jake." Tom picked up the swaddled child that rested in the woman's limp arm. "Poor wee mite. Throttled by the cord, it looks like. Well, come on then, Jake, set that lad in this one's place."

"I hate this, Tom." Jake gently settled the peacefully sleeping newborn he held next to the woman. "T'ain't right. T'ain't right at all. The poor lass has no strength to care for the mite. He will be dying right along with her. Mayhap we could—"

"You just stop right there, Jake Potter," Tom snapped. "You be forgetting what happened to old Melvin when he tried to say nay to that bitch? You want your bones tangled up with his in that pit? 'Course this ain't right, but we got no choice. No choice at all. Better the wee lad dies than gets reared up by that woman, I says. Or e'en murdered by his own mam."

"His lordship'd take good care of the lad."

"His lordship is blind to what that woman is and you be knowing that. Now, let us be gone from here. The bitch wants this poor dead babe in her arms ere his lordship returns and that could be soon as he was sent word that his wife had been brought to the birthing bed hours ago. The fool who did that will be fair sorry, I can tell ye," Tom muttered and shook his head.

Jake started to follow Tom out of the tiny, crude cottage, but then hesitated. "I will come with you in a blinking, Tom. I just—"

"Just what? We *have* to go now!"

"I just want to make 'em warm and comfortable, give 'em a fighting chance, or I will ne'er rest easy."

"Hurry then or soon we be both resting easy right alongside old Melvin."

After making a fire and covering the woman and child with another thin blanket, Jake looked around to make certain Tom was not watching him. He took a sheath of papers from inside his old coat and hastily tucked them beneath the blankets. When he looked at the woman again, he started in surprise. She was watching him.

"Your babe will have a fine resting place," he whispered. "I hate doing this, I surely do, but I got me a wife and five wee ones. Aye, and I be a coward when all be said and done. That vile woman would ne'er hesitate to kill me if I ruined her evil plans. If ye can, take them papers and hide them well. If his lordship survives all his wife's plots, he will be wanting his son and them papers will be all the proof he will be aneeding from you. Tis as much as I and a few others dared to do, sorry poor help that it is. I will pray for you, missy. You and the lad here. Aye, and I will pray for meself as well for I have surely blackened my soul this day." He hurried out of the cottage.

After waiting a few moments to be certain the men were gone, Chloe Wherlocke crept out of the niche by the fireplace where she had hidden herself when the men had ridden up to the door. She moved to kneel by her sister Laurel's bed and stared at the child she held, the living, breathing child. Touching the baby's soft, warm cheek, she looked at her sister, grief forming a tight knot in her throat. Laurel was dying. They both knew it. Yet, her sister smiled at her.

"Tis just as you foresaw it, Chloe," Laurel whispered, weakness and not a need for secrecy robbing her of her voice. "Life appearing in the midst of death is what you said."

Chloe nodded, not at all happy to be proven right. "I am so sorry about your child."

"Do not be. I will join him soon."

"Oh, Laurel," Chloe began, her voice thick with tears.

"Do not weep for me. I am ready. In truth, I ache to be with my love and our child. My soul cries out for them." Laurel lifted one trembling, pale hand and brushed a tear from Chloe's cheek. "This is why I lingered on this earth, why I did not die soon after my dear Henry did. This child needed us to be here, needed my son's body to be here. I recovered from that deadly fever because fate required it of me. My little Charles Henry will have a proper burial. A blessing, too, mayhaps."

"He should not be placed in the wrong grave."

"It matters little, Chloe. He is already with his father, waiting for me. Now, remember, you must make it look as if this child died. Be sure to mark the cross with both names. Wrap the bones we collected most carefully. Ah, do not look so aggrieved, sister. Instead of being tossed upon a pile as so many others dug out of the London graveyards are, that poor child we gathered will have a fine resting place, too. Here in the country we are not so callous with our dead, do not have to keep moving the old out of the ground to make room for the new. Tis a fine gift we give that long dead babe."

"I know. Yet, throughout all our careful preparations I kept praying that we were wrong."

"I always knew we were right, that this was a fate that could not be changed by any amount of forewarning. I will miss you, but, truly, do not grieve o'er me. I will be happy."

"How could a mother do this to her only child?" Chloe lightly touched the baby's surprisingly abundant hair.

"She cannot bear his lordship a healthy heir, can she? That would ruin all of her plans."

When Laurel said nothing more for several moments, Chloe murmured, "Rest now. There is no need to speak now."

"There is every need," whispered Laurel. "My time draws nigh. As soon as I am gone, see to the burial, and then go straight to our cousin Leopold. He will be waiting, ready to begin the game. He will help you watch over this child and his father, and he will help you know when the time is right to act against that evil woman and her lover." Laurel turned her head and pressed a kiss upon the baby's head. "This child needs you. He and his poor love-blind father. We both know that this boy will do great things some day. It gives me peace to know that my sorrows are not completely in vain, that some good will come out of all this grief."

Chloe kissed her sister's ice-cold cheek and then wept as she felt the last flicker of life flee Laurel's bone-thin body. Pushing aside the grief weighing upon her heart like a stone, she prepared Laurel for burial.

The sun was barely rising on a new day when she stood by her sister's grave, her sturdy little mare packed with her meager belongings, a goat tethered to the patient mount, and the baby settled snugly against her chest in a crude blanket sling. One wind-contorted tree was all that marked Laurel's grave upon the desolate moors. Chloe doubted the wooden cross she had made would last long and the rocks she had piled upon Laurel's grave to deter scavengers would soon be indistinguishable from many another one dotted about the moors.

"I *will* come back for you, Laurel," Chloe swore. "I *will* see you and little Charles Henry buried properly. And this wee pauper child you hold will also have a proper burial right beside you. It deserves such an honor." She said a silent prayer for her sister and then turned away, fixing her mind upon the long journey ahead of her.

When, a few hours later, Chloe had to pause in her journey to tend to the baby's needs, she looked across the rutted road at the huge stone pillars that marked the road to Colinsmoor, the home of the child she held. She was tempted to go there to try to find out exactly what was happening. The village had been rife with rumors. Chloe knew it would be foolish, however, and remained where she was, sheltered among the thick grove of trees on the opposite side of the road which would lead her to London and her cousin Leopold.

Just as she was ready to resume her journey, she heard the sound of a horse rapidly approaching. She watched as a man recklessly galloped down the London road and then turned up the road to Colinsmoor to continue his headlong race. He made quite a show, she mused. Tall and lean, dressed all in black, and riding a huge black gelding, he was an imposing sight. The only color showing was that of his long, golden brown hair, his queue having obviously come undone during his wild ride. His lean aristocratic face had been pale, his features set in the harsh lines of deep concern. He was the perfect portrait of the doting husband rushing to join his wife and welcome their child. Chloe thought of the grief the man would soon suffer believing that his child was dead and the grief yet to come when he discovered the ugly truth about the woman he loved. She wondered how it might change the man.

She looked down at the infant in her arms. "That was your Papa, laddie. He looked to be a fine man. And up the road lies your heritage. Soon you will be able to lay claim to both. On that I do swear."

With one last look toward Colinsmoor, she mounted her horse and started to ride toward London. She fought the strange compelling urge to follow that man and save him from the pain he faced. That, she knew, would be utter folly. Fate demanded that the man go through this trial. Until his lordship saw the truth, until he saw his lady wife for exactly what she was, Chloe knew that her duty, her *only* duty, was to keep this child alive.

A fortnight later she knocked upon the door of her cousin Leopold's elegant London home, not really surprised when he opened the door himself. He looked down at the baby in her arms.

"Welcome, Anthony," he said.

"A good name," Chloe murmured.

"Tis but one of many. The notice of his death was in the papers."

Chloe sighed and entered the house. "And so it begins."

"Aye, child. And so it begins."

Chapter One

London—three years later

Struggling to remain upright, Julian Anthony Charles Kenwood, ninth earl of Colinsmoor walked out of the brothel into the damp, foul London night. Reminding himself of who he was was not having its usual stabilizing effect, however. His consequence did not stiffen his spine, steady his legs, or clear the thick fog of too much drink from his mind. He prayed he could make it to his carriage parked a discreet distance away. While it was true that he had been too drunk to indulge himself with any of Mrs. Button's fillies, he had felt that he could at least manage the walk to his carriage. He was not so confident of that anymore.

Step by careful step he began to walk toward where his carriage awaited him. A noise to his right drew his attention but, even as he turned to peer into the shadows, he felt a sharp pain in his side. Blindly, he struck out, gratified to hear a cry of pain and a curse. Julian struggled to pull his pistol from his pocket as he caught sight of a hulking shadowy form moving toward him. He saw the glint of a blade sweeping down toward his chest and stumbled to the left, crying out as the knife cut deep into his right shoulder. A stack of rotting barrels that smelled strongly of fish painfully halted his fall backward.

Just as he thought that this time whoever sought to kill him would actually succeed another shadowy form appeared. This one was much smaller. It leapt out of the thick dark to land squarely upon his attacker's back. As Julian felt himself grow weaker, he finally got his pistol out of his pocket only to realize that he could not see clearly enough to shoot the man who had stabbed him. Even now the pistol was proving too heavy for him to hold. If this was a rescue, he feared it had come too late.

Chloe held on tight as the man who had stabbed the earl did his best to shake her off his back. She punched him in the head again and again, ignoring his attempts to grab hold of her, as she waited for Todd and Wynn to catch up with her. The moment they arrived she flung herself from the man's back and let Leo's burly men take over the fight. She winced at the sounds of fists hitting flesh, something that sounded a lot more painful than her fist hitting a very hard head, and hurried to the earl's side.

He did not look much like the elegant gentleman she had seen from time to time over the last three years. Not only were his fine clothes a mess, but also he stank of cheap liquor, cheap women, fish, and blood. Chloe took his pistol from his limp hand, set it aside, and then, with strips torn from her petticoats and his cravat, bound his wounds as best she could. She prayed she could slow his bleeding until she could get him to Leo's house and tend to his injuries properly.

"Need him alive," Julian said, his voice weak and hoarse with pain. "Need to ask questions."

Glancing behind her, Chloe saw the man sprawled on the ground, Todd and Wynn looking satisfied as they idly rubbed their knuckles. "Did you kill him?"

"Nay, lass, just put him in a deep sleep," replied Wynn.

"Good. His lordship wants to ask him a few questions."

"Well enough then. We will tie him up and take him with us."

"My carriage—" began Julian.

"Gone, m'lord," replied Chloe. "Your coachman still lives and we have him safe."

"Wynn's got the other man," said Todd as he stepped up to Chloe. "I will be toting his lordship."

Julian tried to protest as he was picked up and carried like a child by the big man, but no one heeded him. He looked at the small figure leading them out of the alley and suddenly realized that one of his rescuers was a woman. This has to be some delusion brought on by too much drink, he thought.

When he was settled on a plush carriage seat, he looked across at his coachman. Danny's head was bloody but his chest rose and fell evenly proving that he still lived. The small woman climbed into the carriage and knelt on the floor between the seats, placing a hand on him and the other on Danny to hold them steady as the carriage began to move.

"Who are you?" he asked, struggling to remain conscious and wondering why he even bothered.

"Hold your questions for now, m'lord," she replied. "Best they wait until we can sew you up and some of that foul brew you wallowed in tonight is cleared out of your head and belly."

His rescuer obviously had little respect for his consequence, Julian thought as he finally gave into the blackness that had been pulling at him.

Chloe sat in a chair by the bed and sipped her coffee as she studied the earl of Colinsmoor. He smelled better now that he had been cleaned up but his elegant features held signs of the deep dissipation he had sunk himself in for the last year. She had been disappointed in him and a little disgusted when he began to wallow in drink and whores, but Leopold had told her that men tended to do such things when they suffered a betrayal at a woman's hands. Chloe supposed that, if her heart had been shattered so brutally, she too might have done something foolish. Yet, rutting like a goat and drinking oneself blind seemed a little excessive.

Even so, she had to wonder if the earl was lacking in wits. Three times before this he had nearly been killed yet he had continued to do things that left him vulnerable, just as he had done two nights ago. Did he think he was simply a very unlucky man? She had hoped he knew he was marked for death and at least had some idea of the who and the why. Chloe did not look forward to trying to get the man to heed her warnings, but Leopold felt they could no longer just keep watch over the man, that it was time to act.

For little Anthony's sake she had agreed. The boy saw her and Leo as his family. The longer that was allowed to continue, the harder it would be to reunite him with his father. Her heart would break when that happened but she was determined to see that Anthony did not suffer unduly. The boy also needed his father alive to help him claim his heritage and hold fast to it. Between the earl's increasingly dissipated ways and his mother's greed, Anthony would not have much heritage left to claim unless this game was ended very soon. That was unacceptable to her. Anthony was innocent in all of this and did not deserve to suffer for the follies of his parents.

She smiled at her cousin Leopold when he ambled into the room. Leopold never seemed to move fast, appeared permanently languid in his every action, but it suited his tall, almost lanky, body. Those who did not know him well thought him an amiable but useless fellow living off the wealth of his forefathers. Appearances could be deceptive, however. Leopold had been indefatigable in his surveillance of the Kenwoods, had gathered up reams of information, had assembled a large group of associates who were all dedicated to keeping the earl alive and getting proof of who was trying to kill him, and was himself responsible for saving the man's life three times. England also benefited from dear Leopold's many skills for he was one of their most dedicated and successful agents. Chloe wondered at times if there was something about the earl's enemies that made Leopold think they might be a threat to England as well but she never asked. Leopold held fast to the country's secrets.

"He will live," Leopold said after carefully examining Lord Kenwood's wounds.

"Again. The man has more lives than a cat," Chloe drawled.

"His enemies are certainly persistent." Leopold lounged at the end of the bed, his back against the thick ornately carved post. "Clever, too. If not for us they would have won this game long ago, even after his lordship discovered the ugly truth about his wife."

"Ah, but not *all* the ugly truth."

"I think he suspects most of it. He already strongly suspects that that babe was not his get. And that his wife was never faithful to him, never much cared for him at all."

"How do you know all that?"

"His best friend has become mine. Do not look so

uneasy, love. I truly like the fellow. Met him the first time I saved this poor sot's hide. Thought he could be useful, but quickly saw that he was a man I could call friend. Even more important—he was a man I could trust."

Chloe nodded and set aside her empty cup. "How much does this friend know?"

"Nearly all. Guessed most of it himself. Since I was already disinclined to lie to the man, I *implied* that I had begun to look into the business after the second attempt on the earl's life. He told me that was exactly when Lord Kenwood himself had begun to believe that his wife wanted him dead, that she was no longer happy just cuckolding him."

"Who is this friend?"

"The honorable Sir Edgar Dramfield."

"Oh, I know him. I have met him at Lady Millicent's on occasion. She is his godmother. A very good fellow. He is kinder to Lady Millicent than her own daughter is."

"He *is* a good man and he is very concerned about his friend. That is why I sent word to him this morning about Lord Kenwood's injuries, asking him to keep it quiet. Very quiet. He will undoubtedly arrive soon."

"Are you sure that is wise? Lord Kenwood may not wish others to hear what we have to tell him."

Leopold sighed. "It was a hard decision. Yet, the earl does not know us at all, does he? He has, however, known Edgar all his life, trusts him, and has bared his soul to the man on a few occasions."

"Whilst deep in his cups, I suspect."

"That is usually when a man bares his soul," Leopold drawled and then smiled at Chloe when she rolled her eyes. "I felt the earl would need a friend, Chloe, and Edgar is the only close one he has. We will be telling his lordship some very ugly truths and he needs to believe us."

"You said he already has his own suspicions," Chloe began.

"Suspicions do not carry the same weight, or wield the same blow to one's heart. We will be filling in a lot of holes he may have concerning his suspicions and giving him proof. There is also one hard, cold fact we must present to him, one that would bring many a man to his knees. It would certainly cut me more deeply than I care to think about. We may also need Edgar to help us keep this fool from going off half-cocked and to convince him to allow us to stay in the game."

"What game?"

Chloe joined Leopold in staring at Lord Kenwood in surprise. There had been no warning that he was about to wake up, no movements, not even a faint sound. When he attempted to sit up he gasped with pain and grew alarmingly pale. Chloe quickly moved to plump up the pillows behind him even as Leopold helped the man sit up and drink some cider doctored with herbs meant to stave off infection and strengthen the blood.

"I know you," Julian said after taking several slow, deep breaths to push aside his pain. "Lord Sir Leopold Wherlocke of Starkley." He looked at Chloe. "I do not know you."

"Chloe Wherlocke. Leo's cousin," Chloe said.

There was definitely a similarity in looks, Julian decided. Chloe was also slender, although a great deal shorter than her cousin. Julian doubted Chloe stood much higher than five feet, if that. She had the same color hair, a brown so dark it was nearly black, but her hair appeared to be bone straight whereas Leopold's was an unruly mass of thick curls and waves. Chloe was also cute more than pretty with her wide inky blue eyes. Julian nearly

started in surprise when he suddenly realized where he
had heard that low, faintly lilting voice before.

"You were there," he said. "When I was attacked."

"Ah, aye, I was." Chloe decided it would be best not to
tell the man just how she had known he needed her help.
People often found her visions a little difficult to understand, or tolerate. "Me and Leo's men Todd and Wynn."

With his left hand Julian touched the bandages at his
waist and shoulder. "How bad?"

"You will live. The wounds were deep enough to need
stitching but are not mortal. They also cleaned up well,
the bleeding was stopped fair quickly, and you continue
to reveal no sign of a fever or an infection. You have also
slept most peacefully for nearly two full days. All good."

He nodded faintly. "I should go home. I can have my
man care for me and relieve you of this burden."

"That might not be wise," said Leopold. "This is the
fourth time someone has tried to murder you, m'lord.
The ones who want you dead nearly succeeded this time.
Indeed, they came closer than ever before. I think you
might wish to consider letting them think that they *have*
succeeded. The rumors of your sad fate have already
begun to slip through the ranks of the ton."

Before Julian could ask just how Lord Sir Leopold
knew this was the fourth attack on him he was surprised
by the arrival of Edgar Dramfield. He watched his old
friend greet Lord Leopold with obvious warmth and
wondered when the two men had become such good
friends. It surprised Julian even more when Edgar
greeted Miss Wherlocke as if he had known her for
quite a while as well. Finally Edgar stepped up to the
side of the bed and studied him.

"Either the ones trying to kill you are completely inept
or you are one very lucky man, Julian," said Edgar.

"Tis a bit of both, I think," replied Julian. "Have you come to take me home?" He frowned when Edgar looked at Leopold before answering and that man slowly shook his head.

"Nay," replied Edgar.

"What is going on here?"

Edgar sat in the chair Leopold brought to the edge of the bed. "We have decided that it is time this deadly game was ended, Julian. You have been attacked four times. Four times someone has tried to kill you. Your luck simply cannot hold. Do you really wish to continue to give them the chance to succeed? To win?"

Julian closed his eyes and softly cursed. He was in pain although he wondered what had been in that drink he had been given, for his pain was definitely less sharp than it had been when he had first woken up. Nevertheless, he was not in the mood to discuss this matter. And, yet, Edgar was right. He had been lucky so far but this time, if not for the Wherlockes, he would be lying dead in a foul alley outside a brothel. And what the Wherlockes had to do with his troubles he did not know. He looked at Edgar again.

"No, I do not want them to win, whoever they are," he said.

"I think you know exactly who is behind it all, Julian," Edgar said quietly, his eyes soft with sympathy.

Not ready to say the name, Julian turned his attention to the Wherlockes and frowned. "Just what do you have to do with all of this?"

Chloe felt a pang of sympathy for the man. She knew the pain in his jade green eyes was not all due to his injuries. Even if he had lost all love for his wife the betrayal still had to cut deep and she was soon to add to his wounds. As her cousin retook his seat at the foot of the bed, she clasped her hands in her lap and tried to think of just what to say and how best to say it.

"I believe we can leave the explanations as to *how* we stumbled into this until later," Leopold said.

"That might be best," Chloe agreed and then smiled faintly at Julian. "We have been involved in your difficulties for quite some time, m'lord."

Edgar nodded. "Leopold was the one who brought you to my house the last time you were attacked."

"But did not stay until I could offer my gratitude for his aid?" Julian asked.

"Nay," Leopold replied. "You were not as sorely injured as you were this time and I felt we still had time."

"Time for what?"

"To gather the proof you will need to end this deadly game." Leopold cursed softly. "It is time to be blunt, m'lord. You know who wants you dead. Edgar knows. We know. I can understand your reluctance to speak the ugly truth aloud."

"Can you?"

"Oh, aye, most assuredly. Our family is no stranger to betrayal."

"Fine," Julian said between tightly gritted teeth. "My wife wants me dead."

"Your wife and her lover."

"Which one?" The bitterness in his voice was so sharp Julian nearly winced, embarrassed by the display of emotion.

"The only one who could possibly gain from your death—your uncle Arthur Kenton."

Chloe clenched her hands together tightly as she fought the urge to touch Lord Julian, to try to soothe the anger and hurt he felt. She was relieved when Wynn arrived with tea and food, including a bowl of hearty broth for his lordship. It was best if the harsh truth was allowed to settle in a little before they continued. She proceeded to feed Lord Julian the broth, oddly relieved by the way he grimaced over such weak fare in the normal manner of most patients. Edgar and Leopold moved to the table set near the fireplace to sip tea, eat a little food, and talk quietly while she tended to Lord Julian.

"What are they talking about?" Julian asked between mouthfuls of the surprisingly tasty broth.

"You, I suppose," Chloe replied. "They are probably making plans to keep you alive and bring down your enemies."

"Edgar's interest I can understand, but I still have to wonder what you and your cousin have to do with this."

"What sort of people would we be if, upon knowing someone was in danger, we just turned our backs simply because we did not know him?"

"Quite normal people."

"Ah, well, very few people have ever accused the Wherlockes of being normal." After feeding him the last of the broth, Chloe set the bowl aside and retook her seat by the bed. "Perhaps we just feel that one cannot allow people to dispose of the gentry whenever the mood takes them. Tsk, think of the chaos that would result."

"Enough of your sauce," said Leopold as he and Edgar rejoined them. "Shall we plot our plots, m'lord?" he asked Lord Julian as he sat down at the end of the bed again. "Unless, of course, you enjoy indulging in a slow, catch-me-if-you-can sort of suicide."

"And you reprimand *me* for sauce," Chloe muttered but everyone ignored her.

"No, curse you, I do not enjoy this game," snapped Lord Julian, and then he sighed. "I but wished to ignore the harsh truth staring me in the face. It is bad enough knowing one's wife is cuckolding one—repeatedly. To think one's own uncle is not only doing the cuckolding but that he and said wife want one dead is a bitter draught to swallow. I am not a complete idiot, however. You are all right. They nearly succeeded this time. I am just not certain what can be done about it. Did the man you caught say anything useful?"

"Nay, I fear not," Leopold replied. "He says the man who hired him was well hidden in a large coat, a hat, and a scarf. All he is certain of is that the man was gentry. Fine clothes, fine speech, smelled clean. All the usual clues. He also said that he was paid a crown to follow you about until an opportunity to kill you arose and then grasp that opportunity."

"A crown? Is that all?" Julian felt strangely insulted by that. "An earl's life ought to be worth more than that."

"To that man a crown is a small fortune and he was promised more if he could prove that you were dead. And, nay, there is no hope of catching anyone red-handed. A very convoluted way was set up to deliver the extra payment. One that easily allows your enemy every chance to slip free of any trap set for him. Also, proof of your death must be shown and we cannot feign that. I am assuming that you are rather fond of your right hand."

"You could say that." Julian frowned at his right hand, at the scar that ran raggedly over the back of it. "It was a near miracle that I did not lose it to this wound. A duel," he said when he noticed the curiosity the Wher-lockes could not hide. "The first and last I fought in the name of my wife's honor."

Julian was beginning to feel very tired and he knew it was not just because of his wounds. It was his own emo-tional turmoil that stole his strength, a heaviness of the spirit and the heart. Not only had his pride been lacerated by his wife's betrayal, but his confidence in himself and his own judgment. However, he had wallowed in self-pity long enough. Painful though it was to face the truth, he could no longer try to ignore it, not if he wished to stay alive. Soaking himself in drink and whores might have looked like a slow suicide to others, but that had never been his intent. He was certainly miserable, but not so much that he was ready to welcome the cold oblivion of the grave.

"Edgar and I think you should play dead for a while," said Leopold. "Aside from us, the only one who knows you are alive is the man who attacked you. He will very soon be too far away to tell anyone the truth."

"Your servants—"

"Will keep the secret." Leopold smiled faintly at Julian's look of doubt. "You must accept my word on that, m'lord. Our family and our cousins, the Vaughns, have servants whose loyalty and silence is absolute."

"Something many would pay a fortune for. So, I remain dead. Do I hide here then?"

"Do you trust *your* servants to be silent?"

"Not all of them, no." Julian sighed. "I still do not understand how you became involved in this mess."

"We have been involved from the beginning, m'lord," said Chloe. "From the night your wife gave birth—"

"To someone else's child," he snapped. "That was *not* my child."

"I know, m'lord. It was my sister's."

Julian was shocked speechless. As he slowly recovered his wits enough to start asking a few questions, he became acutely aware of a new, very pressing need. He tried to will it away, but reluctantly accepted that his body was not willing to wait until he got the answers he needed.

"Damnation," he muttered. "We need to talk about that, but, right now," he hesitated then said, "I need some privacy."

"Ah, I understand." Chloe stood up, quickly guessing what he needed and moved toward the door. "I will have the answers to your questions when I return."

"How can she know what my questions will even be?" he asked Leopold the moment Chloe was gone and Edgar quickly moved to help him tend to his personal needs.

"Oh, she can easily guess," replied Leopold.

Julian fought down a sense of humiliation as the two men helped him, washed him down, and put him in a clean nightshirt. He hated being so weak and helpless but had to accept that he was both at the moment and that he needed all the help he could get. Once settled back in his bed, he needed a few moments to still the trembling in his body and will his pain to recede. When he finally opened his eyes again, he gave the two men watching him with concern a weak smile. Then he recalled what Chloe had said and frowned. Julian decided he must have misheard her.

"Did she really say that the child was her sister's?" he asked. "That I have interred her sister's child in my family crypt?"

Leopold sighed and nodded. "Her sister Laurel's child. Laurel married a poor man who died whilst out fishing. She knew she would not survive the birth of her child, that she was too weakened by a recurring fever and grief. Two men came whilst Laurel lay dying on her childbed, her babe born dead, and they took the child away."

"But why? Was Beatrice feigning that she was with child? Was it *all* a lie?"

"Oh, nay, not all," said Chloe as she entered the room

and walked to the side of his bed, allowing little Anthony to remain hidden behind her skirts for the moment. "Your wife was indeed with child. She and Laurel took to their birthing beds at the same time, something your wife was well aware of as she held the midwife in her power. S'truth, I think the midwife made certain that both women birthed their children at the same moment."

"That makes no sense," Julian muttered. "If Beatrice *was* with child, what happened to it? Where is it buried?"

"It is not buried, m'lord, although Laurel and I worked very hard to make your wife believe the child lies in a grave with Laurel. A trade was made. Lady Beatrice's live child for my sister's dead one."

"Again—why? To what purpose?"

"Why? Because the very last thing your wife and uncle wanted was for you to have an heir."

"If the child was even mine. That woman was never faithful."

Chloe stared at him for a moment and then smiled. "Then it seems you won the luck of the draw, m'lord. The child *is* yours."

"You have seen the child? You know what happened to the baby?"

"The baby has been well cared for." Chloe tugged Anthony out from behind her until he stood in front of her. "The child is the very image of his father. My lord, meet Anthony Peter Chadwick Kenwood—your son and heir."

Julian stared into eyes the same verdant green as his own. Thick golden curls topped the boy's head, sharply reminding Julian of his own boyish curls. Julian looked at the three adults all watching him intently and then looked into those eyes that marked the child as his own. Even as he opened his mouth to speak, he felt himself tumble into blackness.

More by Bestselling Author
Hannah Howell

__Highland Angel	978-1-4201-0864-4	$6.99US/$8.99CAN
__If He's Sinful	978-1-4201-0461-5	$6.99US/$8.99CAN
__Wild Conquest	978-1-4201-0464-6	$6.99US/$8.99CAN
__If He's Wicked	978-1-4201-0460-8	$6.99US/$8.49CAN
__My Lady Captor	978-0-8217-7430-4	$6.99US/$8.49CAN
__Highland Sinner	978-0-8217-8001-5	$6.99US/$8.49CAN
__Highland Captive	978-0-8217-8003-9	$6.99US/$8.49CAN
__Nature of the Beast	978-1-4201-0435-6	$6.99US/$8.49CAN
__Highland Fire	978-0-8217-7429-8	$6.99US/$8.49CAN
__Silver Flame	978-1-4201-0107-2	$6.99US/$8.49CAN
__Highland Wolf	978-0-8217-8000-8	$6.99US/$9.99CAN
__Highland Wedding	978-0-8217-8002-2	$4.99US/$6.99CAN
__Highland Destiny	978-1-4201-0259-8	$4.99US/$6.99CAN
__Only for You	978-0-8217-8151-7	$6.99US/$8.99CAN
__Highland Promise	978-1-4201-0261-1	$4.99US/$6.99CAN
__Highland Vow	978-1-4201-0260-4	$4.99US/$6.99CAN
__Highland Savage	978-0-8217-7999-6	$6.99US/$9.99CAN
__Beauty and the Beast	978-0-8217-8004-6	$4.99US/$6.99CAN
__Unconquered	978-0-8217-8088-6	$4.99US/$6.99CAN
__Highland Barbarian	978-0-8217-7998-9	$6.99US/$9.99CAN
__Highland Conqueror	978-0-8217-8148-7	$6.99US/$9.99CAN
__Conqueror's Kiss	978-0-8217-8005-3	$4.99US/$6.99CAN
__A Stockingful of Joy	978-1-4201-0018-1	$4.99US/$6.99CAN
__Highland Bride	978-0-8217-7995-8	$4.99US/$6.99CAN
__Highland Lover	978-0-8217-7759-6	$6.99US/$9.99CAN

Available Wherever Books Are Sold!

Check out our website at
http://www.kensingtonbooks.com

Books by Bestselling Author
Fern Michaels

Bartók

DATE DUE			
MR 3'99			
AP20'99			
MY 27'99			
NO 29'99			
MY 19'00			
JE 2'00			
JE 11'00			
DE 19'01			

In the same illustrated documentary series:

The Illustrated Lives of the Great Composers.

Bartók

Hamish Milne.

Omnibus Press

London/New York/Sydney

Cover design and art direction by Pearce Marchbank.
Cover photography by George Taylor, Rembrandt Bros.
Cover styled by Catherine Cardwell, Marina Cantacuzino.
Properties by Boosey and Hawkes Limited, John Frost, Ben Sutton, The Talking Box.
Book designed by David Morley-Clarke.

Printed in Great Britain by BPC Wheatons Ltd, Exeter

© Hamish Milne 1982.
First published by Midas Books in 1982.
This edition published in 1987 by Omnibus Press, a division of Book Sales Limited.

Order No. OP42464
UK ISBN 0.7119.0260.7
USA ISBN 0.8256.2276.X

Exclusive Distributors:
Book Sales Limited,
8/9 Frith Street,
London W1V 5TZ,
England.
Music Sales Pty Limited,
120 Rothschild Avenue,
Rosebery,
NSW 2018,
Australia.
Music Sales Corporation,
257 Park Avenue South,
New York,
NY 10010,
U.S.A.
To The Music Trade Only:
Music Sales Limited,
8/9 Frith Street,
London W1V 5TZ,
England.

Distributed by
BEEKMAN PUBLISHERS, INC.
P.O. Box 888
Woodstock, NY 12498-0888 USA
(914) 679-2300 • (888) BEEKMAN

Contents

Bartók on an early folk song
collecting tour.

Chapter One

Without a comprehensive knowledge of the political and geographical upheavals which attended the prolonged death-throes of the Austro-Hungarian Empire, it can be a baffling task to track down the birth-place of one of Hungary's greatest sons. One might assume, rightly, that Béla Bartók was born in Hungary, but even the knowledge that he was born on 25th March, 1881 in Nagyszentmiklós, Torontál county, is of limited help, since no such place is to be found on any modern map of the country. If one recalls that a large part of eastern Hungary was ceded to Romania in the peace treaties of 1920, then you still need to know that Nagyszentmiklós was then renamed Sînnicolaul Mare. It is as well to get to grips with the geographical vagaries and polyglot population of the region, as they have an important, indeed crucial bearing on the life and work of the composer, who, it should be remembered, was for long widely referred to as 'pianist, composer and folk-song collector'. Bartók's nationalism will be seen to have sprung from a fiercely racial pride, rather than the sentimental attachment to scenic characteristics, domestic or political traditions, or even the 'homeland' which plays such a central rôle in the nationalist fervour of many more romantic patriots.

Indeed, racial and linguistic tension, that most intractable of all political problems, lay at the heart of the unrest and upheavals that eventually led to the disintegration of the Hapsburg empire and to the formation of the states which make up eastern Europe today. With the benefit of hindsight, it is not difficult to perceive that the Hapsburg monarchy had been fighting a losing battle since the French revolution. Its political achievement in the hundred and twenty years or so which intervened between then and its eventual dissolution can be measured only in its success in delaying defeat. The more or less bloody suppression of revolutionary movements in Austria, Hungary, Czechoslovakia, Poland and Italy (to give them their modern names) in the mid-nineteenth century was effective in restoring an illusion of stability, but, as always, such measures inflamed rather than dampened the underlying aspirations which motivated them. The defeat of Lajos Kossuth's Hungarian insurgents in 1849 was, in the words of Zoltán Kodály, still a grim and living memory. Old men who had taken part in the uprising and who still wore their beards in the style of Kossuth, were still to be seen frequently in the streets.

Red-blooded patriots were unappeased by the Compromise of 1867 (the *Ausgleich*), hastily put together by Austria in the wake of reverses suffered in Italy, which established the so-called Dual Monarchy and introduced a loose package of conservative and liberal measures which more or less negated one another, so unrest continued to simmer beneath the surface.

In Hungary, the revolutionary undercurrents were two-fold, and the various movements were only united in their allegiance to an undefined concept of a 'Hungarian Hungary'. Although it is not always apparent to the protagonists, separatist and proletarian movements are not synonymous and their aims can readily come into conflict, even opposition. In nineteenth century Hungary the repression of the common man stemmed at once from foreign domination and from the power of an unusually numerous and largely feudal-minded aristocracy.

Bartók's nationalism bridged both camps and when, early in his career, it became central to his artistic manifesto, it gave rise to

Below Bartók's father who died when the composer was seven years old.
(Embassy of the Hungarian People's Republic)

Right Bartók's mother who initiated his musical training.

Nagyszentmiklósi m. kir. földmives iskola főépülete (igazgatói lak.)

Örvendettünk a sikerült aro Kéjnek, köszönet érte. — k a dolgom, levélben leg közelebb többet.

90 3. VII/8.

csókk: A.

The Agricultural School at Nagyszentmiklós where Bartók's father was headmaster.

bitter dissentions amongst officials and intellectuals over the validity of his extra-musical objectives. The petty squabbles which followed Hungarian performances of his music and the planning and publication of his researches into folk-music had little to do with their intrinsic artistic or scholastic value.

However, it seems unlikely that Bartók's immediate family was much affected by political discontent for in the two preceding generations they had made for themselves a modest but secure niche in the established order of things. Later, in his student years, Bartók was to chide his mother (and none too lightly) for her unpatriotic lapses into German in the family circle. His grandfather, János, had secured the respectable post of headmaster of the agricultural school of Nagyszentmiklós, and on his death in 1877, the composer's father, Béla senior, succeeded him at the early age of twenty-two. Three years later he married Paula Voit, an accomplished amateur pianist and teacher and in the following year their first child, Béla, was born.

To record the secure middle-class situation of the family should not imply any complacency or lack of imagination in the young parents. On the contrary, Bartók's father seems to have been an unusually energetic and imaginative man, his sense of civic duty enlivened by his enterprise and determination. He drew up extensive plans for farming reform and intensification, as well as writing quite copiously on educational matters. Of more

9

Bartók and his sister in Poszony, 1892.

significance in the present context are his cultural interests which were wide but particularly favoured music. He was a leading light in the establishment of the Nagyszentmiklós Music Society, and even learnt the 'cello so that he could play in its orchestra. Although predominantly Hungarian, the town had large and vociferous German, Romanian and Yugoslav communities, and to reconcile the different groups was in itself no mean feat.

The musical initiation and development of the infant Béla was largely in the affectionate hands of Paula Bartók, and it is lovingly recorded in her account of the composer's childhood. It reveals little more than one would expect from an exceptionally musical child, a ready ability to play folk tunes on the piano with one finger and so forth, hardly intimations of genius. Like any good middle-class family, the Bartóks nurtured the child's talent by playing to him and taking him to local performances, such as the inaugural concert of the Music Society orchestra. Of this occasion, Paula Bartók recalled, with a trace of doting motherliness,

The other guests went on eating and drinking but he put down his knife and fork at once and listened with complete absorption. He was delighted, but annoyed that the other people could go on eating while such beautiful music was being played.

At the age of five, at his own insistent request, he began to receive piano lessons from his mother, and all seemed set for a comfortable bourgeois childhood. But a cruel event was to make the coming years a period of bitter hardship and struggle. Bartók's father had suffered continuing ill-health and, despite holidays and 'cures' in Austria, he was forced to give up his job at the end of 1877. However, his deterioration was unabated and he died on August 4th of the following year.

So poor Paula Bartók found herself bereft of her husband, with no means of support and two children to care for (a daughter, Elza, was now three years old). Her elder sister, Irma, came to live in the house and helped as best she could, while Paula continued for the time being to give piano lessons. Béla had already shown a tendency towards introversion from an early age, and was often ill. Severe chest infections were frequent and his reluctance to play or communicate with other children was aggravated by an unsightly skin complaint. The present crisis and his mother's inevitable preoccupation with practical considerations can only have made his feeling of isolation worse. Throughout his life he left an impression of extreme reserve on all who met him, though few doubted the iron will and unbending principles which lay behind his withdrawn demeanour, and to which he was not afraid to give voice in the face of powerful opposition, as we shall see.

10

After a year or so, as is the nature of these things, the family began to emerge from the shadow of their tragedy and look more positively to the future. Paula found a job teaching at a school in Nagyszöllös, now in Czechoslovakia. They stayed there for three years, during which time Béla's musical development regained its momentum. He began composing short pieces for piano and his talent began to attract the attention of local and visiting musicians. Mrs Bartók was sensibly resistant to predictions of a 'great future' for her boy and sent him off to school in Nagyvárad where her other sister Emma could look after him. It was not a great success, and he returned the following year to Nagyszöllös, but his musical achievements were greater than his academic ones and he appeared with great success at a local concert, playing the difficult first movement of Beethoven's *Waldstein* sonata and his own composition *The Flow of the Danube*. It would be foolish to pretend to foresee greatness in this naïve little tone-poem, but it shows the creative urge emerging, albeit uncertainly. More important, this modest local triumph sufficiently impressed a school inspector who was instrumental in securing for Paula a year's leave of absence. She wasted no time in removing the family to the infinitely more glamorous Pozsony (now Bratislava), an important cultural centre, where she hoped to find a better job for herself and better education for her children. It was not a happy venture, as the job did not materialise and, at the end of her leave, she was forced to accept a post in Beszterce which was considered even less exciting than Nagyszöllös. Her persistence was finally rewarded, though, when,

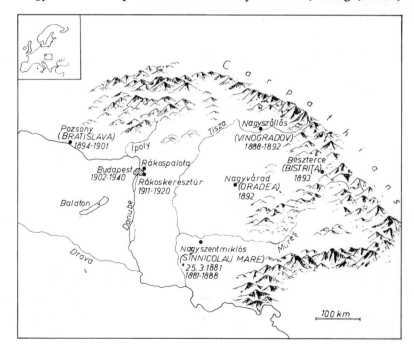

Biographical map of Bartók's early years.

11

in 1894, she was accepted onto the staff of the Teacher Training College in Pozsony. So the five year period of rootless wandering was over.

For Béla, the change was of inestimable benefit.

'In those days,' he wrote in a brief autobiography (published in 1923), 'Pozsony had the most flourishing musical life of all Hungarian provincial towns.'

On the previous, abortive attempt to settle in Pozsony, he had started lessons with László Erkel, the third of four sons (all musicians) of Ferenc Erkel, a composer revered in Hungary, whose operas are still regularly performed at the Budapest Opera. These lessons were now eagerly resumed:

He taught me harmony and the piano until my fifteenth year, and made me go to the opera and to concerts . . . Nor did I neglect to take part in chamber music, so by my eighteenth year I had a pretty good knowledge of music from Bach to Wagner (though only up to *Tannhäuser*). In between, I got down to composition; I was strongly influenced by Brahms and Dohnányi who was four years my senior and whose early work made a deep impression on me.

László Erkel, son of Ferenc Erkel, who taught Bartók in the early 1890s.

Dohnányi was an important figure in Hungarian music, and becoming well-known throughout Europe. An outstanding pianist and teacher and fine conductor, he composed warmly appealing music of immense technical accomplishment in an unashamedly post-Brahmsian style. His elaborate *Variations on a Nursery Song* ('Twinkle Twinkle Little Star' to English speakers) for piano and orchestra remains one of the best of all musical jokes and a witty and invigorating piece in its own right. For a time it seemed as though Bartók was going to be yet another composer in the same mould, and it has to be said that, on the evidence of his earliest works, he was not as good at it as Dohnányi. Of course, when he found his true identity and blossomed into one of the great original voices of twentieth century music, the styles of the two diverged irreconcilably. It is to Dohnányi's credit, though, that his own conservatism did not prevent him from retaining a keen interest in the apparent barbarisms and asperities of the younger man.

In all, then, these five years in Pozsony were a time of retrenchment, of consolidation. The traumas of his father's death and lack of a settled home were laid to rest, and Béla made steady progress towards musical maturity. He put in those long hours of piano practise without which no pianist can contemplate a serious career as a performer, and his knowledge and understanding of the accumulated legacy of the great masters increased daily through his own studies and by the natural absorption of a stimulating musical environment. When László Erkel died in 1896, his work continued

12

Pozsony where Bartók began systematic studies.

without serious hiatus under the now forgotten composer Hyrtl, and as his schooldays drew to an end it was not questioned that his life lay in music.

The geographical, historical and social proximity of Pozsony to Vienna was such that it had longstanding links with the Hapsburg capital, so the choice of conservatoire for Béla to pursue his serious musical studies scarcely merited discussion. In great excitement he set out for Vienna with his mother on December 8th, 1898. He passed his entrance exam with flying colours and was promised a scholarship from the Emperor's private funds, although, with the peculiar inconsistency of autocratic régimes, free places were generally reserved for Austrian-born candidates.

The long suffering Paula was understandably thrilled and bursting with pride. But within a few weeks, Bartók had rejected the offer and made the momentous and far-reaching decision to go instead to the Academy of Music in Budapest. It must have caused a great commotion in the family circle but, characteristically, the autobiography is unemotional and laconic,

At Pozsony in those days the Vienna Conservatoire was considered the only main musical centre. Nevertheless, I followed Dohnányi's advice and chose Budapest.

13

Chapter Two

Musically, as otherwise, Hungary had been very much a satellite of the Austrian empire and in the upper echelons of the aristocracy (who in many cases owed their wealth and influence to their shameless allegiance to the Hapsburg court) there were households who employed sizeable bands of musicians. As a rule, these were imported from Germany or Austria and did much to establish the essentially German-Austrian tradition which dominated Hungarian musical life right up to the early years of this century. Most notable amongst them was Josef Haydn, who was for many years resident composer and musical director to Prince Miklós (Nicholas) Esterházy, so many of the greatest masterpieces of the classical era were in fact composed and first performed in Hungary. Nor was Haydn remiss in acknowledging his debt, as many of his works make reference to the perennial popularity of 'gypsy' fiddling in Hungary. The finale of his G major piano trio, the so-called 'Gypsy Rondo', is but the most celebrated example among many. Zoltán Kodály pointed out that, in so doing, Haydn

was the first to announce to the world at large, in his music inscribed *all'ongarese*, that a musical mode of expression specially Hungarian and differing from any other had come into being.

How far the elements used by Haydn were truly representative of the Hungarian ethos is another matter, and one which was to exercise Bartók and Kodály greatly in their efforts to establish a truly national style. What is beyond argument is the much needed shot in the arm which Haydn, by his very presence, injected into Hungarian musical consciousness. Kodály acknowledged this,

In small Hungarian country towns, wherever there were schoolboys, civil servants or others who could play the fiddle, they sat down and played the string quartets of Haydn. For these people, more often than not, this was the only road leading towards the higher sphere of classical music.

Opposite Bartók in 1899, the year he entered the Budapest Academy. (Embassy of the Hungarian People's Republic)

The material used by Haydn (and by Schubert and Brahms after him) to add a dash of Hungarian local colour to certain

15

Budapest around 1903.

compositions derived from two principal sources — the so-called *verbunkos*[1] style, an amalgam of ancient dance music and popular song, and the gypsy *csárdás* of later date. Amidst the political discontent of the nineteenth century this style assumed symbolic status, and Hungarian composers adopted it whole-heartedly as evidence of their patriotic fervour, regardless of its ethnic impurity. Even so, it was largely a cosmetic veneer and composers like Mihály Mosonyi, Ferenc Erkel and the cosmopolitan Liszt remained essentially in the mainstream of Western European romantic music, their devotion to the cause of nationalism notwithstanding. Ferenc Liszt was by far the most celebrated Hungarian musician of his time (his father had been employed on the Esterházy estates) and although he left his native country at an early age he paid increasing attention to Hungarian affairs in later years. This is reflected in his music, where the dashing Hungarian Rhapsodies of his youth give way to the stark 'Hungarian Historical Portraits' and church music in 'Hungarian' style. His visits to Budapest became longer and more frequent and as, in the face of military and political frustration, cultural ideals seemed a positive step towards national identity, he took pride in accepting the position of first president of

1. The word derives from the German *Werbung* (enlisting). Such music traditionally accompanied the recruitment of soldiers.

16

the National Academy of Music, founded in 1875 and Erkel became the first director.

Nationalist aspiration remained buoyant, but musical influences obstinately Germanic. The situation was much the same when Bartók enrolled for his first term at the Academy in September, 1899. Erkel's successor as director was Ödön Mihalovich, an ardent Wagnerian. The Budapest Opera had reached almost international status, but largely through the invigorating musical direction of the great Austrian composer and conductor, Gustav Mahler in the years 1888-91.

Budapest was not untouched by other great forces of the 19th century, capitalism and industrialisation, with their attendant shrinking of the natural barriers of communication. Whereas Pozsony, for the reasons already mentioned, had preserved its close links with Vienna together with a certain bourgeois conservatism, Budapest had succumbed to more glamorous and cosmopolitan influences and was now, if not exactly a playground, certainly as close to Paris in its daily life-style as to Vienna. The casinos, the opulent restaurants were patronised by the still wealthy aristocracy, but the latest literary and political controversies raged in the street cafés. Not that this was likely to distract the intensely serious young Bartók — who was in any case uneasy in company — but he responded to the excitement and variety of the city's cultural life.

His piano professor at the Academy was István Thomán, a former pupil of Liszt and the teacher of Dohnányi, who was to exert a wholly stimulating and benevolent influence. Thomán saw his rôle as an embracing one; his supervision of his pupil's technical and academic progress was allied to a generously humane concern for his general welfare and the growth of his artistic experience. In a tribute to his teacher, written some twenty-five years later, Bartók shows a warmth and affection which he rarely exhibited in public,

A few months after my performance examination — I didn't even think that Thomán would remember me — I received an unexpected letter from him. It was a brief invitation to come to Budapest as his guest to hear the great conductor János (Hans) Richter and the Philharmonic Orchestra play Beethoven's Ninth Symphony, a musical event that he, Thomán, found very important for the development of a young musician. Needless to say, this letter was but the 'upbeat' of his unparalleled, truly paternal concern for me that he demonstrated a countless number of times when I became one of his pupils the next year.

Bartók also had some interesting observations to make on Thomán's teaching methods,

I must have been a real 'savage' as a pianist when I first came to Thomán. My technique was good enough, but thoroughly crude. Thomán taught

Haydn. Portrait in oils by Thomas Hardy.

17

me the correct position of the hands and all the different 'natural' and 'summarising' movements which the newest pedagogy has since made into a truly theoretical system and which, however, Liszt had already applied instinctively and Thomán, a former pupil of Liszt, could acquire directly from his great master. Thus, the most initiated hands imparted to me the mastery of poetically colouring the piano tone.

Thomán's personal qualities he summarises as a

harmonious entity made up of great circumspection, superior tact, deep love of mankind and superb expertise.

One of the first steps which Thomán took in the interest of his new pupil was to recommend him to János Koessler for composition lessons. The benefits of this encounter are less easy to assess. Koessler was unarguably an immensely capable musician and pedagogue, but a representative of the old school, a staunch Brahmsian and a stickler for correct academic procedures with a mistrust of novelty in any shape or form.

It was particularly unfortunate that this same Brahmsian thinking was precisely what Bartók was struggling to emerge from, having passed through that stage during his year in Pozsony. His bewilderment and depression come through clearly in his letters to his mother almost from the beginning of his lessons with Koessler. In January, 1900,

István Thomán's piano class of 1901. Bartók stands 3rd from the left. On the extreme left is Arnold Székely, distinguished pianist and teacher of Sir Georg Solti and Annie Fischer. Felicitas Fábian, seated third from the right, was an early flame of Bartók and dedicatee of some early compositions.

I took along the quintet. Professor Koessler said that none of it was any good at all, that I should try my hand at simpler things, like songs for example. I have no idea what was so bad about it as he spoke only in general terms — that I should take more care over the choice of themes, and so on. . . . I feel myself that my works are basically sound, but need

18

modification, mostly in connection with form. But if they are so bad that they can't be improved well, that's pretty serious.

In any event, the result was that Bartók's creative urge all but dried up for a period of about two years. As a composer, he was clearly going through a state of self-examination and reappraisal, and it may be unjust to lay the blame entirely on Koessler. Not that his time was wasted; far from it. He worked enthusiastically and profitably for Thomán and gained ever-increasing respect as a pianist. Although shortage of money was a constant problem, he still managed to take full advantage of the riches of Budapest's musical life. He threw himself wholeheartedly into the study of Wagner's mature works as well as the orchestral music of Liszt, perhaps as a way of exorcising the Brahmsian spirit, and he seldom missed a performance by a great visiting soloist or ensemble. His

19

letters home contain careful evaluations and comparisons of such artists as Eugene D'Albert, Emil Sauer, Jan Kubelik and many more. He had to eke out his allowance by giving piano lessons to achieve all this, and Thomán was helpful here, as always,

he secured me free admission to the Sauer recital and so I was able to sell the ticket I had already bought. And now he's given me a ticket for *The Valkyrie*.

Liszt, regarded as the father figure of Hungarian music.

Bartók's health had given his family cause for concern again from the very start of his studentship. In October, 1899, he had gone down with a particularly severe attack of bronchitis and had been forced to return home to recuperate. His doctor was so concerned that he strongly advised that he abandon the stresses and strains of a career in music for something less demanding. This turned out to be an unduly alarmist view. On this occasion the interruption was not too prolonged and he concluded the academic year without any further relapse. However, at the end of the summer vacation, when on the point of returning to Budapest to commence his second year, he was taken ill again. This time it was more serious, a combination of pleurisy and pneumonia. Fears that his life was in danger were perhaps exaggerated, but it was several months before he was fit enough to resume his studies. By then it was too late to join the second year course at the Academy, but he made full use of his time in consolidating his piano technique and learning new repertoire, including the monumental *Sonata in B minor* of Liszt, whose powerful personality was insinuating itself more and more into his own musical consciousness. 'The Problem of Liszt' (the title of a paper which Bartók delivered to the Hungarian Academy of Sciences in 1936) was to occupy his thoughts for many a year. Like so many musicians he was puzzled by the paradoxes of the man, the genius tinged with theatricality, sensuality with asceticism. Despite reservations about the work, which he later ascribed to misunderstanding ('of course, at this time, I didn't understand Beethoven's last sonatas either,' he added), he scored a tremendous success when he performed it at an Academy concert in October, 1901.

Despite this and other notable advances as a pianist, the impasse which he had reached in his work with Koessler remained unresolved, although he continued dutifully to produce compositions which were little more than academic exercises done to order.

In his autobiography he recalled the circumstances with detachment, without reference to the agonies of self-doubt he must have suffered,

I got rid of the Brahmsian style, but did not succeed, via Wagner and

Summer in Poszony, 1901. (Left to right) Bartók (recently recovered from a severe illness), sister Elza, Aunt Irma and Paula Bartók.

Liszt, in finding the new way, so ardently desired. (I did not at that time grasp Liszt's true significance for the development of modern music and only saw the technical brilliance of his compositions). I did no independent work for two years.

However, in the course of his regular attendance at the Philharmonic concerts, 'the new way' opened up before him though not, as it turned out, the road to his true destiny. This time his description of the event leaves us in no doubt of the pent-up frustration from which it brought release,

From this stagnation I was roused as by a lightning stroke by the first performance in Budapest of *Also sprach Zarathustra*. The work was received with real abhorrence in musical circles here, but it filled me with the greatest enthusiasm.

He immediately plunged into a wholesale exploration of Richard Strauss, whose methods, he became convinced, 'held the seeds of a new life.' It was a comparatively short-lived enthusiasm, one might almost describe it as youthful infatuation. With the knowledge we now have of Bartók's later style and creed, Strauss would seem an unlikely hero indeed, an arch-perpetrator of the 'excesses of the Romanticists' from which he turned so decisively but a few years later. But, for now, Richard Strauss was the man of the moment and under his spell Bartók recovered his voice and produced a steady stream of new works. His new obsession also led him to make a piano transcription of Strauss's vast and complex tone-poem *Ein Heldenleben*, of which his brilliant performance gave added lustre to his reputation as a pianist. He was engaged to appear at the prestigious *Tonkünstlerverein* in Vienna specifically on the strength of it. He took a mischievous delight in parading this particular success in front of Koessler who, predictably, had no time for Strauss's post-Wagnerian extravagances.

An agreeable side-effect of this psychological breakthrough (no doubt bolstered by the confidence engendered by his growing status) was a relaxation of his social inhibitions. He began to be seen (and heard) at the various private musical gatherings that were a lively element in the musical and academic life of the city. To Bartók, the most congenial of these meetings were at the house of Emma Gruber who, at this time, was married to a wealthy businessman and amateur violinist. It was here that he first met Zoltán Kodaly, a true kindred spirit, who was to be a life-long confidant and collaborator in all musical matters, especially folk music research and educational projects. This remarkable lady was no mean musician herself, a pianist and composer of genuine attainment, so whether her short course of lessons from Bartók was an exercise in self-improvement or patronage is open to question. In any event, the durability of their friendship was assured when, following a divorce, she married Kodály in 1910.

At the Grubers, too, Bartók renewed his acquaintance with Dohnányi, now renowned as a virtuoso throughout Europe, and arranged to take intensive coaching from him in Gmunden at the end of his final year at the Academy. This had to be arranged clandestinely as Dohnányi, seldom fully master of his own affairs, had too often claimed pressure of work as an excuse to fob off the legions of young pianists who clamoured to study with him.

The richest fruits of this period of regeneration were a group of large-scale compositions which make up the greater part of what is loosely known today as the posthumous works, i.e. those which can be considered an important part of Bartók's *oeuvre* written before the allocation of opus numbers, after discounting juvenilia. A three movement *Sonata for violin and piano* has not found much acceptance, and little is heard of the ambitious and difficult *Four Piano Pieces*. The lavish *Piano Quintet*, published only in 1970, has much to commend it, despite its sometimes clumsy joinery, and it may yet establish itself in the repertoire of a medium that finds favour with audiences though surviving on a handful of master-pieces. But the outstanding achievement of this group is, appropriately, the most luxuriantly Straussian, the so-called *Kossuth Symphony* (more properly *Kossuth — Symphonic Poem for Full Orchestra*), and here, once again, we must digress briefly into the shifting sands of Hungarian politics.

As we have seen, anti-Hapsburg resentment never lay far beneath the surface of everyday life and in 1902-3 a series of events occurred which, at the same time, incited the more spirited elements in the populace to fury and fanned Bartók's own hitherto quiescent political awareness into a raging fire. A bill was put before the

22

Budapest at the turn of the century.
(Corvina)

Hungarian Parliament proposing an increase in its contribution to the Imperial army. The Hungarian army with its primary allegiance to Vienna was a perennial thorn in the flesh of the separatists, and a symbolic issue was made of the continuing use of German as the official military language. In fact, German was still the common language of the upper and middle classes (much as French was spoken in Russia as a sign of education and sophistication) and it also served as a means of communication between the various ethnic groups. But when Emperor Franz Joseph, with autocratic disdain, bluntly refused to countenance the use of the Hungarian language in the army, it was denounced as the blackest treachery, final proof (if such were needed) of the hypocritical sham of the Compromise of 1867. Civil disturbances were almost daily events and Bartók passionately added his voice to the general clamour for freedom from the foreign yoke. He took to wearing Hungarian national costume to the Academy, berated his mother and aunt for speaking German and inscribed his letter headings with nationalist slogans. On a deeper level, far removed from mob hysteria, he wrote to his mother,

Everyone, on reaching maturity, has to set himself a goal and must direct all his work and actions towards this. For my own part, all my life, in every

23

sphere, always and in every way, I shall have one objective: the good of Hungary and the Hungarian nation.

What more natural then, as he embarked on his first great orchestral work, his own *Heldenleben*, that his hero should be Lajos Kossuth, defeated leader of the last great Hungarian uprising?

The omens for *Kossuth* were good from the outset. Even Koessler expressed guarded approval at the piano-score and suggested Bartók orchestrate it in the hope of its being included in an Academy concert. But more exciting things were in store. The Budapest Philharmonic decided to present it in January, 1904, and, even better, at a fortuitous meeting in Pozsony during the summer, the great conductor Hans Richter was so impressed that he promised to arrange a performance with the Hallé orchestra in Manchester.

The nationalist scenario was always likely to produce stock responses in Budapest, and the première induced more patriotic slogans than informed comment from the press. In a sense, Bartók had invited this by writing his own rather naïve and provocative programme notes. Each of the ten movements was given an explanatory heading — 'Danger threatens the Fatherland', 'Come fine Hungarian warriors, valiant heroes' and so on. The representation of the Austrian army by a grotesque parody of *Gott Erhalte* (the Austrian national anthem) was too much for some of the non-Hungarian members of the orchestra who downed their instruments in protest at the first rehearsal. This touch of notoriety did no harm at all to the growing reputation of the young composer.

The performance in Manchester aroused no such passions, of course, and Bartók scored a greater success with piano solos by Liszt and Volkmann (which he played in the same programme) than with the symphony. The unbiased listener probably shared the impression we receive today on the rare occasions it is performed; that the work, despite undeniably striking passages, is so closely modelled on Strauss's tone poems that it can only suffer by the inevitable comparisons.

Amidst this welter of activity, Bartók's student days came to an unspectacular, almost incidental conclusion. He was under no delusions. Although he could justifiably feel that he had made an indelible imprint as a composer, it was by playing and teaching that he would have to earn his living in the foreseeable future.

Chapter Three

Bartók's career as a concert pianist had got away to a highly promising start. Even while engaged in the preparation of *Kossuth* he had to break off from time to time to fulfil performing engagements. Moreover, his name was becoming known beyond the Austro-Hungarian border, partly on account of Dohnányi's enthusiastic recommendation. The Liszt scholarship awarded on his graduation from the Budapest Academy enabled him to spend a few months in Berlin where his reputation already was sufficient to attract the presence of at least two great pianists, Busoni and Godowsky, to his recital, and his performance in Manchester had secured him the promise of appearances in London the following year. Nonetheless, there was never any question that he would be diverted by his successes into the comparatively narrow outlook of the travelling virtuoso, and he felt keenly the need for seclusion, not only to pursue his composing but to ponder the philosophical and moral attitudes that gave his life purpose. Accordingly, he retired to the plains of Gerlicepuszta in the spring of 1904 and stayed there for six months, emerging only briefly in August to make the pilgrimage (obligatory for all Wagnerites) to the Bayreuth Festival. There he met again Hans Richter who was greatly taken with Bartók's latest work, a Scherzo for piano and orchestra, another Straussian monster, virtually a fully fledged concerto. But the most interesting product of that summer was the *Rhapsody No. 1* which exists in several versions of which the one for piano and orchestra is definitive. It is not surprising to learn that Bartók was working hard at the preparation of several major pieces by Liszt at the same time as composing this most overtly Lisztian of all his works. He was evidently well pleased with it as it was on this work, along with the Piano Quintet, that he elected to be judged in the Rubinstein competition, held in Paris in the summer of 1905, for which he had entered as both composer and pianist. This expedition to Paris proved to be a harsh experience, but its effect on his outlook and character was perhaps not wholly negative.

From Bartók's point of view the competition was a humiliating fiasco. The piano section was won by the great German pianist Wilhelm Backhaus whom Bartók conceded to be an entirely worthy opponent, without accepting that he was necessarily a better player in any absolute sense.

'It's a matter of taste whose performance you prefer,' he declared.

It was in the composers' competition, however, that he tasted the real bitterness of failure. The facts presented to the public were simply that the jury had decided not to award either of the cash prizes, but to confer Certificates of Merit on two competitors, the Italian Attilio Brugnoli and Bartók, in that order. What roused Bartók's disappointment into a fury of frustration was, firstly, the incompetent organisation of the practical arrangements for the competition and, secondly, some inside information given him by Lajos Dietl (an old friend, then teaching in Vienna) who was on the panel of judges.

On arrival, Bartók was told that there were mistakes in the orchestral parts of the *Rhapsody*, which he quickly corrected, only to be told that it was too difficult for the orchestra to rehearse in the time available. However, the officials had not reckoned with the tenacity of the young composer and in the face of his stubborn insistence they gave way and 'it was finally played rather well, after all.'

He was not so successful with the *Quintet* and was told 'flatly and categorically' that it could not be learned in time — this after they had insisted that he copy out a second score for the jury to follow during the performance. He was therefore forced to substitute his Violin Sonata (which luckily he had with him) and after an anxious search was fortunate enough to secure a fine violinist, the young Russian Lev Zeitlin, to play it with him.

No wonder, then, that Bartók's letter to his mother fairly fumes with rage at the eventual outcome,

The minute I receive my diploma of (dis)honour, I shall send it back to Auer,[1] to Petrograd. I am not prepared to accept rubbish like that.

I may say that Brugnoli's pieces are absolutely worthless conglomerations. It is quite scandalous that the jury could not see how much better my works are.

And yet my works were quite well performed. That, having heard them, the jury still failed to appreciate them is equally scandalous.

On the face of it, this seems nothing but a petulant outburst of wounded vanity, but Bartók was particularly upset by Lajos Dietl's disclosure that the preponderance of Russian judges, 'where they play nothing but Haydn, Mozart and Beethoven' (not strictly true), gave little or no chance to works in a more advanced idiom. Accord-

---

1. Leopold Auer (1845-1930) chairman of the jury. Hungarian-born violinist who founded a celebrated violin school in Russia. Jascha Heifetz was among his many famous pupils.

ing to Dietl, Richard von Perger, a Viennese Brahmsian, simply couldn't understand it at all, to which Auer added airily, 'Oh yes, this is the new school; we're already too old for anything like that.'

Nor was this the most acandalous of Dietl's revelations. The Russian composer and pianist Anton Rubinstein had bequeathed a capital sum to the Petrograd Conservatoire on which interest amounting to 10,000 francs was to accrue every five years to fund the prizes for the competition. Russian currency had been devalued in the wake of the war with Japan and there was a suggestion that, as a result, the interest fell short of the advertised prize money, the inference being that there had been a tacit agreement all along to withhold prizes to avoid drawing on the capital.

'If that is so,' wrote Bartók venomously, 'it was a monstrous piece of impudence and deception to allow all the composer competitors to flock to the place on a wild-goose chase.'

This blow to his confidence had deep-rooted effects which lingered for several years, but at the same time accelerated his quest for a definitive personal style which, despite his pride in his recent works, he realised had not yet crystallised.

For the time being, he was not so despondent as to be blind to the marvels of Paris — 'this heavenly godless city.' At the galleries he took intense delight in discovering the paintings and sculptures hitherto known to him only in reproductions. He was quite over-whelmed by the Murillo collection in the Louvre,

When I look at them I feel as if I was being touched by a magic wand. It is an experience to be classed along with seeing a performance of *Tristan* or *Zarathustra*, attending the first Weingartner concert in Berlin or hearing Dohnányi play the Beethoven concerto in Vienna this year or catching my first glimpse of the Stephanskirche when I was in Vienna 3 or 4 years ago.

His wonder at the banks of the Seine and at the city's parks and woods was tinged with envy of the Parisian 'who can glory in this sight at any time.' He was particularly entranced by the Parc Monceau with its ingenious and harmonious blend of art and nature — 'a little paradise' — and he had disparaging comparisons to draw with Budapest which he suddenly saw as a bed of petit-bourgeois provincialism.

The insights and revelations of Bartók's visit have remarkable parallels with the Parisian experience of Endre Ady, the foremost Hungarian poet of the period to whom Bartók became attracted a few years later. His *Five Songs for voice and piano, op. 16*, are all settings of Ady poems. At this stage, it seems that Bartók remained unaware of the recent currents and developments in French music which were to profoundly influence his own thinking. In fact, in a letter from Paris to Irmy Jurkovics, he categorically states that,

27

Bach, Beethoven, Schubert and Wagner have written such quantities of distinctive and characteristic music that all the music of France, Italy and the Slavs combined is as nothing by comparison!

He patriotically puts up a case for Liszt being the one who most closely approaches the 'Big Four', but of Debussy there is no mention. (And what has become of Richard Strauss?)

Irmy Jurkovics and her sister Emsy had become devoted admirers of Bartók since the day of his first public recital in Nagyszentmiklós in 1903, so the tone of his letter is superficially bright and informative, but it does little to conceal his underlying depression. He describes the communication difficulties of the English, Spanish, German, Turkish and American residents of his boarding house with detached amusement, but these anecdotes carry less weight than the problems and anxieties which were troubling him even then. He lays down unequivocally his commitment to atheism, and touches on his flirtation with Nietzschian ideals, a theme which recurs in a serious letter to his mother about family problems written a few week later,

I would recommend to anyone the attempt to achieve a state of spiritiual indifference in which it is possible to view the affairs of the world with complete indifference and with the utmost tranquillity. Of course, it is difficult, extremely difficult — in fact the most difficult thing there is — to attain this state, but success in this is the greatest victory man can ever hope to win: over other people, over himself and over all things.

His style, as usual, is matter of fact, dispassionate, but through it his uncertainty and sense of isolation well up like a cry of despair,

I may be looked after by Dietl or Mandl in Vienna, and I may have friends in Budapest (Thomán, Mrs Gruber), yet there are times when I suddenly become aware of the fact that I am absolutely alone! And I prophesy, I have a foreknowledge, that this spiritual loneliness is to be my destiny.

If the fruits of his French experience lay dormant for a while, the seeds of another far more important influence had already begun to take root. In 1903, in the early days of his nationalist fever, Bartók had written home asking his sister to identify two Hungarian folk tunes. Subsequent research has revealed that the Bartóks had a domestic servant called Lidi Dosa from the Székely region and it was from her that he had picked up these and other melodies. The momentous significance of this chance encounter seems to have eluded him at the time, but to the retrospective onlooker there can be little doubt that it marked the beginning of his true life's work. A more thorough examination of indigenous musical characteristics was an obvious step to take in the furtherance of his avowed

28

intention to serve 'the good of Hungary and the Hungarian nation', but he can have had no inkling of the enormity of the task, nor of the extent to which it was to possess him and direct his entire life. Almost immediately he was aware of the gulf that separated true peasant music, handed down from generation to generation, from popular pseudo-folk-art but it turned out to be wider and more complete than even he had imagined. On the one hand, he discovered,

a natural phenomenon, just like the various forms of the animal or vegetable Kingdom. As a result, its individual organisms — the melodies themselves — are examples of the highest artistic perfection,

on the other,

the usual gypsy slop.

It took him not much longer to realise that interest in his chosen field of dedicated research was practically non-existent. Professed intellectuals, he found, tended to be at once 'not sufficiently naïve but not yet sufficiently educated' to appreciate the scientific and artistic value of such primitive material.

The confusion between popular gypsy-style music and folk music was as well entrenched in Hungary as in the rest of Europe, where the *tzigane* formulae adopted from time to time by composers from Haydn to Liszt was accepted unquestioningly as a reflection of earthy Hungarianism. Liszt himself had produced a long book *On the Gypsies and their Music in Hungary* which gave the myth a

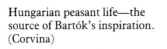

Hungarian peasant life—the source of Bartók's inspiration. (Corvina)

further stamp of authority, although he also expressed a desire to visit the remoter parts of rural Hungary in search of folk material. However, that was never more than a romantic daydream and he never went so far as setting foot in the mud to follow it through. The one dissenting voice, it seems, was a long-forgotten violinist and composer, August von Adelburg (Turkish born, Viennese trained), who challenged Liszt's assumptions in a pamphlet published in 1859 and laboriously entitled 'Reply to Dr Franz Liszt on his assertion in his works that there is no Hungarian national music other than Gypsy music.'

There had been intermittent excursions into the realms of folk-lore by amateur anthropologists throughout the nineteenth century, but, by and large, they had been more concerned with the words than the music of folksong. Such investigation as there had been into folk music had been indiscriminating and unreliable. Even Béla Vikon, who pioneered the use of the phonograph in collecting folksong, was no trained musician and his recordings had to be transcribed by others at a later date. It was Hungary's great good fortune that the two men who rescued and preserved this ancient musical culture for posterity (in the nick of time too, before the explosive expansion of radio and recorded music obliterated it forever) were, in Bartók and Kodály, both meticulous and dedicated scholars as well as composers of genius. Kodály made his first collecting tour in the summer of 1905 (when Bartók was busy with the Rubinstein competition) and in the following year Bartók set off for the Great Hungarian Plains. From a personal point of view, it was a therapeutic venture. Although he had completed his *Suite No. 1* for orchestra during a stay in Vienna following the Parisian débacle, he was heading for another creative impasse. This new passion for folksong research together with performing engagements in Spain and Portugal freed him from any moral obligation to compose for the time being. In fact, his letters suggest he was in rare good humour, making light of, even enjoying the frustrations and absurdities with which the life of the inexperienced traveller is fraught. In Madrid, he and the violin prodigy Ferenc Vecsey were received by the Queen of Spain, who proceeded to trample on Bartók's deepest sensibilities one by one, but his gleeful account of the incident is free of righteous indignation,

My facial muscles were subjected to a severe trial by my efforts not to burst out laughing! She talked a lot of rot, but her prize remark (about Hungary and the Hungarian language) was, 'Your King speaks Hungarian very well, doesn't he? (Old Francis Joe) I agreed, very well. She asked me to play some Hungarian music — czardas. I didn't mind: I let her have her joy. If only she had known what a Hapsburg-hating republican she was speaking to!

30

1908—collecting folk songs in Darázs, now Drazovce (Czechoslovakia).

Similarly, he is more amused than exasperated by the difficulties in tracking down aged peasants and coaxing songs out of them.

The first tangible result of their labours was a collection of *Twenty Hungarian Folksongs* which Bartók and Kodály published in 1906. It is not wholly characteristic of Bartók's work in this field and was soon withdrawn by the publishers through lack of demand. Nonetheless, it remains an important landmark in the growth of Bartók's personality and of Hungarian music as a living force. It is virtually impossible to over-emphasise the importance of this immersion in folk music in considering any aspect of the composer. His experience with the peasants, an ever-present reminder of the corrupting force of social pretension, formed the basis of his gradual shift from a narrow concept of nationalism to the broad humanitarian ideals of a 'brotherhood of peoples' which imbued his later work and attitudes with the universality which lies at the heart of his greatness.

As for his music, he soon realised that he held in his hands the means to his goal, the raw material of a new, individual and uniquely Hungarian style. In his many lectures, essays and pamphlets on his researches and experiences in the field of folk music, he makes it clear that the features that he painstakingly codified and tabulated were gradually incorporated into his own

31

musical thinking. The first and most important discovery was that most of the melodies were based on scales and modes that had not been used in concert music for centuries, if at all. The prevalence of pentatonic (five-note) scales in turn suggested novel combinations and a whole new system of harmony,

For the majority — and most valuable — of the melodies I collected during my research tours, moved in the old church tonalities, that is, in the Greek and certain other even more primitive (pentatonic) modes, and show the most varied and freely changing metrical and rhythmic patterns performed in both rubato (freely) and 'tempo giusto' (exact time). It is now clear that the ancient scales, that are no longer used in our folk-art music, have lost none of their vitality. Their application has made possible new types of harmonic combinations.

Furthermore,

From this music we may learn unique terseness of expression and inexorable rejection of all inessentials — and that is exactly what we have been longing for after the prolixity of Romanticism.

Eventually, his assimilation of these ideals became so complete that it becomes impossible to say, without foreknowledge, where his thematic material is a genuine folk melody or of his own devising.

Whereas Kodály continued to occupy himself in the main with Hungarian material, Bartók felt compelled to follow up connections with folk music from neighbouring territories, to seek out

Bartók and Kodály.
(Embassy of the Hungarian People's Republic)

differences and similarities or to speculate on migratory patterns, and his final tally amounts to many thousands of melodies of Hungarian, Slovak, Rumanian, Bulgarian, Ruthenian, Turkish and even Arabic origin. As Kodály remarked, 'if his interest had turned to money, he would long since have become a millionaire!'

Kodály, 'who guided and advised me in my study of every kind of music,' was also instrumental in introducing the final transitional element in the development of Bartók's mature style — the music of Claude Debussy. Bartók, like musicians throughout Europe, was greatly taken with the novelty, the exotic harmony and colouring of the Frenchman's music, but two other features held a special attraction for him. Firstly, he fancied that he could discern in Debussy's use of simple melodic outlines the very element which appealed to him in Hungarian peasant melody, and, secondly, its utter remoteness from the German mainstream was a virtue in itself. . . .

New ideas were released and the emergence of Debussy signified the replacement of German music by French music as a source of inspiration.

The Academy of Music, Budapest, where Bartók became a professor of piano in 1907.
(Embassy of the Hungarian People's Republic)

Clearly, if this wealth of new experience was to be exploited to the full in a fresh burst of creative activity, he would have to take steps to reconcile the conflicting demands of his career. In November 1906, he had written to Lajos Dietl in Vienna,

The practising has not been at all to my taste; it's a nuisance and I'd far rather have spent my time collecting as many more songs as possible.

The rigours and time wasting involved in his rôle as a travelling performer were becoming an increasing source of irritation, and, in the summer of 1907, an opportunity arose to instil a measure of stability into his life and at the same time to fulfil an ambition that Paula Bartók had cherished on her son's behalf for some time.

István Thomán was due to retire at the end of the academic year, and on the strength of his recommendation, supported by the director Mihalovich, Bartók was invited to succeed him. He took his teaching duties very seriously, and, like Dohnányi, contributed in no small measure to the stream of outstanding pianists to emerge from Hungary in this century. But like most creative artists he often found the work infuriatingly time-consuming and irksome. Nevertheless, it resolved his problems for the moment and he wrote in his autobiography,

In 1907 I was appointed professor at the Academy of Music and I particularly welcomed this appointment because it gave me an opportunity to settle down at home and pursue my research into folk music.

33

Chapter Four

Before taking up his duties at the Academy, Bartók embarked on another folksong collecting tour, this time in the depths of Transylvania. It was to become a regular pattern in the next few years. During term time he remained, perforce, in Budapest, where his mother joined him in his flat in Teréz Körút, but at least once each year he set off into the country to pursue his obsession and, it seems, to fulfil some spiritual need and seek solace in a natural and 'uncontaminated' existence. 'There is peace among the peasants,' he wrote at the end of his days, 'hatred for their brothers is fostered only by the higher circles.' Painstakingly, though with occasional outbursts of exasperation, he pieced together his collection 'in the parlours of pubs, in bootmakers' workshops, sometimes in the open air.'

A Hungarian village scene around the turn of the century. Children's games provided the titles for many of Bartók's short piano pieces. (Corvina)

He explained some of the difficulties the folklorist could expect to encounter in an article written in 1921,

Nothing is more difficult than the collection of melodies of this kind. We have to look for them among the simplest and poorest peasants, far away from the railroad, if we intend to find material untouched by the contaminating influence of the cities. But it is just these peasants of 'untouched' territories who will usually greet with fierce mistrust the stranger knocking at their door! It is in vain that one tries to explain to them why their old, almost forgotten melodies are being collected; they don't listen to reason. They bestir themselves to attribute the most ridiculous explanations to this strange fact, because they never get to understand why a gentleman from the town would leave his accustomed comfort for the sole reason of hearing them sing their old village tunes. Many of them are totally convinced that this means some extra tax, this time on their music! A certain bashfulness joins this fear: they are nearly always afraid that the gentleman might make fun of their ingenuous and simple melodies. The folklorist, therefore, must have much time and patience to cope with so much mistrust.

In spite of his frustrations and discomforts, this brief summer of 1907 seems to have been one of the happiest periods of his life. Although he was appalled by the living conditions of these simple people, he gladly shared their squalor and as the bonds between him

On a folk song collecting trip with Zoltán Kodály and his wife in 1912. (Corvina)

35

and his subjects grew closer, his scientific curiosity acquired new dimensions of respect and affection. In later years, he looked back on 'these days spent in the villages among the peasants' as 'the happiest of my life.' He made a good friend of György Gyugyi Péntek, a village carpenter in Körösfő, from whom he ordered a table for his Budapest home.

'Now I'm quite at home with them,' he wrote.

'His home consists of a kitchen and a very small workshop with a leaking roof.'

Many years later, Péntek's son, Ferenc, recalled Bartók as 'a gentle, smiling little man, always in a good humour.'

It is pleasant to record this more or less idyllic interlude, for it was the prelude to one of the most severe personal and emotional crises of a life regularly afflicted with bouts of deep, though rigorously controlled depression. It is unlikely that the full story will ever be known because Bartók himself was such an intensely reticent and private man, and because he inspired such fierce loyalty in his few close friends that they have been reluctant to shed light on the circumstances. At the heart of the matter lay Bartók's deep but thwarted love for the beautiful and talented violinist Stefi Geyer, then aged 19, a pupil of Jenö Hubay at the Academy, who later married the Swiss composer and concert promoter Walter Schulthess and settled in Switzerland. After Bartók's death, as a contribution to Hungarian research on the composer, she released the texts of three letters she had received from him in August and September, 1907, which lay bare the passionate temperament behind the oddly aloof face, often seemingly contemptuous in its defiance, that he presented to the world at large. Despite the considerable volume of correspondence that has come to light (and few twentieth century composers have been so thoroughlv researched and documented), Bartók admitted that he was a reluctant correspondent and generally only wrote letters through necessity or obligation. Moreover, he was secretive about his private life and feelings to the point of eccentricity, so Stefi Geyer's gesture is enormously helpful in any attempt to reconcile Bartók's icy manner with the fiery intensity of his music.

The first of the letters is cheerful enough — an amusing account of a tortuous but ultimately successful campaign to wheedle a few songs out of an aged peasant woman, set out in the form of a dramatic dialogue between 'The Traveller' and 'The Woman'. The second letter, ostensibly written in reply to a letter from Stefi, followed just three weeks later. It runs to some four thousand words and is virtually a tract on his philosphy of life and on the very meaning of existence.

That he was hopelessly in love could be deduced from his opening paragraph, especially if one compares its agitated manner

36

Stefi Geyer—Bartók's unrequited passion for her is reflected in much of his music of the period.

with his normal blandly informative style. He had evidently given an address in Vésztö for her to write to him, and

I caught a cold on Monday, but I've come here all the same. I was rash enough to make the journey on a wild, wet day — and all because, ever since last Sunday, I have been wondering whether your decision to write to me augured good news or bad. Perhaps you were only going to tell me a few jokes? Or had you something more serious to put on paper? Which part of my letter would you have thought about and commented on? These conjectures gave me a headache, I had to do something about it as soon as possible — and there was almost a calamity. Your letter had arrived one day ahead of me, and as I had not told them I was coming, they had already sent it back to the post-office.

37

His tone becomes altogether weightier when he touches on a reference in her letter to religion.

I was absolutely convinced — although we have never talked about it — that you were 'godfearing'. It wasn't difficult for me to put two and two together. This makes it all the more difficult for me to touch on this subject. I am almost afraid to begin.

But 'begin' he does, and it is almost certainly here that the relationship began to founder. Not content to accept their differences and respect one another's beliefs, he launches into a lengthy, cogently argued vindication of his atheism, his belief in the self-sufficient divinity of Nature and man's control of his own destiny, and pours withering scorn on such concepts as the Immortality of the soul and on the ethics and dogmas of the church in general. The letter is signed

'Greetings from AN UNBELIEVER
(who is more honest than a great many believers).'

If he had hoped to win Stefi's heart by his fearless (if tactless) honesty, then he was clearly disabused of this notion by her reply, although its precise contents are known only in as far as they can be deduced from his third letter, which is perhaps the most poignant document in the entire literature of Bartókiana.

Dear Miss Stefi,
By the time I had finished reading your letter, I was almost in tears — and that, as you can imagine, does not usually happen to me every day. Here is a case of human frailty! I anticipated that you might react like this, yet when you actually did so I was upset. Why couldn't I read your letter with cold indifference? Why couldn't I put it down with a smile of contempt? Why should I be so affected by your reaction? So many 'why's', and I think I must leave you to answer them — provided, of course, that you think them worthy of your consideration.

As he reiterates his fundamental beliefs, it does not seem too fanciful to draw parallels with Beethoven's 'Heiligenstadt Testament' which he set down in the aftermath of his hopeless passion for the Countess Giulietta Guicciardi, dedicatee of his 'Moonlight' Sonata. The precarious emotional equilibrium of the creative artist is similarly expressed.

Beethoven: 'For I have so sensitive a body that even a slight change can transport me from the highest to the most wretched state.'
Bartók: 'One letter from you, a line, even a word — and I am in a transport of joy, the next brings me almost to tears, it hurts so.'

Where Beethoven draws strength from his belief, Bartók

struggles to draw strength from his disbelief. The inner loneliness which he had confided to his mother two years earlier is now more oppressive than ever.

After reading your letter, I sat down at the piano — I have a sad misgiving that I shall never find any consolation in life save in music. And yet. . .

There follow nine bars of mournful music, *Adagio molto*. Above a phrase of four notes he has written, 'this is your *Leitmotif*.'[1]

Consolation in music was what he sought now and in the works which he composed in a steady stream between 1907 and 1911 he gradually achieved the integration of the eclectic and sometimes disparate elements which characterised his output up to this point. He was aiming for a synthesis of the intellectual and structural control of the great classical masters, the novelty and un-German transparency of Debussy and, most importantly, the ancient, primordial elements of Hungarian folk music. His first task was to complete his second orchestral *Suite op. 4* which he had started and abandoned during his stay in Vienna, and the folk element, if mildly expressed, is already clearly to be heard.

He composed a great deal of piano music during this period, much of it for children which may have been a side effect of his teaching involvement at the Academy or more often it seems, a convenient and less arduous medium in which to try out his new ideas. In 1931, he attempted to categorise the methods by which folksong can be 'transmuted' into modern music. The first possibility, he said, was to leave the original melody virtually intact, but to lavish the utmost thought and feeling on how best to highlight its unique characteristics by means of an illuminating accompaniment or by adding an introduction and conclusion. He likened this technique to that of a jeweller fixing a precious stone in its setting. Perhaps the most perfect examples in this category are the 4 volumes *For Children*, 85 enchanting settings of Hungarian and Slovak folktunes which have taken their place alongside Bach's *Anna Magdalena Notebook* and Schumann's *Album for the Young* as a cornerstone of the child's repertoire.

The *Fourteen Bagatelles* are another matter. Often blatantly experimental, sometimes sketchy in detail, they represent decisive steps towards the future and many of the traits of Bartók's mature style can be discerned in embryonic form. In June, 1908, Bartók played them to Busoni who exclaimed, 'At last! Something *really* new.' Busoni, a tireless champion of new music, tried to interest his

---

1. *Leitmotif* (German) Musical term denoting a single short phrase or even a single chord that is constantly associated with a particular character or event (most notably used by Wagner in his music dramas).

A Hungarian folk song sketch which was the basis of one of the piano pieces 'For Children'.

own publishers, the prestigious German firm Breitkopf and Härtel, in them but they timidly rejected them as 'too difficult and modern for the public.' Busoni also invited Bartók to conduct the Scherzo from his Suite No. 2 in Berlin the following year, a novel and exhilarating (if nerve-racking) experience which he never repeated.

Busoni's support was welcome, as words of appreciation and understanding were hard to come by. Etelka Freund, a former pupil, was another patient propagandist on Bartók's behalf and it was thanks to her advocacy that the distinguished Swiss (later American) pianist Rudolph Ganz became one of the first to include Bartók's music in his programme. Bartók was appreciative, and wrote to Ganz

Your kind lines (just received) have given me real pleasure, especially as I have had to endure an unbelievable number of attacks all provoked by these very piano pieces . . . hardly more than one in a hundred will find any pleasure in these works, and I have to be thankful if they are not labelled as products of frenzy or insanity as has often occurred.

He was particularly stung by the remark of the eminent German musicologist, Hugo Leichtentritt who, after attending the Berlin performance of the orchestral *Scherzo*, declared that Bartók 'had no clear notion of the essential requirements necessary to give artistic significance to a composition.'

Happily, such setbacks did not this time stem the flow of inspiration, as had Koessler's grumpy antipathy in his student days, for he was confident that he was on the right path. Performances of his orchestral works, while neither a regular nor frequent feature of the Budapest Philharmonic season, were becoming accepted as occasional events of some importance, even if the standard of

40

performance left much to be desired. Although they were invariably greeted with a more or less equal mixture of cheers and catcalls, Bartók was far from dismayed by this reaction, and even felt sufficiently encouraged to compose further orchestral works. In fact, this mixture of adulatory enthusiasm and hostility was becoming the norm for important premières of those composers who were blazing their respective trails away from the comfortable opulence of late romanticism. Schoenberg, Berg, Hindemith and Prokofiev all had similar experiences and the trend reached its zenith in the notorious riots which attended the Paris première of Stravinsky's ballet *The Rite of Spring* in 1913. Peter Ustinov coined the memorable phrase, a 'fiasco d'estime', which neatly suggests a certain *cachet* which attached to the composer on such occasions.

The very title *Two Pictures* for orchestra op. 10 calls to mind Debussy and his *Images* for piano and for orchestra, and the first of these reveals the influence of the French master more strongly than any of Bartók's other orchestral works. The second, a stamping rustic dance, has, in addition, a new earthiness in its handling of folk material.

A further orchestral work, *Two Portraits (One Ideal, One Grotesque)* op. 5 assumed a peculiar interest in the light of the Stefi Geyer letters. In the summer of 1907, Bartók started work on a two-movement violin concerto for Stefi. Although Bartók scholars had known of its existence for many years, it was not performed during the composer's lifetime, and the complete score only came to light among Stefi Geyer's effects after her death in 1956. However, the first movement of the concerto, serenely meditative but for its soaring impassioned climax, turned out to be none other than the first *Portrait (The Ideal)*, and its thematic base is clearly the 'leitmotif' in the third letter to Stefi. The second, 'grotesque' *Portrait* is an orchestral version of the last of the *Fourteen Bagatelles* for piano, a shrill, hysterical 'Danse Macabre' in which the themes of the 'ideal' portrait are twisted and distorted with strident irony. This scheme is of special fascination to musicologists because Liszt used exactly the same technique in his *Faust Symphony*, where the themes of the Faust movement are grotesquely disfigured to express the evil spirit of negation in the Mephistopheles movement. The last two *Bagatelles*, a lugubrious dirge and this frantic waltz which became the second portrait, are both shot through with the melancholy strains that Bartók jotted down in the letter. According to Denijs Dille, the Flemish researcher, Stefi Geyer severed her relations with Bartók in February, 1908, and the Bagatelles were completed shortly afterwards. So the psychological inferences of this pair of portraits are even more thought-provoking than the musicological ones.

Other piano works, the *Two Rumanian Dances, Two Elegies, 3*

Burlesques (op. 8a, b and c), the *Four Dirges* and the *Seven Sketches* (op. 9a and b), all composed between 1908 and 1910, show notable advances along the 'new road', although Bartók's sporadic lapses into a Lisztian piano style sometimes sit uneasily with his growing terseness of expression. The only chamber work in this sustained creative burst was the *String Quartet No. 1, op. 8,* intense, serious and moving and an important work in its own right, but more especially so as the first in a series of six quartets that have become accepted without argument as true classics of 20th century music. When Kodály said that it concerned 'a man's return to life after travelling to the very borders of non-existence,' he was evidently referring to his knowledge that Bartók had actually contemplated suicide over the Stefi Geyer affair.

In a memorial speech, Kodály described his friend's driving force as 'a thirst for knowledge, perseverance, love of work and a consuming interest in all forms of musical expression.' In connection with his work at the Academy, Bartók took on an additional burden in starting a series of editorial revisions of a wide range of keyboard music. This immersion in baroque and classical music was no doubt the source of a final external influence on his music, although its effects are not really to be felt until some years later.

Among his class at the Academy were two sisters, Herma and Marta Ziegler, daughters of an inspector in the police force. It is clear that Bartók soon formed a particular attachment for the younger girl, Marta, for he dedicated the *Portrait of a Girl* in his *Seven Sketches* to her in 1908. Just how close they had become was suspected by no-one apparently, and the ensuing events reveal that Bartók's mania for privacy had reached almost comic proportions. Jenö Kerpely, 'cellist in the Waldbauer-Kerpely Quartet which was closely associated with Bartók, related the bizarre tale after he had emigrated to America many years later. The sixteen-year-old Marta was having her lesson at Bartók's home one morning in the autumn of 1909, and Bartók told his mother that she would be staying for lunch. The lesson continued into the afternoon and Paula Bartók raised her eyebrows enquiringly on being told, 'Marta will stay to supper, too.' Only then did Bartók grudgingly add, 'We're married.' They continued to keep their marriage a secret from the outside world for a while until Marta absent-mindedly referred to the professor as 'my husband.' The cat was out of the bag and Dohnányi immediately sent them a congratulatory telegram, which Bartók hotly resented as an intrusion into his private affairs!

Bartók's insatiable appetite for work was not diminished by this change in his domestic circumstances. His folk music researches continued unabated and his young wife often accompanied him on

Bartók, Kodály and the members of the Waldbauer-Kerpely String Quartet—the phalanx of the musical avant-garde in Budapest.

his tours. They were fortunate in having Paula Bartók on hand to help in caring for young Béla junior, who was born in August, 1910. There were occasional and much acclaimed concert appearances in popular concertos by Liszt and Saint-Saëns, but from this time onwards, Bartók was really only interested in playing his own music in public.

Two especially noteworthy concerts took place in Budapest and Paris in 1909 and 1910 respectively. At the local event, the brilliant young Waldbauer-Kerpely Quartet (whose oldest member was twenty-five years old, the youngest a mere eighteen) played the first quartets of both Bartók and Kodály which once more aroused the antagonism of the establishment but caused great excitement amongst the burgeoning avant-garde circle. The mouthpiece of progressive intellectuals was a literary magazine of great vitality, *Nyugat* (West), founded by the liberal writer Hugo Ignotus, to which Endre Ady was a leading contributor. Its aims as expressed by Ignotus's son Paul, in his masterly study 'Hungary' (London 1972), were precisely those of Bartók himself,

The *Nyugat* guard were determined to create a totally European Hungary, delivered from parochialism; but, at the same time, to assert the national

Bartók with his three year old son Béla jnr. in the garden of the house in Rakoskerestúr. (Embassy of the Hungarian People's Republic)

Béla Balázs—librettist of *The Wooden Prince* and *Duke Bluebeard's Castle*.

personality and to dig deep into the Magyar heritage of images, concepts, and melodies, and refurbish what had been debased by usage and foreign influences,

so he would have found the perceptive and enthusiastic reviews of Géza Csáth, the magazine's lively young music critic, particularly heart-warming.

The 'Festival Hongrois' presented in Paris the following year by Sándor Kovfåcs, included music by Léo Weiner, Árpád Szendy, Ödön Mihalovich and Dohnányi, as well as by the two modernists, Bartók and Kodály who were branded in the press as 'young barbarians'. Bartók's reply was his *Allegro Barbaro* for piano, a piece of even greater ferocity than anything he had previously produced. It is typical of a certain strain in his music, evoking the primitive violence and indomitable rhythmic energy that delighted him in peasant dances; but it was unfortunate that this single aspect of his work was seized upon by critics of delicate sensibility who could see in him nothing more than a brutal, savage iconoclasm.

'Tonal chaos arising from the diabolical employment of

Endre Ady—leading Hungarian poet and radical. Bartók set five of his poems to music in 1916. (Embassy of the Hungarian People's Republic)

unrelated keys simultaneously,' is typical of the sort of criticism he had to endure for most of his career.

Despite the defiant gestures, there were signs that Bartók's resolve was beginning to crumble; small wonder, when we consider that he had been working at white heat for more than three years only to have inched forward to a position precariously balanced between neglect and notoriety. Antal Molnár, the violist in the Waldbauer-Kerpely Quartet and a new recruit to folk music research, described Bartók's withdrawal,

He spoke as matter-of-factly as a locksmith showing his tools to a new apprentice, but with flattering brevity. Otherwise he stared at me with wide questioning eyes, quite often for fifteen minutes at a time.

It was Béla Balázs, poet, novelist and dramatist, who conjured one last gigantic effort out of Bartók,

I talked to him about the great Hungarian renaissance, the necessity for a Hungarian contribution to the development of European culture, and I

45

encouraged him. . . . But I had never before observed in anyone the tight lips and unchanging deathly pallor with which Béla Bartók listened to me.

Thus Bartók, with Balázs as librettist, embarked upon his first and only opera *Duke Bluebeard's Castle*. Although the source of the one-act scenario was the age-old legend of the murderous Bluebeard and his seven wives, the psycho-analytic approach of composer and librettist is a far cry from the blood and thunder of nineteenth-century operatic melodrama. The critic, Sándor Veress described its theme as 'the eternal tragedy of the dualism of man and woman, the heavenly and earthly perspective of their souls.' Of more significance to Bartók, surely, was the impenetrable loneliness of Bluebeard, inescapably bound by his own nature, from which he cannot be free even by the total self-sacrifice of the woman, Judith. The music, while clearly influenced by Debussy's *Pelleas et Melisande* is a brilliant kaleidoscope of sound imagery and psychological nuance (Stefi Geyer's *leitmotif* is unmistakeably present), but the lack of dramatic stage action betrays the libretto's poetic origins and makes severe demands on the audience's attention.

In a despairing effort to improve the performing standards and general climate for contemporary music, an attempt was made to set up a *New Hungarian Music Society* (*UMZE*), but it ran into one obstacle after another. Before long, Bartók was scribbling furiously on a postcard to Etelka Freund,

This UMZE has been such a nuisance that I would like to consign it to the depths of hell.

Duke Bluebeard's Castle was rejected out of hand in a competition organised by the Lipótvárosi Kaszinó, and the two failures were too much for Bartók, who now gave up the struggle and withdrew from public life. He was still smarting with frustration eighteen months later, when he wrote explaining his reasons to Géza Vilmos Zágan, a colleague who had worked hard in the cause of modern music,

. . . a year ago sentence of death was passed on me as a composer. Either those people are right, in which case I am an untalented bungler; or I am right, and it's they who are the idiots. In either event, this means that between myself and them (that is, our musical leaders: Hubay, etc.) there can be no discussion of music, still less any joint action . . . Therefore I have resigned myself to write for my writing-desk only.

But one flame was not extinguished,

My public appearances are confined to *one sole field*: I will do anything to further my research work in musical folklore.

46

Chapter Five

In the years leading to the first world war the political scene in Hungary had become a farrago of ever-increasing complexity, in which conflicting ideals and vested interests jostled to produce a series of dramatic changes and gestures that were so frequent and impermanent as to result in stalemate. The fundamental obstacles to political maturity (in a present-day sense) would seem to be clear enough — the continuing dependence on Vienna and a restricted franchise. However, these issues were clouded by the reluctance of the various factions to concede their present positions of power — the gentry over the peasantry, the Magyars over the ethnic minorities and the Hapsburgs over all. Although implacably opposed to one another, the active partisans of each power *bloc* were secretly in dread of a genuine popular uprising, and each exploited the others' fear of it. The parties strove to reconcile their conflicting objectives with a startling degree of compromise and often with disregard for logic. Magyar supremacy could be equated with the power of the gentry over the peasantry, hence we find radical intellectuals leaning towards the dynastic camp as their best means of undermining aristocratic wealth and privilege. On the other hand, pillars of the landowning establishment emerged as champions of the common man in retaliation against Hapsburg attempts to clip their wings. The heir to the Imperial throne, the dour and pedantic Prince Franz Ferdinand, was perceptive enough to see the possible advantage in these anomalies, and for a while tightened the Hapsburg grip by granting minor concessions to the opposed sectional interests. But his manner in doing so, together with his charmless personality, succeeded only in antagonising *en bloc* the disparate elements in Hungarian society. In any event, history was against him, for where he had hoped to win support from Romanov Russia and Imperial Britain, hindsight tells us that the Republican movements in France and Italy were more relevant to the Hungarian situation.

The universal distaste for Franz Ferdinand felt by almost every shade of Hungarian opinion makes it the more absurd and inexplicable that the nation's leaders and press should have joined so loudly in the clamour for war that followed his assassination at Sarajevo on

1918—with his friends Ion Buşiţia and Zoltán Kodály.

June 28, 1914. On the face of it, the idea of avenging a Hapsburg could scarcely have been further removed from the mood of the Hungarian people. Paul Ignotus could only explain it as 'a general malaise from which everyone tried to escape into military adventure.'

Bartók's interest in the squabbles of party politics was minimal. He had made his anti-Hapsburg sentiments clear long ago, but by now his Hungarianism was tempered by his affection for the minority races, especially Slovak and Romanian, with whom he had become involved on his collecting tours. He was moving away from a narrow, parochial nationalism towards his ideal of a 'brotherhood of nations'. He had no taste for sabre-rattling and was deeply shocked by the suddenness of the catastrophe.

I have been so upset by world events that my mind has been almost completely paralysed,

he wrote in September, 1914.

He was not called for military service on medical grounds (he weighed only 98 pounds), but his mood of depression and introversion was not helped by the additional threat to his collecting activities. When he did venture out, however, he found that things were not so bad as he feared — for the time being, at least.

It is hard to imagine that anyone could go on collecting folk-songs in times like these. But it can be done. The amazing thing is that you can do it exactly as in peace-time. The peasants are so merry and lighthearted, one might think they don't care a rap about the war.

The collection was growing apace, and by the end of the war he had amassed some 1,000 Hungarian, Romanian, Slovak, Bulgarian, Ruthenian, Serbian, even Arabic folksongs. With Kodály's help he began to classify this mass of material, using a modified form of the system devised by the Finnish folklorist, Ilmari Krohn.

His original compositions between 1910 and 1915 are sparse indeed, and the bulk of his output from this time is derived from the Romanian material he had started to gather in 1909. There are many treasures to be found here, including the enchanting *Sonatina* for piano and the *Six Romanian Folk Dances*, one of his most popular works which has undergone further rearrangement for almost every conceivable instrument. An examination of his original precise transcript of what the peasant musicians actually played him on their strange violins, flutes and bagpipes reveals the subtlety and delicacy with which the definitive piano version imprints his own personal and unifying style on their exotic

48

Below left Marta and Paula Bartók, 1915. (Embassy of the Hungarian People's Republic)

Bartók during his years of seclusion.

nuances and mannerisms, rendering them alive and intelligible to the concert performer, or to the sympathetic amateur.

Bartók formed close and lasting friendships as a result of these Romanian sorties, notably with Ion Buşitia, a schoolmaster of many talents, who lent wholehearted support and companionship to his projects. He was rewarded with a niche in posterity by Bartók's dedication of the *Six Romanian Dances*. Another Romanian contact, the conductor Dumitru Kiriac laid a significant milestone in Bartók's career by arranging the publication (Bucharest, 1913) of the first of his many ethno-musicological monographs, a lesser-known side of the composer's output which gives fascinating insights into his own musical language.

Bartók was fully aware that this surprisingly tranquil and trouble-free situation could not continue indefinitely.

49

He perform the "Wooden Prince" in 1917

Budapest Opera House where the first two stage works were produced.

My long silence has been due to the fact that every now and then I am thrown into a state of deep depression by the war, (he wrote to Ion Buşiţia in May, 1915) a condition which, in my case, alternates with a kind of devil-may-care attitude. In all my thinking there is a *ceterum censeo*: nothing matters, but to remain friends with Romania; it would be a grievous thing to me to see my beloved Transylvania devastated, besides greatly hindering my prospect of finishing, or rather continuing, my work. In fact, I can't hold out much hope for work of this kind; the future seems gloomy indeed!

His fears were well founded. In August, 1916, Romania invaded the Transylvanian territory of Hungary. Marta Bartók and young Béla were in the region at the time and for three weeks Bartók waited in an agony of suspense for word whether they were alive or dead.

As the war tightened its grip on the country, remorselessly isolating his research territory, Bartók returned to his writing desk, and several important works now flowed from his pen. The bleak desolation of the fourth movement of his *Suite, op. 14* for piano suggests a deserted battlefield, while in the ferocious, whirlwind

50

third movement, the Arabic scales implanted in Bartók's mind during his visit to Biskra (North Africa) in 1913 emerge for the first time. The passionate and moving *String Quartet No. 2*, composed at the same time concludes in a similar manner: subsiding into eerie stillness, its fury spent in the barbarous Second movement.

Two song cycles followed, Bartók's only contribution to the *genre*, if we except student efforts and the numerous folksong arrangements. The *Five Songs, op. 16* are settings of poems by Endry Ady, far and away the leading Hungarian poet of the time and *doyen* of the *Nyugat* radicals. The *Five Songs, op. 15* are of more curious origin. For many years, their texts were given as 'by unknown author(s)', but research in Hungary has shown them to be the work of sixteen-year-old Klara Gombossy, a forester's daughter who accompanied Bartók on several collecting expeditions. Their friendship lasted about a year, and the fact that her authorship is not credited on the score has given rise to speculation that their relationship may have been deliberately kept secret.

But the most exciting event of the war years was undoubtedly the production of the one-act ballet *The Wooden Prince*; not for posterity, perhaps, for it has never received the same recognition outside Hungary as Bartók's other stage works (*Duke Bluebeard's Castle* and *The Miraculous Mandarin*), but because it provided the composer with his first taste of unqualified public success and acclaim. The libretto, again by Bela Balázs, was published in *Nyugat* in 1913, a naïve fairy-tale of a princess who spurns the ardent prince in favour of the wooden puppet he creates for her, but

Below right Scene from *The Wooden Prince*.
Below left Scene from *Duke Bluebeard's Castle*.
(Embassy of the Hungarian People's Republic)

Egisto Tango—the Italian conductor and saviour of *The Wooden Prince*.

decked out with elaborate symbolism that today smacks of archness or pretentiousness at times. Bartók was taken by the idea of art (the puppet) being made a rich girl's plaything at the expense of the artist's feelings, but he also wanted to show, by setting a second libretto by Balázs, his faith in their previous collaboration, the rejected *Duke Bluebeard's Castle*. He had started work on the score in 1913, and now, in his latest surge of creative vitality, took it up again. The project was fraught with every kind of obstacle. No Hungarian conductor would touch it, the orchestra said it was unplayable and the ballet master (who understood not a note of the music) pronounced it undanceable as well. Anxious well-wishers advised cancellation to avoid a certain fiasco.

Bartók himself would probably have thrown in the towel, retreating into a fit of righteous indignation reminiscent of his Paris experience.

What is the Royal Opera House anyway?! An Augean stable; a dumping ground for every kind of rubbish; the seat of all disorder; the pinnacle of confusion.

But all was not lost. The dynamic Italian conductor Egisto Tango demanded (and got) no less than thirty rehearsals and Balázs himself took over the coaching of the corps de ballet. Their enthusiasm and dedication infected the whole company, and when the curtain came down after the first performance on May 12, 1917, the doubters were confounded. Balázs recalls that 'the applause broke out in the galleries, and like an avalanche swept down to the boxes and the stalls, carrying before it all the rabble of the press. Many reviews had to be rewritten that night.' Bartók, Balázs and Tango were recalled to the stage fifteen times. In deepest gratitude for 'a musically perfect performance' Bartók dedicated the score to Egisto Tango. The depression and pangs of rejection were lifted for a while. The autobiography reads,

The year 1917 brought a change in the attitude of the Budapest public toward my compositions, I had the wonderful luck to hear a major work of mine, a ballet entitled *The Wooden Prince*, performed in a perfect manner under the direction of Maestro Egisto Tango. In 1918 he also arranged a performance of an older work of mine, *Duke Bluebeard's Castle*.

On a darker note he goes on,

After these promising beginnings there followed, alas! the complete political and economic breakdown of 1918. The sad and troubled times that followed for about a year and a half were not conducive to serious work.

Chapter Six

While Bartók was absorbed in *The Wooden Prince*, the seeds of the collapse had already taken root. As the war dragged on, the spurious bellicosity stirred up at the outset gave way to frustration, boredom and misery. The political manoeuvring and sniping of the pre-war years became increasingly bitter and recriminatory, and by the time the conflict approached its messy and ragged conclusion the hostility between the various shades of authoritarians, democrats and communists was at boiling point. Scapegoats for the deprivation and humiliation of the wasted years were sought by all sides. For a brief spell it looked as though firm but moderate diplomacy might save the day. The disintegration of the Hapsburg empire into some pattern of national units was a foregone conclusion by the summer of 1918, and within days of the German surrender a Hungarian National Council was set up — in effect an alliance of the old Independence Party and assorted leftish groups from outside parliament. It was headed by Count Mihály (Michael) Károlyi, an immensely wealthy landowner but a man with genuine democratic aspirations, for all his inbred aristocratic *hauteur*. The prime minister, Count István Tisza, made frantic last minute concessions in parliament on practically every contentious issue. But it was too late to stem the flood of support for Károlyi's National Council on which people hysterically pinned their hopes for 'peace' and 'people's welfare'. So Count Tisza, who had been in and out of office since the turn of the century through his skill in the art of compromise, was himself cast as scapegoat and summarily shot in his own home in what was otherwise a surprisingly bloodless *coup*.

But it was a false dawn. Although Károlyi's Council achieved the transition from Imperial satellite to Republic, it could not withstand the vengeful dismemberment of the country by her neighbours in collusion with the victorious powers. In panic, the country lurched to the left in the hope that Lenin's new Soviet Russia would support its territorial claims. A new Hungarian Republic of Councils was formed between two workers' parties under the leadership of the communist agitator Béla Kun who had been hastily released from prison. Economic conditions had sunk

Proclamation of Karolyi's
Republic, 1919.
(Embassy of the Hungarian
People's Republic)

even below wartime levels and the shortage in the cities of basic
commodities like fuel and foodstuffs was aggravated by the influx of
trainloads of refugees from the lost territories. Barely four months
elapsed before the inept adventures of Kun's Red Army opened the
capital to Romanian invaders and yet another junta, this time of a
vicious right-wing militarism. A communist witch-hunt ensued,
involving the indiscriminate slaughter of workers, Jews and
peasants and in March, 1920, Rear Admiral Miklós Horthy,
'Supreme Commander of the Hungarian National Army' was
officially 'elected' head of state, a position he occupied for the rest
of Bartók's life. The series of events was not, indeed, 'conducive to
serious work' and its repercussions were to be felt repeatedly over
the next two decades.

As a state institution, the Academy was not immune from the
shuffling of official positions inevitably associated with these rapid
changes. When Ödön Mihalovich retired as director at the
beginning of 1919, the Károlyi administration appointed Dohnányi
to succeed him with Kodály as his deputy. When the Horthy
régime took effective control in the summer, Dohnányi was abroad
on a concert tour. He returned to Budapest in November to find
himself suspended for one year 'while his appointment was being
reconsidered.' Kodály, Imre Waldbauer the violinist and Kerpely

54

the 'cellist were also excluded, pending investigation of their activities under the communist government. Bartók himself had been enlisted onto the Music Committee set up by the Kun régime along with Dohnányi and Kodály, but had undertaken no active political rôle apart from his support for Kodály's radical programme of educational reform. His main interest had been in a projected Museum of Music with himself as director of the folk music section (a post he had long dreamed of as an alternative to teaching). At first, he found the bickering little more than a tiresome farce. He pointed out in a letter to his mother that the suspended teachers

continue to draw full salaries, of course, only do no work. In fact, they come off better than those teachers against whom no action has been taken.

He underestimated the situation. Far from fizzling out, as Bartók predicted, the right wing backlash took an uglier turn the following year.

The Horthy government's choice for the post of director was Jenö Hubay, the eminent violinist and teacher, whose dazzling array of pupils included Stefi Geyer, Ferenc Vecsey, Imre Waldbauer, József Szigeti, Jelly Aranyi and Zoltán Székely, all of whom were closely associated with Bartók at some stage in his career. Hubay had presumably satisfied the authorities that he was amenable to political pressure and, as an administrator, he was given to making airy and sweeping pronouncements to the press without consulting his colleagues. Bartók, who was on a six month sabbatical at the time, viewed his elevation with some cynicism from the start,

Mr Hubay has made his triumphal entry into the halls of the National Academy of Music (probably to a festive march composed by himself) . . . he is handing out statements left and right.

By now it was clear that the 'white purge' was not going to blow over and, although Hubay made friendly overtures to Dohnányi and Bartók in his public statements, they were viewed with some caution. Béla Reinitz, the composer who had chaired the Music Committee of the Republic of Councils, was now in prison and Béla Balázs, an avowed communist, had fled the country. What actually spurred Bartók into action was the implementation by a government commission of the long-threatened disciplinary action against his friend Kodály, who was accused, firstly, of being a member of Reinitz's Music Committee and secondly, in his rôle of deputy director of the Academy, of permitting the *Internazionale* to be orchestrated, allowing recruitment of students by the Red Army, and various petty infringements of bureaucratic red tape.

Ernst von Dohnányi—an early victim of the post-war political intrigues.

Bartók and Dohnányi leapt publicly to his aid. Bartók pointed out that, since he too had sat on the same committee, it was flagrantly unjust to single Kodály out for this 'offence', while Dohnányi declared that anything that had occurred during his directorship of the Academy was his responsibility alone. To the charge of 'unpatriotically' collecting folksongs of the minority 'alien' races, Kodály was eloquent in his own defence,

I have never meddled in everyday politics. But figuratively speaking, every bar of music, every folk tune I have recorded has been a political act. In my opinion, that is true patriotism; a policy of actual deeds, not of mere slogans.

Before long, the Ministry officials let the case drop rather than allow the wave of sympathy for Kodály grow into anything more menacing, but not before they had demoted him from deputy director to rank and file teacher.

The persecution of his friend had sinister implications for Bartók, with his close personal and scientific ties with the Romanians and Slovaks. This side of his work ('as necessary to me as fresh air is to other people') had come to an indefinite halt through the curbs on free travel imposed in the wake of the war, and in other respects his future was uncertain, too. The museum post he hankered after had progressed no further than discussions and a more recent suggestion to make him director of the Opera filled him with horror. His exasperation with the cultural authorities was aggravated by a report in a right wing newspaper that he was to sit on a newly appointed Music Council. He immediately sent a stiff note to the Editor-in-chief,

. . . I feel obliged to inform you that, on the contrary, I have received no official approach in this matter; nor would I wish to be a member of any musical council from which the greatest musicians of the country (i.e. Dohnányi and Kodály) are excluded.

Many of his friends and colleagues had fled abroad to escape the purge, and Bartók himself gave serious thought to the possibility of emigrating. Berlin, Vienna, Transylvania and even London were all considered for one reason or another. He had recently signed a contract with the enterprising Universal Edition of Vienna for his music and he now sent some of his ethnographical studies to Germany in the hope of finding an outlet for his growing accumulation of unpublished findings.

In February, 1920, some concert engagements gave him the chance to test the water in Berlin, where he stayed for two months. Postal services had still not been resumed between Hungary and

Romania, so it was also a good opportunity to get in touch again with his friend Ion Buşiţia,

At home the outlook is pretty bleak; I have come here to have a look around and see what may be done. I have been pleased to find that I am greatly respected here. At any rate, it would be possible for me to settle here.

Rumours, apparently well founded, reached Budapest that Max Reinhardt had approached Bartók with a view to commissioning a score for his production of *Lysistrata*, and mutterings of 'treachery' were heard in the chauvinist press. In the end, it was his passion for folksong which 'drew him east', as he put it to Buşiţia, and in May he returned to Budapest, not to the little house on Rákoskerestúr where the family had lived for ten years, but to a handsome and spacious mansion in Gyoparutca at the invitation of a benevolent friend, József Lukács (the father of the Marxist philosopher György Lukács). They had only two rooms, but Bartók's sick leave and the ravages of inflation and currency problems had wrought havoc with his finances and they were grateful for this refuge where they remained for about two years.

They had barely settled in when rumblings in the press over Bartók's dealings in Germany erupted into a violent and malicious personal onslaught. The bitterness engendered by the final humiliation of Hungary at the Treaty of Trianon incited the chauvinist elements almost to hysteria, and Bartók found himself branded as a traitor for his findings on, of all things 'The Romanian Folk music Dialect of Hunyad'. The opening salvo was fired by one Professor Elemér Sereghy in the newspaper *Nemzeti Ujsag*. The article was dismissive and insulting about the scientific validity of Bartók's work, but the arguments sprang from political bigotry and hinged on Bartók's 'motives' for attributing Romanian ancestry to material collected within Hungary. It may be that Sereghy's rage was inflamed by the knowledge that Bartók's intermediary in negotiations with German publishers on the essay in question was Géza Révész, a communist refugee from the new régime. A further polemic appeared a few days later, in which Bartók's essay was described as 'treacherous poison' and Kodály as his 'evil genius'. At first, Bartók was content to ignore this catchpenny journalism as irrelevant to any serious discussion of the points at issue. But when Jenö Hubay entered the fray, his voice, with the authority of his position behind it, could not go unchallenged.

Hubay was aware of Bartók's growing international prestige and generally anxious to preserve civil, if not cordial relations with him. But in this matter he found it more prudent to toe the party line and, accordingly, he issued one of his lofty statements to the press.

57

He deplored the untimely publication of the essay in a German magazine and thought it 'culpable for us to be in any way concerned with the culture of our minorities.' After sweeping condemnation of Bartók's conclusions, he ended with a burst of jingoism that was as stupid as it was shameless.

These questions must not today be judged from a scholarly point of view, but only from that of the national interest of Hungary, which at the present time is, in any event, more important than details of scholarship to which in general no great significance can be ascribed.

Bartók replied with icy fury, refuting the charges one by one.

I read with amazement in today's issue of *Szozat* that director Hubay has identified himself with the charges brought against me by *Nemzeti Ujsag*. I am therefore compelled to reply publicly and point to the most conspicuous examples of those charges which show ignorance, malevolence, and deliberate distortion. . . . The publication of my article was also desirable in order to show those abroad in what high esteem we hold our minorities, the extent of our concern for their cultural matters, how little we oppress them. Or does Hungary's interest possibly not require that we refute our enemies' charge that we oppress our minorities?

After reiterating his belief in his scientific methods and conclusions, he throws down his challenge to Hubay.

Because I have been doing research for more than a decade, I may be less prone to 'errors' than Director Hubay, who — so far as I know — is not acquainted with my Hungarian and other collections, nor has he ever taken any interest in them. If he insists upon his statement, then let him state which of the 'falsified' melodies he considered to be of Romanian origin and he should prove that they are indeed so.

For the moment, the campaign withered in the face of such unshakeable moral conviction. Bartók was contemptuous rather than bitter about it all and gratified that his true friends rallied round him.

I have no cause for complaint against my compatriots either (he wrote to Busitia). Some of them may not have acted fairly towards me; but others have tried to make up for this with all the more zeal.

Although he only reluctantly involved himself with political squabbles of this nature, he was a shrewd judge of shifting trends.

The dictatorship of the military is crushing the intellectual life of the country, just as the dictatorship of the proletariat crushed its economic existence before,

58

he wrote in 1920, and he was perceptive enough to discern even then signs of the canker that was to poison the fabric of Hungarian society.

Far from being censored for the loss of Tango, (another casualty of political intrigue), or for the present inartistic regime, Emil Ábrányi, the general director of the Opera, has merely been accused of possessing too little-marked a sense of 'Christian Nationalism'! He was, in all seriousness, accused of having engaged several new Jewish members and of having performed two local works by Jewish composers. For with us at present it is no longer a question of whether an artist, a singer, a savant is of good repute in his especial class of work, but whether he is a Jew or a man of liberal tendencies. For these two sections of humanity are to be excluded so far as possible from all public activity.

And how did Bartók's own creative force withstand the pressures of this chaotic and frustrating era? Unsurprisingly, his output was sporadic, but the works he did produce show no wavering in the ever-increasing mastery of style and intensity of expression achieved during the war years. Remorselessly he stripped away the familiar and traditional elements that remained and moved towards an uncompromisingly 'modern' idiom, never abandoning his folk sources but moving decisively into the main vanguard of twentieth century European music where his rightful position was increasingly recognised.

Melchior Lengyel, librettist of *The Miraculous Mandarin*, later a Hollywood script writer.

The unexpected success of *The Wooden Prince*, and the emergence at its première of a fervent and vociferous coterie of supporters, encouraged Bartók to stay with the theatre for his next major work, the ballet, or *pantomime grotesque*, *The Miraculous Mandarin*. The lurid and bloody scenario was a far cry from Balázs' poetic and philosophical abstractions, and its author Menyhért (Melchior) Lengyel belonged to the new group of naturalistic writers associated with the Gay Theatre in Budapest. The script was published in *Nyugat* in 1917 and the composer and librettist were introduced over Sunday lunch at István Thomán's house the following year. The taste for horror and atrocity which had entered the world of literature around the turn of the century in the writings of Poe, Wedekind and Wilde was reflected in music by Debussy's projected (though never completed) setting of Poe's *The Fall of the House of Usher* and Strauss's *Salome* (based on Oscar Wilde's play) which had greatly excited Bartók during his Strauss fever. The apocalyptic horrors of the war provoked a fresh wave of literary shockers, and there may have been an element of opportunism in Lengyel's choice of subject. After his fall from grace in Hungary, he successfully adapted his talents to the requirements of Hollywood, where the Garbo classic *Ninotchka* was amongst his many screen credits. Bartók's reasons for choosing the

59

libretto are harder to assess. He was, of course, not unmoved by the ugliness of war, nor was he unaware of current trends in music and literature. He was keenly interested in the music of Stravinsky and Schoenberg and he berated the Hungarian musical establishment for their indifference to important new developments. Marta and he had been working hard at the piano duet arrangement of Stravinsky's *The Rite of Spring* which he saw as a Russian manifestation of the same primordial force that he found in the peasant music of his own land. His own style was moving towards an apex of dissonance and uncompromising harshness which may have been influenced by external factors but also, in terms of his total output, seems evolutionary and inevitable. The elemental passions of *The Miraculous Mandarin* therefore presented themselves at an ideal juncture in his development as a composer. The staging of the ballet ran into one obstacle after another. Since most of them arose from the subject matter of the libretto, it is worth relating the plot in some detail. The curtain rises on a backstreet room, barely furnished but with an open bed prominently displayed. On stage are three men and a girl, whom they urge to dance at the window in order to lure men in from the street. The first victim is an elderly drunk who is beaten and thrown out when his comic posturing turns to violence. He is followed by a timid youth, for whom the girl feels a tender attraction but he too is ejected when it is discovered that he has no money. At this point the Mandarin makes his entrance, a mysterious, inscrutable and awe-inspiring figure (Lengyel's original conception was a misshapen dwarf). As the girl, at once fascinated and repelled, starts again her erotic dance, he pursues her round the room, slowly at first, then with increasing frenzy. The three pimps emerge from hiding, set upon the Mandarin and suffocate him but, so unquenchable is his lust, he will not die. They stab him repeatedly and finally hang him from the ceiling, but only when the girl submits to him does the blood begin to flow from his wounds and, sated, he sinks and dies.

Although attitudes towards theatrical licence are more liberal now than in the 1920s, even so they were then not especially noted for prudery or austerity. The ballet was open to a number of interpretations — from the overwhelming strength of nature within man himself to the indomitable power of love over inhuman cruelty — but the Hungarian authorities could see no more than a seditious potion of criminal violence and flagrant sexuality. They vacillated and compromised interminably and eventually suggested that the affront to public morality might be mitigated by transferring the action to an anonymous, outdoor Asian setting. Thus it finally reached the Budapest stage, but, by then, twenty-five years had elapsed and Bartók was dead. However, it was given in Cologne, in 1926, where the scandal and outrage of the church and press was so violent that the mayor stepped in and banned the production after a single performance.

Bartók never returned to the theatre. He had no taste for the intrigues of theatrical life and was probably aware that his greatest gift was for instrumental music. This is not to discount the importance of a comparatively small number of vocal masterpieces, any more than to say the same of Beethoven belittles *Fidelio* or the *Missa Solemnis*. It was to this medium that he now returned, first with the *Eight Improvisations on Hungarian Peasant Songs* for piano, which represent his most extreme reworking of actual peasant material. There followed, in 1921 and 1922, two sonatas for violin and piano, neither of them calculated to win mass popularity, but which nevertheless contributed enormously to his standing in the international arena. They represent the extreme point of Bartók's experimentation with logical dissonance and this, together with certain melodic aspects, brings his music into closer proximity with the second Viennese school of Schoenberg than ever before or after. The galloping folk dance movements are, of course, pure

Bartók with his mother in 1925.
(Embassy of the Hungarian People's Republic)

61

Bartók but, if influences are to be discerned, then mention should also be made of the Polish composer Karol Szymanowski, whose works Bartók was studying eagerly at the time. Their composition coincided with a fortuitous re-meeting with the brilliant violinist Jelly Aranyi whom he had known in his student days. Her family had emigrated to London before the war, but she visited Budapest in 1921 and Bartók was thrilled by the fire and imagination of her playing. Both sonatas were dedicated to her although, oddly, she did not give the first performance of either. When she did collaborate with the composer in performances in Paris and London, their success was enormous. The Paris première of the first sonata was a particularly exciting occasion, and Jelly 'excelled herself', Bartók informed his mother. Henri Prunières, the French musicologist, gave a supper party after the concert which 'was attended by "half the leading composers of the world" — that is Ravel, Szymanowski, Stravinsky — as well as a few young notorious Frenchmen whom you would not know.'

The young 'notorieties' included Milhaud and Poulenc who both sent enthusiastic notes to Bartók about the sonata.

Folk music collecting was still moribund due to the continuing restrictions on travel, so activity in this field had to be confined to the organisation and classification of existing material. Bartók and Kodály organised voluntary seminars at the Academy to this end and work progressed steadily, although Antal Doráti recalled that most of the students attended through devotion to their teachers rather than any great enthusiasm for the painstaking chores involved.

Travel of a broader sort was on the increase again. Concert tours took him to England, Germany, Holland, France and Italy, as well as his beloved Transylvania. In the provinces he offered mixed programmes with Debussy and Scarlatti interspersed with the less demanding pieces by himself and Kodály, while the capitals were introduced to his toughest new works, such as the *Studies, op. 18* and the Violin Sonatas. Although the works composed between 1918 and 1923 are few, one can only marvel that he found time to compose at all. His public appearances in Budapest were largely confined to chamber music, but abroad, his reputation and the scope of his activity were growing year by year. English and French newspapers treated his appearances as events of major importance, and the enthusiasm of knowledgeable audiences was heartwarming. The Viennese *Musikblätter des Anbruch* devoted a whole issue to Bartók to mark his fortieth birthday, an event which passed unnoticed in Budapest.

Eventually, the Hungarian government no longer could hold aloof in the face of international acclaim. In 1923, on the occasion of the Jubilee of the union of the old towns of Buda and Pest, it

FŐVÁROSI VIGADÓ

1923. évi november hó 19-én este 7 órakor
ESÍTÉSÉNEK 50-IK ÉVFORDULÓJA ALKALMÁBÓL
RENDKÍVÜLI
ÓNIAI DÍSZHANGVERSENY

yei:
NYI ERNŐ   MŰSOR:
ködik:
IDY FERENC
NA KÓRUS
NYI ERNŐ

Poster for the concert in 1923
which signified the re-
establishment of Bartók,
Kodály and Dohnányi.

swallowed its pride and announced a Festival Concert featuring specially commissioned works by its three leading musicians, thus welcoming the black sheep back to the fold.

The programme read as follows,

Festival Overture	Dohnányi
Psalmus Hungaricus	Kodály
Dance Suite	Bartók

Even then, the rebels had something defiant to say to their chauvinist persecutors. Although Dohnányi produced a thoroughly respectable overture from unimpeachable sources, the other two made thinly veiled references in their scores to their recent experiences. Kodály's setting of a sixteenth century paraphrase of the fifty-fifth psalm contained words of an unmistakeable symbolic significance,

Better it were to dwell in the desert,
Better to hide me deep in the forest
Than live with wicked liars and traitors
Who will not suffer me to tell the truth.

while Bartók drew liberally on 'alien' Romanian and Arabic sources as well as Magyar idioms in his thrilling *Dance Suite*.

In one important aspect this exhilarating work marks the crossing of the last divide for the composer. Every theme in the suite is of Bartók's own invention and yet, never has the earthy source of his inspiration seemed more present. The assimiliation is complete, the mission in search of a 'truly national style' accomplished.

The *Dance Suite* was a more fitting and momentous contribution to this memorable evening in Hungarian music than the commissioning authorities can ever have imagined — or deserved.

63

64

Chapter Seven

The year 1923 was also a momentous one in Bartók's personal life. In the summer he and Marta were divorced and in August he married Ditta Pásztory, a twenty-one-year-old student who had entered his piano class at the Academy the previous year. Bartók may have found Marta's submissive nature oppressive (as has been suggested by one Hungarian researcher) or it may simply have been a case of irresistible attraction between teacher and pupil. The circumstances and background to this domestic upheaval have never been fully revealed and Bartók's nature would clearly have found any airing of his private life distasteful to a degree. In any event, it seems to have been Marta who urged him to take the irrevocable step and, as far as such a rift can be accomplished without undue pain and suffering, this was done. To judge from their letters, the main preoccupation of both was to allay the distress and anxiety of Paula Bartók and to consider the welfare of young Béla who 'understood the "specialness" of the situation.'

Otto Klemperer's recollection of a collaboration with Bartók some years later confirms that the break-up was achieved with a remarkable lack of rancour and bitterness.

He was a strange man — very reserved, very shy but very sympathetic. He had a new wife at the time. But the old one also came to the rehearsal, so he appeared with two wives!

The unnerving mixture of reserve and fanatical intensity made an indelible impact on many people who met Bartók. Their descriptions of his manner and personal appearance would suggest romantic hyperbole were it not for the unanimity of their impressions. Even those Academy students who had no direct contact with him felt the power of his presence as they passed in the corridors, and Antal Doráti's is typical of their reminiscences.

Bartók was rather small . . . very thin, pale, white-haired. (This is no mistake. Bartók had then at thirty-four, white-grey hair). He had thin lips, barely moving for a timid smile, and barely parting to allow softly-spoken words to be heard; a fine, straight nose and eyes! — there was never such a pair of eyes! Large, burning, piercing — his looks had something of a branding iron — they seemed to mark everybody on whom they fixed.

Besides the students and fellow musicians, there was a perceptive and outspoken critical faction, led by Aladár Tóth, which urged Bartók's compatriots to recognise and acclaim the emergence of a Hungarian composer of truly international stature. Foreign orchestras clamoured for the *Dance Suite* and it was presented by Pierre Monteux in Amsterdam, Frigyes (Fritz) Reiner in Cincinnati and Vaclav Talich in Prague within a year of the Budapest première, while, in 1925, it received over fifty performances in Germany alone.

By and large, though, the Budapest public did not really take him to its heart even at that time, and there was still considerable hostility towards him in reactionary quarters. However, the self-doubt and indecision that had afflicted him after earlier rebuffs was a thing of the past, and the fact that he produced only one work between 1923 and 1926 (*Village Scenes* — Slovak folk songs for female voice and piano) should not be attributed to dejection or loss of confidence but to the ever-increasing pressure of work in his other three fields — performing, teaching and research.

Although collecting tours were still not a practical proposition, work on the existing material was never forgotten. It was an enormous task, an unending one really, but this was more an attraction than a deterrent. Bartók regarded folk music as a pure source from whence he could renew his strength and replenish his imagination. A major landmark was the publication (Budapest, 1924) of an extensive treatise *Hungarian Peasant Music,* and the preparation of his collection of some three thousand Slovak folk songs was in progress intermittently from 1922 to 1928. Another collection, and one especially close to his heart, was of Romanian *Colinde* (Christmas Songs) and he had high hopes when keen interest was shown by a visiting representative of the Oxford University Press. However, he had not reckoned with the dilatory expansiveness of English academics and his pleasurable anticipation was succeeded by exasperated frustration at their leisurely ways. He eventually published a curtailed version at his own expense in Vienna but, since the whole saga dragged on over nine years, the eventual outcome can hardly be put down to unreasonable impatience on Bartók's part.

His literary activities were not confined to folk song and he contributed articles to various musical publications on subjects ranging from Schoenberg and Stravinsky to letters exchanged between Liszt and Mosonyi, not to mention all the entries on Hungarian music and musicians in *A Dictionary of Modern Music and Musicians* published in London in 1924.

66

Teaching remained something of a burden, but he was not a man to give of himself half-heartedly and his pupils remembered him with gratitude and affection.

I remember him as being rather soft-spoken and polite (Sir Georg Solti recalled), if he criticised anything, he always did so very gently ... I suppose my foremost feeling about Bartók was a sort of reverance of the kind one has for a priest or a pope. He was tremendously remote from us, and you never heard any gossip about him: he was absolutely pure, like a saint.

If he found it hard to reconcile himself to the administrative chores of teaching, there were incidental benefits which he cannot have foreseen. Many of his pupils were to be a source of help in the troubled years to come, and one of them, the conductor Frigyes (Fritz) Reiner, was already vigorously championing his works in America. The study of early keyboard music (Frescobaldi, Couperin and Marcello amongst them), which he initially undertook as a pedagogic exercise, provided valuable additions to his own repertoire as a pianist and, more significantly, added a new dimension to his next creative outburst.

Bartók's reputation as a pianist has perhaps been unduly overshadowed by his greatness as a composer. István Thomán maintained that, of contemporary pianists, Busoni and Bartók most closely approached the sovereignty of Liszt. One might incline towards indulgent scepticism at the judgement of a teacher on his favourite pupil, but Otto Klemperer's assessment is not to be lightly discounted.

He was a wonderful pianist and musician. The beauty of his tone, the energy and lightness of his playing were unforgettable. It was almost painfully beautiful. He played with great freedom, that was what was so wonderful.

Others remarked on the lucidity and integrity of his interpretations, but this evidently did not preclude the occasional eruption of volcanic energy from his slight frame, as a startled Olin Downes reported,

... he showed a born instinct for the keyboard with poetry of conception and at times a fury of virtuosity and élan astonishing in a man of his modesty and unostentation.

Concert tours in several European countries were now annual events and, although he grudged the time involved, he enjoyed the liberating effects of travel which brought escape from the claustrophobic pressures of Budapest. If official circles at home showed scant appreciation of his worth, the neighbouring Romanians left him in no doubt of the warmth of their admiration, and he was given a tremendous reception on a return visit in October, 1923. An extensive tour of the provinces culminated in a piano recital in Bucharest, and a chamber music concert the following day (organised by the Association of Romanian Composers) brought together the leading musicians of the two countries in a performance of the *Second Violin Sonata* with George Enescu and the composer. The Romanian government crowned this triumphant occasion by bestowing on Bartók an official accolade, the Bene Merenti Order (1st Class).

This shameless fraternisation with the erstwhile enemy was inevitably not to the liking of the right wingers in Budapest and they wasted no time in renewing their wearisome sniping. Despite Bartók's scathing comments on the ineptitudes of the Kun administration, he was regarded as a communist by the hard-liners and repeatedly attacked for his association with left-wing emigrés. There were even threats of violence when plans were announced to revive the two Balázs stage works. In response to persistent pressure, the Ministry of Culture initiated proceedings against Bartók for playing in the still disputed Transylvanian region, now officially Romanian territory. The charge was soon dropped, but Bartók must have derived quiet amusement at the Romanian government's retaliatory gesture in refusing an entry permit to Jenö Hubay who had planned to give some concerts in the country in 1924.

By now, Bartók was fairly phlegmatic about this sort of behaviour and, if he felt a twinge of pique as his major works were consistently overlooked when it came to the allocation of national awards and prizes, he had only to look beyond the Hungarian border to be reassured of his standing. He had been enlisted by the energetic English scholar, Edward J. Dent, into the activities of the newly-formed International Society for Contemporary Music, and, from now on, his works were a regular feature of the society's festival promotions. The Prague newspaper *Bohemia* in a report of a performance of the *Dance Suite* at the 1925 Festival showed that his music was not only admired by foreign musicians, but also increasingly understood.

Bartók gives us no more syncopated pieces in the *Czardas* manner nor over-sentimentalised tunes; he has gone back to the original sources of Hungarian folk song and dance, and has recreated them in a manner of his own. A kind of music of barbaric power in its rhythms and ebullient temperament, that carries itself along with urgent excitement has emerged. . . . No work by any of the other foreign composers was given such a tumultuous reception, and Bartók had to take call after call.

To be singled out from composers of the calibre of Stravinsky, Janácek, Milhaud, Busoni and Vaughan Williams must have warmed even Bartók's reticent heart, but perhaps not so radiantly as a repetition of this brilliant performance (by the Czech Philharmonic Orchestra under Vaclav Talich) in Budapest later in the year which was encored in its entirety. This popular success at home did something to alleviate his underlying sadness that he, of all people, should have been pilloried for 'un-Hungarian activities'. Just a year earlier, in November, 1924, he had ruefully observed to a foreign journalist,

There may come a time when I shall be recognised as a Hungarian composer. Though perhaps by that time I shall no longer be alive.

As a pianist, Bartók was necessarily presenting a somewhat out-of-date image of himself. His last piano work had been the *Improvisations* of 1920, so his programmes could give no hint of the enormous strides made in the *Dance Suite* and the two *Violin Sonatas*. Consequently, when he took up his pen again in 1926, he concerned himself almost exclusively with his own instrument and, after a summer of furious creative work, his repertoire was enriched by the *Piano Sonata*, the suite *Out of Doors*, the *Nine Little Piano Pieces* and his *First Piano Concerto* which, taken as a group, admirably exemplified his current position, encompassing characteristics of both his recent instrumental works and those which were shortly to follow.

The *Nine Little Piano Pieces* bear witness to his studies of the early keyboard composers, and introduce a new contrapuntal ingenuity which was to be an integral feature of his music from now on. They have been cited, too, as an excursion into the 'neo-classicism' then in vogue. The retreat from romanticism took many forms and the objectivity of the baroque masters seemed to many composers an ideal worth recapturing. Poulenc, Hindemith and, especially, Stravinsky went along this road at various times, and so too did Debussy and Ravel, though without the same self-conscious ostentation. Bartók certainly knew Stravinsky's early 'neo-classical' works, but was repelled by his aesthetic argument that music is incapable of expressing anything other than itself.

'Bach also expressed something — some moments of life,' said Bartók, and these pieces (though hardly to be counted among his greatest) conspicuously avoid the element of artifice and pastiche that has so rapidly dated so many works of the school.

Nevertheless, the polyphonic experience added a further rich dimension to his language, and his ability to absorb and profit from fresh ideas and influences without compromising his individuality is a measure of his ability to transmute life's experience into art.

69

The harsh, brutal drive of Bartók's piano music had ruffled the sensibilities of conservative souls ever since he had unleashed the *Allegro Barbaro* on the world in 1911. In 1915, the critic of the learned *Musical Quarterly* had likened his pieces to

Unmeaning bunches of notes apparently representing the composer promenading the keyboard in his boots,

and he wrote himself into the history of philistinism by concluding

Some can be played better with the elbows, others with the flat of the hand. None require fingers to perform nor ears to listen to.

'Ugly and incoherent,' grumbled *The Sunday Times*, and the name Bartók came to symbolise everything that the bewildered layman associated with 'modern music' in much the same way as Picasso symbolised 'modern art'. The *Piano Sonata* must have confirmed the uneasy expectations of traditionalists, just as it thrilled the more adventurous. Although its ebullient rhythmic vitality has much in common with the *Dance Suite*, the monochrome nature of the instrument and Bartók's unequivocally percussive treatment of it underlines the atavistic barbarism of the peasant rhythms and the starkness of the melodies. The slow movement, traditionally the expressive core of a sonata, begins with a single note struck twenty times without nuance and with the barest rhythmic inflection, before resolving downwards to complete the melodic statement, and this is accompanied by colourless, impassive dissonances in the left hand. Some of the pianistic devices can be traced back to Liszt and it is possible to point to parallels with Beethoven in the adaptation of traditional forms to accommodate specific threads of argument, but these are superficial comparisons when viewed alongside the boldness and sheer originality of the conception which make the sonata a major landmark in piano literature. These observations apply to many aspects of the *First Piano Concerto* which features the same percussive piano writing and primitive thematic material. Bartók was sorely in need of a new vehicle for his appearances with orchestra. He had hitherto been relying on the *Rhapsody No. 1* which was no longer representative, although he always retained a special affection for it partly, no doubt, on account of its rejection at the Rubinstein competition. The significance of a fully-fledged concerto was quickly acknowledged and the first performance (in Frankfurt under Furtwängler) was followed by others with such important conductors as Erich Kleiber and Pierre Monteux.

The central movement of the *Out of Doors* suite, *Night Music* (dedicated to Ditta), introduces us to a further uniquely Bartókian

sound-world, a magical evocation of the sounds and atmosphere of
nature at night; not the langourous nocturnal dreams of Chopin,
still less the vapid effusions of the countless nineteenth century
piano pieces entitled 'At the Brook' or 'Forest Murmurs'. Nor has
Bartók's vision much in common with the romantic, pantheistic
view of Beethoven's *Pastoral Symphony* or Smetana's *Ma Vlast*. His
natural world is alive with the chirping and twittering of insects,
the eerie rustle of twigs and undergrowth, the sudden screech of a
frightened bird.

These sounds evoke the reality of a night beyond the realm of earth,
Bartók's own night (wrote the critic Aladár Tóth after the first
performance). This is one of the most marvellous masterpieces to capture
the poetry of nature in Hungary.

Bartók's absorbing interest in the natural world was nothing
new. Back in 1907, had he not proclaimed to Stefi Geyer, 'if I ever
crossed myself it would be in the name of Nature, Art and Science'?
Folk music itself he regarded as a natural phenomenon and in the
course of his explorations he had amassed a sizeable supplementary
collection of insects, moths and shells and a thorough knowledge of
natural history to go with it. In his last years in America, onlookers
were startled at the sight of a frail old man prodding at cowdung
with his stick and peering intently at the teeming life within.

71

Bartók—as seen by a New York cartoonist.

It was at this time that Bartók paid his first visit to the land that was to be his final resting place. An extensive concert tour of the USA was arranged for December, 1927 and January, 1928. His first impressions were mixed. Though bewildered by 'the maddening hubbub everywhere,' he admired the exuberant vitality of the people but found the unquestioned supremacy of commercialism depressing. The schedule was an exceptionally arduous one, not only in the sheer number of engagements but also the vastness of distances travelled. Orchestral performances, chamber music and solo recitals jostled with one another in bewildering profusion. An additional strain was the half-hour lecture with which he prefaced his solo recitals, which taxed his command of English to the utmost. Nonetheless, he welcomed the opportunity to spread a little propaganda for Hungarian music and to clear up a few misconceptions about his own work.

There was little time to indulge his insatiable traveller's curiosity, but he did visit a Chinese theatre in San Francisco ('I was the only white man present except for the doorman') and also had his first taste of real jazz. Contrary to some reports, he did not disapprove.

72

In the past few days, I have heard real Negro jazz in a speakeasy in Chicago. This was really good. They played from a score but many times they improvised and this was fascinating.

But he did make it clear where his allegiance lay,

We have no need for jazz. We have beautiful folk music of our own and it is superfluous to fling ourselves into the arms of jazz.

By the end of January, the wear and tear of incessant travelling and waiting listlessly in stations and overheated hotel rooms had taken its toll of his frail constitution and he was more than ready to return home, and on March 6th he was on his way.

Two other masterpieces adorn this richly productive period. Bartók's string quartets, like Beethoven's, present a kind of résumé of his achievement, crystallising the stages in the development of his mature style with a conciseness that makes the individual works stand out as peaks in a panoramic view of his achievement.

The *Third String Quartet* of 1927 is the shortest but perhaps the hardest to assimilate of the series, and thus sums up what is some-times described as Bartók's 'expressionist' period, which encom-passes *The Miraculous Mandarin,* the two violin sonatas and certain aspects of the piano music of 1926. The harmonic idiom is harsh and grating, the structural organisation intensely compressed and the percussive chordal conclusion rivals the piano music in its barbaric violence. Bartók submitted this work for a competition organised by the Musical Trust Fund of Philadelphia and, to his surprise and delight, he and Alfredo Casella shared the first prize of six thousand dollars, which caused great commotion at home.

You can hardly imagine what sensation this created in Budapest. Six thousand dollars! I told everybody from the outset that it just couldn't be as much as that — but all to no effect; it is by now common knowledge that I won 6,000.

Even so, his share of three thousand dollars was a wonderful tonic and his first major financial reward. By a curious anomaly, the forgotten composer H. Waldo Warner, who was awarded joint second prize and outright third, won more in actual cash than the two first prize winners.

The *Fourth String Quartet* followed about a year later, after Bartók's return from the States. It shows the same rigorous logic as its predecessor, but the design is expanded to five movements. Overall structure becomes an increasingly dominant consideration from this point, and the 'arch' form is a prototype for several later works. In simple terms, this 'arch' can best be described as a

73

Bartók with the violinists Zoltan
Székely . . .

palindrome, the outer movements being closely related, the second and fourth likewise, with the central slow movement forming the cornerstone. This increasing preoccupation with architectural design should not in the least imply a dilution or supression of expressive intensity. The 'cello's passionate Magyar lament in the slow movement, the magical sounds of the night, the scurrying whirlwind *Prestissimo* could hardly be more direct in their emotional impact.

The string quartets have been analysed inside out by subsequent generations of musicologists but, although Bartók relished the intellectual grappling that their researches have unearthed, he was not insensitive to practical considerations, and his friendlier face is nowhere more disarmingly revealed than in the two virtuoso *Rhapsodies* he composed for the violinists József Szigeti and Zoltán Székely during this period. His was not a facile talent, but, through unflinching perseverance and artistic integrity, he had now acquired the complete mastery to give unfettered expression to his genius no matter what external factors were to govern his choice of forces or medium.

. . . and József Szigeti, dedicatees of the two *Rhapsodies*.

Chapter Eight

The complete assurance with which he now approached his work enabled Bartók to free himself from any self-protective limitations. Although he never once throughout his career stooped to anything which could be remotely described as commercialism, he was able to capitalise to a limited extent on his success. People now came to *him* with pleas and commissions for new works and he was able to adapt to their requirements. He orchestrated the piano *Sonatina* (under the title *Transylvanian Dances*) and some of the *Fifteen Hungarian Peasant Songs* which he freely admitted was

Bartók in March 1927.

now an orchestral suite which I put together for the money. This is the sort of thing that will be performed because the music is pleasing, it is not very difficult to play and it is by a 'known' composer.

In the two *Rhapsodies* he also overcame his earlier aversion to urban popular music, making use of nineteenth century 'verbunkos' elements for the first time. He had made his point that this sort of thing did not represent the true basis of Hungarian folk music, and he was now able to see it as part and parcel of his country's musical culture. He emerged from his ivory tower secure in the knowledge that his own musical personality was fully formed and incorruptible.

After his travels in Europe and the United States, there was but one field left to conquer, and that was put in hand for the very end of 1929 and the first half of January, 1930. There was naturally considerable antagonism at government level between the Soviet Union and Horthy's Hungary, but tenuous cultural links had been maintained. There was much musicological nonsense written in Soviet journals about 'bourgeois heritage' and 'leftism' in the arts, but the dictates of 'socialist realism' had not yet taken its stranglehold on the development and dissemination of modern ideas and, in Moscow and Leningrad at least, there was a lively avant-garde.

Bartok's tour of the USSR began in Kharkov and thence to Odessa and Leningrad. Political considerations at once took a backseat to his perennial passion,

The folklore collections I saw, particularly those in Petersburg, were impressive and most valuable,

and his comments on the economic situation were restricted to practical observations,

There are practically no good pianos at all; the old ones are worn out and cannot be repaired because all the materials have to be imported.

The friendly warmth of the people was very appealing and Bartók was good humoured and indulgent about the sometimes chaotic disorganisation of his schedule. Concerts had to be cancelled because insufficient time had been allowed for travelling between venues, and it was by no means certain which trains would run or how long they would take to reach their destination.

But apart from this, (he wrote to Ditta), they are very charming people, and they have loaded me with scores and folk song publications (I shall have plenty to drag home with me). The audience also proved to be very enthusiastic at the end of the concert; they shouted bis! bis! (encore! encore!), and there were 3 encores. After the concert we went to a 'lordly'

76

mansion, now owned by the Ukrainian People's Commissariat, where a banquet was held to seal the Hungaro-Ukrainian friendship.

It was refreshing to find that audiences were genuinely 'of the people' and not restricted to an élite section of society as was often the case in European and American halls. And everywhere their enthusiasm was heartwarming and spontaneous.

The whole tour lasted barely three weeks, so there was little time for idle tourism, but he found plenty of incidental delights to add to his store of traveller's memories.

Moscow looks just as one knows it from pictures: the roofs loaded with snow, so that they seem ready to cave in, and little one-horse sledges tinkling everywhere . . . Maupassant is right when he says that one ought to come here in the middle of winter (just as one ought to go to Africa in the height of summer); it is then that the country is at its most characteristic.

Once again, he arrived home feeling ill and exhausted, but there was scarcely time to recuperate before he was off on his travels again — this time to Switzerland where he appeared in two concerts of his own music at the end of January. It would be irksome to record all of his concert appearances in Europe, as they were now a routine feature of his existence, but this visit to Basle and Zurich (under the *aegis* of the ISCM) was significant for a number of reasons. In the first place, it marked a reunion with Stefi Geyer (now living with her husband in Zurich) who appeared with Bartók along with the singer Ilona Durigo, and it was also the occasion of

Bartók with the composer Conrad Beck and Paul Sacher, the conductor who secured the commissions for some of Bartók's greatest works of the 1930s. (Embassy of the Hungarian People's Republic)

The Congress of Arab Music.
Paul Hindemith and his wife
are on the left.

his first meeting with Mrs Müller-Widman of Basle, an admirer who was to become a close and devoted friend in time of need. Paul Sacher, the energetic young conductor of the Basle Chamber Orchestra, came into Bartók's life at this point too. Sacher was one of the great champions of twentieth century music, enlarging the repertoire of the chamber orchestra with commissions from several major composers, and it is to his friendship and influence that we owe three of Bartók's greatest masterpieces of the late 1930's, the *Music for Strings, Percussion and Celesta*, the *Sonata for Two Pianos and Percussion* and the *Divertimento* for string orchestra. In a tribute delivered shortly after Bartók's death, he presented a vivid portrait of the composer.

Whoever met Bartók, thinking of the rhythmic strength of his work, was surprised by his slight, delicate figure. He had the outward appearance of a fine-nerved scholar. Possessed of fanatical will and pitiless severity, and propelled by an ardent spirit, he affected inaccessibility and was reservedly polite. His being breathed light and brightness; his eyes burned with a noble fire. In the flash of his searching glance no falseness or obscurity could endure. If in a performance an especially hazardous and refractory passage came off well, he laughed in boyish glee; and when he was pleased with the successful solution of a problem, he actually beamed.

It was not just his music that took him abroad, but also his reputation as a musicologist. Such ventures were not always rewarding; he was happiest working in the field or in his study, and the world of congresses, seminars and academic one-upmanship was not his natural milieu. Once such event was the congress of Geneva in 1931, organised by the League of Nations Committee for International Co-operation. As a social occasion it had its attractions and he enjoyed the company of such eminent men of letters as Thomas

78

Mann and Paul Valéry, but the attendant official functions were not so palatable. A dinner given by the Hungarian Minister came in for acid comment in a long letter to Paula Bartók.

There were 5 or 6 wine glasses at each place of expensive Venetian glass, with dolphin shaped stems. Before lunch, delicious cocktails (brandy), at the end of the meal — Tokay (this, of course, is as it should be at the Hungarian Minister's). Nevertheless the lunch wasn't pleasant; what with the horrid screeching of Mrs X (the Minister's American wife) and these smooth and cunning diplomats — there's no getting away from it, they are an artificial crowd, quite different from artists.

The proceedings of the congress soon got bogged down in protocol, sub-committees and points of order, but Bartók refused to be disheartened, and he shows an unsuspected gift for humorous irony as he describes his own contribution. As the only musician present, he was urged to table a proposal:

I explained that I could only propose things that would cost a lot of money; they answered that it did not matter. So far so good; so I went ahead that evening and drafted something (about gramophone records) . . . A sub-committee was formed, we drafted a resolution, which was of course far different from the original and of no use, but it needed no money.

This was his first experience of the subtle cut and thrust of academic backbiting, and he looked on with fascinated amazement.

It is very amusing to see one speaker's reactions to another. They all begin by saying that they heard the proposal made by the previous speaker with the greatest pleasure and enjoyment, that the ideas were excellent, but that this wasn't quite accurate, and needed slight changes before being put into practice, or that something else was incorrect — in the end it turned out

79

that nothing said by the previous speaker was any good at all. However, politeness is the prime consideration. One thing you can be quite sure about, and that is that there will never be any violence on this Comité.

This sort of thing he could take lightly and with an engaging touch of self-mockery — as he did the farcical episode of a summer school at Mondsee where hardly any of the pupils turned up — but there were disquieting political developments on which his conscience forbade him to keep silent. He had been outspokenly critical of the anti-semitic tendencies of the Horthy government from the start, as we have seen, and as fascism crept into the fabric of Italian and German life his anxiety and disapproval demanded public expression. When, in 1931, Arturo Toscanini was beaten up and virtually drummed out of Italy by fascists for refusing to conduct the *Giovinezza* (fascist march), Bartók drafted a resolution to the ISCM urging the society to take immediate action at the forthcoming session in Oxford to counteract the growing state interference with artistic freedom and to formulate proposals 'for the protection of the integrity and autonomy of the arts.'

He was, of course, far from happy with the political situation in Hungary itself. The Horthy régime was now solidly entrenched and, despite its nationalistic posturing, did little to improve the lot of the common people. Horthy himself relied heavily on the support of the old ruling classes and his two henchmen, Count István Bethlen and General Gyula Gömbös were, respectively, a died in the wool aristocrat and an out and out careerist. Little if anything was done to alleviate the appalling poverty amongst the peasantry, and the occasional outbursts of left-wing intellectuals failed to arouse a genuine popular response. The traditional restrictive measures of authoritarian régimes — for instance, the banning of trade unionism in key areas such as agriculture and public services — kept a tight rein on the status quo, and it seemed to some democrats that the Hapsburg court had simply transferred from Vienna to Budapest. Official historians seemed to be advocating a return to feudalism, and these reactionary forces were unrelenting in their attempts to belittle the work of Bartók and Kodály. One such writer who particularly infuriated Bartók was the critic and composer Emil Haraszti, who derided Kodály's 'faithful folklore and artistic primitivism,' at the same time eulogising the gypsy musician 'whose like as an artist cannot be found anywhere in the world.'

In 1930, the Romanian folklorist and scholar, Octavian Beu, prepared a radio programme on Bartók and submitted his text for the composer's approval. Bartók's reply has been much quoted, and rightly so, for it contains a serious and valuable attempt at self-assessment, as well as some amusing side-swiping at Haraszti.

80

I must inform you that Haraszti is a stupid and, in addition, a malicio
man who, moreover, understands as much of music as a hen does of the
ABC.

Elsewhere in this revealing document, Bartók is at pains to
clarify the relative importance of Hungarian, Romanian and Slovak
folk music in his own work, and at the same time reveals a deep
humanitarian concern which is a far cry from the narrow
nationalistic road which he started out along thirty years before.

My creative work, just because it arises from three sources (Hungarian,
Romanian, Slovakian), might be regarded as the very embodiment of the
very concept of integration so much emphasised in Hungary today. Of
course, I do not write this for you to make it public; you will yourself
beware of doing so, for such ideas are not for the Romanian press. I only
mention it as a possible point of view which I encountered about ten years
ago, when I was attacked in the most violent manner as a musical Scotus
Viator. My own idea, however — of which I have been fully conscious
since I found myself as a composer — is the brotherhood of peoples,
brotherhood in spite of wars and conflicts. I try — to the best of my ability
— to serve this idea in my music; therefore I don't reject any influence, be
it Slovakian, Romanian, Arabic or from any other source. The source must
only be clean, fresh and healthy! Owing to my — let us say — geographical
position, it is the Hungarian source that is nearest to me, and therefore the
Hungarian influence is the strongest. Whether my style — notwithstanding its various sources — has a Hungarian character or not (and that is the
point) — is for others to judge, not for me. For my own part, I certainly
feel that it has. For character and milieu must somehow harmonise with
each other.

Bartok's fastidious conscience could be positively obstructive at
times. In January, 1931, shortly before his fiftieth birthday, he
received a letter from a Mr Tamasiu inviting him to attend the
festivities associated with the unveiling of a plaque in his honour at
Nagyszentmiklós, his birthplace (now in Romania and renamed
Sinnicolaul Mare). Bartók replied coldly that he was not fond of
ceremonies, nor did like the idea of 'squeezing money out of people'
for such a project. On receiving assurances that the cost was trifling
and the money already collected, he yielded slightly but imposed a
condition that the plaque be inscribed in Hungarian as well as
Romanian. The deterioration in relations between Hungary and her
neighbours meant that Bartók's friends in Czechoslovakia and
Romania had to fight to protect him from attacks by their own
nationalist cliques. In any event, it all came to nothing and a
suitable memorial was not erected until 1951.

An appetite for public acclaim was never a driving force in
Bartók's life and by this time he was so disillusioned with political
and cultural conditions in Budapest that he had again virtually

81

retired from public life there. All his major works were premièred
abroad, and for six years he made only occasional appearances as a
pianist in the capital, and then only to play music by other composers or to renew collaborations with old friends such as Dohñanyi
or Imre Waldbauer. Plans had been afoot again to revive the stage
works and Béla Balázs, from exile, waived his rights to royalties and
public billing in the hope that this might ease their path, but to no
avail. Yet another attempt to get *The Miraculous Mandarin* onto the
stage at last met with a similar fate.

The French recognised Bartók's fiftieth birthday by making him
'Chevalier de la legion d'honneur', and the Hungarian authorities
made a belated attempt to match this by awarding him the Corvin
Wreath. Bartók did not attend the ceremony, and his feelings were
probably accurately divined in a moving tribute by Aládár Tóth in
the paper *Pesti Naplo*:

It is not for us to hasten with gifts to an artist when we made no haste to
accept the gifts he had to offer; it is not for us to disturb the privacy of an
artist whom we ourselves would have none of. We have no right to feel
proud of an artist who was born among us and lived for us, but whom we
did not accept as one of ourselves. The time is not ripe for a Bartók
celebration in Hungary. First we must work for this genius, then we can
honour him.

Indeed, Bartók's depression was deepening. Wherever he looked,
he saw evil poisoning the everyday lives of ordinary people. He was
one of the first to set his face implacably against Nazism, and from
1933 he never played in Germany again. Likewise, Franco's victory
in the Spanish civil war signified the end of his association with that
country with all its happy memories of his early concert tours. He

82

fostered his connections in England, Belgium, France, Holland and Switzerland but, from this time, he held little hope for the future of Europe.

Happily for subsequent generations, his zest for composition was undiminished. In 1932, he moved with Ditta and their young son Peter into a comfortable house on the Csalan-ut, their last home in Hungary, where he was able to work in peace in his studio on the second floor, and it was here that a new series of major works was born. This new wave had begun two years earlier with the great *Cantata Profana* for two soloists, full choir and orchestra, to his own text based upon a Romanian folk ballad which expresses something of his hopes and dreams for the destiny of man. There is good reason to believe that Bartók had in mind a triptych of cantatas, the other two to be based on Hungarian and Slovak folklore — thus serving the ideal of the brotherhood of nations outlined in his letter to Octavian Beu. The idea never came to fruition, so the *Cantata*

Bartók's shorthand 'aide-memoire' for the *Second Piano Concerto*.

83

Profana stands as a unique edifice in Bartók's oeuvre; although the ballad style shows some affinity with *Duke Bluebeard's Castle* and the nature imagery some echoes of *The Wooden Prince*, its style is unlike either and the forces employed are dissimilar to those in any other of his works. The cantata is shot through with Bartók's most earthy melody, enriched by strong, woody colouring and an amazing contrapuntal fecundity (Kódaly stated that Bartók was studying Palestrina's choral style at the time). The ballad tells of an old man whose nine sons go hunting in wild country. They come to a mysterious bridge and, on crossing it, are turned into stags. The old man begs them to return, but they choose to remain in their transformed state, united with nature. The message is unmistakable; that sacrifice must be made if man is to find his way back to a pure way of life — in Bartók's words, 'to drink only from the clear spring.'

Then there is the magnificent *Second Piano Concerto*, a brilliant virtuoso vehicle for the soloist and the work of a virtuoso composer too, revelling in his mastery of every facet of his craft, juggling with all manner of contrapuntal devices with effortless legerdemain and bewitching his audience with the bright, clean 'baroque' flavour of the first movement, the still, soulful Adagio with its whirring 'night music' intermezzo and the barbaric splendour of the finale. Bartók spoke disarmingly of the 'light' and 'popular' character of the themes in this Titan among piano concertos. The first performance in Frankfurt was also Bartók's last appearance in Germany. Even for this brilliant vehicle, he was not to be persuaded to emerge from his withdrawal from the Budapest stage and the Hungarian première was entrusted to Lajos (Louis) Kentner.

Between 1930 and 1935 Bartók wrote an unusual amount of vocal music, and besides the cantata, mention should also be made of the *Twenty Hungarian Folk Songs* with piano accompaniment and, for chorus, the *Four Hungarian Folk Songs* and the *Six Székely Songs*. Young musicians benefited during this period from the *44 Duos* for two violins and the eight volumes of choruses for school choirs (with and without orchestra).

Finally, the great series of string quartets received fresh impetus in the shape of a commission from the Elizabeth Sprague Coolidge Foundation. This, the *Fifth Quartet*, which continues the five movement format established in the fourth, was composed at white heat in exactly one month at the end of the summer of 1934 and the first performance was given in Washington by the Kolisch Quartet the following April.

An unexpected blessing came to ease the tribulations of the aging composer. In September, 1934, he was relieved of his teaching duties at the Academy and offered a long coveted research post by the Hungarian Academy of Sciences, of which he became a member in May, 1935.

84

Chapter Nine

This change in Bartók's routine did not entail any lessening of his workload; far from it. He had been pressing for an officially sponsored collection of Hungarian folk tunes since 1913, and had frequently castigated the government for allowing neighbouring countries to steal a march on them by publishing their own collections. There was a mass of work to be done and, although his dream did not come to fruition until after his death (when the Hungarian Academy of Sciences published the first of a series of volumes in 1951), much of the source work was the result of Bartók's steadfast endeavour. In all, he sorted and categorised some 13,000 Hungarian melodies, in addition to his ancillary work on folk music of other nations which continued at the same time. There were inevitable but infuriating obstacles to overcome, now that the whole business had become so entangled with the nationalist squabbles of Eastern Europe. Bartók, although he could not ignore the problem, tried to stand aloof from all political considerations and he made his attitude plain in a letter to the Croatian folklorist, Vinko Zganec.

Please believe me when I say that in my studies I have not been, and never shall be, guided by any chauvinistic bias; my sole aim is to search for the truth and to conduct my search with as much impartiality as is humanly possible. As the clearest proof of this I can point to my explicit statement in this booklet (of his radio talks) that approximately 38 per cent of the Hungarian material is of foreign, chiefly Slovak, origin, while only about 20 per cent of the Slovak material is of Hungarian origin (all this, of course, on the basis of the material collected so far; additional collecting might change the picture).

The reality of political obstructionism was firmly brought home to him when the booklet was returned by the Yugoslav customs marked 'Forbidden Material', and the elusive nature of his scientific objectives is indicated by the proviso in parentheses. Time and time again he had to revise his conclusions as new probabilities and inter-relationships emerged from his studies of Bulgarian, Slovak, Ruthenian, Serbo Croatian and other source material. Some understanding of the problem involved can be gathered from his important essay 'The Folk Music of Hungary

Transcribing recordings of folk music.

and the Neighbouring Peoples' (1934). Information gathered from his visit to the Congress for Arab Music in Cairo, in 1932, and to Turkey, in 1936, further complicated the picture. At times, he inclined to the belief that all the world's folk music would eventually be traced back to a handful of simple scales.

Some musicians, notably Stravinsky, have expressed regret that a composer of Bartók's genius should have expended so much time and energy on the pursuit of folk music, but, in truth, Bartók the composer and Bartók the folklorist are so inextricably intertwined that there is good reason to suppose that the one could not have existed without the other. His own view is cogently expressed in two further essays on 'Why and How Do We Collect Folk Music?' (1936) and 'The Influence of Peasant Music on Modern Music' (1931). The latter piece pinpoints Bartók's own position succinctly, even if the generality of the title elicits some special pleading when applied to other composers.

At the beginning of the twentieth century there was a turning point in the history of modern music.

The excesses of the Romanticists began to be unbearable for many. There were many composers who felt: 'this road does not lead us anywhere; there is no solution but a complete break with the nineteenth century.'

Invaluable help was given to this change (or rather let us call it rejuvenation) by a kind of peasant music unknown till then . . . It is the ideal starting point for a musical renaissance, and a composer in search of new ways cannot find a better master. What is the best way for a composer to reap the full benefits of his studies in peasant music? It is to assimilate the idiom of peasant music so completely that he is able to forget all about it and use it as his mother tongue.

From the earliest days of his discovery, Bartók never questioned the validity of this course. For him, it was both the alchemy of his creative genius and an absorbing passion in its own right, and never did he begrudge the hours of toil involved. Letters had to be written to colleagues in other countries and the interplay of scientific data was painstakingly recorded and correlated with his own material.

Inevitably, he ran into chauvinistic criticism from time to time but he accepted it, as a rule, as an irritating concomitant to his work. Nevertheless, it pained him that he should be the subject of attacks from xenophobes in Romania, where he had so recently been the object of adulation. Smears against him were initiated by various obscure informants (a bank manager from Brassó seems to have started it all) which resulted in his being banned from entering the country for a while, but the petty absurdity of the whole affair can best be seen from the final episode in 1937. Bartók had been

In the field—with members of the nomadic Kumarli tribe.

87

taunted beyond endurance by an article by Coriolan Petranu, a teacher at Cluj university, which accused him of distorting his information in the interests of 'Hungarian revisionism'. He published a blistering retort refuting the charges one by one, and this comment (on one of Petranu's more purple passages) conveys something of the acid contempt of Bartók's reply.

We must acknowledge that these lines could have embellished any novel written a century ago; it is nevertheless impossible for us, although we are most willing, to detect in them any scientific value.

And what was the subject of this acrimonious exchange? The very same article on 'The Romanian Folk Music Dialect of Hunyad', written way back in 1915, over which Bartók had already weathered the insults of his own countrymen for its alleged anti-Hungarianism.

His compatriots did not leave him in peace now either. Under the Horthy government there had arisen an influential body of reactionary Catholic intellectuals who were strongly represented in the Ministry of Education, and it was from this quarter that the next attack came. It seemed to the adherents of this group that official condemnation of the progressive views of Bartòk and Kodály was weakening, and it is certainly true that there was a gradual, if belated, shift in the establishment press towards recognition of the country's two outstanding composers. Kodály had been an energetic advocate of educational reform at the most fundamental level ever since his days on the ill-fated Music Committee of 1919, and it is to his unflagging zeal in this direction that Hungary owes its lively and widely admired musical education system today. Bartók, though less active in this field, wholeheartedly supported Kodály's aims, and the performance of his children's choruses gave him especial delight.

I shall never forget this impression of the freshness and gaiety of the little ones' voices. There is something in the natural way these children from the suburban schools produce their voices that reminds me of the unspoilt sound of peasant singing.

The clerical press did not share his enthusiasm. Their attack was partly political, but at least equally philistine in motivation. The campaign began in 1937, with an unsigned editorial in *Magyar Kultúra*, a paper owned by a wealthy Jesuit preacher, Béla Bangha. The article deplored the increasing official support for the work of the two composers and took the view that this progressive nonsense, like Ady's poetry, reflected the spirit of 'a bleak and destructive soul' and that its consumption should be confined to adults only. Its official encouragement in schools and youth choirs, it continued, could only lead to the pollution of the ideals of the young, and its use in church, the writer felt, was little short of blasphemous (Kodály's exciting motet 'Jesus and the Traders' had recently caused quite a stir).

The progressive intelligentsia reached for their pens and a lively battle of ink ensued. It was all something of a storm in a teacup and Bartók, on this occasion, was not to be drawn.

When a person is in the public eye, anything can be said about him . . . What is destructive about my music? Even the writer of the article could not say. I cannot try to improve my work since I do not know what they are complaining about. I consider the whole thing beneath my attention.

However, the passion which the episode aroused does indicate the predominance of reactionary aesthetics in influential circles which militated against Bartók throughout his career. The learned Kisfaludy Society had already furnished evidence of this when they decided to award him their prestigious Greguss Medal in 1936. This was a decidedly back-handed compliment, for the society made it clear that the award was not in respect of any of the internationally acclaimed masterpieces of the preceding ten years, but specifically for the immature, but comparatively euphonious *Suite no. 1* for orchestra of 1905. Bartók spat the trinket out in disgust, and his letter of rejection to the society is worth reproducing *in toto*.

Gentlemen:
I have read in today's papers that the Kisfaludy Society has awarded to me this year the Greguss Medal for my Suite for Orchestra No. 1 (Op. 3). I would like to add the following remarks to that:
1. The Society's statement of motivation is erroneous in regard to the first complete Hungarian performance of this work: it was performed in its entirety not in November, 1929 but, thank God, in 1909 by Jenö Hubay and later by Antal Fleischer on November 29, 1920. I say 'thank God' because it would be peculiar if in Hungary twenty-four years had passed before the first complete performance of a work composed in 1905 and of such excellence that it is deserving of the Greguss Medal.
2. Even if this statement of motivation is true — just as it is untrue — there would be something amiss in the award. I do very much like this work of mine; it is really an outstanding achievement for a young man twenty-four years of age. But in the period of 1929-1934 much better and more mature works were presented in Hungary, for instance, *The Spinning Room* or *Dances of Galanta* (both by Z. Kódaly).
3. Though unbidden I give friendly advice: it is urgent that you appoint another adviser in this matter. How can someone judge the value of a work, who is unable to decide — on account of external chronological conditions — which compositions are to be considered?
4. And in conclusion may I declare that I do not wish to accept the Greguss Medal in the present or in the future, neither alive nor dead.

89

Fortunately, it need not be assumed from this saga of persistent aggravation that Bartók's last years in Hungary were in any way stunted in achievement. In 1936, he gave his inaugural address to the Hungarian Academy of Sciences with a paper on 'Some Liszt Problems', a subject that had long fascinated him, and his performance of the solo part in Liszt's *Totentanz* for piano and orchestra, given as part of the composer's centenary celebrations, was talked about for many a year. Moreover, his opponents were justified in detecting an increase in official support for his music. In 1935, at long last, *The Wooden Prince* was seen again on the stage of the opera house to another overwhelming reception and a revival of *Duke Bluebeard's Castle* followed a year later. His more recent *Cantata Profana* was finally heard in Budapest a month later, albeit more than two years after its première by the BBC in London. Bartók felt sufficiently encouraged to enter again into the musical life of the city and, in 1938, the capital was finally able to hear the composer's own definitive performance of the *2nd Piano Concerto* under the baton of Ernest Ansermet.

In 1937 he began to assemble the *Mikrokosmos*, his unique collection of 153 instructive piano pieces, progressively graded from the elementary five finger exercises of Volume I to the demanding concert pieces of Volume VI. This compilation had occupied Bartók intermittently over a period of fourteen years, and it would be a short-sighted student who dismissed even the simplest ones as being beneath his attention, for their significance is far wider than their sterling pedagogic value. The collection is nothing less than a key to the world of its composer. Almost every facet of

In recital with Imre Waldbauer.

Bartók's last concert in Vienna. Liszt's *Totentanz* with Dohnányi conducting.

his music is here, reduced to its barest essentials, and as such affords a priceless introduction to the world of modern music for the young pianist. Young Péter Bartók had a hand in the proving of this unusual masterpiece, as his father acknowledged.

In 1933, my little son Péter begged us to teach him to play the piano. I thought about it for a long time and finally, greatly daring, set to work on what was for me an unusual task. Apart from vocal and technical exercises the only music given to the child was taken from the *Mikrokosmos*; I hope this was good for him, but I must confess that I too learned a great deal from the experiment. . . .

By this time, Bartók was well into what is sometimes described as his 'classical' period. Certainly, he now composed with the orderly confidence and fluency of the great classical masters (witness the lightning speed with which he completed the *Fifth Quartet*) and although his formal procedures never ossified — he was always moulding and adapting his intricate structures — the experimentation with style and language was over. Virtually

91

With his second son, Péter, the first young pianist to study *Mikrokosmos*.
(Embassy of the Hungarian People's Republic)

composed during the 1930s is immediately identifiable as quintessential Bartók; all influences are so deeply absorbed and synthesised as to have become integral parts of a single unified personality.

The three great works for Basle, the *Music for Strings, Percussion and Celesta*, the *Sonata for Two Pianos and Percussion* and the *Divertimento* have a unity of form and content that can truly be described as classical. Moreover, this fluency of inspiration which had taken wing in the *Fifth Quartet* did not desert him. The *Divertimento* and the *Sixth Quartet* (for his friend Zoltan Székely's New Hungarian Quartet) were almost entirely composed during a four week 'vacation' at Paul Sacher's chalet in Saanen. These commissions, as he reported with some satisfaction to his elder son Béla, 'make my situation similar to that of the old composers.'

If there were natural justice in this world, then this resolution and reconciliation of his artistic struggles would have presaged a peaceful and productive old age. That this was not to be can be laid at the door of the man who dashed the hopes and aspirations of so many at this time — Adolf Hitler.

92

As we have seen, the rise of Nazism had been a source of grave anxiety to Bartók from the beginning. Hungary was ripe for its doctrines, like a rotten apple ready to fall. The guiding principles of its leaders were expediency and opportunism. Bartók had been one of the first to complain about the exclusion of Jews from public positions and anti-semitism made further inroads during the premiership of General Gömbös who, while maintaining ostentatious friendships with Jewish industrialists, at the same time concluded a secret pact with Goering in 1935, which virtually undertook to turn Hungary into a Nazi-style state 'within two years.' After Gömbös' death in 1936, the rot continued and successive premiers vied with each other in ingratiating themselves with the mighty Third Reich, and were rewarded with the return of a disputed strip of Czechoslovakian territory which was held up to the people as a symbol of nationalistic independence. 'You can't imagine to what extent this has strengthened his (Hitler's) following in this country,' observed Bartók morosely.

Were it not for its evil cruelty, this sycophantic parade would sometimes appear to have elements of high farce, as in this anecdote from the career of Premier Béla Imredy, caustically related by Paul Ignotus:

In support of a Second Anti-Jewish Law which he published, with a picturesque touch of cruelty, on the eve of Christmas, 1938, he declared that 'one drop of Jewish blood' was enough to infect a man's character and patriotism. No sooner had he said so than he turned out to have more than one drop — a Jewish great-grandmother in his German-Bohemian ancestry. When the Regent (Horthy) at a dramatic audience showed him the relevant document, he fainted.

There was no humour in the situation for humanists like Bartók, nor for the thousands of Jews who headed for the free countries of Europe and America in order to escape the inevitable.

By this stage, open opposition would have been suicidal, so Bartók had to resort to subterfuge. He had refused to play in Italy or Germany for some time, but he had to invent a contractual pretext to prevent these countries from relaying a Hungarian Radio broadcast over their national networks.

Once again his thoughts turned to emigration, but the thought of having to take up teaching again, at the age of fifty-eight, to earn his living in a foreign country was so distressing that he 'could hardly bear to think about it.'

For the time being, he did not have to think about it, for he soon decided that it was out of the question to desert his aging and ailing mother in her last years. He expressed his mental and spiritual torment in a moving letter to Mrs Müller-Widman (now a regular

Brussels, 1938.

correspondent and confidante) in April, 1938, shortly after Hitler's take-over in Austria.

I think it is quite superfluous to write about this catastrophe — you have very concisely and eloquently put into words the main issue. This is exactly how we feel. There is one thing I want to add, concerning what is at this moment — at least for us — the most terrible prospect. That is the imminent danger that Hungary will surrender to this régime of thieves and murderers. The only question is — when and how? ... So much for Hungary, where, unfortunately nearly all of our 'educated' Christians are adherents of the Nazi régime; I feel quite ashamed of coming from this class.

There were other practical problems to consider, too. After the *Anschluss*, Bartók had to urgently consider the question of his Austrian connections. Both he and Kodály were members of the Austrian branch of the Performing Rights Society and his publishers, Universal Edition, were also in Vienna. Within weeks, the German organisation STAGMA had taken over the PRS offices, and both Hungarians received a questionnaire to complete in order to establish their Aryan credentials to the satisfaction of the German authorities. Both refused angrily and Bartók used this 'illegal document' which, he claimed, infringed the statutes of the PRS, to transfer his membership to the London branch. He also concluded a hasty deal with the London firm of Boosey and Hawkes

Bartók with his eighty year old mother, whose age and frailty delayed his departure from

94

who, opportunely, were looking to build up their list of contemporary music at the time and took over the publication of his works from then on.

Then there was the safety of his manuscripts to think about. He began to send them surreptitiously to his friends in Switzerland but, as the situation deteriorated still further, even this seemed a chancy way of ensuring their survival, so he wrote again to Mrs Müller-Widman:

I would like to ask you to send my manuscripts to my publishers, Boosey and Hawkes, 295 Regent Street, London . . . After all, London is further away from the land of the monsters.

Life was hectic. 'I have so much to do and arrange whenever I am in Budapest that it defies description,' he wrote, and yet he still had to find time for 'little money-making tours' abroad. With all the pressures that crowded in on him, it is hard to imagine how he found the time to compose. We must assume that he acted upon his own advice, given in response to a despondent letter from his American pupil Wilhelmine Creel:

As a musician, you should try to get through your difficulties by giving yourself entirely to your art.

Amidst this frenetic activity and growing apprehension two other works were born, remarkable instances of a great artist's ability to transcend and triumph over the adversities of external circumstances. The glowing, passionate *Violin Concerto*, written for his friend Zoltán Székely, established itself almost from birth alongside the concertos of Beethoven and Brahms as one of the very greatest of the genre. In lighter vein, *Contrasts* for violin, clarinet and piano, was commissioned by the great jazz clarinettist Benny Goodman (at the instigation of Szigeti) and fairly bubbles with swaggering *verbunkos* rhythms and bravura treatment of the two melody instruments (the piano has a surprisingly supportive rôle). The three artists recorded the work together for Columbia, in April, 1940, during Bartók's next visit to America.

Before this visit took place an event intervened which affected Bartók deeply and at the same time threw his plans into turmoil again. In December, 1939, Paula Bartók, who had struggled and suffered greatly to set her son on his path to greatness, died at the age of eighty-two. Bartók felt keenly his special debt to her, far beyond the ordinary bonds of filial devotion, and he suffered the inevitable pangs of remorse that he had perhaps neglected to attend to things which might have made her last years a little easier. At the same time he knew that the last tie which bound him to his homeland was now severed, and he set out for America with a heavy heart, but determined to pave the way for a new life.

When he returned to Budapest at the end of May, his official story for the press was that a further American tour had been arranged, starting in October, but his friends were in no doubt that his absence would be indefinite, perhaps permanent, and that the concert given by the Bartóks on October 8th was a farewell gesture. Ditta, who had recently been joining her husband on the platform in two-piano works, made her solo début in Mozart's Concerto in F. 'She played beautifully,' wrote Bartók, who had opened the evening with a performance of Bach's Concerto in A, and the couple united in a performance of Mozart's Concerto in E flat for Two Pianos under the direction of János Ferencsik.

The warmth of their reception from an audience which (according to a newspaper report) included 'the leading figures of our cultural life,' must have done much to ease the bitterness which, four days earlier, had prompted Bartók to add the following codicil to his will:

Recording *Contrasts* with Szigeti and Benny Goodman.

The farewell concert in
Budapest, October 8th, 1940.

. . . as long as there shall be any squares or streets in Hungary named after these two men (Hitler and Mussolini) no square, street or public building shall be named after me in this country; and until then no memorial plaque shall be put in any public place.

Emotional farewells had to be curtailed to ensure that preparations for the voyage could be completed on time, and a few days later the couple set out on their hazardous journey across war-torn Europe to Lisbon, whence they sailed on October 20th.

Their feelings can easily be imagined, and they are poignantly recorded in a letter to Mrs Müller-Widman from Geneva, the last Bartók wrote from Europe.

It is hard, very hard to say farewell. And to see this wonderful country, your country, perhaps for the last time, wondering all the time; what sort of future awaits it and all our friends who are here!

Mrs Stefi Geyer came yesterday afternoon and was with us until this evening, helping us and seeing us off. The voyage is, actually, like plunging into the unknown from what is known but unbearable. If only on account of my none too satisfactory state of health; I mean my periarthritis, still incompletely cured. God only knows how and for how long I'll be able to work over there. But we have no choice; it isn't at all a question whether this has to happen; for it must happen.[1]

I send my thanks to you and your family for all the beauty, love and friendship you have bestowed on me, and we send you every possible good wish for the future.

1. In the original German text of this letter these words 'muss es sein; denn es muss sein' are a reference to the last movement of Beethoven's String Quartet, op. 135, where these words are inscribed over the two leading phrases.

Chapter Ten

Omens were not good as they stepped ashore in New York on October 30th. Most of their luggage had been held up for so long by the Spanish customs authorities that they had had to abandon it for fear of missing the connection to Lisbon. Their first concert was only four days hence, so they had to rush out and buy replacement evening clothes almost as soon as they arrived.

For the first few months, a reasonable income was assured from concert engagements, but this in itself made it all the more difficult to find time to attend to all the practical necessities. Early in December, they moved from their hotel into an apartment in Forest Hills, and in the meantime coped as best they could with the innumerable problems that beset them. Communications with Europe were slow and unreliable, but there were matters concerning his family at home that Bartók simply had to attend to, so endless hours were taken up with correspondence and enquiries about his Hungarian pension, his passport, currency, royalties, and, of course, the even more pressing business of the whereabouts of their luggage. In addition, they had to satisfy the US immigration regulations and they reported, in fairly good humour, to the local Post Office to have their finger-prints taken.

Bartók's last years in America were not happy ones, as is well known, and his feelings of disappointment and disillusion probably started from the beginning. Although he never expressed any sense of wounded pride, he must have felt hurt that his arrival in the USA was accorded so little attention. At this time, he well knew, European refugees were flooding into America in their millions, so it would have been unrealistic to expect that his sacrifice and personal stand against Nazism would arouse admiration or even recognition, but, whether he knew it or not, the previous wave of immigrant composers (such as Schoenberg, Stravinsky and Hindemith) had attracted far greater publicity. As it was, the couple felt bewildered and disorientated and were deeply grateful to the handful of friends, mostly Hungarian emigrés and former pupils like Wilhelmine Creel and Dorothy Parrish, who went out of their way to make them welcome.

A bright spot on the horizon was Bartók's research appointment

A two piano recital in New York Town Hall.

at Columbia University. In 1933, Milman Parry, then Harvard Professor of Classical Philology, had set out for Yugoslavia in pursuit of ethnic material which he hoped would yield connections with the Homeric epics. On his death in 1935, the material, which included over two thousand recordings of Serbo-Croatian folk songs, had been deposited with Columbia University. During his tour in the spring, Bartók had been invited to undertake the task of unravelling and classifying this collection under a temporary research fellowship funded by the Ditson Foundation. Even this arrangement was to be the source of disappointment and frustration as Bartók had not realised at the time that the appointment was not a secure one, but depended on funds being available for annual renewal. For the present, though, the prospect was an enticing one and, as a preliminary to his appointment, he was awarded an Honorary Doctorate by the university.

This sort of work was his natural habitat, but there were other aspects of American life to which he was less easily able to adapt, from the trivial,

human beings ruminating like cows (every second person is chewing gum); railway carriages in semi-darkness; the cheque-book system.

to the more serious matter of accommodation. They moved in May, 1941, to a quiet apartment in the Bronx, but up to then

we were piano-played and radio-blasted from right and left; a lot of noise came in from the street night and day; every five minutes we heard the rumble of the subway which made the very walls shake. Lastly, it took more than an hour to get to Columbia.

At least his work on the Parry collection took his mind off his worries for part of the day, but on every other front the clouds were gathering fast. His wife Ditta was not of the independent and resourceful mould of European immigant, and her feelings of estrangement and depression were aggravated by her anxiety about their son Péter. It had always been the plan that he would rejoin the family as soon as he left school and his father had to expend valuable time and energy (not to mention lawyer's fees) in frustrating and protracted legal formalities to procure his entry visa. Bartók himself had to travel to Canada and re-enter the country to renew his own permit, which only gave him 'visitor's' status. But the most worrying thing was the financial insecurity which was becoming more threatening with each month that passed. Concert bookings for the coming season were not forthcoming and, for the first time, Bartók considered going home, on the grounds that,

if things are bad everywhere, one prefers to be at home.

99

Life would indeed have become unendurable were it not for the constant support of their friends. At this bleak moment in their lives the Bartóks were invited to spend the summer months in Vermont at the seaside home of Ágata Illés, whom they had met through their old friend Ernö Balogh, a former piano student in Budapest, who had emigrated after the first world war. Under the pseudonym Agatha Fassett, Miss Illés wrote a disconcertingly novelettish account of Bartók's last years under the title 'The Naked Face of Genius', but her kindness and concern was immeasurable. Wilhelmine Creel, too, did her utmost to secure a more advantageous academic post for Bartók at the University of Washington in Seattle, but he preferred to cling to his job at Columbia where he felt his involvement with Eastern European folk music preserved at least some links with his old life.

At the end of the summer, he was alarmed to discover that his arthritis was so bad that he could barely lift his arm to play the piano, and although it was greatly relieved by X-ray treatment, it was the prelude to more serious bouts of illness over the next eighteen months.

Their financial plight was becoming desperate, and in March, 1942, he wrote to Wilhelmine Creel,

All I can say is that never in my life since I earn my livelihood (that is from my twentieth year) have I been in such a dreadful situation as I will be probably very soon.

Everything about the current musical scene in America was against him. Royalties from European performances of his works could not be remitted to him because of the stringent currency restrictions in force everywhere, and performances of contemporary music in America were at their lowest ebb. The recording industry was virtually at a standstill owing to a dispute between the Musicians' Union and the recording companies, so there was no hope of work or publicity from that source.

In April, 1942, a single shaft of light penetrated the gloom when Péter Bartók was joyfully reunited with his parents after a hazardous journey lasting almost four months, and this probably confirmed their resolution to stay in America.

For over two years it had seemed that Bartók's creative spirit was broken, for he had composed not a note since his landing in America. He had just heard that his contract with Columbia University was unlikely to be renewed, although his work there was not half finished, but now, when his fortunes were at their lowest ebb, he took his first tentative steps towards a renewal of his powers. Another old and devoted friend, the conductor Frigyes (Fritz) Reiner, had arranged an appearance with the New York

Philharmonic and for the occasion Bartók produced a *Concerto* for
Two Pianos, Percussion and Orchestra, in fact a reworking of the
Sonata. It is not one of his most successful achievements, as the
addition of an orchestra merely dilutes and sometimes even nullifies
the unique and delicately balanced *timbres* of the original, but it was
perhaps the spark which rekindled his creative urge. Sadly, this
concert was his last public appearance as a performer.

The disastrous financial implications of the termination of his
contract with Columbia University were to some extent alleviated
by an invitation from Harvard to give a series of lectures, starting in
February 1943. His health was deteriorating steadily by now, and
an evening temperature of over 100°F was a daily occurrence, while
his weight had fallen to eighty-seven pounds. Doctors were baffled
as to the cause of his condition and were therefore unable to
propose treatment. As a result, he collapsed in the middle of a
lecture at Harvard and was rushed to hospital. The horrified
university authorities offered to pay all immediate expenses and,
shortly afterwards, Ernö Balogh approached the American Society
of Composers and Publishers who undertook to meet the cost of all
further medical treatment.

Comprehensive tests at the hospital finally came up with the
incontrovertible diagnosis of leukaemia, but Bartók was told that he
had an obscure, but infinitely less alarming disease, polycithemia.

Meanwhile, his friends rallied around him in the most magnificent fashion. This was no easy task, for Bartók had a stubborn
streak of resistance to anything which smacked of charity.
Nevertheless, by the end of 1943 they had lifted the threat of
financial disaster from his life and, from then on, his means, though
modest, were never again a major source of anxiety.

Victor Bator, later to become the trustee of Bartók's Estate in

101

America and founder of the New York Bartók Archives, arranged for Columbia University to renew the research facility that meant so much to his friend, on the understanding that he and Szigeti would raise the additional funds required by subscription. Although the response from official bodies was poor, generous donations by private individuals, including Eugene Ormandy and Benny Goodman, ensured that this was done. Douglas Moore, chairman of the University Music Department, secured a donation from the relief fund of the National Institute of Arts and Letters which had to be deposited in Bartók's bank account in the guise of a prize award.

Finally, Serge Koussevitzky readily agreed to Szigeti's suggestion that he should commission an orchestral work with funds from the Koussevitzky Foundation which he had established in memory of his wife Natalie, a wealthy tea-heiress, and he visited Bartók in hospital to make the proposal personally. The suspicious composer at first refused to accept the thousand dollar cheque that the flamboyant conductor thrust in front of him then and there, protesting that he was in no position to undertake commitments that he might well be unable to fulfil for some time, if ever. Eventually a compromise was reached to pay half the fee immediately and the balance on completion.

Through the dedicated attention of his doctors, Bartók gained a temporary respite from the disease and at the end of June, through the continuing benevolence of ASCAP, he went to convalesce at Saranac Lake, NY. The creative spark which had flickered hesitantly at the beginning of the year now roared into flame and, when he returned to New York in October, he had with him the complete score of the *Concerto for Orchestra*. This was a tonic for everyone, and he could not have more amply repaid the loyalty and generosity of his friends and colleagues than with this life-enhancing symphony in five movements. The word 'concerto' is used in its baroque sense, and Bartók explained his choice of title 'by its tendency to treat the single instruments or instrument groups in a *concertante* or soloistic manner.' He described the grand design of the five movements as 'a gradual transition from the sternness of the first movement and the lugubrious death-song of the third, to the life-assertion of the last one.'

Koussevitzky was thrilled with the work and Bartók wrote with some relish to Wilhelmine Creel that he

said it is the best orchestra piece of the last 25 years (including the works of his idol Shostakovich!)

Bartók felt that Shostakovich's success had been out of all proportion to his worth as a composer, and in the fourth movement

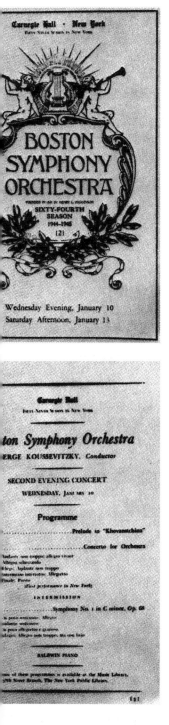

Programme for the premiere of the *Concerto for Orchestra*, Bartók's most popular orchestral work.

of his *Concerto*, the 'Interrupted Serenade', a swooning Hungarian love song is obliterated by the raucous intrusion of the brass ('a band of rowdy drunkards', according to one interpretation) and there follows a snatch of trite fairground music which turns out to be a parody of Shostakovich's seventh symphony.

His doctors imposed strict limits on his activities, but they were persuaded to allow him to travel to Boston to attend the first performance in December 1944, by which time he was able to write,

For the next three years a modest living is assured for us.

There were still immense difficulties in collecting and transmitting royalties from Europe but Ralph Hawkes, the head of his English publishers, arranged to pay an annual advance of fourteen hundred dollars over and above anything that might be forthcoming from sales and royalties.

Another commission followed and in the most agreeable circumstances. Yehudi Menuhin, now safely through his *wunderkind* period and established in a great international career, had taken up the *Violin Concerto* and Bartók was entranced with his playing of this and also of the *1st Violin Sonata*.

He really is a great artist, (he wrote with enthusiasm) . . . It is altogether a happy thing that a young artist is interested in contemporary works which draw no public, and likes them and — performs them *comme il faut*.'

Menuhin's championship of the ailing composer did not stop short at 'liking and playing' his music, and soon after their first meeting, he commissioned a sonata for solo violin, and made many helpful suggestions of a practical nature in the course of its composition.

To avoid the rigours of a New York winter, Bartók retired, on doctors' advice, to the milder climate of Asheville, North Carolina. It was a beneficial move in every way.

At present I feel quite well, I have no temperature, my strength has returned, and I am able to take nice walks in the mountain forests — yes, I climb mountains (only very cautiously, of course). In March my weight was 87 lbs now it is 105 lbs.

and he not only completed the Sonata for Menuhin but also embarked on a massive scientific work on Romanian folk music, which eventually appeared in print in 1967, through the tireless endeavour of Benjamin Suchoff, Victor Bator's successor as Trustee of the New York Bartók Archives.

These were trying times for poor Ditta. She had no career as a pianist except as her husband's partner, and those days were now

103

One of the last photographs of Bartók. (Corvina)

over. The pain of her enforced separation from Béla was now compounded by Péter's enlistment in the US Navy. At the conclusion of a training course in electrical engineering, he was drafted to Panama for the rest of the war. They had given up their flat in Riverdale and moved into the Hotel Woodrow during Bartók's stay in hospital, and the outlook was still too uncertain to tackle the problem of finding a permanent home with any resolution. With the help and encouragement of friends, she was installed in a small two-room flat on the West Side and this became their last home in New York.

With the easing of their immediate worries concerning health and wealth, their thoughts turned increasingly to events in Europe and the fate of their country and loved ones at home, and they suffered agonies of suspense as a result of the garbled and conflicting reports that reached them.

In the latter part of 1944 they were able to re-establish some sort of orderly routine. They spent the summer at Saranac Lake again and the miraculous improvement in Bartók's health stabilised for a while. In February 1945 he contracted pneumonia, but even this responded quickly to the new wonder drug, penicillin.

They had been invited to spend the following summer with the Menuhins in Alma, California, but, at the last minute, Bartók felt unable to undertake the long journey and, besides, Ditta ('by way of variety') was not well herself at the time. So they headed once more for Saranac Lake, where the *3rd Piano Concerto* was all but completed, and work on a *Viola Concerto* for William Primrose reached an advanced stage.

On his demobilisation in August, Péter joined his parents at their summer retreat, but this happy reunion was almost immediately plunged into catastrophe. Bartók's condition deteriorated alarmingly and rapidly, and the family rushed back to New York early in September. For a week or two he was treated at home, where he continued to work on the piano concerto. On September 21st he was admitted to West Side Hospital and given blood transfusions, dextrose drips and oxygen, but these desperate measures only delayed the end for a few more days and he died on the 26th September.

The *3rd Piano Concerto*, his parting gift to his wife, Ditta, was complete but for the orchestration of the last seventeen bars, and his friend Tibor Serly was able to construct a plausible performing version of the *Viola Concerto* from the piano outline. Of a seventh string quartet, only jottings were on paper.

As his weary spirit and emaciated body sank beneath the weight of his illness, Bartók murmured to his doctor,

I am only sorry to be going with my luggage full.

104

Chapter Eleven

Bartók was a solitary man, a 'loner'. At an early stage in his career, he developed a stubborn integrity which won him more admiration than affection, except from a small handful of really close friends. From the early 1920s he had absolute conviction in his stature as a composer, and he clearly felt that his time would come. The Hungarian scholar, Bence Szabolcsi, compared Bartók's relationship with his public to that of Beethoven. Like Beethoven's, his new works were often met with angry incomprehension and then, as they became accepted, his latest productions were condemned as wilful novelties and compared disparagingly with the earlier ones. It was particularly hard, then, that his American works, the *Concerto for Orchestra* and the *3rd Piano Concerto*, should suffer the sneers of certain critics and musicians, this time on account of their alleged 'commercialism'. Bartók had gone soft, they said, and was pandering to the American masses, though the gritty *Sonata for Solo Violin* should have been enough to disabuse them of this notion. In fact, the simplicity, directness and radiance of these works continue a trend that had begun to manifest itself in works he composed before he left Hungary, notably the *Violin Concerto* and the *Divertimento*. To decry it as cheap populism was sheer intellectual snobbery. If we stand back and look at Bartók's output as a whole, we can see it as a great arch from the naïve romantic excess of *Kossuth* to the unforced and humane intelligibility of the *3rd Piano Concerto*, an arch which reaches its apex in the extreme harshness and dissonance of the works written in his forties in the period roughly spanned by *The Miraculous Mandarin* and the *Fourth String Quartet*. Viewed in this way, the increasing clarity and lucidity of his 'classic' period — the 1930s — leads naturally and inevitably to this last American phase.

Since his death, Bartók research has become a thriving industry for musicologists, especially in Hungary. Scarcely a year passes which does not yield some new revelation to their persistent probing. A Béla Bartók Archive has been set up as a permanent department of the Hungarian Academy of Sciences and in 1981, the centenary of the composer's birth, a Bartók Museum was opened in the house of Csalan Street, Budapest, where the family lived from

1932 to 1940. The music has been analysed, it would seem, from every conceivable angle and the results have sometimes proved startling. Ernö Lendvai, in his brilliant study *Béla Bartók; An Analysis of his Music* (1971) caught the academic world napping when he disclosed that several of Bartók's works conformed very precisely to Golden Section proportion, a phenomenon observed in ancient Greek and Egyptian architecture. No one has been able to deny this demonstrably mathematical fact, but there are still eminent scholars who claim that it was fortuitous, not deliberate.

Tonal axes, Fibinaccian series, heptatonic scales, polymetric synchronisation and all the other paraphernalia of Bartók analysis lie well beyond the scope of this general biography, but the interested reader is directed to Laszlo Somfai's admirable résumé of these findings in the Bartók entry in *The New Grove's Dictionary of Music and Musicians*.

The first serious analysis of Bartók's music was undertaken in 1930 by a German musicologist Edwin von der Nüll, and it is always wise to bear in mind Bartók's comments on that occasion:

. . . in spite of all honest efforts, with such things intuition plays a far more prominent rôle than one would imagine. All of my music and, last but not least, this problem of harmonisation depend on instinct and emotion. It is no good asking why I wrote a passage as I did, instead of putting it differently — I can only reply that I wrote down what I felt. Let the music speak for itself; it surely speaks clearly enough to assert itself.

Bartók's international reputation was not really established until the late 1920s, so was not a factor in the movements which, in the two preceding decades, determined the course of European twentieth century music. Hence, he founded and left no 'school' and pursued his musical career with the same solitary idealism as he led his private life. And yet Bartók, perhaps most of all the great twentieth century composers, has reached the hearts of concert audiences in the way that apologists have always predicted for their avant-garde heroes, while other notable, even great figures are still more cherished by scholars and musicians than by the public at large. It may seem odd that Bartók, whose uncompromising intellectual discipline would seem likely to discourage the uninitiated and whose preoccupation with localised folk song would seem to make him exclusive, if not parochial in appeal, should win this genuine popularity whilst others have retained an intimidating relationship with concert goers. Yet this is surely a measure of the greatness of the man; that, of all the accepted masters of the first half of this century, he speaks with the most universal appeal. Like Bach and Beethoven before him, he possessed that rarest of gifts, to express the most complex thoughts and feelings with a directness that explains itself to the receptive ear.

106

It is sad that in his life he rarely experienced the same warmth of communication that his music has enjoyed posthumously. And yet his work was by far the greater part of his life, and in that he no doubt achieved a certain rarefied happiness that is not attainable to lesser men. Towards the end, he looked wistfully again towards Hungary, 'I should like to return home, and that for good,' and the Provisional Hungarian National Government, set up by the Russians at the end of 1944, elected him a member *in absentia*.

Modern Hungarian biographers tend to blame his difficulties onto the reactionary forces that controlled Hungary between the wars. But Bartók had been just as scathing in his condemnation of the short-lived communist Republic of Councils of 1919:

Protectionism and bureaucracy flourished as never before. The Councils' Government was just as narrow-minded as the former bourgeois administrations had been.

So it is doubtful whether, granted good health, he could have settled happily into an official position in the Soviet-dominated post-war establishment. He had long since decided to go his own way, to do nothing with which he could reproach himself and to shut his face to compromise and the fickleness of official approval. Ernst Roth, an executive of the publishers, Boosey and Hawkes, perhaps enshrined his life more pithily than anyone when he wrote,

It was his misfortune to have been born and to live in such troubled times; for ultimately they overwhelmed him.

Selected Bibliography

Ferenc Bónis: Béla Bartók—*His Life in Pictures and Documents.*
                        Boosey and Hawkes, London, 1972
ed. János Deményi: *Béla Bartók Letters.*
                        Faber & Faber, London, 1971
Agatha Fassett: *The Naked Face of Genius—Béla Bartók's Last Years.*
                        Gollancz, London, 1958
Paul Ignotus: *Hungary.*   Ernest Benn Ltd., London, 1972
Lajos Lesznai: *Béla Bartók.*   J. M. Dent & Sons, London, 1973
Serge Moreux: *Béla Bartók.*   Harvill Press, London, 1953
Halsey Stevens: *The Life and Music of Béla Bartók.*
                        New York University Press, 1953/1964
ed. Benjamin Suchoff: *Béla Bartók Essays.*
                        Faber & Faber, London, 1976
József Ujfalussy: *Béla Bartók.*   Corvina Press, Budapest, 1971
Percy M. Young: *Zoltán Kodály.*   Ernest Benn Ltd., London, 1964

List of Works

Note: Juvenile works (i.e. works composed before 1900) are not listed. Several works by Bartók exist in more than one version (i.e. orchestrations, transcriptions, etc.). Only the original versions are given here. For a complete list of Bartók's works, see Grove's Dictionary of Music and Musicians.

Stage Works

1911   Duke Bluebeard's Castle, opera in one act   46, 51, 52, 84, 90
1917   The Wooden Prince, ballet in one act   51, 53, 59, 87, 90
1919   The Miraculous Mandarin, pantomime in one act   51, 59, 60, 73, 82, 105

Orchestral Works (including Concertos)

1901   Rhapsody no. 1 for piano and orchestra   25, 26
1903   'Kossuth' — Symphonic Poem for full orchestra   22, 24, 25, 105
1904   Scherzo for piano and orchestra   25, 40
1905   Suite no. 1 for orchestra   30
1905-7 Suite no. 2 for orchestra   39
1908   Violin Concerto no. 1   26
1907-16 Two Portraits for orchestra   41
1910   Two Pictures for orchestra   41, 42
1912   Four Pieces for orchestra
1923   Dance Suite for orchestra   63, 66, 68
1926   Piano Concerto no. 1   69, 70
1928   Rhapsody no. 1 for violin and orchestra   74, 76
1928   Rhapsody no. 2 for violin and orchestra   74, 76
1931   Piano Concerto no. 2   84
1938   Violin Concerto no. 2   90, 95, 101, 105
1939   Divertimento for string orchestra   78, 92, 105
1943   Concerto for orchestra   102, 105
1945   Piano Concerto no. 3   104, 105
1945   Viola Concerto (reconstructed and orchestrated by Tibor Serly)   104

Chamber Music

1903   Sonata for violin and piano   22
1904   Piano Quintet   22, 25, 26
1908   String Quartet no. 1   42
1917   String Quartet no. 2   51
1921   Sonata for violin and piano, no. 1   22, 26, 68
1922   Sonata for violin and piano, no. 2   68
1927   String Quartet no. 3   73
1928   String Quartet no. 4   73, 105
1931   44 Duos for two violins
1934   String Quartet no. 5   84, 91, 92
1937   Sonata for two pianos and percussion   78, 92
1938   'Contrasts' for violin, clarinet and piano   95
1939   String Quartet no. 6   92
1940   Sonata for solo violin   105

109

Piano Music

1900	Variations on a theme by F.F.
1903	4 Pieces 22
1907	3 Hungarian Folk Songs
1908	14 Bagatelles 39, 41
1908	10 Easy Pieces
1909	2 Elegies 41
1908-9	For Children (43 pieces in 4 volumes) 39
1910	2 Romanian Dances 41
1908-10	7 Sketches 42
1910	4 Dirges 42
1908-11	3 Burlesques 42
1911	Allegro Barbaro 44, 69
1915	Sonatina 48, 75
1915	6 Romanian Folk Dances 48, 49
1915	20 Romanian Christmas Songs
1916	Suite 50
1914-18	15 Hungarian Peasant Songs
1918	3 Studies 62
1920	8 Improvisations on Hungarian Peasant Songs 61, 69
1926	Sonata 69
1926	'Out of Doors' 69, 70
1926	9 Little Piano Pieces 69
1916-27	3 Rondos
1926-39	Mikrokosmos (153 pieces in 6 volumes) 90, 91

Vocal Music (all for voice and piano)

1904	4 Hungarian Folk Songs
1905	'To the Little "Tót",' (5 songs)
1906	20 Hungarian Folk Songs (in collaboration with Kodály) 31
1907	4 Slovakian Folk Songs
1915-16	5 Songs (texts compiled by K. Gombossy) 51
1916	5 Songs (texts by E. Ady) 27, 51
1907-17	8 Hungarian Folk Songs
1924	Village Scenes 66
1929	20 Hungarian Folk Songs (in 4 volumes) 84
1945	Ukrainian Folk Song

Choral Music

1910	4 Old Hungarian Folk Songs, for 4 part male chorus, a cappella
1915	2 Romanian Folk Songs, for 4 part female chorus, a cappella
1917	5 Slovak Folk Songs, for 4 part male chorus, a cappella
1917	4 Slovak Folk Songs, for 4 part mixed chorus and piano
1930	4 Hungarian Folk Songs, for mixed chorus, a cappella 84
1930	'Cantata Profana', for tenor and baritone soloists, double mixed chorus and orchestra 83, 90
1932	6 Székely Songs, for 6 part male chorus, a cappella 84
1935	25 Choruses for 2 and 3 part children's choir, with and without accompaniment
1935	'From Olden Times', for 3 part male chorus, a cappella

Index

Illustrations in bold type

111

112